The Anti-Marriage Pact

ALSO BY LINDSAY MACMILLAN

The Heart of the Deal

Double-Decker Dreams

Summer on Lilac Island

The Anti-Marriage Pact

A NOVEL

Lindsay MacMillan

HARPER MUSE

The Anti-Marriage Pact

Published by Harper Muse, an imprint of HarperCollins Focus LLC, 501 Nelson Place, Nashville, TN 37214, USA.

ISBN 978-1-4003-4810-7 (TP)
ISBN 978-1-4003-4811-4 (ePub)
ISBN 978-1-4003-4812-1(downloadable audio)

HarperCollins Publishers, Macken House, 39/40 Mayor Street Upper, Dublin 1, D01 C9W8, Ireland (https://www.harpercollins.com)

Library of Congress Cataloging-in-Publication Data

CIP data is available upon request.

Art Direction: Halie Cotton
Cover Design: Faceout Studio, Brian Mellema
Interior Design: Chloe Foster

Printed in the United States of America

26 27 28 29 30 LBC 5 4 3 2 1

To EJ—for cracking me up and cracking open parts of myself I didn't know I was ready to meet. I adore you.

Chapter 1

I GUESS IT'S BEEN A LONG time coming, really. For a while, the four of us have been getting spooked about the settling-down-with-one-person-forever thing. That's why we moved to New York in the first place and leaped off the marriage-and-baby train. We refused to dull our fabulous edges to fit the Midwest's archaic definition of a successful woman: married by twenty-five with two kids before thirty.

Our friends back in Michigan have been following that life plan (or death plan, more accurately) without questioning who made it or why. It sort of feels like watching blindfolded captives walk the plank. Except domestic life is way less exciting than jumping into an ocean full of piranhas. Maybe dissolving into nothingness is the better analogy.

No dissolving for the Redstockings. That's what we call the four of us roommates. We named ourselves after the 1970s feminists who performed street theater with all these brilliant political messages about how they were caged by the patriarchy. They even crowned a sheep as Miss America to protest how society turns women into objects through beauty pageants. Talk about icons.

Every January, the four of us modern-day Redstockings re-sign our two-bedroom Brooklyn lease. For a fleeting moment, there was a fifth Redstocking who slept on the pullout couch, but she defected to be a tradwife instead. Four is a stronger number anyway.

Sturdy and even. We've declared our apartment the global headquarters for the new wave of the Women's Liberation Movement.

So the origins of the Anti-Marriage Pact go way back, but the thing that really solidifies it is the night I babysit for the Andersons. Yes, twenty-eight-year-old me babysitting on the Upper East Side on a Friday night. Such is the life of an up-and-coming playwright. Emphasis on the "and-coming" part as I haven't sold any of my scripts yet, but that has less to do with my talent and more to do with the gatekeepers who run the show. Only 13 percent of Broadway plays are written by women, so the odds aren't just stacked against me, they're stacked on top of me, pressing my head down, eyes facing the pants of the old men who expect me to quite literally suck my way up.

It's fine, though; I'm not freaking out about needing to make it big in my twenties. Do you see men putting that kind of pressure on themselves? Only women do it because of how we're force-fed all these coded messages that say everything is downhill once we hit our thirties. That we've missed the boat and are no longer desirable and our biological clocks are expiring, *tick tick tick*. And even if we do manage to have a successful geriatric pregnancy, well, there go any other dreams we might have because we're supposed to spend every waking and sleeping minute being the perfect wife and the perfect mom, sacrificing our own needs and desires, wearing invisibility cloaks like badges of honor.

I'm not succumbing to that brainwashing. Someday I'll make it big, but for now I'm just trying to have fun and scrape together enough money to pay my portion of the rent and walk into a thrift shop feeling rich.

Anyway, there I am babysitting in that swanky Park Avenue apartment and trying to wrestle the twins into bed. I'm so fed up with the whining and hair pulling that I let them stay on the couch chugging Dr Pepper and watching violent cartoons. I'm thinking I still have a while before Mr. and Mrs. Anderson come home, but they end up returning early. Apparently Mrs. Anderson had so much separation anxiety from her little demons that she insisted on boxing up their entrées and leaving the restaurant mid-meal.

Mr. Anderson doesn't seem pleased about it. He scowls as he hands me two twenties for the short amount of time I was there. Pocketing the money fast before he realizes he overpaid me, I scurry out the door and ride the elevator twenty-two stories down to the ground floor, where I tip my imaginary top hat to the doorperson on my way out.

Taking the 4 train down to Union Square, I transfer to the L to take me back home to Bushwick. It's the gritty part of Brooklyn with block-long street murals, converted warehouse coffee shops, and dive bars with delightfully mismatched vintage furniture.

These two mansprawlers are sitting next to me in the urine-and-pickle-scented subway car. They're trying to crowd me out with their thighs, but I don't let them. I spread my jeans wide and jam my knees into their legs to teach them the long-overdue lesson about what century we live in and the kinds of things women won't tolerate anymore. The men scowl at me in that New York kind of way, but they seem to realize I'm not letting up, so they exhale these dramatic huffs and change seats. I congratulate myself because this is how equality comes about, one mansprawler victory at a time.

My cell service flits back in once we get to the other side of the East River, safely in Brooklyn territory. The shift in energy is palpable even underground. I'm free from the Manhattan clutter. Doing a quick Google search of Mrs. Anderson, I try to find out her backstory because it seems important somehow. After a couple false starts, I dig up some articles and photos of her before she was married.

Bonnie Beaumont was her name. She was an NYU film school grad and had an edgy bob like mine and a glimmer in her eyes like she's thinking, *Just watch*. I get this pit in my stomach over how a woman like Bonnie with such an artsy, independent streak ended up evaporating into just another Wall Street housewife.

Bonnie Beaumont's ghost haunts me even after I get off the train at Myrtle Avenue. Emerging into the hornless Bushwick air, I walk along the cracked sidewalks back to our place on Knickerbocker Avenue. It's three or six blocks to get there; I never like to count if I don't have to. It's so constrictive to make the brain move in linear patterns like that.

I descend the stairs to the front door of our apartment, and yes, I mean *de*scend, not *a*scend, because we live on the garden level, which is just a New York aphorism for basement—how quaint. The Dunge Inn, we call our place. It's a punny nod to how the only windows are these grilled slivers at the very top of the walls, too high for any of us to see out of and too skinny for rapists to crawl through, though who knows these days with the rise of Ozempic. We're not as safe as we used to be.

Less enlightened people—our families, for instance—say we're too old to be living like this: four adults squished into a cellar and sleeping in bunk beds. But their judgment only makes us double down on our decision to stay. If they don't like it, we know we must be doing something right. It's a pretty good litmus test. What some people see as a decrepit dungeon, we see as the mecca of freedom, and that just shows what a difference perspective makes. Maybe I'm not right all the time, but I'm right about this.

We're designing our lives from scratch, lives that are free of all societal expectations, and that kind of thing requires sacrifice. I wouldn't be happy in a spacious penthouse, not if it meant grinding it out in a soul-crunching office job. The other Redstockings feel the same; that's why we're soulmates. We've known we were ever since we met in Western Michigan University's Gender Studies class that Professor Riley called the most progressive syllabus ever to sneak into the Midwest.

Our bright and irreverent energy is splashed all over the Inn.

We painted the walls a yellow and turquoise base coat and then layered on the Redstockings' logo from 1969—a red fist thrust in the air with the female gender sign encasing it, only we added the nonbinary sign too because it allows more room for evolution.

We keep adding more designs to the walls the longer we live here. The homemade art makes up for the lack of natural light, and the colorful ambience is worth losing our security deposit over, though we'll put up a sublime fight if our landlord denies it from us when we move out—not that we're thinking about moving out anytime soon. We're going to live in the Inn for many years to come, and then once we've established ourselves as cultural icons, we'll move somewhere exotic together. Ibiza or maybe just California, wherever the whim blows.

Hal is sprawled out on the striped slipcovered couch watching a show on her laptop. Jenni's in the kitchenette, wringing out lacy underwear under the lurchy tap water. The closest laundromat is too close to justify driving to, so we always walk but regret it afterward. On the trek back, we end up tossing out half our clothes just to lighten the load. That's why we've taken to washing most of our clothes in the sink with dish soap. Laundry detergent is an environmentally evil, overpriced scam anyway.

Classic rock ricochets out from our thirdhand turntable. It's a Stevie Nicks record tonight. Tara's singing along from the bathroom, slaying every note. She always does best when it doesn't count for anything, when she's not convincing herself that she's not good enough.

The Inn smells vaguely of weed, like it has fully seeped into the ceiling cracks and leaky pipes. I notice it today only because I haven't been smoking much lately—not because I'm trying to reform myself or anything; I just got bored of it like I get bored of everything and everyone except the Redstockings. They're sort of my one steady fixture. Knowing they're always there for me lets me swing up and down and off the rails in every other part of my life. It's a good gig.

On nights like tonight, I'm especially thankful to come home to them.

"That's it," I say upon entering the apartment. I fling off my high-top sneakers and stuff my oversized coat into the closet rather than trying to find a hanger in the haystack. "Promise me you'll never let me turn into *that* kind of woman."

Hal closes the laptop and sits up straighter on the couch. There are few things she likes better than a good rant. "What kind of woman?"

"The kind who's completely consumed by her offspring." Fuming, I walk to the pathetically small fridge and scowl at a huge wedding invite drooping under flimsy magnets. It's from Lilly, that sellout who used to be our fifth. The mere sight of her name makes me sick. The only thing more pretentious than a cursive *L* is a cluster of three cursive *L*'s.

I rummage through the mini fridge's motley contents—coconut milk, wilting arugula, two mangled slices of buffalo tofu pizza from Tony's down the street. I locate a lone IPA, and even though there's a bottle opener right there on the counter, I break the beer open with my teeth because I like to feel my own power like that. Taking many gulps in one, I carry on. "The kind of woman who forfeits herself to her husband and kids," I elaborate.

Tara emerges from the bathroom in a scaly costume gown and lipstick the color of ripe papaya. Her gorgeous Afro is matted down with a taming product. "But don't you think you're being kind of harsh?" she says. "Isn't the whole point of feminism that women can choose what they want to do? Some people are happy with the tradwife thing. It's not for us to judge."

"But that's the thing," I say. "I don't believe any women actually *are* happy with that life; they just pretend to be. Or maybe they *think* they're happy but only because they've forgotten what real happiness is, or they've never known it at all. But deep down, they're all aching for more. I just know it."

There's a dramatic beat as the record reaches the end of side one and the needle scrapes the silence like it's agreeing with me.

"Just look around," I say. "At all the women who've done the 'right thing' and settled down—which, by the way, just means settling. All this buildup to marriage and then—boom—it's all downhill from there, watching *The Bachelor* on TV because you never go on dates anymore. Living vicariously through romance novels because you never get laid. And don't get me started on the kids thing . . ."

"I think maybe you're just stinging because of the whole Lilly situation," Tara says gently. "But we knew she was always going to move back to Oregon and marry that boy she grew up with."

"Did you see her wedding dress, though?" Jenni gushes now. "It's *stunning*. She sent it in the group chat today." She takes out her phone to show us. "Oh wait, maybe it wasn't the group chat. It was just to me, I guess."

My whole body winces. "I removed Lilly from the group chat," I say. "Obviously. And please read the room, Jenni."

Jenni sheepishly tucks her phone away. "My bad."

"None of this is just about Lilly," I go on. "Sure, maybe she's the catalyst for the combustion, but the match was struck ages ago. Now it's time we burn it all down."

"Is this one of your bits?" Jenni asks, looking to the others for confirmation. "It is, right?"

"I don't think so," Tara whispers back.

"Of course it's not a bit," I say, pouncing onto the couch between Hal and Jenni. Hal hands me a beer because I guess I've already finished my first. "Think about it," I go on. "The highest compliment that society bestows on a woman is that she's selfless. A selfless wife, a selfless mother, a selfless friend. Self-*less*. A lack of self! How fucked up is that?"

"I think I heard that on a podcast," Hal says. "How martyrdom is glorified."

Hal is always listening to "enlightenment influencers," as she calls them, and then writing stand-out quotes in permanent marker on the ceiling of the Inn to help them stick.

"That's how I felt," Jenni says, voice hoarse like she's just seen Bonnie's ghost too. "Like I was going to lose myself by taking his name."

Of the four of us, Jenni came closest to walking the plank. Two years back, she left her high school sweetheart before the wedding; she had a panic attack at her final dress fitting and ripped off the constrictive corset right there. She drove straight to New York with her bridal tiara still on and moved in with us that day. We were tempted to sell the tiara to buy some softer toilet paper, but we had Jenni smash it with a hammer instead. It was the catharsis she needed.

"And think about all our other friends back in college," I say, because I'm really on a roll now. "Who swore we'd be that close forever, and then one by one they dropped off the face of the earth when they got married, like we were just the opening act."

"You're not the opening act for me," Tara says. "You're the main-stage performance."

Hal and Jenni agree right away. Their assurances make me feel a tiny bit better but not much. My heart physically indents at the thought of ever losing them.

"I bet a lot of women have had this same exact conversation, though," I say. "But then one by one they started to get hitched, and then the others got scared they were falling behind so they got hitched too. It's a vicious cycle."

"The whole thing is like some kind of twisted game theory, isn't it?" Hal says. "No one wants to be the last single one standing."

Hal's right. That's exactly what this marriage pressure is: twisted game theory.

"If people would just keep their friendships strong," I say, "they wouldn't need to latch onto spouses to keep from being lonely. They could lead thrilling romantic lives, perpetually high on love or lust, and have the stability of their friendships to ground them. It's the best of both worlds."

"That's what we do," Jenni points out proudly.

"And very successfully," Tara adds with a wink that hints at our delicious lifestyle.

"I don't deny that," I say. "I just don't think we'd be the first women to have all these radical ideas of liberation and then end up as domestic prisoners, too trapped to even see the bars on their own cell."

"Have you met us, though?" Tara asks. "We're the most modern inventions ever to come out of the Midwest."

"But at the end of the day, we're still from the Midwest," I say. "And our families expect things, society expects things. It's programmed into us, always will be on some deep, dangerous level. It's a case of our wild nature losing out to our tamed nurture."

"I agree with Tara, though," Jenni says. "We're not the get-married-and-settle-down type. That's how we ended up here, remember?"

Tara and I drove east first, right after college graduation. We were both set on becoming Broadway actors with our faces on taxi ads and our names lit up on Times Square billboards. That's still in the cards for her, but I switched to playwriting after a few years of rejections got under my skin. It didn't make me question my talent, just the industry's ability to appreciate it. I hate sticking to a script. I'm much more about improvisation, but the casting directors rarely commended my creativity. So I started writing instead to give the actors more original dialogue and break free of all the recycled, clichéd plotlines. I've only written drafts and scraps so far, nothing phenomenal. But the genius is building, bubbling beneath the surface, ready to explode like a fucking volcano. I can feel it.

The year we turned twenty-five, Hal came out to her parents as bisexual, which was a complete mess, so there was no way she was going to tell them she actually didn't like men at all except for using them to get free drinks. Needing to get away, Hal visited us in New York and never left. She's the entrepreneurial type, spilling over with billion-dollar ideas. The ideas usually come in the form of her venting about something being dysfunctional and then making PowerPoint pitch decks for all her future investors. She scrapes by on grants and scholarships she has a knack for winning.

Jenni joined us after Hal. She's Korean American, the daughter of immigrants, and has been deep in the unlearning of all the pressures to "be successful" in the conventional sense. She's a recovering management consultant who's still figuring out what her dream is. I kind of envy it, how new the whole liberation thing is for her, but there are some perks to being an old pro at it too. I don't feel guilty that I'm sinning or straying like Jenni does. Once you've been free long enough, you realize morals are all man-made, designed to keep women in our tiny little boxes so we don't disrupt the status quo.

Lilly was the last to join the Redstockings and the first to leave. We met her at a Bed-Stuy rave and she moved in the next day. Turns out the rebel life was just another of her performative eras, a character she was cosplaying.

I'm worried Jenni might follow in Lilly's footsteps, and maybe even Tara and Hal too. There's no way I can let that happen.

"I think we should formalize our rejection of convention," I tell the Redstockings now. "So we hold ourselves accountable to independence and never ditch each other for a spouse."

"What do you mean, formalize it?" Jenni asks, sounding wary, as if I've ever proposed a bad idea.

"We'll make a pact," I say, the idea hitting me hard in the head and soft in the heart, like all great things do. "To never get married."

My words soar through the air and somersault a few times just to show off how unshackled they are.

"You want to go full-on 4B movement like my cousins in Korea?" Jenni asks. "My parents would officially disown me."

"I'm already there with decentering men and only dating women," Hal chimes in. "Wouldn't be hard."

"Not full-on 4B," I say. "We're not banning men or sex, just marriage and confinement."

"You're deadass?" Hal asks, as Tara and Jenni exchange a look.

I'm kind of annoyed at how slow they're all being to support an objectively brilliant proposition. I don't say that last part aloud, or maybe I do. The lines between my speech and my thoughts are blurry, and I like it like that, the constant state of flow.

"But no pressure to join if you see yourself settling down with one of your admirers," I shoot back at Hal.

Hal has one of those magnetic auras where she has a hard time picking up coffee without someone picking her up—or at least trying to. The other person nearly always fails. It's good fun to watch.

"Don't be ridiculous," Hal says. "You know I can't stay interested in someone for more than a few weeks, forget about a lifetime. Just the thought makes me claustrophobic." She shudders, as if trying to worm her way out of a hive of hornets before they attack.

"But what about kids?" Jenni pipes up.

I say, "Well, what about them? I thought we'd agreed that they're dream-sucking monsters with egregiously big carbon footprints clogging up an overpopulated world." I try not to sound too impatient. Jenni still needs some help as she adjusts to this loose way of life. "Loose" is a positive quality around here. It means free. We don't let men try to convince us that being loose is a bad thing, a soiled thing. We're too smart for that.

Jenni says she supposes I'm right, but she hasn't ruled out adopting a child, maybe one that was found in a dumpster or something equally grim. "There's a nice social impact angle there, don't you think?" she says.

We pause to consider it, or at least I pause to pretend to consider it, and Tara says maybe it could be alright if we raise one kid among the four of us. "We could trade shifts; it wouldn't be that much work."

It still doesn't appeal to me, but I'm not going to lose all the good momentum over that one sticking point. I say we'll revisit that particular clause at a later time.

Then I ask everyone who's in on the Anti-Marriage Pact to please raise their right fist or their left one, who cares, just raise a fist nice and high.

The Redstockings look at me, then at each other.

Hal is first to raise her fist. Tara quickly follows.

Tara was shuffled through the foster system as a kid, and she still has abandonment issues. I can tell that this appeals to her, a formalized commitment to stand by each other forever.

"It's genius," she says now.

"Genius," Jenni repeats, fist in the air too, wavering ever so slightly.

"Of course it is," I say. "The patriarchy stops with us." I'm pleased with my persuasive ability. Maybe I should be a director instead of a writer, not that the gatekeepers would let in a visionary like me. They'd be too threatened. "Rejecting marriage is the least we can do to build on the work of the women who came before us. Now, time to take our vows."

The lights flicker overhead. Our upstairs neighbor must've gotten in the shower, which somehow always has the effect of dimming our electricity. It's kind of spooky, and I feel more confident than ever that Bonnie Beaumont's ghost has come to warn us away from her fate.

I kick things off. "We, the Redstockings, vow to enter into an Anti-Marriage Pact."

Hal and I make eye contact, and she takes over. "The four of us take each other to have and raise hell with from this day forward," Hal says, and our eyes dance at how she changed the words from the boring version we've heard at way too many weddings. "For better or worse, sober or . . . let's face it, mostly high."

"To have and to hold . . . each other accountable," Tara adds earnestly.

"I vow to love and honor you all the days of my life," Jenni says. "Until a billionaire proposes—then I'm cashing out," she adds with a grin.

"Business proposals only," Hal clarifies.

"Till death—or death by bridal shower games—do us part," I close out.

We punch our fists in the air, 3D versions of the mural on our wall.

"Welcome to the resistance, bitches and witches," I whisper happily. "Let the Friendship Soulmate Revolution begin."

We sit back in the glow, slowly lowering our fists and breathing a collective sigh of relief that something as old-fashioned as matrimony will never steal us from each other.

Chapter 2

ALL WINTER WE FLIT IN AND out of the Inn, staying at a base level of buzzed so we don't feel the cold slap our legs through the runs in our tights, the holes in our jeans.

The pact brings us even closer together. We get all the benefits of lifelong commitment without any of the daily confinement.

We never bring anyone back to the Inn with us, though. It's one of the only ground rules we have, along with always restocking the freezer drawer with a new carton of vegan ice cream before you finish the prior one. We try to be vegan for environmental reasons, but we're too poor to be fully vegan, so sometimes dairy ice cream finds its way in. And once it's there, we're not going to throw it out. That's even worse for the earth, so we're morally compelled to finish it.

Staying over at our lovers' places rather than bringing them home helps us keep the power since we can be the ones to escape before dawn. Plus, there's the bunk bed situation and paper-thin walls to deal with. The Inn isn't exactly renowned for its privacy, but it's the only square footage in the world that we actually own, or at least lease. That's why we're so adamant about not letting outsiders disrupt the energy. And the kind of people we go for would definitely disrupt it. That's why they catch our attention.

I tend to like other theatrical types because they're not confined by a preconceived sense of self. They're down, or up, to play with neon-light personalities, knowing they can drop them or draw new ones whenever they want. I do it too, parading sides of myself I've never unveiled before or making up new sides altogether, conjuring wings that I wear to fly high, high, higher into the night before the sun burns off the fragile magic of the moon.

I'm addicted to the rush, but the thrill is never as sharp, the sensations never as exquisite, the second time around. Even if my brain doesn't remember, my body does, and I can always guess at least half of what's about to happen, so I let my flings fizzle into nothing before they try to tell me we had something.

I collect lovers like travelers collect postcards, looking back fondly on the quaint, two-dimensional images that never have to be ruined by the reality of tourists and sewage and scaffolding.

The Redstockings don't all share my allergy to monogamy. They'll usually pair up with someone for a little stretch of time before the itch to quit them kicks in. My way is kinder when you think about it. At least I never give anyone the impression that I might commit.

For a few weeks now, Hal's been seeing this rich college girl from the Manhattan debutante circle. Hal is attracted to a certain lifestyle, says it can't be helped; it's just the natural consequence of having grown up on a bankrupt blueberry farm. She can spin that story for all it's worth. It got old a while ago, but she just keeps embellishing it.

One night in February, or maybe it's March, Hal invites us to Williamsburg for the opening of a modern art gallery that this girl's parents own. Usually we'd say no because we're anti-Williamsburg. It's a grotesquely bougie neighborhood that brands itself as bohemian. The tidy streets are stuffed with formulaic trust-fund artists who aren't actually artists at all because true art comes only from necessity, from lacking, from having no other choice than to take the pain inside you and eject it in a new shape.

A decade or two ago, Williamsburg really was a wonderful cluster of creatives, but enter gentrification and all the actual artists got priced out to deeper parts of Brooklyn. Bushwick, for instance, which is why we've found our people here.

We agree to venture into Williamsburg tonight, though, because of the free drinks and munchies promised. And we're also kind of curious to catch a look at Hal's girl. It's rare that any of our lovers last long enough for an introduction, so it's hard to pass by the opportunity to scope.

The gallery is exactly what you'd expect—a yawningly square space rimmed with abstract paintings so bad that people start believing they're good just because the alternative is too obvious. The con artist is easy to spot. He's surrounded by a sheeny orb of admirers, each fawning over his work because the person next to them is fawning over it and New York isn't a place where you want to be left out of a trend.

A particular kind of disgust fills me as I watch. No doubt this silver-spoon swindler has booked a lavish vacation to Barbados with the profits. Or maybe he's already too wealthy, so he'll donate the money to charity just so everyone will coo over what a good person he is. I'm not jealous; I just don't like frauds.

Even if my parents knew anyone in show biz, which they don't, I wouldn't let them catapult me to stardom. It would taint it for me. Success is respectable only if you have to suffer for it, sweat for it, spit in the face of the critics who rejected you time and time again, and carve your own path with the machete you stole when they were sleeping the day away in their Hamptons mansion.

I don't warm up to Hal's girl. She's all bubbles and chic. It seems like she's using Hal to check the box of the sexually experimental college experience, though to be fair, Hal's using her for the rich-people perks, so I guess you can call it even.

The two of them pair off, and Tara and Jenni go to the bathroom for a coke break. I hang back, not in the mood for it tonight, not in the mood for anything I've done before.

I scan the crowd for anyone interesting to mingle with. No one stands out. Half the people are in suits, clearly thinking themselves very hipster for having taken an Uber out of Manhattan all the way into *Brooklyn*. It's all so predictable that I could rock myself to sleep right here, but drinking sounds better.

It's an open bar. I order two cocktails. One with rum and the other with vodka because I don't like even pairs. Carrying one in each hand, I pace the perimeter of the gallery, tilting my head and trying to imagine myself swimming in the artwork. None of the pieces give me that feeling of lava lapping up against my naked body, which is how I verify they're no good, not that I didn't know that before.

This old guy starts following me from painting to painting. It's like he thinks I don't notice him stalking me, so I round on him and ask what his deal is.

He eats me alive with his eyes, from my tits to my toes and back up again. I wish I could fold my arms to cover my chest, but I'm double-fisting the drinks, and why would I drop a drink for a man?

"I've been observing you as I soak in the art," he says. "You're a beautiful sight."

I'm wearing these great corduroy overalls of Tara's. We share a closet, which means we share a wardrobe, and it's mostly full of costume fragments that Tara takes home from her different shows. My hair is streaked with maroon, and I've got some gold flash tats crawling up my neck. I don't do real tats because of the commitment. Turquoise contacts enhance my dull gray eyes. I look like a fucking vision, and I don't need this pig to validate that.

"I'm not an object," I tell him.

The pig chuckles to himself, like he finds my rebellious spirit endearing. Like I'm doing it to flirt or something.

I keep moving along but he doesn't back off. He asks me which of the paintings I'd buy if money weren't a constraint. I tell him I can already afford them but wouldn't waste a penny on this junk. That doesn't shut him up. He keeps hovering, getting closer.

"There you are," a voice says. It's different from the one I was expecting. Softer, like a metal that accidentally melted and now can't go back.

I look up and there's this other guy standing there, in between the stalker and me. My first thought is that I've met this guy before, but then I realize that's just because he has that formulaic look, like he was created in some human genome lab with a perfectly controlled environment. He's trim but not skinny, not short but not tall. His clean-shaven face is an unnervingly symmetrical oval, anchored by solid brown eyes and a right-triangle nose with a bridge as thin as a pencil. His olive skin is clear of acne scars and sunspots and any other evidence of interesting stories.

I suppose he's objectively attractive, but subjectively he's not my taste at all. Far too bland. His neck seems choked by his collar and tie, and that's a turnoff if I've ever seen one. He's probably about my age but has an older air about him. Maybe it's the deep groove of his part line, like his hair has been raked by the comb so many mornings in a row that it's lost the spirit to dissent, or maybe it never had any free will in the first place.

I'm not that intrigued by Mr. Suit—or Mr. Suitor, more accurately, since he's clearly interested in me—but I am a little intrigued. There's a stirring of the unexpected that such a follow-the-rules kind of person would have gone out of his way to develop a scheme to get this pig off my tail. I want to see if the plot might take another twist, so I go along with it.

"Darling, I've been looking everywhere for you," I say, all drama and delight, like I'm back in my audition days. I shove the rum drink into my faux partner's hand and loop my free arm through his.

The old guy frowns. He asks if we're together, and Mr. Suitor says that together is an understatement; we're getting married next month. His voice is way too even-keeled, but it's perfect for this ruse since it rings of reliability.

"I don't wear my ring in public," I explain, "because there's too big of a risk of it getting stolen, what with the size of that rock and all."

The pig snorts disapprovingly, then recovers enough to wish us his sincerest congratulations and skirts away, scouting his next prey.

Mr. Suitor shakes his head. "Why do men think they can act like that?" he asks.

It's my turn to round on him. "Why do you think *you* can act like that?" I yank my arm free of his.

He looks perplexed, like he can't possibly imagine why I'm not kissing his shiny loafers right now, thanking him for rescuing me, the damsel in distress.

I'm already furious with myself for going along with such a story, but I couldn't resist how different it was from my Redstocking life. There's no greater bait than the allure of the opposite and the way its hook snags my skin, leaving scars I'll brag about later.

"I didn't need saving," I tell him. "And just for the record, I don't believe in marriage."

"What do you mean you don't believe in it?" he asks.

I explain how I'm part of a feminist pact to never get married. "So if you were hoping that little engagement story back there would come true, so sorry, you're out of luck."

He puts on this injured expression. Guys like him love playing the victim card. He says he was just trying to help, he really wasn't hitting on me. I sort of believe him, which pisses me off even more, so I slice him with my fiercest glare and march off into the crowd.

He follows me nearly as closely as the pig did, but I'm not half as bothered by it. Beneath his banal face, an inquisitive energy flickers. It's like he's gotten bored of himself and wants something else but just doesn't realize it yet.

"Why don't you believe in marriage?" he wants to know.

I think about freezing him out, but I'm hit by a spontaneous burst of generosity and indulge him with the quick facts.

"Marriage is a cage," I say. "The best possible outcome is contentment, and that's really just a synonym for complacency."

"And what's the worst outcome?" he asks. "Divorce?"

"No, of course not. At least divorce provides the opportunity for new beginnings. The worst outcome is total invisibility or maybe total indifference. Take your pick."

He considers it for a moment. Impatience presses on me from all sides, seeking out the friction, creating some itself. "That's a dismal view," he finally says. "My parents are still crazy about each other."

It's so typical that this golden boy grew up in a picture-perfect family. I could choke on the cliché of it. "Chances are they've had affairs," I say, hoping the phrase will soften the prick, throw a blanket over the barbed-wire fence I'm scaling.

"No, they haven't," he says, sounding very defensive about it, like I've crossed a line. It makes me want to cross the next one too.

"You can't be sure of that." I try to sound like I have the evidence to prove their infidelity. Life is all about projecting confidence. Fake it till you make it, Hal is always reminding me. I've just about mastered the trick.

He asks if my parents are still together, and I say no, I'm actually an orphan who was never adopted. I deliver the lie convincingly, but he doesn't seem to buy it.

He reaches out his hand. "I'm Chris," he says, as if I asked for his name, as if I gave him the faintest sign that I was interested. I am sort of interested, though, not in him, just in how I can press his buttons. It's not like there's much else to do at this hoax of an art show.

As I shake his hand, there's a light shock when our palms touch. It's not a spark of chemistry, just a by-product of his static-collecting suit. I squeeze his hand as hard as I can, trying to crush every bone in his knuckles to make up for all the women before me who've shaken hands too lightly and given men all the power right from the start.

"EJ," I say.

He asks how I spell that, and I half expect him to take out a fountain pen and write it down. He has that look of someone who's never caught without his spiral notebook and stack of business cards.

"E-J," I answer. "Very phonetically difficult, I know."

A toothy smile tumbles onto his face. Once it has landed, it's perfectly symmetrical, down to the mini dimples on both sides. I'm filled with an urge to reach out and pull one side of his mouth downward, just so it's not so balanced.

He asks what EJ stands for.

"Ever Joy," I say dryly, making it up on the spot and pleased with the outcome.

"You're lying," he says. "I can see it in your eyes."

I've got to admit this scares me for a second, especially since I'm wearing colored contacts. But then it fills me with a bizarre relief, the idea that a complete stranger can call me out on my bullshit. Usually people just gobble down whatever feces I feed them.

"Emily Jane," I tell him because it almost feels like he's earned it somehow. "But those are the two most boring names ever. My parents lacked a certain creativity."

"Well, you seem to have inherited a lot of creativity from somewhere." Chris's even-keeled voice should lull me right to sleep, but it seems to be waking me up instead. Or maybe I'm just wired from the drink that I guess I've chugged in the time we've been talking.

"I got it all from my friends," I say, looking around the gallery to locate the rest of the Redstockings. Three shooting stars in a room full of space junk. I feel a tug to join them, but it's overridden by the tug to stay and put another wrinkle or two in Chris's ironed-out life.

"You're an actress?" Chris asks, not in a way that implies he recognizes me from anything before, but as if he expects to someday.

"Act*or*," I correct him, though I'm pleased that he sees the star potential in me. "But no, I'm not. I leave that to my roommate." I nod over to Tara. "I'm an Uber driver," I elaborate, which is actually true.

I whiz around the city a few times a week, raking in a hundred dollars a night; it's not bad. We kept the old Ford Focus that Jenni drove out from Michigan—the Red Rocket, we call her, even though she's a rusty brunette by now. I love the rush of racing taxi drivers along the avenues, edging them out. Few things are more satisfying than provoking others' road rage. So many people think they have to sell their souls to corporate America to survive in New York, but there are actually unlimited alternatives if you're not burdened by the weight of other people's expectations.

Chris seems to be carrying a lot of expectations. I ask what he does, if he's a bond trader on Wall Street. He has that look about him.

"Close." His eyebrows wiggle slightly. Self-effacing or arrogant, it's hard to tell. "I'm a tax accountant."

"Even more thrilling," I deadpan. "How'd you end up in Brooklyn tonight? Did someone kidnap you?"

He says the owner of the gallery is a client of his.

"Yup, checks out," I mutter.

"You're a writer," Chris says, staring at me like he's trying to pin down the real color of my eyes. I thought he'd let the career topic drop after I gave the Uber line, but I guess not. Guys like him think that what you do is who you are.

"No, I'm not." But I grow tired of the lie as soon as it's out of my mouth, so I backtrack to the truth. "Okay, sure, I write plays but I've never sold anything. The theater kings don't think I'm very good at all."

I say this with defiant pride, like I'm not scared to look myself in the mirror and see the mascara sinking into the early stages of eye wrinkles that I refuse to buy night cream for because the whole anti-aging industry is rooted in misogyny. The truth is, I actually hate looking at myself in the mirror and nearly always pee in the dark, but that's not because of the wrinkles. It's because I don't want to send the wrong messages to my brain that my looks are tied to my worth.

Chris asks what I'd write about if I was going to come up with a play about tonight.

"That's easy," I say. "It would be about a conventional man falling in love with a modern woman who finds monogamy monotonous. And him not hearing her when she says that she doesn't do commitment, so he tries and fails to get her to change her mind."

Chris seems to find this answer amusing, which wasn't the point at all. "And how would the plotline end?" he asks.

"Depends if it's a comedy or a drama," I say. "It would probably be the former because my comedic talent is really too good to waste. But either way, it would involve significant pining on the man's behalf."

"Nothing like some good male pining to please an audience," Chris says.

"I don't care about writing an ending that pleases the audience," I say, a little more sharply than I mean to because it hits a nerve. "I care about writing an ending that pleases the characters."

"Can't those be the same?" he wants to know, and I have to

explain that no, audiences want the characters' fates to neatly tie together in the end, whereas characters want to break free in the end.

"But can't those outcomes overlap?" he presses. "Things tying together and also breaking free?"

"Of course they can't," I snap, but it's weird that I'm not fully confident in my answer. The Redstockings are at the door now, waving me over. I tell Chris I have to go, my soulmates are calling. He asks where we're off to, is it the House of Yes?

The infamous Bushwick club is our social calendar staple and I'm annoyed that Chris guessed it. It makes me feel like he thinks he knows me, which couldn't be further from the truth. I defy every stereotype, you just can't always tell right away, and I like it that way.

"Care to join?" I ask him. I know he won't, but I'd give a lot of things to see him in that place, the sheer juxtaposition of it. He predictably declines but then asks for my number, which actually makes me laugh aloud, a chunky syllable adding some texture to this two-dimensional gallery.

"Believe me," I tell him, "I'm not your type."

He seems to realize I'm probably right. "Okay," he says, fiddling with the buttons on his blazer, making sure they're lined up just so. "Well, maybe you could base a character off me in one of your future plays. Just make sure he's not the villain."

"He won't be."

I don't tell him what I'm thinking: that he's not interesting enough to be a villain, or a hero either. I just kiss his cheek and leave a flaming orange lipstick stain, a souvenir for him to remember me by.

Following the Redstockings out of the gallery, we hop on the L train at Bedford and skid off at Jefferson right across the street from the House of Yes.

The club doesn't look like much from the outside, just another graffiti-streaked warehouse with a falafel food truck out front.

But when you walk inside, it's a different world—trapeze artists and strobe lights and glitter and flesh. It's unapologetically loud and accepting. The only place in the city that still dazzles me every time.

I fall in love more than once that night, locking eyes, locking lips, locking legs. The reason most people are so miserable is that they buy the myth that love has to last in order to be real. The trick to love is letting it flow in and out, not trying to trap it or freeze it or morph it into the mold you think it should fit. Ordinary people choke love to death, that's the problem.

My knack for plunging into love and bursting out of it again, drenched in its holy water, is all part of the playwriting thing, I guess. Experience the full range of human emotions, break the bounds in all directions, then spill the excess onto the page.

At some point in the night I realize I'm wasted. This frees me even more because I'm no longer constrained by any bad habits I've learned over the years. I'm back in touch with my primal instincts, floating up to the stage and taking my place as the rightful lead of the dance troupe, rearranging the choreography like I was always destined to do.

I can't pick out the Redstockings and don't try to. But I feel them with me and we're dancing, swaying together, changing the angles of our galaxy and every other galaxy too.

Then I'm popping some pellets with the mannequins in the bedazzled bathroom, and next thing I know I'm up on the roof in the hot tub. The air is cold, but it's got me sweating and my thoughts are spinning in a gorgeous non-pattern. Sideways, upward, outward, then backward to Chris and how stiff he looked in that suit.

I wonder if he wants to take it off. I wonder what his body looks like underneath, if his skin is so taut that his spirit can't dance, if his spirit wants to dance at all. It probably doesn't because a person who's lived under a candle snuffer his whole life wouldn't know what to do if he were suddenly on fire again.

I'm on fire now, and I flip over so my other side can burn too, and then I'm back on the stage, wrapped around a new body. Our energies sync as we sink into each other and tangle on the trapeze bars, crossing in and out of the big birdcage that's suspended above the stage. We fly into the sky, liberated in this single moment and therefore liberated for eternity.

And it's so clear in the haze why I'm never going to let myself be locked to loving one person forever. I mean, what kind of a prison is that?

Chapter 3

AS THE DAYS AND WEEKS OOZE onward, I keep coming back to that thing Chris mentioned about whether the ending the characters want and the ending the audience wants can be the same. It's not like I've been thinking about him or anything, just the premise.

I'm not giving his theory much weight. It's just like an accountant to try to turn art into math and think that everything can fit into an overly simplistic Venn diagram. I want to disprove him, but the problem is I haven't actually made it far enough in any of the plays I've started writing to reach the ending, and even if I did, it's not like I'd have much of an audience to test it on.

I'm tempted to debate the whole thing with him just so I can win and let it go, but there are way too many "Chris accountants" in this city to track him down. Not that I haven't toppled down a few rabbit-hole internet searches. It's better that I can't find him, though. The only reason I'm pulled to him at all is the sense of the unfamiliar, the magnet in me that sticks to anything new before inevitably repelling it the next day.

It's on my mind one afternoon a month or three after the art gallery opening as I head outside to the shared courtyard behind the Inn that we treat as our own private garden. Occasionally some other tenants from the adjoining apartments will come over and smoke with us, but mostly they just let us do our thing. It's pretty clear that the space belongs to us.

Jenni has strung some colored Christmas lights that we leave up year-round, Tara feeds the squirrels all the best Lucky Charms marshmallows, and Hal is always out there absorbing inspiration from the clouds or typing up some new business proposal. I sort of float around like an urban nymph doing whatever the fuck I want. Occasionally I even remember to water the weeds that we call ivy. I like helping them climb up the walls and go wild.

Hal's out there now in her throne. It's one of those hanging egg chairs, swinging back and forth to induce creative flow. Her laptop is perched on her folded legs and she's punching away at the keyboard.

I start to ask about the character versus audience thing, but she disengages with that I'm-in-the-zone look. She's been honoring a burst of entrepreneurial energy, up straight for the past who knows how many hours or days, surviving on cold brew and cold ramen. I've got no idea what Hal's working on, but she'll tell me when she's ready. Poking the bear never works even though it's fun.

I pick up Hal's empty ramen bowl and a stray dishrag to take back inside. But she pounces and claws the rag back from me like I've just stolen her most prized possession.

"What're you doing?" she shrieks. "That's the demo!"

"The what?" I ask, taken aback by her attachment to this scraggly little rag.

Hal shrieks again. "It's the demo for my start-up."

"Are you inventing a dishrag company?" I guess. "Made for men, so they start doing their fair share of domestic duties?"

"No," Hal says. "It's a bra-humbug!"

I ask what a bra-humbug is and she impatiently explains that it's a bra for people who hate bras. You know, all the beautiful Scrooges out there like us. Like a bandeau but actually comfortable and supportive, not just some flimsy fashion statement to please the male gaze. "And it's made 100 percent of recycled material."

Landfill material might be the better term, but I start to see the vision. That's the thing with Hal—she's almost too brilliant. It can take a while for other people to catch up, even me sometimes.

"Very innovative." I applaud. "We can get scrappy and plaster your logo onto the Red Rocket, and I'll give you free advertising as I speed around the city."

Hal makes a face like I don't understand how start-ups work. To be fair, I don't know a ton but I hate it when she gets all condescending. She says first she needs to get the frat bro investors to see the vision and hand over the money to scale the production and build a robust direct-to-consumer sales operation, but it's an uphill battle.

"Less than 2 percent of venture capital dollars go to women-founded businesses, you know," she says. Her jaw hardens into that pissed-off-but-determined-as-anything expression that's basically a prerequisite for success. It gives me that warm, proud feeling to be on this ride with her.

"You've got this," I say. "You're a literal genius."

"I know," Hal snaps. "I've just got to keep grinding."

Hal shoos me away, so I walk back inside where Jenni and Tara are sprawled out on the couch, looking as hungover as I feel. We went out last night to celebrate Jenni quitting her latest job, some gig at a think tank that wasn't half as creative as it sounded. She used a portion of her paychecks to buy a Polaroid camera and film, and now she's going to pursue photography. It's all part of the process of elimination to help her find her passion.

"No, it's not anti-feminist," Tara's telling Jenni now as they both gulp giant mugs of something—maybe coffee, maybe whiskey, probably both.

"Let's ask EJ," Tara says and turns toward me. "Do you think it's anti-feminist for Jenni to ask out her ex-boss Peter?"

I think about it, tip it on one side and then the other to see how it stands, how it falls. "It's not anti-feminist," I decide. "I mean, sure, there's the concerning power dynamic from your origin story, but the fact that you're the one asking him out subverts that. And you don't work together anymore, so it's not like you have to do what he says. He can take directions from you this time around."

Tara says yup, that's exactly what she said too, and Jenni says that settles it, she'll text him now. "Should I suggest drinks or coffee?" she wants to know.

I say "drinks" at the same time Tara says "coffee," and Jenni looks flummoxed.

"Jenni," I say, "you can do whatever the fuck you want. You don't need our permission."

I lay a quick hug on her to make sure she feels my softness. It's hard to detect sometimes, but they're not my soulmates for nothing. They're fluent in EJ.

"You're an ooey-gooey marshmallow at the center," Jenni tells me. "You're just always coated in charcoal on the outside."

It's a pretty good summation, I've got to admit. "What can I say, I like the flames and the crunch," I reply.

"Well, here goes nothing," Jenni says. She exhales a pent-up breath and starts drafting a text.

"I'll be out driving," I say, grabbing the car keys and heading out the front door.

It's that kind of day where I can't sit still for too long. Technically I'm sitting when I'm driving, but the rush of the motion soothes the fidgety feeling. I'm as deranged a driver as you'd expect, but no tickets yet—just a couple dozen warnings that I always flirt my way out of and call theater rehearsal.

I drive for a while on my own tonight, and then when I get bored of myself, I start picking up riders. I'm very selective about who I let into my car—no one who's got an Uber rating above three stars out of five. The lower the rating, the more interesting the person; it's basically a scientific correlation. And it's not like I'm that concerned about anyone wrecking the Red Rocket. There's negligible monetary value left to lose; it's all emotional at this point. The bumper is duct-taped together and the wipers smear the chipped windshield with stale ash and dirt.

I accidentally press Accept for someone named Olivia who's got a 4.9 rating, nearly perfect. I'm about to cancel it, but I'm already at the pickup destination in the West Village. It's the corner of Greenwich and West 11th Street, the part of the city where everyone dresses like they're expecting to be mistaken for a celebrity at all times.

This woman on the curb, Olivia it must be, is carefully cross-checking my license plate like she already doesn't trust me. She's with a guy who opens the car door for her. It's just like men to think that they're being all kind and considerate when actually they're just propagating society's chauvinistic order. Because while chivalry is alive, sexism can't be dead.

Olivia is nothing but chic and bones. She'd blow away in a mild wind, maybe already has. She's got that vacancy about her, no aura at all. I stare her down in the rearview mirror as she gets into the back seat.

She looks like cashmere and smells like cashmere and is the type of person I might've been jealous of in middle school, back before I awakened to the perks of being different. Or maybe she's someone I'd see now at a fashion week after-party, the kind of event I'd crash just to piss off the people who are on the list, waiting their turn for admission. We'd start hooking up until I'd realize there was no flavor to it, no pulse, so I'd dash out before doing anything memorable enough that I'd need to forget.

Or more likely we'd never start hooking up in the first place because she's probably never delved deep enough into herself to realize that she's not totally straight—no one is. Her parents are definitely the kind of people who make snarky comments about how the world is going to hell with all these gays with blue hair cluttering up the streets.

The guy gets into the car after Olivia. I can't see his face, but I already know who he is. People like Olivia always date the same kind of guy.

If it seems like I'm being judgmental, I am. I don't ride around this city on a high horse saying I don't judge people. Judging people sparks joy, so why should I quit?

They buckle their seat belts right away. It makes me want to weave in and out of the other cars even more recklessly than usual. Olivia clasps both her hands around one of her partner's arms like she's clinging for dear life, and I feel a surge of gratitude that I'm not chained like that to a man.

"They're going to adore you," Olivia gushes when we're stopped at a red light in bumper-to-bumper traffic.

She's talking to the guy like he's some kind of show pony that she can't wait to parade around. They must've just started dating and now they're off to the big meet-the-friends event that the Redstockings rarely have to deal with since we don't play for keeps.

I get this urge to butt into the conversation, and I could control myself, but where's the fun in that?

"Oh, do you think so, Olivia?" I say. "I don't always make the best first impression, but it means a lot that you have that kind of confidence in me."

Olivia doesn't say anything. She just sits there like she's trying to convince herself that I didn't actually speak. Then she starts whispering to her man in a serpentine sort of way, asking for advice no doubt. It pisses me off because she should be able to make up her own mind about what to say, and also it's such a rich-person thing to do, for Olivia to see her Uber driver as merely a means to an end. You can always tell the character of a person by the first five words they say to their Uber driver. If they say five words at all, which they usually don't.

"I asked you a question, Olivia." I turn off the radio to amp up the awkward silence as I wait for her to answer.

The guy has to speak on her behalf. "Sorry, I think she might've been talking to me," he says to me. "But how's your night going so far?"

My stomach recognizes his voice before my ears do. I whip my head around while I'm zooming up the Seventh Avenue circus, nearly clipping the side mirror of a Tesla that's incompetently parked.

"Chris!" I think and say at the same time. There's no gap between the two.

He looks just like he did the last time I saw him—the same dark parted hair and mellow brown eyes and those lips that need more of a shape. He's not wearing a suit this time, but he still has a button-down shirt and dry-clean-only pants. It's really not any better, but it seems better.

I'm weirdly relieved to see him. It almost feels like I've been driving around the luxury neighborhoods where I thought he'd hang out, just on the off chance that something like this would happen. That's not what I've been doing; it just kind of feels like that.

"Emily Jane?" He seems uncertain, which I guess is fair since I've bleached my hair and buzzed part of it too, and I'm wearing these amber contacts today that make me feel like I'm a cheetah that just escaped a zoo.

"Just EJ," I correct, though hearing my full name doesn't bother me as much as I would have expected.

Olivia murmurs something, only to Chris, but I can still hear it. "You know her?" is what she says.

The way she puts that othering emphasis on *her* makes me scream inside. I mean, why do women always have to go pitting themselves against each other? I'm not pitting myself against her; I'm just reacting to her hostility.

They're the kind of uninteresting people that dating app algorithms pair together because they're programmed to match like with like, as if people are trying to find their clone, not their lover.

"Did you meet on a dating app?" I ask, hoping to confirm my theory and get Olivia more involved in the conversation so she can give me a chance to disprove the judgments I've made. Or maybe just confirm them more.

"We did," Chris says, and I make a clucking sound to congratulate myself on being right.

It strikes me that there should be a dating app that deliberately matches opposites to keep things interesting. Maybe I'll pitch the idea to Hal later and share in the profits.

Olivia is doing her little mumbling thing again and Chris is explaining to her that he met me at an art gallery once. There's not much emotion in his voice, but there never is so I don't take it personally. He's probably just being extra careful not to arouse any suspicions.

"Chris asked me to marry him," I elaborate for Olivia's benefit, just so she understands the context. "But don't worry, I said no."

He tells her it wasn't anything, just a practical joke, but I see Olivia withdraw her hands from his arm. There's a victorious lurch in my stomach.

He reaches for her hand again but she resists. It's so petty. We're all going to be dead in the blink of an eye, and here she is wasting her life being miserable, punishing a man she's choosing to be with. It doesn't even seem like the makeup sex will be good, so what's the point?

"Don't worry," I say to Olivia. "I told Chris he wasn't my type."

That just makes her prickle up even more like she's a desert cactus. I'm really wondering what Chris sees in her. Maybe she gives better blow jobs than she looks like she would.

"Chris, feel free to text me if you ever need a private ride," I say, dripping temptation over the words *private ride*. Then I rattle off my phone number. I say the numbers pretty fast because I don't want to make it too easy for him. He blinks twice and I'm pretty confident that he memorized it on the spot. I mean, he's an accountant, so numbers should be his thing.

We're still some blocks from their Midtown destination, but traffic is all backed up. I'm starting to feel suffocated by having them in my car, so I pull over and eject them with pomp and circumstance.

"Here you are," I say. "We've arrived."

Olivia doesn't point out that we're not there yet. She just slithers out like she's relieved to be rid of me and my stench. Chris thanks me for driving and follows her out. He seems to know it's not safe for him to linger, that he might fall victim to my charms like he did the last time.

"See you soon!" I call out with cherry-flavored cheer as they walk down the sidewalk.

They're not holding hands. It's like Olivia is still trying to freeze Chris out. Not enough that their relationship will fall apart, just enough so he'll take her out to a Michelin-starred dinner tomorrow night. As if that's where happiness lurks, in the shallow shells of hundred-dollar oysters.

They should be thanking me, really; I've given them conversation fodder, no doubt more interesting than whatever they'll talk about at their posh little party. Everyone sitting around comparing six-figure salaries and planning their next European vacation so they don't have to find anything original to bond over in the present.

I keep driving for a while longer.

I'm all wound up after that, and sometime after midnight I start thinking about sleeping with my riders. It's the easiest way ever to have a one-night stand, all these people going home from the clubs after failing to find someone to go home with, and then they luck out with an irresistible Uber driver.

I'm not in the mood for it tonight, though, so I drive back to Bushwick and park the Red Rocket outside the Inn in the parking spot that we've painted with a big "Private Parking—Violators Will Be Towed" sign to scare off the other cars. The police around here have bigger things to worry about than coming for us.

I'm not ready to go inside. Privacy appeals, so I walk around the neighborhood. Emptied spray paint cans litter the gravelly potholes of Knickerbocker Avenue. Spotty streetlights illuminate sidewalk graffiti with shapes I've never seen before but immediately recognize as true.

This is what art is supposed to be. Communal and evolving, on full display for everyone and their mother to see and stomp their feet on, scream out for. Not something private and static that's caged away in galleries and museums where you get arrested for touching it, hushed for expressing the uncouth emotion it stirs within you.

Revolutions aren't born in fancy theaters where rich people pay an arm and a soul for tickets. Revolutions are born on grimy city blocks where broke communities refuse to break by walking together, dancing together, dreaming together, banding together.

Feeling a surge of affection for Bushwick, I try to scope out a street fight, a drug deal, a shoplifting bust. I'm not going to insert myself in the middle of it; I just want to watch something interesting swirl around me, swirl within me. But it's dead quiet.

I'm not a fan of silence; it makes everything louder inside. It makes me wonder when I'll hear from Chris. Because the question is "when," not "if." I know he'll text me once Olivia stops censoring his phone. He's obviously bored out of his bones. The problem is that all his friends are bored too, so he just thinks that's the way relationships have to be: pairing up with someone who makes people say, "Oh, what a perfect couple," when you post photos on social media. Little do they know your faces sag back to apathy right after the camera flashes. Guys like Chris want someone who seamlessly fits into their life, as if it's a good thing to fit in. As if it doesn't mean that you hardly even notice the other person's existence and don't evolve in their presence at all.

It's late. Chris and Olivia are probably in bed right now. The thought makes me itchy, so I take off my patched denim jacket, and then I peel off my T-shirt and then my bra too because the metal wiring is poking into my skin. Talk about a grassroots advertising campaign for liberation. I continue down the block, past Blazin' Skinz Tattoo Parlor, which looks as reputable as it sounds. Tony's Pizzeria, our no-frills anchor, is wedged beside it, just dilapidated enough to keep the swarm of Manhattanite foodies from invading and propagating our deep Brooklyn culture into a social media hashtag.

The streets are nearly empty. I'm not scared for my safety. My aura oozes invincibility. The neighbors would come help me anyway, at least the ones who aren't far away on a trip where screams sound like seagulls.

I expect to be noticed, but the few people I pass don't glance twice. They barely glance once, too absorbed in their phones or their pizza or the real or imaginary music in their ears. And isn't that the truth about Bushwick—you can walk around topless and not even stand out. Kind of great but kind of sad too. It almost makes me miss Michigan, how I could be guaranteed to cause a scene just by going running in a crop top. *Gasp*, the scandal of a belly button.

Refusing to slump under the defeat of it all, I maintain the strong neck of a sphinx as I return to the Inn and take a scorching shower. No one else in the building is using the hot water this late; it's all mine to hoard. One of the best perks of being nocturnal.

I take out my contacts. The gray irises bleed through again. Looking away from the mirror fast so I don't have to see myself like that, I bumble into my room and settle into the bottom bunk. The thin little mattress bends to my body like most things do.

I try to conjure up a steamy scene for a lucid dream, but all I keep thinking about is how Chris blinked twice when I gave him my number, like he was trying to tell me he got it.

Chapter 4

CHRIS DOESN'T END UP CALLING, WHICH is completely fine. It's his loss. It's more just annoying because I had that sense that he would and I don't like being wrong.

But it's probably better to keep him as a stranger and preserve the mystery of illusion before the uninspired reality of being with an accountant ruins the vibrancy of the things I can fantasize about it. Not that I *am* fantasizing about it, but I could if I wanted to. That's all I'm saying.

Spring slopes sharply into summer and the Redstockings spend basically all our free time out in the garden, begging for a breeze. Our window A/C units work only when they want to. I'm torn between being proud of the A/C's rebellious streak and furious because we're basically reflective with our own sweat, that's how shiny we are.

One afternoon we're all out there in the garden and I'm practicing lines with Tara for a musical she's been cast in.

I'm standing in for the lead. It's this character who travels through time and breaks a heart in every century. I'm really pouring myself into the role, ad-libbing left and right and left again. It makes me wonder if I threw in the towel a little too soon when it comes to acting. Then I remember how the directors would try to squash my creative liberty, demolish it under the formulaic treads of their shoes. I won't stand for that, so I'll have to keep my talent underground. Sometimes darkness is the brightest place.

Tara has landed a supporting role for an off-off-Broadway show. That might not sound like a big deal, but it is by New York standards. It's a huge fucking deal. The only problem is she's got imposter syndrome. I think it traces back to the whole foster kid thing and how she tried to fit into all these different families that only half wanted her and she felt like she was never enough.

No imposter syndrome for Hal. She's abandoned the bra-humbug idea, deciding that the most progressive and environmentally friendly bra is no bra at all. I must've inspired her when I shared about my late-night topless stroll, plus the original Redstockings burned bras back in the seventies, so that's really the precedent to beat all prejudice.

Now she's onto something new, a horoscope/telescope app that maps your zodiac chart with stars in the sky that are giving off vibrations on any given day so you can physically sync up with the stars. Hal hasn't actually built the app yet, but that doesn't deter her.

"All the guys out in Silicon Valley do it," she keeps saying. "It's all about getting investors to buy into the idea before the product exists, then using their money to build it."

I'm not big on zodiac signs. Looking to anything external for guidance is just a capitalistic ploy or patriarchal tactic to keep women from realizing we're in control of our own destiny. But I'm obsessed with Hal's confidence. It's contagious and it's always easier to believe in the unbelievable when I'm around her. She says the same about me.

Today Hal is curled up in the egg chair working on a business plan, and Jenni is sitting at the wobbly patio table, scrolling through her phone.

Jenni has started posting pictures of her Polaroids across her socials so she can get a following and monetize the talent. It's slow going right now. She hasn't exactly reached influencer status yet, but I think it's better that way. It's a slippery slope when you start pandering to a social media audience. I know because I posted some writing on there for a bit, but then I deleted my account. It wasn't because I only had forty-three followers; it was because I felt like I was writing to get other people to click Like rather than writing something that I actually liked myself. I have too much artistic integrity for those games.

Jenni speaks without looking up from her phone. "Peter's going to stop by the Inn for a few minutes," she says very casually, like she's announcing that she's putting in our usual pizza and garlic knots order from Tony's.

Tara stops her line mid-sentence. Hal lifts up her heavy-duty headphones, like a bomb just detonated, which it basically has.

I respond first. "Peter?" I try to keep my voice calm, try to give her the benefit of the doubt that perhaps I was so swept up in my lines that I misheard her. "As in your boyfriend?"

Jenni's plan to ask out her old boss went very well, she'd tell you. Or very badly, I'd say. He's snatching her away, bribing her with air-conditioning and laundry machines; the man has no shame. He's gotten her crawling into a cage and thinking it's a castle. They've gone from zero to serious in no time flat. Hal and Tara have assured me it's just a phase Jenni's going through, but I don't like it, and here's the proof that things have escalated to a dangerous level.

"Yep, that's the one," Jenni says, like she thinks I'm being playful. "He wants to meet all of you and see our place before we go to dinner. Don't worry—he's not staying over or anything."

I don't try to muffle the scornful sound that comes out of me. I just try to recall if we ever explicitly said that we wouldn't bring romantic partners over in the daytime. Even if we didn't, it still feels like a violation of something sacred as well as a grievous oversight on my end as the unofficial but unanimously accepted leader of the Redstockings.

Jenni seems to mistake our shell-shocked silence for acceptance. She bounces up and hops inside through the broken screen door. "I need to clean up before Peter gets here," she says.

That helps me find my voice. "You're not actually conforming to that 1950s housewife shit, are you? Don't you remember how far you've come?"

Jenni tosses me an exasperated expression. "Come on, EJ, you're blowing things out of proportion. Peter just wants to come by and say hi. It's not a big deal."

I look to Tara and Hal to back me up on this, but Hal's not in the mood for combat; it's too distracting. "Let it rest, EJ," she says in her business voice, putting her headphones back on and resuming with the *click click* of the keyboard.

Tara's my last hope. I know she doesn't want Peter over here. I know she likes the stability of our space and feels threatened by an outsider. But the thing is, she's also terrified of disappointing anyone, and so she winds up just half shrugging her shoulders. "I should go wash my dishes in the sink," she says. "They've been there too long anyway."

As she starts walking inside, I remind her that no, we're not caving to those gender-normative pressures—we're going to finish rehearsing. "Opening night is only eight weeks away, Tara," I say. "You can't afford to blow your big opportunity just because you're cleaning up for some guy who's stealing our friend from us before our very eyes."

I realize it sounds harsh, but these are dire times. I can't go easy on Tara and tell her how amazing she is and that she'll slay either way, no matter how much I want to.

The doorbell buzzer goes off. It sounds more haunting than usual, and I feel proud of our little Dunge Inn. It's like it knows this intruder doesn't belong and is doing its best to scare him away.

It doesn't work, though. Peter bounds in, big and burly like a washed-up college athlete who's still clinging to his glory days as the only evidence of his importance in the world. Jenni's beaming when she introduces him, and I catch a glimpse of her younger, sheltered self. Her hair and clothes and posture are different now, sharper now, but there's still a softness in her face, a softness that I'm worried Peter has turned into a pillow to lay his inflated head on.

Peter doles out bottles of wine, the expensive-looking stuff we mock people for buying when they could get just as drunk on the grocery store stuff.

"One for each of the Redstockings," he says very proudly, like it's some big deal he's remembered our name or knows how to count to four.

Jenni gives him a tour of the apartment, and you've got to give her some credit, she doesn't even bat an eyelash to show him the top bunk she sleeps on. Her self-confidence has certainly improved over the years. That's something at least.

Everyone goes out to the garden except for me. I stay and sulk for a bit.

Eventually I cave and join them because I don't feel like being that dramatic friend who shuts herself in her room when things don't go her way. I'm more mature than that. Also, my room is basically a boiler and I need the breeze.

Jenni passes out the terra-cotta cups that we use as wineglasses. I slurp greedily from mine to take the edge off the insufferably dull questions that the others are asking Peter about where he grew up and what he likes to do in the city and on and on. Finally, I can't take it anymore.

"What's your favorite bar in Bushwick?" I interject, keeping my voice nice and flat so he won't suspect how I'm trying to get him to walk into my trap and reveal his total ignorance of everything beyond his immaculate Manhattan bubble.

He makes a joke that it's this garden right here, then admits it's actually his first time in Bushwick. I feel smug because my trap worked, but the satisfaction slips away as Jenni says it's exciting that she gets to introduce him to Lone Wolf and General Deb's and Le Garage and Public House. "How fun is that?" she gushes.

Peter is the dry kind of guy whose idea of a good time is talking about stock markets and sports. I wonder if he and Chris would be friends. At first I think they would be, but ultimately I shake out that they'd only be acquaintances. They really aren't that similar at all because Chris at least has this underlying irony about him, this self-awareness that he's not very interesting, whereas Peter seems perfectly oblivious to the fact.

He's overly transfixed by Jenni too, draping his arm around her the whole time, his fancy watch catching the sun and blinding us like a white-collar weapon. He laughs too loudly at everything Jenni says. It feels like he's entranced by the idea of dating someone poor, someone artsy, someone outside his echo chamber. But the novelty could wear off tomorrow and he'd be gone in the blink of a drink. This wouldn't bother me except that I know it will bother Jenni. She still hasn't gotten the hang of letting love in and out the revolving door every night. She'll be pretty crushed when Peter moves on, but that's what the Redstockings are for. We pick up the pieces and arrange them in glorious mosaics.

After tossing back a couple more glasses of wine, I'm not drunk, but I probably wouldn't pass a sobriety test either. Unless I tried to pass it and then I could.

My phone starts buzzing. It's a number I don't recognize, probably some political pollster asking my opinion on gun control or abortion. I nearly always talk to pollsters because I respect their commitment to the cause, whatever their cause is, and I also like to tell them the opposite of what I actually believe. It's a good time, leading people on like that.

I'm grateful for this call now. It gives me an excuse to stop paying attention to Peter—not that I was waiting for an excuse, but I'll still take it. Walking to the far end of the garden, I pick up.

"What do you want?" I bark into the phone.

I'm all ready to give some hugely believable spiel about why I think marriage should only be between a man and a woman and everyone who thinks otherwise is going straight to hell. This is the only way to make sure the progressives don't get too complacent, because the day that all the polls say the overwhelming majority supports gay marriage is the day that people lose the fire to keep fighting the good fight and forfeit fifty years of progress.

"Emily Jane," the person on the phone says.

It's so invasive how these people know my name and probably my address, maybe even my Social Security number. It'll only be a matter of time before they sell my data to the highest bidder. I pity the fool who tries to steal my identity. I'll sue them for all they're worth and take the Redstockings to Amsterdam with the winnings. I'm lost in those happy little thoughts when my brain backs up and hears the voice behind the words.

"It's Chris," the pollster says and I realize it's not a pollster at all. It's Chris.

My insides flip over themselves a few times before I can calm down enough to land on the appropriate flavor for a reply—sriracha sauce and toasted sesame seeds. After a pause, I get it right. "Why're you calling me?" I ask. "Have you never heard of texting?"

He lets out a shaky laugh and I get the feeling he's already wondering if he made the wrong decision by calling. This makes me certain that it's right. Guess it was only a matter of time after all.

"I have a favor to ask you," he says. "And I thought it would be more polite to call than text."

Now I'm awake. I can think of a lot of favors Chris would want from me, but unfortunately I don't think he's asking about those. I can't pass up the opportunity to poke about it, though. "Let me guess," I say. "You're inquiring about a threesome with you and Olivia?"

I swear I can feel him trying not to smile a guilty sort of smile. "Not quite," he says and informs me that he and Olivia are going to her parents' place on Long Island for some long weekends in August.

I choke on my own eye roll because *on Long Island* is how rich people refer to the Hamptons. It's like when the prick from Harvard says they went to *a small college just outside of Boston*. I've got no patience for this. If you're going to be privileged, then at least wear your privilege on your sleeve so I can yank on it and cause a scene.

It's not clear where Chris is going with this, but I pretend I know. "Oh, you're inviting me to the Hamptons?" I say. "I could be persuaded. I'll dance on broken beer bottles on the beach until my feet bleed and paint the sand red. It'll be spectacular."

That gets him nice and flustered. He says sorry, he's not getting this out right—he was wondering if there was any chance that maybe I might take care of his dog, Arnold, on the weekends he's gone. "I'd pay you, of course, and you could stay at my place, but really no pressure. Just wanted to check."

I don't even dwell on how wishy-washy the request is. I'm too busy being surprised because no one has ever asked me to collect their mail before, let alone take care of a living, breathing pet. I love animals and they love me right back, but responsibility isn't exactly my strong suit. I can be objective about that.

"You want me to take care of your dog?" I clarify.

Chris says yeah, he can't stand kennels and he just thought Arnold and I would get along well.

I catch a whiff of his motive, sniff it right out.

"I'm the only person you know who doesn't summer in a no-pets-allowed Hamptons palace, aren't I?" I ask.

He says no, that's not it at all; I'm just the only one he'd trust his dog with.

That makes me laugh. "Oh yeah, because I've given off such trustworthy vibes from the thirty minutes you and I have spent together."

"I think I've got a decent sense of who you are," he says.

I've got to admit that this freaks me out. It almost feels like he knows something about me that I don't know. But then I remember he's just doing what men do: talking a big game when they've got no facts to back it up.

"Of course you don't," I say. "And you should just use one of those dog-walking apps. Find someone there who's got good reviews and all that."

"I haven't had great luck with those apps," Chris says. "Arnold is family, and he's got to be in good hands."

I nearly make an innuendo about my good hands, but I can't get it out. Because out of nowhere and everywhere too, my throat is filled with stupid pebbles of nostalgia. I'm missing Melon, the Shetland sheepdog my parents got my little sister and me the Christmas I turned seven. I named her Melon because I was in a phase of life where I was obsessed with melons; it doesn't really have much of a backstory. Sometimes the best things are the simplest.

I was Melon's favorite. No one could argue with that, though they did anyway. The day after my little sister went to college, Melon died, just never woke up. It was like she'd been doing her best to hold the family together and now that my parents were empty nesters, her duties were done—she knew it was a hopeless cause to make those two fall back in love, if they'd ever been in love in the first place. It's hard to picture even with an imagination like mine.

"What's your offer?" I ask Chris, and I'm pretty taken aback at how high of a number he gives. I negotiate it up 20 percent anyway because women are always getting the short end of the stick when it comes to compensation.

He agrees to my terms and asks if I can come by next week to walk through Arnold's routine.

"Sure, that works," I say, and then I jab the End Call button. I always like to be the first one to hang up.

There's all this charged energy looping through me as I walk back over to the table. I sit in my chair again, tapping one bare foot on the gravel, then the other. I've got to get this restlessness out but it won't budge. It's lodged inside like there's a blockage in my veins. But my bones feel unstuck, fresh from an oil change.

"What was that?" Hal asks me.

"Oh, nothing," I say. "Just a delightful NRA caller reminding me to fight for my rights."

"Right, because our children dying in mass shootings every day is the epitome of freedom," Hal says.

"And the Constitution should be taken literally," Tara adds. "With no exceptions, given it was written nearly two hundred and fifty years ago when *arms* meant rifles, not machine guns."

"Precisely," I say, feeling an extra wave of gratitude for these beautiful humans that I get to call my best friends.

Jenni murmurs in Peter's ear that we're just joking.

"It's not a joke," Hal says. "Gun violence is now the second-leading killer for teens, behind car accidents. It's pandemic territory."

"Of course the shootings aren't a joke," Jenni says. "Just how EJ trolled the caller."

"You really shouldn't pretend to agree with those maniacs," Tara tells me, as if people-pleasing isn't her entire personality. "It just gives more fuel to their fire."

"Fighting fire with fire," I say. "It's the only way."

I zone out for a bit, enjoying the way that not telling them about the dogsitting for Chris makes it seem like a secret, or something exciting enough to be a secret.

Anything that isn't worth hiding isn't worth keeping. That's one of the EJ aphorisms of life.

I tune back in when they're talking about women's basketball, and I start being a little warmer to Peter, only because being cold is getting kind of old and I'm too preoccupied thinking about Chris and why he called me of all people. The feeling I keep coming back to is that he doesn't actually know why he did, that he's just as confused as I am right now.

Victory splatters me like paint, vibrant and vivacious. I knew Chris wouldn't be able to stay away from me. I knew he'd cave eventually.

I top off everyone's wineglasses and propose a toast to winning bets. The others don't understand the meaning, but I don't elaborate. I just lap up the wine and squirm happily in my seat from side to side, avoiding the center, the evenness of it there.

Chapter 5

CHRIS TELLS ME TO COME OVER to his apartment on Thursday evening at seven o'clock.

This makes me snort some laughter because he thinks everyone's life revolves around such confining things as days and hours. I can nearly always distinguish a sunrise from a sunset and that's about all I need. I've got no interest in shoving my life inside the tiny squares of a calendar. Time is nothing but a construct meant to make people feel behind. Women, specifically, with all the wedding-and-kids pressure.

I make an exception for the dogsitting, though, and set a reminder on my phone. Once I get done rolling my eyes at the rigidity, it's actually quite exhilarating to have a specific place to go, a time someone expects me to arrive. Defying defiance feels good sometimes.

Chris lives in Tribeca, the highest-income neighborhood in Manhattan, bordering the Hudson River on one side and the Financial District on the other. All the corporate sellouts live there so they can sleepwalk to their Wall Street skyscrapers and fulfill their noble calling as disposable cogs in the wheel of capitalism.

I drive over to Tribeca rather than take the subway because I haven't yet hit my road rage provocation quota for the week. When I finally get below the stop-and-go traffic of SoHo, there's an eerie hush that falls over the cobblestone streets. It feels like everyone in this zip code has died an early death, and now it's just their bodily shells marching on in their puffed-up routines because they wouldn't know what to do or who to be if they stopped.

The tidy sidewalks are nearly empty. All the tourists are tied up in Times Square and the homeless know better than to waste their time begging from the wealthy. The streets are still packed with parked cars, though—Range Rovers and Jaguars, it's all so predictable. I have to squiggle around for a while until I can snag a spot. I'm no good at parallel parking. Perpendicular things are nearly always more interesting, so I hold up the cars behind me by taking my sweet time until finally the Red Rocket is wedged into the spot, the back tire up on the curb.

I get out of the Red Rocket and walk east, or maybe west. It's hard to tell because the sun hasn't sunk yet but the buildings are tall enough to block the light, so it feels like night already. That's a metaphor if I've ever heard one.

Eventually I get to Chris's place. He lives in one of those obnoxiously tall towers, a total eyesore in the sky. Thirty or sixty stories tall—I don't feel like craning my neck to check.

The Windemere is written in loopy cursive on the frilly awning out front; it's so typically English try-hard. There are these two doorpeople guarding the place like it's Buckingham Palace. They have to wear these ridiculous uniforms and top hats that make them look like little props in a show; it's so demeaning. They see everyone but no one sees them. It's sort of like being an Uber driver, I guess, but at least I get to wear whatever I want.

I strut into the building like I belong. As I'm making my way toward the elevator bank, the guy at the front desk calls me over and asks my name. If I were on staff here, I'd rather take the outside shift. It beats sitting in this stuffy lobby all day in the sickly light of the crystal chandelier, passing fake niceties with multimillionaire tenants who don't remember your name or more likely never even ask for it in the first place.

I try to bond with the guy at the front desk, laugh about what a joke this place is. I figure he'll appreciate that I'm another outsider, but he's all formal and serious and won't break character. It's not his fault. There are probably security cameras rating his professionalism, waiting for the slightest misstep so they can fire him and hire someone younger who doesn't expect to be paid a penny above minimum wage.

He calls up to Chris's apartment to verify that I'm allowed to be here, that I'm not plotting some heist to steal all the jewelry in this place. The thought makes me giggle, makes me feel unbridled and alive.

In the elevator, I jab the number 27 for Chris's floor. I've never been in an elevator that moves so fast. It's a rush and leaves my ears popping with pleasure.

I try to open the door to Chris's apartment, but it's locked so I rap on it to the beat of a song I was listening to on the radio on my way here. It's my new favorite jam that I know I'll overplay and won't be able to stand by tomorrow.

A dog barks from inside. It's a good bark, assertive without being arrogant, a rare combo. You can always tell about a dog from the bark. It seals in the sense that I've done the right thing by agreeing to help Chris.

The door opens and the dog leaps on me like he's been impatiently awaiting my arrival, like Chris has been prepping him for just how great I am.

I pretend to be put off by the sudden attack, but the pup's got my heart from the start. He's an Australian shepherd, a mash-up of grays and whites and browns and blacks. His eyes are delightfully mismatched too, one golden and one navy blue. I'm wearing navy contacts today and it strengthens the bond between us.

"That's Arnold," Chris says. It's pretty cute, the way he's bursting with pride over this slobbery creature. I wouldn't have expected it from Chris. He's not exactly touchy-feely. But that's the magic of dogs, how they bring out the best in all of us, even stoic guys like Chris who've been trained to think that showing emotion is a sign of weakness.

Chris is looking alright despite the fact that he's wearing pastel khaki shorts, plus one of those golf polos with a little whale logo. It's the classic Hamptons garb, a code to let everyone around you know that you went to an Ivy League school and now work in finance and make more than enough money to buy everyone's drinks at the are-you-on-the-list beach bar, not that you will because you want to hoard it all for yourself. I'm not sure if Chris means to be sending those messages—he may have just fallen into the trap without knowing it, but that's really no excuse. I have the urge to cut off the constrictive collar of his shirt or at least untuck it, but I restrain myself with pure decorum.

The apartment is modern and sterile with gigantic floor-to-ceiling windows that couldn't be more of a contrast to the Inn's. There's central air-conditioning and I realize how sweaty I am only when the beads of perspiration start drying on my skin. The living room windows face south, down toward the Financial District's steely skyscrapers, pompous and sleek. The only respectable building is the Freedom Tower, standing a hundred and some stories high, the spire pointing into the sky like a giant middle finger to the terrorists. I don't do patriotism, but the sight does jab me with a certain pride that America wasn't scared to build another tall building after the Twin Towers fell, that we won't be bullied into meekness. I wonder if Chris ever thinks about these things. He's probably immune to the view by now. That's how it goes.

Arnold's not a puppy anymore, but he still has that spunk like he doesn't plan to calm down anytime soon, like he's not subscribing to the conventions surrounding age and maturity. It's a good outlook. We're on the same page, so I get down on my knees and we start wrestling each other right there on the tasseled rug. I call him Arnie, not Arnold. We're on nickname basis already.

Chris asks if maybe we could take it easy. "I don't want Arnold to wreck the apartment."

By that I know he means he doesn't want *me* to wreck the apartment, though that's what the apartment clearly needs—some wrecking. It's all sharp angles and beige furnishings, like Chris ordered the whole thing straight from a showroom. Nothing personal about it.

The only exceptions are some framed photos of him and Olivia, hanging vexingly straight and centered on the cream-colored walls. Looking around, I notice more pictures of them jammed onto the glass coffee table and granite kitchen counter. I bet there are even photos in the bathroom, so I walk in to check. It's all ceramic and swirls, and sure enough more pictures are right there by the opulent little soap dispenser. I get the feeling that Olivia put all these up. She must've surveyed the apartment from all angles to ensure that there was never a place where Chris couldn't see her face, because out of sight means out of mind. It reeks of insecurity, but what do I know about relationships?

"Olivia lives here too?" I ask, making a point to show respect by using her name. I choose the high road sometimes, just not all the time because then it's not a choice, it's a default.

"No," Chris says. "I live by myself. Olivia and I have only been dating five months."

Doing the math, I conclude they must've met soon after Chris fell for me at the art gallery. Very briefly and very rashly, I wonder what would've happened if I'd agreed to go out with him then. Perhaps this apartment might have more color and less order. Probably not, since we would've fizzled out long ago and he would've met Olivia or someone identical to Olivia by now anyway.

There are two bedrooms, and the entire spare room feels like a gross display of income inequality. I could hate Chris for it, but I'm feeling extra agreeable today so I decide to just hate the system instead.

"Why isn't Arnie going to the Hamptons with you?" I ask.

Chris explains how he wanted to take him, but Olivia's dad has a bad dander allergy and Chris is trying to make a good impression since it's the first time they're meeting.

He seems nervous about it, which makes zero sense. Chris is the textbook definition of the ideal guy to bring home. My mom would be over the goddamn moon if I arrived back in Michigan for Christmas with Chris in tow. My dad would be all for it too since he's worked himself into an uproar thinking I'm never going to settle down, that my Brooklyn friends are bad influences. All the Wendys becoming Peter Pans, the most wonderful plot twist of our generation, but my parents don't see it that way.

Chris starts reciting a bunch of directions that he wants me to follow for watching Arnie, like the exact route to take him out on a walk twice a day. North on Greenwich Street, west on Hubert, down to the end of Pier 26, and back. And it's the same thing for the dog food. One and a half scoops at 8:15 a.m. and 7:30 p.m. with a half scoop at 1:45 p.m., and on and on he goes. There's no question he's an accountant. All that attention to detail makes me crazy just listening to it. It feels like a construction drill is pressing into my skull.

"You can sleep in the spare room," Chris says. "The sheets are fresh."

My toes curl and my lips too. "Does Olivia know I'm staying here?" I ask.

He blushes rose gold at that, flattering evidence of how he really feels about me. He says that no, he didn't mention to Olivia which of his friends was taking care of Arnold; it just hadn't come up, and he's not trying to hide it or anything. That makes me smirk like sunshine.

Chris starts arranging color-coded lists with all the information, displaying them so prominently on the counter that no one could miss them unless they were really trying to.

"You know I'm not really going to look at those, right?" I say.

His forehead creases into well-practiced lines, probably written by all that vapid stress about work and relationships and the life track he thinks he's supposed to be on. "That's what I'm afraid of."

"Remember why you asked me to dogsit?" I say.

"I'm having a bit of a hard time now."

"It's because I'm different," I say, and we both know I'm right. If he'd wanted just another follow-the-directions type, he never would've called me.

Arnie wags his tail like he's trying to tell Chris not to worry, that he wants a change of pace with a zany playmate. I expect Chris's risk-averse nature to take over and talk himself out of it, but he just nods and swallows his anxiety in one gulp.

Chris gets his luggage, a wheely suitcase that's excessively large for just a weekend away. It's like he's packed four backups of everything, just in case. He spends a long time triple- and quadruple-checking that he hasn't forgotten anything and that all the outlets are unplugged and that the windows are locked and that the spare key is in the envelope on the counter. It makes me feel a rush of compassion at how hard it must be for him to need everything to go a certain way. It's easy for me to make fun of routines because of how free-spirited I am, but it's just not how some people are wired.

An uncomfortable sensation shifts inside me, like a hug is trying to paw its way out. I don't embrace Chris; I just arrange my face in a way that I hope he'll interpret as genuine.

He tells me to help myself to whatever food I want, and he'll be back Sunday night by seven thirty. "Oh, and please give Arnold the filtered water. I don't trust the quality of the tap water in the city."

"I've got it taken care of," I say. "Arnie and I are going to have a grand ole time."

Still looking apprehensive, Chris turns around as he's halfway out the door. I expect him to rattle off one last instruction, but he just meets my eyes like he's seeing straight through the navy of my lenses. "Thanks, Emily Jane," he says. "This means a lot."

I get sort of squirmy inside because I don't like making direct eye contact when I'm sober. It's too intimate. But there's also a part of me that wants to hold the gaze longer.

I look away, back to Arnie. His tail is swinging back and forth like it's swatting invisible flies or maybe fairies.

"You're paying me," I remind Chris. "You don't thank your employee."

"Sure you do," he says, and he's right. It boosts my view of Chris a bit more. It's actually pretty high by now.

Arnie doesn't react well to Chris being gone. He goes berserk, like he's scared he'll never see him again. I have to keep telling him that everything's going to be okay, that we're going to have lots of fun together and Chris will be back in just a few days.

It's weird, but I miss Chris right away too. It's probably just because I'm never home by myself at the Inn. Hal or Tara or Jenni is always around so I'm not used to being alone. I'm not really alone, though, because I've got Arnie. He's great company once he settles down.

We curl up together on the couch and watch an action movie that's way too predictable. The ending doesn't surprise me at all and it doesn't surprise Arnie either. He doesn't bark once, sees through it all. I bet he'd like my scripts way more.

After the movie, I explore the jarringly large fridge and raid some ripe avocados and hummus. The hummus doesn't have enough flavor, so I find some minced garlic in the spice drawer and dash it on until it's gone. After poking around all the brass-knobbed cabinets stocked full with blenders and air fryers and bread machines that look completely unused, I rummage through the items on the coffee table. It's all very predictable—*Economist* magazines, Yale coasters, a book of top-ranked golf courses in the world with certain pages earmarked as if Chris has planned out every vacation from now until his eighty-third birthday.

On the shelf above the coat closet, there's a leather-bound photo album that I flip through. It's from Chris's childhood. He had these huge circular glasses and an underbite. He was a cute kid and probably not part of the popular crowd, which is always a nice trait. But it seems he's been wearing a corporate costume his whole life. There's a photo of him in a full suit in church when he's probably eight or nine. Looks like his first Communion.

I think back to my own first Communion, how I wouldn't even recognize that girl anymore, how it was the first and last time I'd ever wear a puffy white dress and a veil. I'm proud of my transformation, how I've broken free, but it makes me sad too. I'm not sure why and I don't want to know, so I just shove the feeling away and focus instead on all the pictures with Chris and this boy, his big brother. He looks a lot like Chris but blonder and less nerdy, standing confidently in his Little League baseball uniform like he knows he'll be recruited by college scouts one day.

Chris's parents don't look as prim as I'd expected. They've got this warmth about them even in 2D and they do appear to be in love, but pictures lie like that. I've got a whole stack of happy-looking pictures of my own parents, and that doesn't mean a damn thing.

I want to have a drink but I feel like Arnie wouldn't like it if I evolved or devolved into my drunken state, so I stick to the lime seltzer and then draw a hot bath in the Jacuzzi-sized tub. There are some bath bombs next to the faucet. I bet Olivia has left them there. It makes me want to use all of them up, so I go a little wild dropping them into the tub, watching them explode with colored foam. They're too saccharine in their smell, but I love the way they froth up around me and make the water all murky so I can't see myself under it.

After my bath, I go into the spare bedroom. The queen bed feels big, too big, so I return to the couch and fall asleep there instead with my arm wrapped around Arnie and his paw wrapped around me.

I never cuddle humans, only dogs. Except for the Redstockings, of course. They're the exception to every rule.

Chapter 6

MY SISTER CALLS ME WHILE I'M dogsitting Arnold.

I don't pick up. It goes to voicemail but my mailbox is full, so the line just disconnects.

We're not close, never really have been. She's four years younger and had it so much easier than I did growing up, though I guess I'm glad I had it harder. It forced me to push back against my parents' ridiculous rules and evolve into my own person. Not like my sister, marrying her college sweetheart and settling down one town over from where we grew up. Let's just say she's not exactly following in my liberated footsteps.

A little while later my phone pings. It's a text from my mom.

FYI the RSVP for your sister's baby shower is overdue. Assuming I can count you in?

My mom has at least stopped calling so much since she's realized that her voicemails don't go through anymore, but these passive-aggressive texts are just as bad.

I have my read receipts on but don't reply.

The fact that she just assumes I'm going to drop hundreds of dollars to travel across the country to celebrate my sister's entrance into martyrdom—oops, I mean motherhood—says just about everything about my family dynamic and how I was raised.

I don't need therapy; I have more than enough self-awareness and pattern recognition to connect the dots.

All of this gets me thinking more about Chris and his brother. They're probably best friends to this day, though I can't recall Chris ever mentioning him.

Arnie nuzzles up against me like he knows I need some love. We wrestle on the floor for a while and then go outside for a walk. I let Arnie lead rather than sticking to Chris's directions, which gives the pup quite the thrill. By the time we return, he has a new buzz about him.

"I know, freedom is intoxicating," I tell him. "Just don't overdo it all at once. We have to pace ourselves sometimes, don't we?"

Arnie nuzzles up against me, burrowing his head into my shoulder like he understands every word.

When Chris gets back on Sunday night, he's got these ridiculous sunglass tan lines. He looks like a raccoon and I tell him that right away.

His peeling face twitches, just a little. It frustrates me, but I like it too, how he doesn't smile or laugh in that over-the-top way. He doesn't waste expressions that he doesn't mean, and that's a rare thing these days.

"How did it go with Olivia's parents?" I ask oh so nonchalantly.

"Oh, it was fine." He leans down to wrap Arnie up in a big fat hug. Chris is looking way too relieved to see his pup alive and well after spending the weekend with me. I should find it offensive but I just find it endearing.

I raise my eyebrows at Chris's answer, let them stick to the top of my forehead. "'Fine'?" I echo back. "'Fine' is the dullest word in the entire dictionary. 'Fine' isn't even really a feeling at all; it's the absence of feeling."

Chris looks at me like I'm overreacting, which just makes me want to react even more. "Alright then, it went well," he says. "Very well. How's that?"

"Fabulous," I mutter, though I'm not feeling very fabulous. I'm all ruffled inside. I was sort of hoping he'd tell me it was a giant fiasco, only because I like conflict and all. No deeper reason than that.

The next week I'm supposed to come by on Thursday again, but I lose track of the days, maybe on purpose or maybe not. I come over on Wednesday night, or at least that's what Chris tells me.

He's just getting back from work, and rather than turning me away, he says he's about to order some dinner for delivery and asks if I want some.

It's against my principles to pass up free meals, so I say sure, if it's vegan. He makes a face at that but goes along with it and lets me pick the restaurant. We order from Le Botaniste in SoHo. I've had it a few times before, ordered it for delivery to the Inn, and it's my favorite despite everything being over twenty dollars. I get the Tibetan Mama bowl and he tries to order pasta, but I tell him no, that's way too safe, he's got to branch out of his comfort zone. I talk him into the Magic Miso instead and he's very skeptical of all the spices, but when it arrives, he admits that it's really not bad at all. That isn't a compliment but it's not an insult, so I take it for now and figure we'll work our way up the enthusiasm spectrum.

I feed some of my food to Arnie under the table. He's a more adventurous eater than Chris. It's a pretty great night and I come back the next day too, which is when Chris is actually leaving for the weekend.

I'm sort of scared to see him again, I'm not sure why, but it just feels like he's been intruding into my life a lot lately. I want some personal space, so I make sure to get there late so he has to head out right away. He probably thinks I'm being irresponsible, but I can live with that.

Once he's gone, I take Arnie out for a late-night stroll and let him lead again. He heads straight to the Hudson River. The water is breathing calmly as it rocks the docked yachts and sailboats up and down, up and down, with far too much compassion for what the obscenely lavish vessels deserve. The river is a smooth mirror for the jagged skyline, and I wonder if it ever wishes it could reflect back something else, a simple farmhouse or just the open sky.

Arnie and I look for stars. We like spotting a few stubborn ones that won't be thwarted by all the light pollution. They'll make sure they're seen from everywhere.

Back at the apartment, Chris has stocked the freezer with four pints of my favorite coconut milk ice cream. I think I mentioned the brand to him once, and it's a thoughtful thing for him to do. I know I'm doing a big favor for him and all by watching Arnie, but still, it shows that he values me. I tell myself this makes me feel good but really it makes me feel bad, almost like I'm not worthy of it, which is a ridiculous thought, but I can't really help it. I guess I'm just feeling like there's a lot of potential to Chris, but he just needs to break out of his own body and mind and let his heart do some cartwheels. But it's probably a lost cause by now. You can't teach old dogs new tricks.

Arnie barks, like he's saying that's not true, he can learn new tricks even though he's kind of old. I wonder if there's something to that, so I try to teach him how to do a fist pump, like the Redstocking symbol, the one we have painted onto the wall of the Inn. Sure enough, he learns it in two days with a little help from the peanut butter cookie dog treats that Chris said I should use sparingly. But "sparingly" is subjective and this is important.

When Chris gets back from the weekend, I have Arnie fist-pump him hello. I tell Chris about the significance of the fist pump and the Redstockings' role in the Women's Liberation Movement and how they didn't wait for anyone to open a door for them, that they went outdoors instead, into the streets. Chris says he likes the fist pump trick, but he seems hesitant about all the feminism stuff, like it's too out there for him.

This gets under my skin. "Do you identify as a feminist?" I ask.

He thinks about it for a moment, which says it all. "I'm not sure," he finally decides. "I'm all for women's rights and everything, but the word *feminist* has kind of a radical connotation, doesn't it?"

"Only if you think equality is radical." It makes me remember just how far apart Chris's universe is from mine. How their orbits would never ever overlap and I'd never even want them to.

"I support equality," Chris says. "I just don't like how some feminists make women feel bad for staying home to raise kids when it's what some women want to do. Like my mom. She loved it."

"She probably felt like she *had* to do that," I say.

"No," Chris says, standing his ground in an infuriating but impressive sort of way.

"She made the choice on her own and wouldn't have traded it for the world. She's told me that verbatim."

"Well, then it's a classic example of patriarchal brainwashing," I explain. "It runs so deep in our society that the women themselves don't even notice it. They're tricked into thinking they've won some great prize by staying at home with the kids when actually they've lost their whole identities. All their big dreams shriveled up to fit inside their kids' lunch boxes."

Chris says he's tired and that he's got to do some work before bed. I know this is my cue to leave, but I can't let this drop now that I've picked it up.

"How many women do you work with?" I ask him.

"Quite a few," he says.

I probe into what jobs they do and how much they make. My suspicions are confirmed as Chris says most of them work as administrative assistants or in the marketing department and generally get paid significantly less than the accountants.

"This proves my point," I say. "Discrimination is just as real as it's ever been."

Chris goes on the defensive. "The firm I work for barely receives any applications from women for the accounting positions. How are men at fault for that?"

"*How?*" I parrot back. "First of all, it's because our society conditions girls to think they're not good at numbers from the time they're babies. They're given Barbies that say things like 'Math is hard!' and dress up as princesses for Halloween while the boys are astronauts. And there's all this other sexist conditioning; it's an endless list. But women have still somehow overcome those barriers, and there are actually more women than men getting degrees in math and business now. But women don't have the same network and old-school connections with the men at the top, and they also don't feel welcome in those environments, so that's why they're not applying to your firm. And if you really want to walk the walk when it comes to gender equality and racial equality and all kinds of equality, you have to seek out diversity and go where you haven't gone before. You can't just wait for résumés to fall in your lap or they'll be the same country club white guys you've always worked with before."

I pause for a gulp of air to refill my lungs, but it still feels like they're empty, like everything is. "You want to know what the real problem is?" I ask Chris.

"Sounds like you've just told me what the problem is." He's wearing that blank expression, so I have no idea what he's thinking or feeling. It makes me want to put some kind of emotion on his face, even if it's a bad one.

"Wrong," I say, slashing the syllable. "That's all just the minutiae of it, but the big sweeping problem is that you don't see any of this as a problem."

On that note, I drop two tender kisses on Arnie's nose and hurry out of the apartment before Chris can think up any kind of rebuttal. Arnie barks after me like he's distraught to see me go.

I don't like that Arnie's upset, but it's kind of nice to feel like someone's missing me, wishing I'd stay.

Chapter 7

I END UP WATCHING ARNIE SORT of regularly. It becomes an unspoken agreement that I'm Chris's go-to dogsitter. My time with Arnie ends up being one of the highlights of my summer, maybe even *the* highlight, not that I'd admit it to Chris. There are some other bright spots too, but I never remember them in the morning the same way. The experiences don't stick between my toes like being with Arnie does.

By the time Labor Day rolls around, I'm kind of wishing that Chris and Olivia would just stay in the Hamptons forever. I've started sleeping in Chris's bed when I stay over, not the spare. I'm not trying to roll around in his scent or anything; it's just a Tempur-Pedic mattress and I like the way it holds my shape and shows me the indents I make in the world.

I haven't lost my populist soul, no risk of that, but I really don't mind playing with privilege for the weekend, using the bougie espresso maker and having a quiet place to crash without Tara mumbling lines in her sleep and Hal banging things around in the living room for her latest product invention.

I wouldn't want this life for good, but it's fun to put on the costume and ridicule the rich from the inside. I understand more why Hal was dating that trust fund girl, though they've broken up now. Hopefully Jenni catches the hint and splits from Peter too, but it's not looking promising from how things are going. Her autonomy is fading by the day.

On my last weekend watching Arnie, I return Chris's spare key. I've made a copy of it just in case I ever need it. I don't tell him about that, no need, but I just thank him for employing me. "It's been better than expected," I tell him. "I wish you bad luck with nothing." It's a less mawkish way of wishing him good luck with everything.

"Well, it's not goodbye," Chris says, looking caught off guard. "There might be some weekends in the fall that I'm out of town that I might see if you can come by. Arnie has really grown fond of you, I can tell."

I know Chris means that he's grown fond of me too, but I don't ask him to say that explicitly. It's easy enough to interpret.

Opening night for Tara's show arrives a little bit after that, sometime in early fall when the city has finally shed the humidity because it was too clingy. I can relate to that.

While Hal, Jenni, and I are getting ready at the Inn before heading out, Hal barges in on me in the bathroom and flicks on the lights.

"Hello there," I say from the toilet.

Hal shrieks. "EJ, why the fuck do you always pee in the dark?" she says, like I'm the one with poor manners here.

"I like to conserve electricity," I say. "Now you're welcome to hang out in here with me, but FYI, the aroma might not be divine. I'm ejecting last night's Thai dinner."

"Unbelievable." Hal makes a face and exits the bathroom, turning the lights off as she goes. "And hurry up, we need to leave in five," she calls back to me.

Moments later, Jenni bangs on the door. "EJ, hurry up, I need to fix my makeup."

"You don't need makeup," I yell back to her as I adorn my own face with glittery eyeshadow while sitting on the toilet. It's peak multitasking, and I have the muscle memory down so well that I don't even need to look in the mirror.

After a bit more ruckus and revelry, we head over early to the Metropolitan Playhouse in Alphabet City to warm up the audience for Tara's show.

Audiences are such malleable things. They hardly ever have an opinion of their own; they just react however the person next to them is reacting. The key is to have enough enthusiasts in the crowd that the applause catches on like wildfire until everyone believes it's the best thing they've ever seen.

The three of us split up and find our seats. We're all in different sections to spread out the euphoric reactions across the crowd so they don't seem manufactured. I plunk down toward the front and start feeling secondhand nerves for Tara. She's got to be freaking out backstage right now, all those self-doubts flapping around inside her.

I try to picture what I'd be feeling if I were about to go out there and perform. It makes me itchy and sweaty at the same time, or maybe that's just the sound of the too-loud piano that's playing in the background while people are taking their seats. Either way, I'm reminded why I'm meant to be the writer, not the actor. I want to give life to it all without the responsibility of having to deliver every line just right. I'm not enough of a perfectionist to enjoy that.

Sitting there in the sold-out theater inspires me to put more time into writing, to earn my own moment to shine. I vow to go straight home after the show and stay up all night working on a script so it can be performed in a place like this. But even as I think the thoughts, I know they're flimsy. I know I'll be out at the after-party until morning or noon and then dip into a fidgety sleep the moment I get back. It's kind of disappointing to admit that, but it's also validating that I'm living such a liberated life that I don't have anything to prove to anyone.

That damn piano finally stops and the theater falls quiet. It's that delicious liminal space before everything starts. I take a swig of the vodka I've snuck in and prepare to rally the crowd.

But as it turns out, Hal, Jenni, and I aren't needed at all. Tara slays the first song. Her voice doesn't shake and she hits every note. But the second song is a blazing dream. She loosens up and pours every last drop of herself into the empty containers of our bodies until we overflow.

That's the power of art: how it can turn secondhand experience into firsthand experience, dissolve all the walls between the past, present, and future until you wonder how your eyes ever saw them as separate at all.

When Tara finishes, there's this pause and I can feel her wondering if she flopped because no one's clapping. But it's just that we all needed a second to catch our breath after she rocked us like that, threw us from our safe little lifeboats into the churning seas, soaking us with water, with salt, with soul. Suddenly the whole place is alive in that way that makes you realize how dead it was before, how dead *you* were before.

The lead comes on next and performs something, but it falls flat next to Tara's solo and the whole theater feels it. This woman with coiffed white hair and jangly pearls who's sitting next to me grumbles about it to her husband. "That's racism right there," she says. "The Black girl should've gotten the lead; there's no justifying that."

I swell with pride and ask the woman if she can say it again while my phone is recording so I can play it back to Tara later. The woman looks offended and scared too, like I'm trying to catch her, cancel her. I explain that I'm Tara's best friend and that I really don't have a higher motive than that. But that doesn't help; she stays tight-lipped and tight-eyed the rest of the play. Next time I'll just record the whole thing without telling anyone. People only speak the truth when they don't think anyone is listening.

When the cast comes out at the end, I spring to my feet for a standing ovation, but I'm not even the first one up. The whole crowd is clapping and they're swaying too, which is the real sign of success in showbiz—if the performance seeps into people's essences, beyond their muscles and bones and bodily organs, and gets them moving to some imaginary beat that's truer than any reality.

I meet back up with Hal and Jenni. Peter's there too. Apparently Jenni invited him, but I'm in too good of a mood to let that fester in me. I just plow my way backstage and tackle Tara in a massive hug.

Her makeup is all smeared like she's been crying tears of joy, and I feel that shot of pinch-me-is-this-real-life because here we are in fucking New York City and my best friend is making it as an actor despite all the gatekeeper bullshit she's had to break through. Sometimes the improbability of the odds is the most empowering feeling, knowing how you defied the statistics just by being born and now are defying them on a whole other level by thriving with the best friends in the brightest city of them all.

In the movies, this is where the big break comes and the no-name person gets instantly famous. But things don't happen like that in real life. That doesn't make it any less incredible, though. It just means we soak up this night even more fully because we know it's not about to become the norm.

The after-party is at a loft in Bed-Stuy, grungy and crowded. We enjoy the party games and ride the euphoria all the way to the top and then higher, giggling in unison as the world shifts around us, reminding us that we're the epicenter of it all. We get emotional in that ethereal way and it feels like the good old times again, the glory days of the Redstockings before Lilly moved back to Oregon and before Jenni started ditching us for Peter and before Hal and Tara were too busy chasing their dreams to join me in choosing this dream.

"I don't tell you enough how much I cherish you," Hal coos, draping her arms around Tara and me. "I wish we could just freeze time right here."

"Same," Tara says. "But impermanence is the only thing we can count on."

"Permanence and impermanence can coexist, though," Jenni muses, her photographer's eye seeping through. "The permanence of our friendship and the impermanence of the exact arrangement of our friendship in this particular moment. They're not mutually exclusive."

"Hope not," Tara says. "I never ever want to lose any of you. Success means nothing without soulmates to eat pizza with at 3 a.m."

"You're the great loves of my life," I say, my affection bleeding out as I sponge it all up, hoping this moment might stretch longer.

It doesn't. Tara is recruited for photo booth pictures with the cast, Jenni peels off with Peter, and Hal reigns over a new ring of admirers. I glide around the party trying to fall in love with someone or everyone, but there's this fake aura following me that I can't shake. Anxiety clenches. It feels like I'm stuck or something. It's probably from the energy of the cast. They're so keyed up and focused on themselves that they can't let anyone else into their sphere. But there's a part of me that has this horrible feeling that I'm the stuck one. Last year I would've fallen in love with five of these people on the spot, but now things just aren't flowing.

I have a couple drinks to try to loosen up, but that just makes it worse. I get paranoid that everyone is looking at me and wondering why I'm here, like I didn't earn it the way they did. Everything starts sinking at different speeds, and it's hard to stay on the ramp. All I want is to get outside and flap my way over to Tribeca and curl up with Arnie on Chris's couch, but they wouldn't want me. They'd tell me I don't belong there either.

So I stop thinking about that and just keep willing myself higher, up into the lights that might point me toward love or pull me into it.

The next morning I stumble home from somewhere in the East Village. I tell myself that this is good, that the world is in its natural order again. I'm doing the walk of pride back to Bushwick just like usual, but it doesn't comfort me much. I don't feel well at all, probably just the side effect of mixing too much and sleeping too little, but everything aches. Not the type of ache that has a clear origin, an easy fix. The kind that sprawls everywhere, plugging up my pores from the inside out, making me cynical about everything except my own cynicism.

Chapter 8

AS THE AUTUMN DAYS WIGGLE ALONG, the slump wears off, but there's still that lingering guilt that I'm not writing enough, that I should be creating stuff and seeing people applaud it in theaters. It's not like the applause is the motivator. I want it for intrinsic reasons, but I'm not going to tell people to stop applauding if they want to. It's hard, though, because the only creativity I've got right now is how to find new ways to procrastinate.

One October afternoon, I bring my laptop to Kora's. It's my favorite neighborhood coffee shop. The walls are dotted with art by local painters and there are pool tables to play at, or you can just grab a stick and poke someone for the fun of it.

I plop down in one of the antique armchairs in the corner and dabble with some concepts for a script. I sort of feel like Hal, with so many ideas I don't know which one to pursue. I make myself work for a long stretch before I go up for another coffee. It's an act of frugality as well as bribery, but it doesn't work. I keep slamming against a wall, deleting one first page after another because I don't even want them sitting on my desktop polluting the energy.

It might sound like I don't have a good work ethic, but it's not that; it's just that I set a very high bar for myself. A lot of people go around submitting things they vomited onto the page. Not me. I won't submit any of my work until it impresses me, and I guess I must have a more refined eye for quality than most.

Chris asks me to dogsit again. He and Olivia are headed to the Hudson Valley to see the foliage.

I try to disguise my snort as a sneeze when he tells me that. I mean, I don't try that hard; I don't mind if he knows I think it's ridiculous, the whole leaf-peeping craze, this obsession with colors. Why should trees get all this praise for being different colors when people are punished for it, murdered for it?

Chris asks what I have against foliage and I tell him that people shouldn't focus on color because it fosters subliminal racism. He listens to my argument, disagrees. "I think we should admire the foliage in humans as much as we do in nature."

I've got to say it's a pretty good answer, and it almost makes me wonder if I've been seeing things wrong. I don't think I have been, but I just didn't expect something like that from Chris.

"What woke podcasts have you been listening to?"

"No podcasts," he says. "But I learn more from you than any show."

If it were anyone else, I'd think he was giving me some line so I'd take off my clothes, but Chris doesn't have game like that, and I also don't think he's preoccupied with seeing me naked. It's kind of a shame but also flattering in its own way, that he likes me for other reasons.

"That's good, but you can't just sit back and listen to my genius," I say. "You've got to get out on the streets, use your own voice and be heard. You should come with me to a women's march. I think there's one next week in Fort Greene."

He says marches make him nervous. "The potential for violence."

"Well, how do you think people of color and women and gays feel every time they step outside? Being nervous is the norm. You do realize how much privilege you have to be able to feel safe on a daily basis, don't you?"

He clams up after that, goes into OCD mode checking everything before he leaves. He puts out only three lists this time, not ten, but he still seems stressed that I'm going to screw something up. I don't get offended by that anymore; I know that's his issue, not mine.

After he heads out, Arnie and I troll around town, walking down the West Side Highway bike path. It's on Chris's list of places not to take Arnie, but I don't believe in coddling. Arnie's got to learn about the world sometime.

The cyclists go whizzing by, ringing their silly little bells as if that's going to intimidate us, get us to move. This one guy screams at me, "Get the fuck out of the bike lane, you fucking idiot!" to which I call out, "And a very merry evening to you, kind sir!"

Arnie gives a friendly bark too, which multiplies the man's fury, and it's all great fun. I'm cracking myself up with our antics, but I do make sure Arnie's walking off on the side over in the bushes so if one of the cyclists really does have the balls to take me out, Arnie won't get hurt in the process; he'll be there to avenge my murder.

Later that night, I'm scrolling through social media when I see a whole carousel of baby shower photos from my sister, all pastels and princess aesthetics. It's a girl, if I forgot to mention that, so naturally they're indoctrinating her into every gender stereotype before she even takes her first breath.

My sister's Instagram stories are packed with videos of the nursery (ten shades of pink—surprise, surprise) and updates about how they're expecting the baby any day now. She's already made the baby her entire personality and it's not even here yet.

I don't usually watch my sister's Instagram stories. I wonder if she'll notice that I did, or if she'll even care.

A week or a month ago, I'd texted her to say I wouldn't be able to go to the shower, and she'd replied, *Yeah, I figured*, which actually felt worse than the much longer, much more impassioned voice note that my mom left. (Having a full voicemail box was a nice reprieve before my mom figured out the voice note function.)

I had told my mom that work was busy and I was already planning to come for Christmas, so I could only add an additional trip if my flight was paid for. That sent her into a spiral about how I'm thirty years old (not true—still twenty-nine) living in the most expensive city in the world (not true—that's Zurich) and that if I valued my family at all, I would find a way to be there for the shower and the birth. It was all very fitting of the dysfunctional family trope with me cast as the big-city villain once again, surprise, surprise.

Being with Arnie puts me in a good mood now, and I'm struck with the spontaneous desire to leave my mom a voice note of my own.

I tap the Record button and tell her that I hope the shower was great and that all goes well with the delivery and that I'll look forward to seeing the baby over the holidays. I don't say the "I love you" part aloud, but I imply it with my tone, and it's really a very sweet message that is sure to disarm her. She'll probably vent afterward to my dad, tell him I'm trying to butter them up for money, and my dad will say that if he had any extra money, it would go toward Lions football tickets, not his blue-blooded rebel daughter.

The family stuff makes my legs feel restless, so I decide to go out and explore the Tribeca scene. Arnie's napping and I'm not too fond of sitting alone with myself, so I get ready to go out. I find a blazer in Chris's closet and put it on. It's more formal menswear than anything I've worn before. It's not like I'm picturing how his body has touched exactly where my body is touching now; I just want to experiment with a new style. When in Rome and all that.

Walking through the cobblestone streets, I pass all these swanky bars with twenty-four-dollar cocktails, what a deal. Finally I find a dive bar on Chambers Street. The Patriot Saloon, it's called. It stands out like a sore thumb, which would usually be a good thing, but not here. The *Patriarchy* Saloon would be a more fitting name as I can basically smell the misogyny drifting out.

I walk inside for a better look. It's a total filth show. Country music belches out from all sides and it's almost like I'm back in Michigan, all these men reigning supreme, most of them in their suits and ties, rich but miserable, wishing they'd been born rednecks instead, wondering if it's too late to jump ship.

Hanging from the ceiling, rusty chandeliers are draped in bras and thongs. Men must've flung them up there over the years, trophies from their sexual conquests since guys are worshiped for sleeping around while women are ostracized for it.

I get the feeling that one day perhaps I'll return here to set this place on fire so "arsonist" can be added to my epitaph. I could do it tonight, but I really just want to get back to Arnie.

I'm not going to roll over without doing anything, though. That would make me complicit. So I go up to the bartender, this bearded guy with a fleshy belly and a sleeveless tank that he probably calls a wifebeater because he doesn't see any kind of problem with normalizing violence against women. He fingers me with his eyes and pours me a beer from the tap though I didn't ask for one. I ask if the manager is here and he says nope but anything I need he can take care of.

I throw my sharpest rant on him, but it hardly seems to hit him. He looks at me like I'm a little kitten or something, so I just go over to one of the only other women in the place.

"Let's get out of this hellhole," I say to her. "Dismantle misogyny one unpaid tab at a time."

She snarls at me, says she's here because she wants to be, then calls me a bitch and says to get the fuck out of her face.

It just shows that you can't save someone who doesn't want to be saved. This gets me thinking about my sister and my ex-friend Lilly, as well as Jenni, who hasn't fully gone to the dark side yet.

I text Jenni as I leave to see if she wants to get high this weekend, just the two of us. She gets back a few minutes later, says that's so sweet of me to ask but she actually already has plans with Peter. She doesn't say what the plans are, which is how I know it's total bullshit. They're probably just staying in bed all weekend, watching Netflix and popping each other's back pimples, how romantic.

It makes me lonely for a second before I remember I don't get lonely. I decide I'll pour the extra time into writing instead. It's about time to finally see one of my plays through to the finish line.

—

"Maybe you're putting too much pressure on yourself," Chris says when he gets back and finds me furrowing my brows at a blank Word doc on my computer.

I was hoping to make some progress on this little retreat of sorts, but Tribeca's corporate energy hasn't exactly been conducive to creativity.

I roll my eyes at that. "Oh please," I say, shutting my laptop quickly before he can have a peek. "Have you met me? I'm the opposite of type A. I'm a sovereign woman who isn't trying to please anyone else."

But there's also this lingering whisper that makes me wonder if Chris is right. Maybe I am getting in my own head about this, comparing my success to Tara's and everyone else's. It feels like I've got this ball of ambition inside me that's begging to get out and bounce along the streets but it can't escape. There's no opening.

It'll get out someday, though, I know it. I have this feeling that I won't be someone who makes it big till later in life, but that will position me well. I'll be fresh in the public's memory when I die and they'll levy a tax on the rich to build the EJ Museum. Not that I'd want a museum. I'd much rather have some street mural, but it would still be flattering having so many people bunched around my artifacts, celebrating my contributions to the Women's Liberation Movement. Piecing together chunks of my life, trying to trace back to the root of my genius and coming up short.

"Have you tried a writing workshop?" Chris asks, and I can tell he's really racking his brain to try to help. If I were in a better mood, I'd find it nice, but right now it's just annoying. "One of Olivia's friends does one every week," he says.

Just the vibration of Olivia's name in the air makes me sink even lower. "Those things are Ponzi schemes for amateurs," I say dismissively. "They make you *pay* so they can tell you what's wrong with your writing and they force you to submit a certain number of pages by specific deadlines. It's all about quantity over quality, just for people who've got no confidence or no discipline. I've got both. I'm just in an ebb phase of the ebb and flow right now, that's all."

Chris says maybe I need a vacation, a change of scenery, and I laugh at that and say my whole life is a vacation. "That's the way life should be," I declare. "If you need an escape from your life, you're living wrong."

I go on to explain to Chris how I could sell my scripts in two seconds flat if I sold out and conformed to the industry's bad taste, but I'd rather never be remembered than be remembered as a sellout. He looks uncomfortable at that, like it's triggering his own introspection.

"For clarification, I don't think you're a sellout even though you do work for an evil capitalistic corporation," I say. "You've just leased your soul for a while, not sold it. You'll get it back eventually. I've got a good feeling."

"High praise," Chris deadpans. His soft brown eyes twinkle with embers that look like they'd have potential to catch fire if he let them. I always like it when I have that illuminating effect on Chris.

He looks happy, like he had a great weekend. This makes me kind of bitter but I'm also glad he enjoyed himself. He needs a break from all those people who send urgent emails with too many

ASAPs. He's a manager at his accounting firm, but he's told me he still feels like he's far down on the totem pole and the stress really gets to him. He confides in me like that.

"Glad to hear it," I mutter. Dropping his eye contact like a hot potato, I kiss Arnie and then scurry out of there, walking east along the cobblestones toward Delancey Street. I need to find my rhythm again and there's nothing like the Williamsburg Bridge for that, stretching over the East River with complete grace and authority. It's a piece of art with purpose, and that's all I aspire to be, really.

The walking and cycling path is a level above the cars, between the purple-pink beams of the bridge. There's all this graffiti there that I like to read. Graffiti poetry is the only decent poetry there is because it's not trying to be anything it's not. This bridge always gives me exactly the words I didn't know I needed. Today it's this: *Whatever happened to slow, slow dancing?*

There's something so simple but piercing about it. It rises and then falls inside me and makes me want to slow-dance right now—just stop and rest my head on someone's shoulder and sway to an old-fashioned symphony, both of us bundled up in sweaters and coats, cozy clothing only. I want Chris to be the one I'm dancing with, but then I remember how ridiculous that is. We live on two different sides of the bridge, which might as well be two different sides of the world. Also, I don't even like slow dancing. It's too boring.

As I keep walking, my mind bounces all around but doesn't land on a new plotline long enough for me to jot it down in the notepad on my phone. I think about how constricting it is to plaster ideas onto the page where they can never move around again. The most beautiful stories are the ones that have never been written. The ones that are still floating to their own bohemian beat, never speared by a pen, never captured by a keyboard.

Maybe I'm not supposed to write stories after all. Maybe I'm just supposed to dream them up and launch them into the universe and then they'll fall back down to Earth as cosmic energy. Land as stardust in a woman's coffee mug, be the inspiration she needs to break free of an abusive relationship, to trust the power in her own legs and run away. Follow her wild and never look back.

But I'm not spiritual enough to believe in that. There's no divine justice in this universe; just look at the news headlines. And even if my stories did make it into the ether, I wouldn't like how no one would know that I was the one to create them in the first place. My own greatness wouldn't be attributed to me. I wouldn't even get a footnote in the history books, so what's the point really?

Chapter 9

FALL COMES TO AN END AND December arrives, that clichéd time of the year when the city is choked in garlands and there are all these dehydrated Christmas trees being sold at every other street corner. The Redstockings never get a tree; we don't support deforestation. But this year Hal drags one back to the Inn one night.

It's a Charlie Brown situation. The tree isn't actually a tree; it's a shrub that's basically scraped clean of needles. Apparently it was being thrown into the dumpster because it was such a sorry sight, but Hal took pity on it and rescued it at the last second. It's got Hal thinking about starting a company that finds homes for rejected Christmas trees. It could expand to rejected groceries and clothes and stuff, too, so the revenue wouldn't be so seasonally dependent. Not only would it be good for the planet, but it would help low-income neighborhoods too.

"Show me a more progressive business model," Hal says, then tunes out Tara when she starts explaining a new law she read about, proposed in one of the socialist countries in Europe—Sweden, or maybe it was Spain.

"The law would insist that in order for billionaires to purchase a second or third piece of property, they have to build affordable housing structures on the land," Tara says as we take the tree into the garden, hauling it by its little stump.

"That's politics, not business," Hal says. "Business is a more efficient agent of change, not mired in all the bureaucracy."

"Business can be bureaucratic too," Jenni says. "Remember that think tank I worked for? Completely allergic to innovation."

"Everything is tainted when there's commercial value attached to it," I say. "Business, politics, even art. Especially art."

"Which is why you're opting out of participation altogether?" Hal asks.

"I'm not opting out," I say. "I'm just honoring my own creative process, not cramming myself into the industry's rigid little box in order to be chosen."

Tara speaks up. "Like I've done, you mean?" she asks, jawline even stronger than usual. She only ever provokes things with us when she's looking for an excuse to be mean to herself.

"Of course not," I say. "You've managed to achieve success and stay authentic. A unicorn, you are."

We all agree and Tara looks relieved though unconvinced. She sets about hanging her most flamboyant earrings as ornaments on the tree while Jenni drapes it with lights as if nothing were wrong with it, as if it were the damn Rockefeller Center Christmas tree. The branches sag nearly to the ground, but they don't snap. They're resilient like that.

I make some spiked hot chocolate for us as we sit out there and exchange gag gifts. We never buy anything for each other—that's against the rules—but we have this tradition of regifting things from around the Inn. The point is to make it ironic.

Tara raises a mug to the four of us. "To the best platonic soulmates out there," she says.

"The Anti-Marriage Pact was the best thing we ever did," Hal chimes in, making it seem like it was her idea, not mine. I don't correct her because that's the proof of great leadership, when other people feel ownership of your ideas. Hopefully the historians will be competent enough to uncover the truth. I'll leave some journals documenting the whole thing to help them out.

Jenni shifts in her chair. "I know I've been spending a lot of time with Peter," she says, guilt dribbling from her words like water from a faucet that appears to be off but isn't. "And I appreciate how accepting you're being."

"I wouldn't say 'accepting' is the adjective that fits best," I mutter, but I withhold calling her out on it much more. It would just put her on the defensive and push her closer to Peter.

Tara and Hal seem to know that too, so we all just toss in some subtle hints.

"The best thing about romantic relationships is how they inevitably end," Hal says happily.

"And how the Redstockings' bond never will," Tara pipes in. "It's the one thing in life we can really count on."

Jenni nods along but doesn't add much, which raises some alarm bells. I've got this irrational fear that Peter's planning a holiday proposal. It's actually not that irrational at all; I've seen these engagement ring ads pop up on Jenni's computer as we're streaming true crime shows on her laptop, and she says she doesn't know how they got there, the algorithms are highly dysfunctional.

I mention it to Hal and Tara the next day, but they wave off my concerns.

"Don't overblow it, EJ," Hal says, patting my shoulder. "Jenni might like having a boyfriend, but she'd never think about getting *married* right now. She's committed to liberation, she really is."

Chapter 10

THE TIME COMES FOR MY ANNUAL Christmas trip back to Michigan.

My family is pretending to be excited to see me, but I know they probably have a more enjoyable time when I don't come home. No one at the table hitting them with the hard facts about how nonsensical their worldviews are. Their little echo chamber is all they know and they like it that way.

I should really start skipping the holidays altogether, but I guess I still feel like I'd be a bad daughter if I completely dropped out of my parents' lives. They're the type of bad parents who think they're good parents and don't leave mounds of evidence, just little breadcrumbs, that prove the contrary. When the breadcrumbs add up, it's a mountain, but I still haven't been able to justify the case for going full no-contact. I also don't like the feeling that my family can just move on from me so easily. Physically being there sometimes is good so I stay fresh in their minds.

Plus I'll be meeting my new niece this Christmas, so I suppose I'll try to infuse some nonconformist energy into the little one before it's too late. Jessica Hannah Davies is her name, how basic, but my sister seems happy and healthy so that's good news.

When I arrive at my parents' house, my sister puts the baby in my arms before I can tell her I don't want to hold her. The baby is still tiny and wrinkly, only six weeks old with this big, horrendous pink bow that reminds me of the ones my mom used to put me in. But she has piercing blue eyes that seem to see right into me. I don't like the feeling but I admire her for it, like she's tuning in to extrasensory vision so she can see through the bullshit programming that will be forced on her.

"She's a very alive baby," I say, handing her back to my sister. The rest of the conversation revolves around the baby—her sleeping habits, what this gurgle or that babble might mean, how utterly exhausting it is to be a parent. Then in the same breath as lamenting all the trials of motherhood, my sister turns to me and says unironically, "You know, Emily Jane, I feel like having kids will be so good for you."

"Hmm, and why is that?" I say, keeping my voice neutral or at least as neutral as I can. She's trying to rile me and I won't let her.

"Well, it's impossible to be selfish when you're a mother." She smiles, but it doesn't reach her baggy, sleep-deprived eyes.

"Impossible to have a self, you mean," I correct. "What a compelling proposition."

"Girls, don't bicker," my mom says because that's how she thinks conflict is resolved. By avoiding it altogether. "It's time to get to church—seats will fill up early."

"You sure about that?" I say. "I've read that church attendance is way down."

"In *Brooklyn*, maybe," my mom says, her intonation making it perfectly clear just what she thinks about where I live. "But here we're doing just fine."

"You missed the baptism, Emily Jane," my sister says, as if she hasn't brought that up twelve times already. "But you should've seen how Baby Jessica felt right at home in church."

"Good thing the priest was there to cleanse her of her sins," I say, straight-faced. "Given she must have racked up quite a lot of murders in her few weeks on Earth."

My mom snaps at me to stop being sacrilegious. My sister looks like she almost wants to laugh but doesn't.

We all pile into the old minivan for Christmas Eve Mass. I could put up a fight and not go, but it's honestly easier just to tag along and dissociate to another planet, somewhere where outcasts are celebrated, not stigmatized.

I keep my coat hood up through Mass, partially to convey my spite about having to go to church and partially to hide. My old classmates probably wouldn't recognize me because of how different I look, but still, you can't be too safe. There's nothing and no one from high school I care to see again. Let's just say I didn't peak back then.

Going back to my hometown is such a horrendous time warp. I think I've made all this great progress, transformed into this endlessly large and independent self. And then when I'm back here, I shrink right up to fit inside the two-stoplight town limits.

My sister's baby starts shrieking nearly right away, and I decide I'm pretty fond of this tiny creature after all. The only problem is the preferential treatment she gets. I would be thrown out for causing a fit and speaking my mind, and she's just given little sympathetic smiles as people accept that it can't be helped. The baby also achieves her goal of being removed from church. My sister takes her outside, so it seems the little nugget is figuring life out pretty fast. Perhaps she sees me as a role model; she probably does.

Back at the house after Mass, my sister puts the baby to bed and my mom starts making her famous chili. It's not actually famous; that's just what she calls it. My dad ends up saying there's not enough spice in it, and back and forth they go about the proper ratio of chili powder. These really are the important things in life, being solved one snippy comment at a time.

My dad goes into another room to watch some sports game on TV.

"Turn it down, George," my mom calls out from the kitchen. "The baby is sleeping."

"It's fine. She'll wake up every fifteen minutes anyway," my sister says, as if she's quite proud of how difficult this has been on her, how she has had to mold her entire life around someone else.

"Facts," my sister's husband says, and then he slinks away to join my dad in the other room for the game.

My sister starts retelling all her grisliest motherhood stories.

"Yes, you've already told me about the varicose veins and your twenty-seven-hour labor and that night when you thought the baby was dying but it was just gas," I tell her.

"You could *pretend* to be interested in the fact that I just gave birth to an entire human," my sister says, all huffy. "Otherwise I'll ask about your dating life."

She knows that will provoke me, so I stay nonplussed. "Fine," I say. "Ask away."

"Did you see Dylan Flanagan at church today?" my mom interjects, then says what a nice young man he's turned into and how we should invite him over for pecan pie tomorrow.

"I'm pretty sure Dylan is engaged now," my sister says, which sets my mom off about how all the good guys are dropping like flies and she just can't understand what I'm doing, wasting my prime childbearing years.

"Honestly, Emily Jane, you're almost thirty and still running around like a teenager," she says.

I could fight back and spell out exactly how I took an oath to never ever get married, or tell them maybe I'll bring a woman home next year. But I'm not feeling motivated enough to cause a scene, so I just sit there and play my own drinking game where I have to take a swig of wine every time my mom says the phrases "settle down," "nice guy," or "almost thirty."

My phone starts buzzing. It's Jenni, FaceTiming me. I know right away this can't be good because she's aware that I hate Face-Timing. I'd always rather text.

I step out of the kitchen to answer.

"EJ!" Jenni squeals through the screen. "Hang on, let me loop in the others."

My worst fears jolt awake, the kind of foggy consciousness that says they were never asleep, not really. Then we're all on the call together, four tiny rectangles on my phone screen. Jenni is wagging something sparkly in our faces, holding it up to the camera so the rock is all we see, abrasive and unfaithful. I brace myself for the blow of the engagement, reminding myself that she was engaged once before and that didn't last. There's still time to get her to see the light before she goes through with it.

"We got married!" Jenni shrieks. The phrase circles around a few times, looking for an escape, before it lands and detonates.

Tara and Hal are as silent as I am. We're all waiting for the punchline that doesn't come.

Jenni storms ahead, says she and Peter had been talking about getting engaged at Christmas, but she had such bad flashbacks from her last proposal that they decided to skip an engagement altogether and just run down to the courthouse this afternoon, just the two of them. "How modern is that?" she squeals proudly. "And I'm keeping my last name, so I'm not caving to the patriarchy. I know I've technically broken the pact, but I'm still going to stay true to the Redstockings my whole life. Don't worry."

I glare at the screen because those statements completely contradict each other. She can't be married and still be loyal to us.

None of us are saying anything and Jenni says she thinks her Wi-Fi is spotty because the screen is frozen and she can't hear us. Hal says the screen isn't frozen; we're all just processing this news.

"Well, can you process faster?" Jenni wants to know. "Because I want you to get on my level. We're having a party over here."

Sure enough, there's champagne popping in the background, probably Dom Pérignon or something just as bad. Peter comes up behind Jenni and they kiss right there on camera. The whole thing is like one of those spiraling nightmares where you keep trying to wake up but your body won't move; it's paralyzed.

I hang up, but I doubt Jenni even notices. She's too high on her own bliss. Hal and Tara both call me, but I banish them to voicemail. I'm not in the mood for talking. I'm not in the mood for anything, so I go outside without a coat and trek through the snowy streets I grew up on, boots dragging like they're wary of leaving the ground, or just tired from trying.

My parents still live in the same cookie-cutter house in the same cookie-cutter neighborhood where I grew up. All the houses look exactly the same, everyone scared to stand out. I retrace my old path to the bus stop, past the overgrown field where the neighborhood kids would play capture the flag and never invite me because they thought I cheated.

There's a clenching in my chest, that stupid nostalgia that makes me miss something I hated at the time. It just feels very cruel suddenly, how time races by but gets snagged in the branches, keeping little bits of us in places we don't want to be.

And it's cruel too, even crueler actually, how friendships can seem so strong, so sturdy, and then one person can defect just like that and reveal how shaky the foundation is, how the concrete has all these cracks. Maybe it's not even concrete at all. Maybe it's sandstone or just mud, caked dry by a drought, ready to return to mush the moment a storm strikes.

Hal and Tara text me, assuring me that they're still 110 percent in on the Anti-Marriage Pact, that we always knew Jenni was the weakest link, that it doesn't change anything.

But that's a lie. It changes everything.

I pass by Mr. Hubert's green-shuttered house, where I used to go for piano lessons. I hated those piano lessons so much, but my mom still made me go for two whole years because she wanted me to be the docile, domestic, piano-playing daughter of her dreams. She never heard me, she never saw me, and she still doesn't now.

My body seizes up even more. I have to sit down in the snowbank and feel the ice burn my bare hands just to prove I can still feel anything.

I just want to hug our old family dog, Melon. She's been gone for many years now, but I can still picture her so clearly, too clearly, on this cul-de-sac where I always walked her. She never liked the leash and I loved that about her. I'd let her run free, take the heat from crabby Mrs. Benson next door, who took her lack of orgasms out on everyone else, or at least that was the story I crafted back then, the story I repeat to myself now.

Taking out my phone, I scroll for a moment to numb the numbness. Chris answers the phone before I realize I've called him.

"Emily Jane," he says, voice warm like an old sweater, tucked in a bottom drawer because it's not fashionable enough to be seen in but you can't bear to donate it. "Merry Christmas Eve."

"Merry Christmas Eve," I hear myself echo.

There's laughing and hollering in the background. It sounds like people are playing a game or something. The sounds revive me somehow. I have an absurd desire to be there with Chris's family, around a fire, drinking hot cider. It doesn't even have to be spiked.

I just have this vision of cracking up over the stupidest things or maybe nothing at all. The vision dissipates as quickly as it came, but something about it lingers in my legs and helps me stand back up and continue walking.

"I was just missing Arnie." I hate how weak I sound admitting to missing anything.

"He misses you too," Chris says. "You'll have to come by and see us in the New Year."

"Yeah, sounds good," I say. "If my jam-packed calendar allows for it."

Chris seems to pick up on the sarcasm, which shows how far we've come, or at least how far he's come, this past year. He's really started to appreciate the full range of my humor and break out of his accountant box.

I ask him if Olivia is there and he says no, that she's with her family down in Florida. This cheers me up a bit—not that I actually care. It's just kind of a game at this point, trying to stir up trouble because I like the constant churn of swirling motion.

"Give her my best," I say and he says he'll do that. I have a feeling he means it too, which makes me feel good picturing him telling her about how we had this intimate phone call on Christmas Eve, which is pretty much the most romantic of all days because there's none of the letdown of Christmas itself. But then it makes me feel a bit sad actually, that Olivia might freak out at Chris for no reason, just because I called him and he picked up. So I tell him that he actually doesn't have to mention anything. But he still says that he will.

I guess I respect his integrity, but I'm also annoyed that this means he still doesn't think he has to hide me.

Chris says he should probably get back to his family; they're in the middle of a game of Balderdash. "They're very competitive about it," he whispers, like he's confiding in me.

"Right." I hang up first, shuffling down the street back to my parents' house, back to the TV room that everyone has migrated to, back to my dad yelling at the screen, waving his hands this way and that.

I don't say much, just watch my sister and her husband sit on opposite sides of the couch, not even touching. They act like friends, not lovers. It makes me feel sorry for them but also oddly sorry for myself. Then I start watching my mom and dad, which makes me feel sorry for everyone.

I rifle through the presents under the tree and count how many are for me. It's one of my only traditions that's worth keeping. I always like presents best before I unwrap them, when I can still imagine them as whatever I want to. Before the disappointment of their underwhelming reality pops the iridescent membranes of hope, swelling then stinging like bubbles of soap.

My phone buzzes and I expect it to be more about Jenni's betrayal, but it's Chris. He's texted a photo of Arnie wearing a pair of reindeer antlers and grinning at the camera like a total goon. I stare down at the photo for a long time, and my sister asks who I'm texting and why I'm smiling.

"What's with the interrogation?" I scowl at her. "Smiling isn't a crime in this house, or is it?"

"Knock off that attitude, Emily Jane," my dad says without peeling his eyes away from the TV.

"And this is why I come home so often." I send myself to my bedroom just to get away from them. My room still has these heinous pink walls that explain so much about who other people wanted me to be.

There's this little toy piano I used to practice at. I sit down on the too-small bench, my spine slouched and my legs wedged, and try to play a song from muscle memory. It's just senseless notes, nothing fits together, nothing comes out cohesively, not even "Hot Cross Buns." It's like I've forgotten every single song. My brain tries to tell my body that this is success, that this is what we wanted, to leave the past behind. But my body isn't buying it. It's all tense and wobbly again.

Standing up shakily from the piano, I get this childish urge to look out the window for the Christmas star, the one the wise men followed all those years ago, or so I once believed, back before I knew better. I'm too tired to fight the desire, so I push aside the checkered curtains and look up at the sky. It's too cloudy. I can't see anything, not that I'd see anything even if it were clear. We're alone in this world. We only have our family and friends, but you can't trust them either. We really just have ourselves.

I crawl into bed and pull the tattered comforter up over my head and stay like that all night. It feels suffocating but also safe, and I like to believe that I'm a caterpillar, transforming into a new creature. It's not that I don't like who I am now; it's just that I wouldn't be opposed to growing some wings. Not butterfly wings, those are too flimsy, but maybe some dragon wings. Flying while breathing fire sounds pretty ideal to me, but when I wake up the next day on Christmas morning, I'm still fully human. Still just me.

Chapter 11

AFTER WE'RE DONE UNWRAPPING THE PRESENTS on Christmas, I make a little comment to my sister about how she got twice as many gifts as I did. My sister stiffens at that, goes into full attack mode, though she talks in a coddling whisper because she's holding the baby, or maybe she just likes to talk like that because of how passive-aggressive it sounds.

"You can't complain. Mom and Dad gave you so much more attention than me growing up," she says. "It wasn't even close."

"If by attention you mean judgment and pressure, sure," I tell her. "Lucky me."

"You loved it," my sister says. "You always tried to keep me from ever one-upping you."

She looks bedraggled by the lack of sleep so I should just give her some grace, but she's the one who started it. "What the fuck are you even talking about?" I slash back.

"Don't swear in front of the baby," she says, covering the little one's ears as if that's what's going to wreck her, not the entirety of the patriarchy and traditional gender roles suffocating her 24-7.

"It's like when I begged Mom and Dad to pay for piano lessons for me like they did for you," my sister carries on. "And then you threw a fit and told them piano was the worst thing ever and that you'd run away if you had to keep going, which ruined it for me too."

"I never said that." I'm not just disagreeing with her to be a contrarian. I truly have no recollection of what she's talking about.

"You literally did," she insists. "You threw the biggest fit until they pulled you out of lessons and made us both do sports instead. I might've been a musical prodigy, but now we'll never know."

"What a shame," I deadpan, wishing I were back at the Inn with the Redstockings, not here in this suburban house where all my expired identities collect like dust, making me sneeze.

But there's that lingering dread of returning too. Because I know that when I go back, the Redstockings won't be the same friend group I left.

"Time for family photos," my mom says, appearing in her ugly Christmas sweater that she earnestly thinks is fashionable. "Emily Jane, please don't make that face."

"What face?" I say, hardly feeling the contorted expression. "This is just how I look. Natural beauty, it's called."

My sister's baby opens her eyes at that and lets out a little gurgle that I swear is a giggle. She's the only one who seems to get me around here.

After all the quality family bonding over the holiday, I head back to New York and have the Inn to myself for a few days. The apartment feels too big and creaky without the others, but it's better than being with my family at least.

Our ex-friend Lilly is getting married in Oregon over New Year's. Naturally I've declined, but Tara, Hal, and Jenni go and all post photos together like they're having the time of their lives.

Why are you fraternizing with the traitors? I text Tara and Hal, hoping they pick up on the plurality of *traitors*, though I'm not sure they do because I've already removed Jenni from the Redstocking group chat twice though Tara added her back both times.

Hal puts the little laugh emoji on the text like she thinks I'm being funny and Tara texts me individually.

We'll talk it out when we're all back home! she says, like that's going to magically fix everything.

I have to admit, though, it does help having us all together. Or at least the three of us since Jenni and Peter popped down to Saint Croix for a honeymoon because of course they did.

Bundled up in the garden together one night, in the glow of the twinkly string lights, Hal, Tara, and I pass a joint around and strategize where to go from here.

"It's not like we're going to burn Jenni at the stake," Tara says, looking distraught at the slew of not-too-dissimilar ideas Hal and I have been spewing in a highly prolific brainstorm. "We're not a cult."

Hal and I aren't such pushovers. "Of course we're not a cult," Hal says. "We're a commune, a revolutionary blueprint for how women of the future will live. But with that, we have to systemize a process for defectors. Jenni broke the pact and there have to be consequences. It's the only way this model will be scalable."

I don't care about the scalability of it, but I do agree with Hal about the consequences. "We need to eject her from the group immediately," I say. "Let her feel the weight of her decision."

"Jenni can't have her cake and eat it too," Hal says, summing it up nicely. "But we'll have to have some parameters. A one-month taper period that we give her to move out before officially exiling her."

"What was that thing we said about this not being a cult?" Tara prods.

"Jenni isn't going to want to live here anymore even if we let her," I say. "We're doing her a favor making her path clearer. You know how she hates making decisions."

"I guess you're right," Tara says glumly. She leans her head on my shoulder and I drop a big kiss on her forehead, leaving behind a stain from the purple lipstick I'm wearing. I decide I don't like the color, but I do like the texture, how it sticks and stays in place.

When Jenni returns from her honeymoon, all bronzed and bedazzled, she announces that she's moving in with Peter straightaway. This shouldn't be surprising, I guess, given the whole they're-technically-married thing, but I still thought maybe they would opt for a less conventional arrangement, be one of those modern couples that lives apart. Or at least they could've phased in this new era, had some kind of transition period rather than just blowing everything up. I'm typically all for a good dynamite explosion—who doesn't love a pyro?—but not now, not when the Redstockings are what's being destroyed.

"He got us a new two-bedroom on the Upper West Side," she says, totally blind and tone-deaf to the mutinous glares from Hal and me. "Seventy-Second and Central Park West, so close to the park."

"Told you so," I tell Tara, who volunteers to help Jenni pack up.

"That's okay. Peter is sending movers," Jenni says, staring down at her ring like it's her savior, not her jailor. "They get here in an hour. But I guess you could help direct them?"

"Yeah," Tara says, and I wonder how Jenni can't hear the hurt in Tara's voice, or if she's just willfully ignoring it. "No problem."

Hal and I go out for a drink so we don't have to watch the heinous act happen. When we come back, we find that Jenni has taken just about everything she ever touched, including the light strands from the garden.

"How petty is that?" I say, looking around at the courtyard, stripped of its usual twinkle.

"I'm surprised she didn't snitch the utensils while she was at it,"

Hal says, sharing in my revulsion. "Just to make a clean swipe of it all."

"At least she left the Red Rocket," Tara points out. "Said she wanted us to have it as her parting gift." Tara gulps, close to tears.

"You're not buying that, are you?" I say. "It's just because Peter already has a Mercedes and they don't want to pay for two parking spots."

"And Jenni's too embarrassed about what her fancy new Manhattan neighbors would think of a rusty old Ford," Hal adds.

"So much for all her vigilante shit," I say.

Walking outside, I give the Red Rocket a good kick in the bumper like it's the car's fault. But the Rocket is tougher than it looks, escaping unscathed as my toes burn and bubble with pain.

A couple weeks later, I take the Red Rocket for a late-night spin over to Jenni and Peter's apartment on the Upper West Side. I've got this feeling that I can spite Jenni by doing loops around the block, channeling some witchy energy and drawing an ominous square around her new life.

In my head, Jenni would look out the high-rise window and see me down here. She'd come running out and hop in shotgun, confessing she made a huge mistake, begging me to take her back to the Inn as she tossed her criminally large ring through the sidewalk grate and felt the weight of the release.

That doesn't happen, though. I guess I have to get over my savior complex. Jenni's an adult and she chose to trade in her sovereignty for suitability. There's really nothing I can do about it except make sure that Hal and Tara never do the same.

I know they won't. They've actually got these things called spines made of bone, not rubber. What a concept.

I rev the engine of the Red Rocket and hightail it out of there, hoping the exhaust pollutes the air. As far as farewell gifts go, it's a pretty generous one. I could've burned her whole block down. A prison sentence for arson isn't the most appealing, though at least incarceration comes with free rent, and a play written from a cell would probably sell. It's got the hook.

Chapter 12

THE NEW YEAR STARTS IN THE same way they all do in New York: everyone flocking to the gym and starting new authoritarian diets that ban every food group except kale.

I swear people only like working out and dieting because it gives them something microscopic to obsess over so they don't have to focus on the bigger issues at play, like the fact that they're living a life that makes them feel dead.

The three of us Redstockings decide to make resolutions this year, just so we can show off our willpower and gloat over everyone else. My resolution is to not call or text Chris until he reaches out to me. It's a facetious one because it's not like it's hard to do at all. Besides, he'll probably call me tomorrow and ask me to watch Arnie while he and Olivia go to Hawaii for a couple's getaway because they're not in love enough to make it through the New York winter. They have to rely on things like tropical islands to keep the spark alive.

Tara's resolution is to go to the House of Yes only one time per week. It's just about the worst resolution ever made, and I have zero intention of following suit.

Hal's is to get a queen-sized bed, and she achieves that one in short order. We unceremoniously dump the old bunk bed she shared with Jenni out on the curb. It's gone by nightfall. There's a market for anything free around these parts.

We adapt to Jenni being gone by not adapting at all. It's the best way to handle change: ignore it until you hardly notice it anymore.

It's kind of nice having more space at the Inn too. We can sprawl out and keep things messy like they're supposed to be. She's not scurrying around tidying up for her man anymore.

Tara starts hosting weekly roommate dinners for Hal and me. She puts a lot of effort into cooking and setting the coffee table with folded paper napkins and clean forks and all this other weirdly formal stuff.

I can tell she's terrified that she's going to lose us, that Hal and I are going to go the way of Jenni. I get it, I do, but Tara's got to stop clinging so hard. There's zero risk that I'll handcuff myself with marriage. I remind her of that every day until she stops freaking out so much if the black bean burgers she cooks are overly charred, or if the sweet potatoes are a bit soggy. Our love isn't dependent on her culinary skills.

"Let's just go back to ordering pizza from Tony's," I tell her one night, and she looks relieved.

The biggest thing I'm upset about with Jenni gone is that my share of rent goes up. Hal says we should split it evenly among the three of us, but that's a scummy business move if I've ever heard one since she's got her own room now while Tara and I are still sharing. Hal finally agrees to pay more but still not fifty percent like I wanted. It means I need to rake in some more money, so I pick up more Uber shifts.

The Red Rocket has this traitorous Jenni vibe to it. Ideally I'd trade it in for a U-Haul truck or something else that sits high and mighty and reminds me that I can run this city if I want to. But I don't have the funds to upgrade, and even if I could afford the gas, the carbon footprint wouldn't sit right. So I end up just giving the Rocket a new coat of paint, mustard yellow. It doesn't quite mask the rusty color underneath, so it's kind of an orange hue when it's all done. I stash some lemon peels and coffee grounds from the compost bin into the cup holders to give it a fresh new scent and call it good.

Sometime in late winter, I realize I'm sick of driving Ubers. I've been sick of it for a while, so I talk my way into a job at Kora's, the coffee shop I love that's a little ways down Knickerbocker Avenue. I figure it'll be good inspiration because I can brainstorm ideas for my next plays based on the characters that walk through the door.

It's not a bad gig. The customers aren't too demanding and most of the orders are simple: black iced coffees or espresso shots. Nothing high-maintenance like you'd get in Manhattan—*matcha latte with oat milk and a splash of vanilla, but no, actually not that much; make me a new one in two seconds or I'm taking my business elsewhere.*

That's not to say that everyone who comes into Kora's is an angel, but it's generally a more low-key crowd. The downside is that the tip jar is always empty except for a few pennies and dimes, pity donations. They're not worth pocketing but I do anyway. Tip jars are a terribly antiquated concept. Who carries cash anymore?

Sometimes I don't show up for shifts or I'll get there late on purpose or by accident, it depends. I'm less scared of losing my job than I am of getting trapped by a repetitive schedule. It's nearly as suffocating as monogamy.

Outside of work, I'm too restless to write so I take long walks through Bushwick and beyond. I stay in Brooklyn because what's to see in Manhattan? Chris hasn't reached out yet. It's been a couple months now since our Christmas Eve conversation, and I've decided I was wrong about him. He never cared about me like I thought.

"Enough with the moping," Hal says one day when I get back from my shift at Kora's and plop down on the couch with a bottle of red and a bowl of chocolate-covered espresso beans slathered in peanut butter for an EJ touch. "Just call him."

"Call who?" I ask.

"Chris, obviously," Hal says. "Don't tell me that you don't think Tara and I have caught on to what's going on."

Tara appears cautiously in the doorway of our room, facing out into the living room. "Don't bring me into this," she says.

I scowl. "Nothing's going on between Chris and me."

"But you *want* something to be going on," Hal says. "Just break your New Year's resolution and text him. Who cares?"

"I've broken mine already," Tara says, and it's true because we've been at the House of Yes as much as ever.

"That's not the point," I say. "The point is that Chris isn't worthy of my friendship. He hasn't even made any kind of effort to stay in touch after I took care of Arnie all summer. It's just human indecency, that's what it is." The thought gets me very agitated, so I take a guzzle of wine straight from the bottle to wash it away.

"Have you thought that maybe it's because he has a girlfriend?" Hal poses. "And he might be trying to be respectful to her?"

"You can't fault someone for being loyal," Tara adds. "Someone like that is what you deserve."

"I deserve way more than Chris," I say, and there's a sense that I need to hear the words aloud before I can believe them. But even when they're lingering in the Inn, there's a concavity to them, a hollowness. "He's not confident enough in himself to go after what he actually wants," I ramble on, eager to fill the space with something, even if it's only my own voice. "He's probably scared that being friends with me would disrupt his calm, boring life. It's not my problem."

"I mean, it's fine if you don't want to be friends with him," Tara says. She joins me on the couch, nuzzling up next to me because she knows I need it. I let myself soften into her. "But maybe seeing him again could help give you closure."

"I don't need closure," I insist. "Nothing was ever open between us, so there's nothing to shut."

"Just remember it's okay if you change your mind," Tara says, gently tucking my hair behind my ear, one strand at a time. "You don't always have to clench your principles so tightly."

"Of course I do," I say. "If I hold on weakly, everything crumbles. Take Jenni, for example."

"That wasn't your fault," Hal says. "Nothing could've saved her."

"I didn't spot the warning signs early enough," I reply, and I realize how much I've been beating myself up over this. "Or at least I didn't act on them. I was too wrapped up in other things."

Other things meaning Chris. Tara and Hal understand but don't make me say it, which I appreciate more than I let on.

Hal piles on top of us in a big bear hug, and that's when I know she's actually worried about me.

"I'm sorry," I say. "I'm really sorry."

"It's not your fault," Hal says again. "You have to let go of that."

But right here in this moment, I don't want to let go of anything. I just want to hold on to everything. It's one of those moments when my heart feels like it's trying to break out of its cast, shatter the encasement to smithereens, but it can't quite push through the plaster.

"And maybe you could consider reaching out to Chris again," Tara suggests. "It might be good for you."

"Not a chance," I say, terrified that any other answer will result in my picking up the phone and calling him right this moment, right this minute. "You two are all I need."

"Don't forget about Maryjane," Hal adds playfully.

"Right." My smile emerges from the cloud coverage, and I hope Hal and Tara can tell how grateful I am for both of them and the way they see me even when I have a hard time seeing myself. "Can't forget about her."

Chapter 13

A FEW WEEKS LATER, I'M IN the middle of designing an artistic swirl on top of a cappuccino for a customer when Chris's name flashes up on my phone.

It's an incoming call.

My mood lurches forward and upward and in new, undiscovered directions too. It's just the smug satisfaction of winning my New Year's resolution. I knew my willpower was rock solid. I don't pick up. No need for him to think I'm awaiting his call. He doesn't leave a voicemail, but then he texts asking how I'm doing. It's basically a booty call by his standards.

Maybe he and Olivia broke up. I doubt it but I like keeping it as a possibility, so I don't text back. I just squirt the rest of the whipped cream straight in my mouth and swallow. Things are instantly brighter. There's this gloriously petty yet empowering feeling about keeping him waiting on my text, picturing him checking his phone every two minutes to see if I've replied. Games like that rile me up in the best way because I'm in control of whether I win them, and I always do.

He doesn't call or text again, which is disappointing. I thought he'd try harder to win me back, but maybe he's feeling rejected. I don't like the idea of him sitting there thinking I'm mad at him. He's probably stuck in a mind loop of anxiety, regretting that he took so long to reach out. He can be so hard on himself—it's pretty cruel actually.

So the next day I ditch work early and take the subway over to Tribeca.

Finding myself outside the Windemere awning, I walk inside the building and go straight into the elevators without pausing to make eye contact with the workers at the front desk. They don't come after me. Confidence is everything; Hal's right.

I knock on the door of Chris's apartment, just a formality since I have my spare key. It's in the keyhole when the door opens from the inside. Olivia is standing there, dressed in leggings and a crop top, looking even more like a mannequin than I remembered. She doesn't show even a flicker of recognition that we've met before. Sure, my hair is black and chin-length now and my contacts are violet, but still, you'd think she'd connect the dots given how much interest she showed me in that Uber. How suspicious she'd been that Chris was going to run away with me, leave her in the glitter that she could only see as dust.

"Hello, Olivia," I say with admirable cordiality. "Is Chris home?"

She says Chris is at work and asks how she can help me, which is code for how she can get rid of me. She's not fooling anyone.

"Do you live here now?" I ask as Arnie leaps on me, licking and sniffing and zooming all around in delight.

Olivia doesn't answer my question, just asks who I am. So I tell her that I'm EJ, Arnie's surrogate mom, here to take him out for a stroll. "Chris asked me to come by," I say, and I get that happy feeling that comes from splashing a lie in someone's face and having it blind them for a second or six.

Olivia gets Chris on the phone, says there's an EJ here to take Arnie for a walk and wants to know if it's a scam. Chris must vouch for me, which I appreciate since I didn't even give him the heads-up I was coming. Olivia hangs up and tells me I can take "the dog" out but have him back in an hour. She seems glad to have Arnie off her hands. I can tell she never gets down on the ground and wrestles him. There's barely any dog hair on her clothes at all. That's always a warning sign, a red flag. I'm surprised Chris hasn't taken note.

I put on Arnie's harness and we both bound out the door. Arnie tugs me down the hallway. He's wild with glee that we're reunited, that I'm helping him escape that dull afternoon. I follow him where he wants to go today. That's really how dogs should be walked so they don't get conditioned to be obedient to humans and lose sense of their own intuition.

He trots east until we're at the Williamsburg Bridge. I realize he wants to be free of Manhattan, so I let him lead me over the bridge. He sniffs and paws the graffiti poetry and seems to be a big fan of it too.

Then we're walking down Bedford Avenue and he's dragging me right past that art gallery where Chris and I first met. I don't go in the gallery, but I pause and look in for a while, repressing a few regrets.

Arnie wants to explore East Williamsburg too. He's loving the streets as they empty out. Soon enough we're back in Bushwick. I let him off his leash and he romps through the overgrown grass and clovers in Irving Square Park like he's been reborn.

The dusky sky is draped with gauzy, violet-gray clouds. To the west, a golden halo swells up from behind the buildings, where the horizon should be. I start to wonder if Olivia has even noticed that Arnie's still gone. Doubtful. She's probably too busy scrolling through social media or lounging in the Jacuzzi. It gives me this ugly jealous feeling that I clamp shut.

I bring Arnie back to the Inn since we're basically there already and he's probably pretty thirsty by now. I pour him water in the only clean bowl left in the cupboard. Tara's out and about but Hal is home, and she rolls around with Arnie on the floor and asks if we can keep him. She's high and getting all emotional about how much she misses Jenni, how she's been burying herself in her start-up incubation process to numb the pain.

I think about Chris getting back from work and finding Arnie still gone. He knows Arnie's with me, but he still might get panicky. I don't want to prey on his anxiety, so I text him not to worry, that Arnie led me back to Bushwick and asked to stay the night.

Hope that's alright, I add.

Chris calls me right away sounding stressed. He says Arnie has to stay at his apartment, that he needs to get his Michelin-star dinner and mineral water and mani and pedi and all that. Maybe I'm exaggerating a little but not much. The mile-long to-do list that Chris rattles off makes me remember why he and I would never work out. Not that I was thinking about that anyway.

In the end, I say that I'm not making an extra trip back into Manhattan tonight when Arnie is perfectly happy playing in the garden here and we've got plenty of vegan-ish leftovers in the fridge that will toughen up his constitution. "But if you come by here," I tell Chris over the phone, "then I'll return him for a pretty ransom."

Chris doesn't seem to find this funny; he just says he's leaving work now and is taking an Uber straight over. I tell him to take the subway because it'll be faster with the rush-hour traffic this time of day. I don't expect him to take my advice, but by the time he arrives, he's covered in the kind of grime that can only come from a long trek underground, snaking through the city's crumbling bowels on a century-old train that rattles violently and then jerks to a stop just when it's finally picked up speed, sending you careening into strangers' spiky shoulders unless you're gripping the germ-infested pole with both hands. But Chris looks better for it all, his hair mussed up, skin splotched with sweat.

I'm waiting for him out by the street because I have this weird feeling when I think about Chris coming inside the Inn. My hands get clammy and I have to check to make sure I'm wearing underwear.

Not because I'm expecting to take it off or anything; it just makes me feel better knowing I've got an extra layer underneath.

Arnie goes happy-crazy when he sees Chris, leaps right up into his arms. Chris coddles him like a baby, telling him how much he missed him all day. It's very heartwarming and makes me feel kind of bad for taking Arnie away.

Arnie tries to lead Chris down the stairs into the Inn. That's just like Arnie, stirring up trouble by putting Chris and me in the same small space, tempting us both.

"You'd better get home," I tell Chris. "Arnie's had a long day." I don't offer to drive them and Chris doesn't ask; he just orders a pet-friendly Uber. As we wait for it, I fill him in on how I'm working at a coffee shop now. I casually drop the cross streets in case he wants to swing by. I figure he won't since it's in Bushwick, but you never know with Chris. He goes out of his way to see me. Take tonight as an example.

I ask him if Olivia has moved in and he says no; she has a remote job and just likes working from his place because the Wi-Fi is stronger. I'm good at reading between the lines so I sense there's some resentment there, like Chris wants his space. I bet she's messing up his routine and it's getting under his skin. The thought makes me bounce a little in my knees, a jovial kind of jitter.

"How are Tara, Hal, and Jenni doing?" he asks. Hearing Jenni's name scrapes a little. Not like a fresh wound but not an old one either. It mostly catches me off guard because I think I've only mentioned their names to him once or twice, just in passing. Chris is a good listener, I've got to give him that.

"Jenni defected from the pact." I briefly fill him in. "But we're better off without her. You can't have someone who's one foot in, one foot out. She would've dragged us all down sooner or later."

"It'll be okay," Chris says, which irks me intensely because why do some people think that "okay" is a good thing? That word scares me senseless. It reeks of forgettable mediocrity. My biggest fear in life is to be "okay." I'd never get books written about me for that.

Sharpening the blade on my tongue, I tell him that of course it's not going to be okay; it's going to be fucking incredible.

A laugh spills out of Chris, like it was suddenly uncorked. The sound is a precious thing and I want to hear more of it. But his Uber arrives so I deposit a few kisses for Arnie on the beautiful black streak that runs between his multicolored eyes. Chris confirms with the driver that it's a pet-friendly ride. The driver says yes, and Chris thanks him profusely. It all makes me wish I'd just driven them home myself.

The car door closes and I'm alone again, or at least it feels that way for a few seconds before I remind myself that Hal is right inside and Tara should be back from rehearsal soon.

Chris texts me as I'm walking inside.

Good seeing you again!

It's a lot for Chris to use an exclamation point and it makes me feel all inflated on the inside, like a hot-air balloon soaring up over the city, seeing how everything connects from the sky in ways you never can down here on the street level.

U2, I reply, but I don't like how cold that sounds, so I add two smiley face emojis and call it a night.

Chapter 14

LATER THAT WEEK I BRING UP my new idea to Hal and Tara. I gather them around the table in the back garden because we're getting a burst of springtime in February.

"What's all the fuss about?" Hal wants to know, clicking away at her computer, working on a new pitch deck.

"You're not moving out, are you?" Tara asks, eyes wide with concern.

"Of course not," I say. "I'm actually here to suggest an addition to our Redstocking family."

I pause dramatically, and it gets Hal to look up from her laptop. "You want us to have a fourth roommate?" she asks. "How well-connected are they? Ivy League pedigree?"

"Why would that be your first question?" I snap.

"To secure investors in my business so I can become a billionaire," Hal replies, as if I should have considered this from the start.

"There's no such thing as an ethical billionaire," Tara says.

"We'll split the billion so we're all multimillionaires, how's that?" Hal amends.

"Except that you don't have a business yet," I point out.

"Because I don't have investors. It's the chicken-or-egg dilemma."

Tara turns to me, re-centering our focus. "Who is it?" she asks. "Who do you want to move in with us?"

"It's not a person," I say.

Now Hal is really listening. "An extraterrestrial?" she says, thrilled by the prospect. "I'm in. We can finally unearth the truth of what the government's been hiding all these years."

"It's a dog," I say, smiling as I think of the idea of snuggling up with a little pup after a long day. "I suggest that we adopt a dog to join our family. It's about time, don't you think?"

Hal wrinkles her studded nose. "Absolutely not. Have you ever heard anything less liberating than owning a pet?"

"You don't *own* a pet," I say, prickling. "You steward a pet and help them retain their own autonomy."

"The sheer commitment of it is absurd," Hal barrels on. "I can't believe that you of all people would suggest this. It's because of Chris, isn't it? How you've fallen head over feet for him, plus that dog."

"That dog's name is Arnie," I say, and it's the closest I've ever felt to a maternal instinct kicking in. "And don't forget how you loved playing with him the other day."

"That's only because I was high," Hal says. "I can't have a dog around with all of my entrepreneurship demands. It would disrupt my productivity."

"You don't need a dog for that," I mutter, and Hal shoots daggers my way. "Tara," I say pointedly, turning away from Hal. "What do *you* think about the idea?"

"I don't know," Tara says, following Hal's lead like she always does. "I love dogs, of course, but it does feel like a lot of responsibility. I mean, we've never even successfully kept a houseplant alive. Even the succulents."

She glances at the dead cacti atop the bookshelf.

"That's because you watered them too much," I say. "Cacti don't need water."

"Unless they're named EJ," Hal says, and I glare at her. "Just kidding," she adds hastily. "But I guess that settles it then. We reject the dog proposal by a vote of two to one. Now if you'll excuse me, I need to get back to building my business."

And just like that, she returns to the *click click click* of her keyboard.

I don't even bother thinking of a clever retort. I just go and lie down in my bunk bed for a while. They're probably right; getting a dog was a stupid thing to consider. Having an animal depend on me makes no sense, not when I can't even depend on myself. I still think I would've risen to the occasion, but now we'll never know.

Some mornings later, I wake up and go out to the kitchen. Tara and Hal are gone for the day already. On the counter, there's a fishbowl with a little goldfish darting about. A yellow sticky note is tacked onto the bowl.

Let's start here and work our way up to a dog? Love you lots.—Tara & Hal

My eyes feel dewy, and I blink away my emotions before I have to feel them on my cheeks. I've never thought of myself as a fish person, but there's instant affinity between me and this little swimmer in the bowl.

I text Tara thank you right away. She says it was actually Hal's idea, which surprises me. Moving over to the Redstocking group chat—Jenni long removed—I thank them both. Then I trot over to the nearest pet store in Williamsburg to buy a second goldfish so the first has a friend. I load up on organic fish food and pebbles and plants for the fishbowl and go a little crazy with all the decorations.

The hypocrisy between being an advocate of freedom and keeping animals captive in a fishbowl is something I'm aware of. I don't like it, but I'd at least rather have the little fishes be with us than with other people who treat them worse. They're doomed to captivity either way; that's the sad truth of it.

What should we name them?? I ask the group. They tell me I can pick, so I think on it for some time until the names emerge from my thoughts, flapping up like old friends.

Mango and Squid.

Chapter 15

IT'S A GOOD SPRING FOR MY playwriting. I don't write much in terms of word count, but I conceptualize this whole new genre, unfurl it with my hips and then my fingers. I touch the fabric, cut its shape, design its texture. Gritty like sandpaper. A slippery streak too, the flat side of a skipping stone.

The premise is that all the dialogue comes from one master voice that you hear from behind the curtain but never actually see. Kind of like an Oz figure but the actors onstage don't speak. They just mime to what the voice is saying.

It's satire about how the theater industry takes away the individual voices of the actors by making them stick to constrictive scripts and paying them nothing, exploiting their talent and turning them into puppets.

We think about pitching it to some directors, but we know it's a lost cause. There's no way they'll go for something that paints the industry in a shady light, no matter how true it is.

The "we" refers to Elliot, this total smoke show who comes by Kora's a lot and inhales nitro cold brew, spilling it into the cracks of their keyboard without care. Elliot wears a look that less enlightened people might mistake as constipation. But as I know too well, it's actually the expression of a virtuoso whose talent is lodged so deeply inside that they can't quite squeeze it out.

Elliot runs the theater circuit too. We hit it off venting about all the nepotism and elitist gatekeeper shit that goes on. It's even worse for the nonbinary community. They gave up on acting because they'd audition for female roles and get told they were too masculine, then get turned down for male roles for being too feminine. And the tricky thing is most of it was this subtle coded language so they wouldn't have great evidence for a lawsuit even if they could afford a lawyer.

Elliot sees my talent, says I'm the leader the world needs. It's validating but frustrating too, that everyone doesn't see it that way. Though maybe some of my charm lies in its controversy.

We find some creative ways to work our disgruntled muscles before they tell me I've inspired them so much that they're moving to LA to conquer the screenwriting scene. I'm pretty relieved by this because I'd probably keep seeing Elliot for a while if they stayed in New York. Not monogamously, but still, it was getting a little too serious. The choking feeling, which begins as a soft tickle in the throat, would soon have become a set of talons clenching my neck.

The day that Elliot leaves, I head over to Lone Wolf, the matchbox-shaped dive bar on the corner of Dodworth and Bushwick Avenue, home to three-dollar picklebacks—a shot of whiskey chased by pickle brine. Picklebacks originated in Bushwick, one of our many claims to fame.

Even at nighttime, it's nearly always darker inside the bar than outside. The lightbulbs in the ceiling lamps are either too old or too grimy to shine properly. Probably both. Tara has started bartending at Lone Wolf for extra money. I like keeping her company. Hal is here tonight too, on the rickety barstool beside me as Tara pours draft beer and whiskey for the motorcycle-and-Medicare crowd. They're the kind of people you can rest around, no sleazy pickup lines or anything like that.

"Let's invent a Redstocking drink to put on the menu," Hal suggests.

"I don't think I have the power to make that happen," Tara says, looking hesitant, as if her manager is going to catch wind and fire her.

"Of course you do," I say. "A Redstocking cocktail is a good idea. It'll cement our legacy. Gin, vermouth, and Sprite? With pomegranate for the red color, plus some maple syrup and bitters to make a statement. And excess salt on the rim so it's nice and crunchy. Tough on the tongue."

I expect Hal to shoot it down and propose her own grand recipe instead. But she just nods in approval and claps my back. "Nice work, EJ," she says. "Might hire you to be on my product development team soon enough."

"Like I'd ever work for you, Hal," I say, giving her a stern do-you-even-hear-yourself look. The ice breaks, and the two of us fall through into laughter that feels like lake water. Tara joins in too. It's like we're hollering extra hard to mask the fact that there are only three of us now, not four.

There's an old, duct-taped jukebox pressed up against the back wall. Hal and I go over and give it a good shake. We've developed a special talent for shaking jukeboxes so hard that the coins they've gobbled up fall into place and we get to pick songs for free. If I had a résumé, which I don't obviously, "Jukebox Pirate" would be front and center in the "Special Skills" section.

Sure enough, things rattle and click into place and we're able to get "Wild Horses" going. It's one of our favorite Rolling Stones songs, though it's on the slower side. Hal and I dance to it together, swaying as we hold each other and twirl this way and that through the narrow bar, cloaked in the liberation that comes from dark lighting and a crowd of heavy drinkers.

Tara won't come out to dance with us for fear of repercussions while she's on the clock, so Hal and I have to hop up and over the bar and join her back there. We're not too unhinged but we're not tame either.

"Better to be fired and free than employed and tethered," I say.

"Well said," Hal agrees. "We should add that to the ceiling quotes at the Inn. You're really on your A game tonight, EJ."

"I'm always on my A game," I say. "Except the days I don't want to be, for risk of my brilliance becoming monotonous."

"Here," Tara says, handing us two cocktail glasses, the rims drowned in salt. "I made you the Redstocking."

"Make one for yourself too," Hal says. "Per our no-Redstocking-left-behind policy."

"The only form of governance we tolerate," I add.

And so, still looking a bit nervous that she might be caught drinking during her shift, Tara hastily conjures up one of her own.

"You gave yourself the worst one," I observe, trading glasses with her before she can protest.

We raise our glasses and sip. It tastes like the beginning of summer, bright and spritzy with confidence that the best is just beyond the next bend.

"Where are you going?" Hal asks, as I hop off the barstool.

"Mango and Squid," I explain. "They've been home alone for several hours now." I don't like the thought that they might feel abandoned. Or a bird might have pecked its way in through the grilled window, on the prowl. Implausible but not impossible.

"They're goldfish," Hal says with an exasperated sigh. "They don't need to be babied."

"As much as I appreciate your input on my pet parenting abilities," I say with an upbeat salute as I head out, back toward the Inn, "I've got this covered."

Chapter 16

AS THE SPRING DAYS SKID ALONG, the guilt starts amping up about holding Mango and Squid hostage. I'm tempted to release them into the East River, but there's zero chance they'd survive. So I use my Uber profits to buy a massive tank that takes up the entirety of our tiny kitchen counter at the Inn.

As carefully as I can, I transfer the wiggly little loves from the fishbowl into their new home. It takes them some time to realize they have more room to swim, but once they figure it out, they're all jubilant, showing off how far they can swim and somersault without hitting the walls. Squid is the rascal of the two, playing hide-and-seek in the weeds, nipping at Mango's tail. Mango doesn't seem to mind. She likes keeping up.

After feeding them and measuring the pH level of the water, I wash out their old fishbowl and decide to repurpose it into a flower vase. Taking it with me into the back garden, I prepare to fill it with a bouquet of ivy and wildflowers.

Hal is out there in her egg chair, except she's not alone. There's someone else squished in next to her. A svelte figure with silky dark hair that falls to her tiny waist, the snatched kind of thing that looks shaped by a rib-crunching corset but seems to just be a by-product of unfair genetics.

"EJ," Hal says, and it sounds like an accusation. "I didn't think you were home."

"Where else would I be?" I ask.

"At the coffee shop or with Chris or something," she says.

"You know I never hang out with Chris." It gets me all agitated because I wish this wasn't the case, but I'm also not going to do anything to change it. "Who's this?" I ask expectantly because we don't invite visitors over to the Inn. Hal knows that.

"This is Astrid," Hal says. "I put in the group chat that she was coming over. We met at a women-in-tech event a few days ago. She's from Norway, a grad student at NYU's school of social entrepreneurship."

Astrid just sits there, looking like a supermodel as she lets Hal deliver her bio. I dislike her straightaway. There's this stormy energy about her. Usually I'd enjoy that, the potential for thunder and lightning and fire, but not now.

"Very good to meet you," Astrid says. Her accent is as angular as her cheekbones, and there's a palpable danger to her beauty. She already seems to have Hal wrapped around her long, bony fingers.

"What're you two up to?" I ask as caustically as I can so they get the message to relocate, vacate the grounds.

"Working on a pitch deck," Hal says. "We came up with this idea together last night and we've been up all night honing it. It's like all the others have led me to this one."

It's unclear if she's talking about her failed businesses or failed relationships, and I'm unnerved that she could be referring to either.

I'm not worried because I know how Hal jumps from person to person as quickly as she jumps from start-up to start-up, but it's still got me on edge a bit.

"Well, you know what they say about mixing business and pleasure," I warn, hoping this will encourage them to put at least a few inches of separation between their bodies.

"What do they say?" Astrid asks, sounding genuinely curious. Perhaps the adage hasn't yet reached Norway.

"They say it's a bad idea," I elaborate. "A recipe for disaster."

Astrid and Hal look at each other, like they're privy to the same inside joke. "Well," Astrid says, "our start-up is called Bad Habits, so perhaps it's fitting."

"Bad Habits?" My interest is piqued. "What's it about?"

Astrid opens her mouth like she's about to tell me, but Hal hushes her. "We're in stealth mode, remember?" Hal whispers to Astrid.

"Oh, come on," I say. "I'm not going to run off blabbing to *The New York Times*. Though you should thank me if I did; you'd benefit from the PR."

"Sorry, EJ," Hal says. "Stealth mode means keeping it secret from everybody until you're ready to launch and make a splash."

"Splash and sink, more like it," I mutter. "You can't keep everyone away or your product won't have any buzz."

"She has a point, Hally," Astrid says. I don't like how she already has a nickname for Hal. It feels like they're moving way too fast, like Hal's full-steam-ahead approach has gone too far this time.

Hal seems to consider Astrid's viewpoint, which isn't what I expect. "We'll tell you soon," Hal says to me. "Just not quite yet. We need to refine our business model before we open ourselves to the noise and input of the outside world."

"I'm not the outside world," I remind her. "I'm your best friend."

"Who has very strong opinions," Hal says. "We just need to make sure our own vision is clear enough before other people start projecting their opinions onto us."

"I'm not going to project onto you. I'm just going to help you make your idea better," I say, irritability rising. "But fine, if you don't want my help, I'll just be over here tanning."

"Don't eavesdrop," Hal warns.

"It's my garden as much as yours," I say. "If you want a coworking space, go rent an office."

"You know we can't afford that."

"Then I guess I have a bit of bargaining power, don't I?" But not wanting to upset Hal too much, I add, "Don't worry. I have my own calls to make anyway."

And so I lie down on my beach towel and call Chris because he's the only person I know, except my parents, who'd actually pick up a phone call. And also because we haven't talked in too long, not since that night he came to Bushwick to collect Arnie.

"Chris," I say, when he picks up. "It's me."

I like being able to identify myself as just "me." I've never had that with anyone before, apart from the Redstockings.

"Emily Jane," he says. He hasn't dropped the habit of calling me by my full name, and now I'm starting to hope he never does. It's a grand thing, making new memories with my old name. Like new life being injected into something I'd left for dead. "What's up?" he asks.

"Lots of things are up," I say. "And lots of things are down. We wouldn't want one squall of emotion without the other, would we?"

"Guess not," Chris says, and I get the feeling he's already not following me. He can get lost in my words a lot, and lost in my eyes too. Not that we're looking at each other right now, but it sort of feels like we are, with how closely I'm holding my phone to my mouth. "I was actually going to call you," he says.

"I know," I say.

"You do?"

"I mean, I know you like talking to me," I say. "And that talking on the phone is your preferred method of communication. So I connected the dots, right after I disconnected some others."

"Right." He sounds nervous again, almost like the very first time he called to ask me to watch Arnie. "I wanted to ask you a favor. Olivia and I are going to the beach for Memorial Day weekend . . ."

"The Hamptons. Time to start calling a spade a spade. And yes, of course I'll watch Arnie," I say to save him the trouble of groveling for my help, as enjoyable as that sequence may have been. "It would be a delight."

"Awesome," Chris says. "Really appreciate it."

"I mean, I basically kidnapped Arnie last time, so don't thank me too much."

"You didn't kidnap him," Chris says. "You gave him an adventure. He was in a better mood all week because of it. I was going to let you know, but . . ." He trails off, and the O word is the obvious barricade between us.

"All good," I say. "I'll need a pay raise, though. Due to inflation and tariffs and FX rates and favorable macro headwinds." I toss around the buzzwords that I've accumulated from Hal.

I can tell Chris is smiling on the other end of the line. "Forgot what a good negotiator you are," he says and then suggests a number that's quite a bit higher than last time. I could probably wrangle him for even more, but I'm not trying to take advantage of him.

"You've got yourself a deal," I say. "I'll be over tomorrow so you can show me the routine again. I'm forgetful, as you know, so I'll need retraining." It's really just an excuse for me to go see Chris sooner than Memorial Day, which is still two weeks away.

"Sounds good. I'll be back from work around seven. I'll leave my key at the front desk if you want to get there early to see Arnold."

It's a nice gesture and reinforces how much he trusts me. I decide not to tell him that I have a key of my own, the copy of the spare he lent me. No need to make him question my character. "Great," I say. "I'll head over after breakfast. Which means I'll probably get there late afternoon."

Chris laughs. "Your life is something else."

"You know what they say. Opposites attract."

He goes quiet, then clears his throat. A phlegmy sound ejects as if something small and sharp is stuck in his esophagus. “Well, I’ve got to get back to work now,” he says. “But I’ll see you tomorrow.”

“Right.” I’m kicking myself for making that comment, for upsetting the refound balance, not that it was going to last long anyway. Nothing thwarts adventure quite like equilibrium. If Chris wants back into my life, he’s going to have to do it on my terms, unstable as they are. “See you then.”

Chapter 17

MEMORIAL DAY WEEKEND IS A DELUGE of fur and fun, just the way I like it.

Of course, Arnie is thrilled to see me, slobbering all over me and egging me on to mess up the overly tidy apartment with him. I gladly join in, though I have to check in with Tara and Hal now and then to make sure Mango and Squid are getting along alright without me. It's the first time I've left them home alone overnight, and there's an unfamiliar sensation pressing in on me. I'd call it anxiety if I didn't know better.

After cooking up veggie burgers I've found in the freezer, I flip again through Chris's family photo album, the one I'd found tucked away in the closet before. It just appeals for some reason. As I'm going through the photos, I narrow in on Chris's older brother more and think about how Chris never mentions him. Maybe there's some kind of intense sibling rivalry going on, though that doesn't fit with Chris's peacemaker personality.

I decide to ask Chris about it when he gets back that weekend. Olivia's not with him when he returns, which is nice, mostly for Arnie's sake. I don't want him getting too attached to Olivia if she's just going to disappear from his life, which seems probable. Not that there's much risk of Arnie getting attached to her. Arnie's too smart for that.

"How was *the beach*?" I ask with a smirk, not the cruel kind.

"Pretty good," he says. "Olivia's family hosted their annual lobster roll cook-off for charity."

"Ah yes, because there's nothing more charitable than slaughtering our marine life for the enjoyment of the elite," I say.

A beat passes and then he says, "Maybe I'll suggest a vegetarian substitute for next year."

The words *next year* make me scowl. It means he's thinking long-term with Olivia.

"I have a question for you," I say. "Who's that?" Photo album open, I point to a slightly faded photo of Chris and his brother. They're wearing these argyle sweaters, different colors, same pattern, and have matching bowl cuts. Chris is probably six or so and has a couple teeth missing, his smile all gap-toothed and gummy. It's pretty cute. His brother is taller and resting one elbow on Chris's shoulder, like it's his favorite armrest.

Chris's face blanches, losing any color he's absorbed from the beach. Silence slashes the air, but not in a way that makes me think of a machete cutting its way through the jungle to build a home among the trees. It's more like a cold ruler scraping against my cheek.

"That's my brother, Luke," he says, and then he goes into his bedroom to drop off his bag. As if I'm just going to let it slide, as if I'm not the expert on avoidance tactics.

I've clearly hit a nerve. Luke must be estranged for some reason. Maybe he's in jail, or there's another juicy family secret. I'm bursting to find out, but I don't want Chris to feel like I'm cornering him, so I just hang back on the couch with Arnie, who's back to snoozing.

My subtlety pays off. Chris emerges from his room and goes about organizing everything in the fridge, even though I hardly changed around anything, just the milk and eggs and meats that I moved to the bottom because I don't eat those.

Chris's voice is muffled from talking into the refrigerator, but I pick up on every syllable like he's right next to me. "Luke died in a car crash," he says.

The news grinds into me. I sink farther into the couch cushions, only now realizing how fluffy, too fluffy, they are. "Oh," I say. It's horribly insufficient, but I can't beckon anything better. I'm too busy feeling sorry for myself about how Chris has withheld this massive piece of information about himself, how he didn't trust me enough to confide in me sooner.

"It was a few years ago now," Chris says, closing the fridge and coming over to the living room. He slides onto the couch on the end opposite from me, with Arnie sprawled out in the middle, ready to play. "It's still kind of hard to talk about." He scratches Arnie's ears, avoids my eyes. "But yeah, that's what happened."

"Why didn't you tell me?" I'm aware I shouldn't be accusing him, but it's still probably better than the hollow sympathies he usually gets. Bluntness has a nice way of distracting the heart from its hurt.

"Sorry," Chris says, and it makes me detest myself, how I always try to steal the attention at the worst times.

"No, no, there's nothing to be sorry about," I say. "It's not like we're that close or anything."

He looks a little sad at that and I want to wrap him in a hug. But since I can't do that, I just prod Arnie to leap up into Chris's arms. Arnie takes my hint, pounces on Chris in that hey-Dad-I-love-you way until Chris takes him in his arms and holds him like a baby.

"Do you still hang out with him?" I ask Chris. "Luke, I mean."

Chris looks at me like I'm not understanding the whole premise about Luke being dead. So I explain my theory of the afterlife, which I invent as I'm speaking. Working under pressure suits me, accelerates my efficiency. "Humans are just individual globs of energy," I say. "And when we die, we lose our bodies but our energy survives. It transfers form or just does some solo victory laps around the universe now that it's free of the confines of a human container."

I don't believe what I'm saying, but it's a nice image to paint and I think it might help comfort Chris. Besides, who really knows what happens when we die anyway? No one can disprove my theory. It's incontrovertible by definition.

The poetic explanation doesn't seem to suit him much. No surprise given he's all prose.

Chris says he grew up believing in heaven but now he's not sure he believes in anything. "I haven't seen any signs or anything that might be from Luke," he says, and I get the feeling he hasn't talked about this with many people at all. "And I just think if there were a heaven, he would've found a way to say he was okay or play some kind of practical joke on me or something. He had the best sense of humor. Kind of like yours," he adds.

The comparison surprises me, flatters me. "Well, maybe Luke is trying to communicate in other ways," I suggest.

"What kind of ways?" He seems skeptical but a little hopeful too, which makes me feel bad. I don't want to lead him on, take advantage of his grief, when I've got no clue where I'm going with this.

"Maybe you need some mushrooms," I say, because it's the most helpful thing I can think of. It would loosen him up and let him get close enough to his pain to touch it without jerking back in fear. He'd be able to crawl curiously into the caves with a psychedelic flashlight.

Chris says he doesn't think mushrooms are the answer.

"Well, you at least need a good cry," I say. "If you keep it all in, it's really going to come back and bite you in the balls."

Chris deflects the comment. "When was the last time you cried?" he asks.

I'm not prepared for that laser beam. The truth is that I haven't really cried in years, but it's not because I repress things. It's because

I process them so well that I don't bottle them up, so there's no need to unleash them through my eyes.

"I cried yesterday," I say, though we both know I'm lying. I wish I didn't have to lie to Chris, but that's just who I am. I keep the Redstockings close and that's it. No need to lower my shield around anyone else.

"Okay," Chris says. It's clear the conversation is over. If I'm not going to open up with him, he's not going to with me. It's fair but feels unjust. "Your money's in the envelope on the counter," he says.

It doesn't feel right taking anything from him, not when he's already lost so much. I know that he has a lot of money and that's not his limiting resource, but it still feels like I'd be exploiting him somehow. Or maybe indebting myself to him, which would be even worse.

"Keep it and take Arnie on an adventure," I say, leaving the envelope untouched. After kissing Arnie goodbye, I pat Chris on the shoulder. There's a moment where I think about going in for the hug but it's too much, so I dash out the door and down the hall.

The elevator ride down is excruciating. My ears pop and my chest pops too, swelling with scruples that make me want to go back up and find a way to make Chris feel better. But I know myself well enough to admit that I'm not good at fixing situations. I just make them worse.

I'm beginning to think that if I'm remembered for anything, it'll be that.

Chapter 18

IN THE DAYS THAT FOLLOW, I can't stop thinking about how Chris reacted when I brought up Luke. It makes me wonder how things used to be, before the car accident.

I look Luke up on the internet and find his college sports profile. He played varsity baseball at Vanderbilt and was captain his senior year. Another few clicks lead me to an old bio at a New York accounting firm. It looks like Luke earned his CPA and moved to Manhattan after college. My sleuthing also uncovers an engagement announcement in *The New York Times* for Luke and his fiancée, a Miss Tiffany Eloise Rockwell. Tiffany has the same blonde, bony look as Olivia. It seems the accident came before the wedding. I try to find Tiffany on social media but can't. She might have a new last name by now. It doesn't feel right that she could just move on and marry someone new when Luke's whole life was snatched.

Luke's obituary is one of those short generic ones that feels like it was written from a template where you fill in the name and dates and—presto—death certificate, please. I can't think of anything more offensive than having such a measly obituary. It gives off the impression that his whole life was only two puny little paragraphs, written in size 8 Times New Roman, the least expressive of all fonts.

"Maybe I should be an obituary writer," I fume to Tara and Hal one night when we're eating pizza and garlic knots in the back garden. Astrid's there too, attached to Hal's hip like she always is these days.

Summer has stuffed its way back into the city. There's not much of a breeze in the courtyard, so Hal has ripped off the top of the pizza box and repurposed it into a fan. It's not her worst invention to date.

"That sounds like the most dismal of all professions," Hal says. "Making your living from other people's deaths."

"I don't know," Tara says, head tilted as if she's assessing the angle of it, the art of it. "It's a beautiful way to honor the dead."

"Exactly," I say. "It's a way to share their legacy, carry it on."

"What's got you on this death obsession, EJ?" Hal wants to know. "Did someone kick the can?"

"Yes," I say. "Luke did."

The rest of them sit there for a moment, looking at each other as if trying to feel out whether they should know who this is, if he was one of my flings they can't keep track of.

"Chris's brother," I elaborate. "He died a few years ago, but the obituary was abysmal. An insult to his memory, really. I wish I'd known him so I could've written a better one."

Tara and Hal exchange a look that reeks of misplaced suspicion. "Does he still have that girlfriend?" Hal asks.

"Of course Luke doesn't have a girlfriend," I snap. "He's six feet under."

"Not Luke, obviously," Hal says. "Chris."

I tell her that yes, Chris and Olivia are still together, but I have a theory about that. "Olivia looks exactly like the woman Luke was engaged to before he died," I tell them. "So it's pretty clear that Chris isn't actually in love with Olivia. He's just trying to live out his brother's dream life and call it his own. It's probably why he's still working that boring accountant job, because he always looked up to his brother and followed in his footsteps. And now that he doesn't have anyone to follow, he's following a ghost."

Hal and Tara appear skeptical and concerned, but Astrid is nodding along.

"I've seen that happen before," Astrid says, and her accent draws me in more than I want it to, the way it carves and contours every word. "After my father died, my mother couldn't make a single decision without asking if it was what my father would've done. It was sad to watch, because in a lot of ways she lost her own life, too, when we lost my father. That was a long time ago now. But still, it sometimes feels like she's trying to live two people's lives at once."

I feel a deep fondness for Astrid in that moment. Part of me wants to initiate her into the Redstockings and fill Jenni's place. But the dynamic with her dating Hal feels like it would disrupt the platonic values of the group. Still, I'm actually glad she's here and hope she sticks around for a while.

"Did you ever tell your mom you felt like that?" Hal asks, leaning her head on Astrid's shoulder.

"Not really," Astrid says. "I tried to go along with everything she wanted so I wouldn't make her life harder. Probably why I ultimately rebelled and moved to America." Her tilted front teeth jut out, the kind of smile that's prettier because it's not perfect. "And fell in love with a woman," she adds.

Hal does a double take. We all do.

"You love me?" Hal balks.

"Of course I do, Hally," Astrid trills, looking into Hal's eyes like she's translating a book from Norwegian to English and back again. "And you love me too."

Hal looks stunned and I think she's going to dispute it. But after a moment, her edges fold inward like origami.

"Guess I do," she admits, with the movements of a child who's been caught stealing candy, then told she can keep it.

Tara and I look at each other. We've never seen Hal in love before, and my own fear is reflected back on Tara's face like flares of a forest inferno we thought was only a campfire. Hal is too non-conformist to go the way of Jenni. It's not marriage we're worried about, but Astrid has still become a threat. Though chances are that once whatever start-up they're working on goes bust, their relationship will follow suit. I'm not rooting for it, but I won't be heartbroken when it happens, that's all.

"Just be careful," I say to Hal and Astrid, like I'm the subject matter expert here. "Love is the worst kind of vine. Sometimes it's hard to realize you're getting choked until it's too late."

Hal and Astrid divvy up a giggle that makes me feel like I'm the outsider here, not Astrid. "And sometimes it's hard to realize when you're getting un-choked too," Hal says.

I don't know what she means and I don't really want to. I just want things to go back to how they were. "Who wants to go out tonight?" I ask. "House of Yes?"

"I would, but I've got a shift at the bar," Tara says.

Hal's out too. "We've got to get back to our business plan."

"Next time, though," Astrid chimes in. "Definitely next time."

"Well, what am I supposed to do tonight?" I sulk, not bothering to keep the thought to myself.

"You could come hang out at Lone Wolf while I work," Tara suggests. "Entertain the crowd with your jukebox dancing."

"I'm tired of that," I brood. "It's the same people every night. I need variety."

"Why don't you go see Chris?" Hal says. "Ask him more about Luke."

It appeals more than it should. "Bad idea," I decline. "He doesn't want to talk about Luke."

"Sometimes the things we want don't match up with the things we need," Hal says in her guru voice.

"But sometimes they do match up," Astrid whispers to Hal, inducing my gag reflex once more.

"Look, I'm not going to force it out of Chris," I say, steamrolling over their moment. "I'm not his therapist."

"That's true," Tara agrees. "But you are his friend. And sometimes friends are supposed to pry, if it's coming from a place of truly caring about the other person."

"I don't care that much about him," I say. It feels important to state that aloud so my brain might interpret it as truth, play it back later while I'm sleeping, persuade my subconscious to register it as fact.

"Well, you're a very empathetic person," Tara says. She hands me the last slice of pizza because she's a true friend like that. "You feel things deeply."

I've never thought of myself as particularly empathetic. At least not since I was a little kid, when the weight of the world encased me in a gravitational vortex set in motion by my own mass. Before I learned how to break the curse of caring about what everyone thought and felt about me.

"I guess that's right," I say. Tara has that way of making me take her side, even if I don't intend to. "Chris is lucky to have me."

"He is," Tara says. "But not as lucky as we are."

"Enough with all the mushy confessions," Hal says, but she's glowing. "Time to get back to business." She opens her laptop, furrows her brows at the screen again, as if taking this one night off might send everything careening off course.

Tara hops up to change into her bartending attire. I follow her into our bedroom so I can get some space from Hal and Astrid.

"You sure you don't want to come along to the bar?" Tara asks, pulling on jean shorts and a black V-neck. The Lone Wolf uniform is casual, no surprise there.

"That's alright," I say, though it means a lot how she goes out of her way to ensure I'm not left out. "Think I'm just going to drive Uber; it's been a while since I have."

"Over to Tribeca?" Tara asks lightly.

I try to arrange my face as neutrally as I can. "Only if someone needs a ride over there."

Tara doesn't pry, just dabs Vaseline on her lips and eyelids.

"I'm just driving Uber so I can pay rent," I remind her. "Nothing else."

"EJ," Tara says, nipping up her purse and hurrying out the door so she's not late. "I know you pride yourself on being a great liar, but I can always tell. Your voice goes up two octaves."

"No, it doesn't." I lower my pitch to prove my point, hammer it home.

"And you don't blink, like you're trying to overcompensate and prove how trustworthy you are."

"I blink," I say, but I know she's right.

"Your antics might work on most people," Tara says. "But not on me. We've been friends for over a decade now, EJ. I've had some time to figure you out."

"Or maybe I just want you to know when I'm lying," I say, and it feels like the truest thing I've said in a while. "Have you ever thought about that?"

"Hmm," Tara says. "That theory makes me feel kind of good."

"It should," I tell her. "You and Hal are my people. You always will be."

Tara shifts on her feet. I can sense her own fears over Hal and Astrid's relationship becoming serious. "Always?" she asks. Her eyes are so wide and vulnerable. It gives me a glimpse into younger Tara, who was shuffled through the foster system from one temporary home to another.

I nod and loop her into a hug, my lips brushing her cheek.

"Always," I say. "Unless you join a polycule with Hal and Astrid and leave me out."

Tara laughs, but the vibration is off. "Yeah, right," she says. "Hal seems perfectly happy having Astrid to herself."

It hits me slowly but all at once. "Shit," I say, looking at Tara with fresh eyes. "You and Hal?"

"No, of course not," Tara says quickly. "Nothing's ever happened."

"But you love her."

Tara doesn't say anything. She's staring at her feet. "I love all the Redstockings."

"It's nothing to be ashamed about," I say. "Everyone's been in love with Hal at some point. Lucky for me, I got my crush out of my system back in college."

"Mine is proving a little trickier to overcome," Tara says. "But it'll pass. I guess you and I are both in our unrequited love era."

"No, I told you I got over Hal in college. Freshman spring, actually, when she was such a know-it-all in that economics class."

"I wasn't saying your unrequited love is with Hal," Tara says. "It's Chris, obviously."

"Are you high?" I ask, then tilt the conversation back to Tara's problem. "Have you ever tried sitting by Hal during one of her work sessions when she talks out loud to herself in all that jargon with all those acronyms? It's the most repelling thing."

Tara smiles, even if it's a limp little thing. "Good point," she says. "I should do that more often."

"It should work instantly," I tell her and squeeze her hand. "Or your money back."

Hal appears in the doorway, coming in from the garden. "What're you talking about? A new type of magic mushroom?"

"Yeah," I say, grinning at Tara as we share our private joke. "Something like that."

"Well, count me in," Hal says. "I need all the biohacks I can get to reach peak performance and optimize my efficiency as Astrid and I incubate the beta prototype of our proprietary software platform."

Told you so, I mouth to Tara over Hal's shoulder, and Tara giggles, the glimmer back in her eyes.

Chapter 19

CHRIS IS HARD TO PIN DOWN in the days that follow.

There's no allure in the chase, just a bloated sort of annoyance. Here I am, trying to get to know him more, trying to help him heal from losing his brother, and he just keeps saying that he's out of town. Sure, it's summer, but there's no way he's gone all the time or he'd be asking me to dogsit. Unless he's found someone new for Arnie. The thought depresses me in the shape of a punch.

Guilt-trapping him is the only way forward. I'm not proud of exploiting his kindness, but there's really no alternative.

"Hey, Chris," I say to the voicemail because once again he hasn't picked up the phone. "I'm having kind of a hard time. There's a problem I'd like your opinion on. Let me know if you're free for dinner or a drink this week. I can come over your way."

He replies via text rather than a phone call, not like him. But at least he agrees to meet up, though he suggests brunch rather than dinner, way less intimate.

I get there early, all keyed up though there's nothing in my system but my own blood. He chose Bubby's, a legendary breakfast spot in the city, or so I've heard. I've never been here, but a line twists out the door and down the block, nearly reaching the West Side Highway.

Inside, exposed brick wraps the family-style joint, and the tables are packed together with the sort of efficiency you'd expect out of

Manhattan. The clientele is a mix of soccer parents taking their kids out to a postgame feast, young couples mopping up hangovers with corn bread and iced coffees, and gaggles of postcollege girls animatedly sharing every negligible, essential detail of their lives as they snitch each other's hash browns without having to ask. Nostalgia for the Redstockings rises, the olden days and golden days when Jenni was still around, and Lilly too, and we could fill a restaurant booth.

Chris arrives and manages to slide into the chair across from me without jamming up against the person behind him. "You're early," he says, and I pick up on the insinuation that he expected me to be late.

"Am I?" I ask, pretending not to be aware of the time. Pretending not to have changed at all since I first met him.

"So what's going on?" he asks. "Everything okay?"

"Not really." I'm enjoying the idea that everyone else in the restaurant likely assumes we're a couple. "First, there's the fact that Hal is *in love*."

"In love or in jail?" Chris asks. "You make it sound like the latter."

"They're one and the same. Both are cages."

Chris pulls his mouth in an oh-so-it's-going-to-be-this-kind-of-day way. It makes me want to hurry on to the next subject, the reason we're here.

"And also, I have this other friend who seems to be pulling away from me," I say, fiddling with the cloth napkin that I refuse to fold on my lap. "I found out something about his life. Something bad he went through. And instead of letting me in, it just feels like he's shutting me out." I pause so the effect of using the third person can sink in, help him feel less attacked. "What advice would you give me? To connect with this person?"

Chris is staring down at the laminated menu, transfixed on the same spot. Reading it over and over, or more likely staring right through it. "I'd tell you to respect his space," he says, words sheared like hedges pruned into compliance. "Not everyone processes things by sharing them."

I ask how someone might process them then. Chris says that actions probably do the talking, that the person probably lives his life differently based on what he's been through.

I want to reach across the table and put my hand over his, be the lid of a frying pan, keeping the heat in. But it would just make him feel like he should further clarify that we're not a couple. No need for that. "I just want you to have people you can talk to," I say.

"I do have people." The statement goes down my throat like an ice cube, catching partway, not melting fast enough.

Olivia's airbrushed face appears in my thoughts. I try to rise above the envy, remind myself it's good if Chris is opening up to her. It shouldn't matter who his outlets are so long as he has them. But I'm not a big enough person to imbibe logic through the arteries to my heart. It stays upstairs, stuck in the head, fucked in the head.

"Good," I say, picking up my own menu, wielding it like a shield. "Glad to hear that."

Later, after the blowup that follows, I skirt off the subway at Knickerbocker, dashing over to Lone Wolf.

"Where are those french fries from?" Tara asks as I walk in. I'm holding a basket of fries. My shoulders are rolled back to their full height, the surest sign that I feel small and saggy inside.

"Stole them from brunch," I say. "And left Chris with the check." There's a cackle in my voice, a pride, but it's the artificial kind, susceptible to the poke of a pin, a fingernail, even the dull side of a butter knife.

"Well, don't carry the fries around like a flower bouquet," Tara says. "Bon appétit." My appetite is still gone, but I pass them over to Tara, hoping this proves I'm not a bad friend after all. Not rude and nosy like Chris said.

"So what happened?" Tara asks, filling in the gaps from the multi-paragraph, punctuation-less text I fired off to Tara and Hal on the subway ride back. "He stiff-armed you when you asked about Luke?"

"He accused me of stalking his family," I say. "Just because I knew a few things about his brother, like that he was an accountant and lived in New York. And that Luke's ex-fiancée was named Tiffany and they got engaged at Gurney's Beach Club in Montauk and lived in a Brooklyn Heights brownstone on Clark Street. Basic stuff like that, and he called me 'obsessive' and 'unhinged.' Can you believe him?"

Tara hesitates a little too long. It's too much to handle, the fact that she might side with him or even contemplate it. I plop my face into my arms, the whole puddle of me leaking onto the countertop, fitting in among the mess of cigarette butts and beers.

"He's the unhinged one," Tara says vigorously, as if to make up for her vacillation. "He doesn't know how to deal with someone who has as big of a heart as you do, that's all." She whips up a Redstocking cocktail, going heavy on the pomegranate maybe because she sees I need the color. "It's a guy thing, and even as far as men go, Chris sounds like he's on the emotionally stunted end of the spectrum."

"The most stunted," I agree and tell her how Chris freaked out when I very gently, very kindly asked if he thought there was any chance that perhaps he was trying to honor his brother by living out Luke's dream life and losing sight of his own along the way.

"I mean, I can see how that would be a bit upsetting to him," Tara says, doling out another round of draft ale to the guys at the bar, the regulars who come at lunch and stay through closing. "If he's never thought of it like that before."

"But how couldn't he have?" I say, certain that no dots have ever been easier to connect. "He's working the same job as Luke, living in the same city, dating a literal dead ringer for Luke's ex. It's so blatant and yet he's gaslighting me for pointing out the obvious."

Hal joins us at the bar. She's solo, which I appreciate. "Just saw the texts," she says, plunking down beside me, gearing up for combat. "And for the record, I never liked Chris. Too wishy-washy, too dense to figure out he should be dating you."

"Dating is completely off the table," I say. "Not that it was ever on the table, but it's fully in the dumpster now." I repeat the brunch story for her with more theatrics this time.

"He needs to go to therapy," Hal says at the end, like this settles it. "Maybe you should go too."

I glare at her. "Yeah, couples therapy sounds like the ideal solution for two platonic friends at an impasse."

"Not couples therapy," Hal says. "Though I'd pay money to sit in on that. Just go on your own, vent about each other, and evict the negative energy from your aura. Wait until Mercury is out of retrograde, though. That's probably why this happened in the first place."

"EJ doesn't believe in astrology," Tara says.

"Maybe I do," I say, just to be difficult, just to take my anger out on the only people in the world who are actually there for me right now, trying to help. "But why would I pay for therapy when I can just vent to you two?"

"Therapy is free in Norway," Hal says, as if this is relevant to the conversation. As if anyone brought up Astrid's home country.

"Chris will come around," Tara says. "Just give him time."

"Time for what?" I ask. "I'm not just going to sit here and take his punches. The ball is in his court to apologize. Until then, he's done to me, dead to me."

I throw back the rest of my drink, wash it down with a pickleback, and then finish off the fries I didn't pay for, the oil coating my fingers, sinking into my dirty nail beds.

Under the wan lighting of the single-stall bathroom, I scrub my hands clean, though I have the sensation I'm absorbing the muck via osmosis. It's all grunge and grime back here, no toilet paper to be used, though plenty strewn across the floor like several mummies were unraveled, their stench lingering. The concrete walls are plastered with magazine cutouts, page corners peeling. Graffiti is streaked, little hearts and initials and skulls, each with its own story that will never be told, never even seen except by Lone Wolf patrons who have to piss, or people like me just trying to get slippery grease off their hands so they don't drop something important. Except maybe they already did.

Chapter 20

BACK AT THE INN LATER THAT day, I turn off my phone and stash it in my pillowcase so I won't have to see how Chris hasn't reached out. I don't want to think about him, expend one more iota of energy on someone who clearly doesn't value my presence in his life, doesn't see how I'm the best, most vibrant thing ever to happen to him.

In spite of, or perhaps because of, this intense focus to not focus on him, on us, I plummet into obsession, replaying the brunch in all its grisly details, berating myself for saying too much and not enough, berating Chris for how he should have acted, might have acted. The angst engorges, pushing up against my bodily walls in a torrent of rain and fire. I have to eject it, have to let it come coursing out of me in whatever form it pleases. I'm not the captain, only the vessel.

So I open up a blank Word doc and submit to the feelings, my fingers flying over the keyboard to keep up with the voices, the visions, the vices. A mini play pours out, my most prolific work in ages.

The dialogue is an alternative version of the debacle that took place. A version of our brunch in which Chris thanks me for being such a caring friend and breaks down his walls and we talk more about Luke and the impact his death had on Chris and how his relationship with Olivia is little more than a misplaced coping mechanism.

The words, the pages, start to stack like dominoes filmed in reverse motion, standing up one after the other, an accordion of creation. It's the kind of tunnel vision I've been wanting to feel with my playwriting, so I keep riding the wave and soar, soar, soar straight into the mouth of the serpent.

Tara appears at my shoulder sometime later, though I'm only half aware. "I thought you said you didn't want to think about Chris anymore," she says, snooping at my work before it's even half baked, greedy for the gooey batter.

"Don't ask me to make sense," I say, refusing to peel my eyes away from my screen, from my characters, from my calling. "Or you're asking me not to be an artist."

Hal comes over to join us on the couch, some chemical energy drink in one hand, homemade green juice in the other. "Now you understand what it's like to be in flow," she says. "And why I don't like to be interrupted."

I tilt my computer away from Hal. Tara's snooping is one thing, but I'm not ready for Hal's judgment, her lectures about how I need to hone my value proposition and develop my pitch.

"I've been in flow before," I say, though I'm starting to wonder if I ever really have been. If all the times before were just imposters and apprentices of the real thing. The exposition slanting up, gradual until the parabola shoots up to the climax, propelling me here, into the eye of the storm that I hope never subsides.

It does let up after a while, but first it doubles down on itself, carries me out into the white-capped waves of a second draft. In this version, I scrap all the sentimental lines and trade them in for biting humor, so dry it crumbles like sun-cracked clay.

I don't edit myself based on what my audience may think of it, if I reach an audience at all. But I still enjoy how the deviations from the facts of what really happened make it harder to compare my life to this play. There's a freedom that comes from letting real life bleed into make-believe, making it impossible to prove or disprove. The trick is making sure that the fiction still reverberates with the solid thump of fact.

—

"When can we read the script?" Hal asks late one night when we're out back in the garden. Astrid is there again too. The two of them still haven't shared what their stealth-mode start-up is all about. If you ask me, it's just an excuse for them to be spending all this time together, fooling themselves into thinking that they're being productive. I could hack Hal's computer and find out if I wanted to, but I don't because I'm busy enough.

"It's not done yet," I say, editing it on my laptop, wobbly on the patio table whose uneven legs teeter on the gravel. My eyes are strained from staring at the screen in the dark. Bitterness resurfaces at how Jenni pulled a total Grinch move, taking all the light strands when she left us.

Tara spritzes her water bottle onto the plants, abetting the ivy in its quest to crawl up the whole wall, over the roof, and up into the sky or down to the earth, whichever path it chooses, maybe both. "Writing is never done, though," she says.

Leave it to Tara to spoil my bad excuse with a good rebuttal.

"There's just a time when you have to say 'good enough' and put it out into the world," she carries on. "Otherwise, art would always stay hidden and only be discovered after the creators died."

"Maybe that's not the worst thing," I say. "No positive recognition, but no negative recognition either."

"That doesn't sound like you," Tara says. "Taking a moderate stance."

"What can I say? I'm *evolving*." I put a dramatic spin on the word, wag my fingers ominously.

"Start-ups are like that too," Hal says, pivoting the conversation back to herself, like she does best. "They're never fully done. It's all about just getting to the MVP—the *minimum viable product*," she explains importantly, as if we don't know this from the thousand times she's used the acronym. "And then sometimes you have to launch before you're ready so you can be the first mover, capture the market share before your competitors. Sprinting is the only speed in the start-up world."

"That means you should be close to launching by now, right?" I ask Hal. "How about this? I'll let you see my script if you tell me what your start-up is."

I know she won't take me up on it, so I'm safe.

"That's not the same," Hal says, shooting down my proposal. "There are intellectual property concerns for my business. *Our* business," she corrects quickly, as Astrid emits an acerbic "ahem."

"Writing is intellectual property too," I retort.

Astrid comes to my defense. "Hally, love," she says. "We can tell your friends. We can trust them."

I've got to admit I like Astrid more than I was expecting to, despite the fact that she's started staying over sometimes, breaking our sacred ground rules. Hal says those rules were made during a different era when we were sharing rooms, and now that she has her own, she should be able to fill it however she likes.

"Fine," Hal says, unable to resist Astrid. She pauses for a dramatic crescendo. "It's a software app."

Tara and I exchange a look, reciprocal underwhelm. "Aren't all apps software by definition?" Tara poses. She does it in a gentler way than I would have, but Hal still gets prickly, like we've attacked her baby, gone straight for the jugular.

"I wasn't done yet," Hal says. "It's a social impact platform that fosters global diversity and inclusion across an array of end markets."

The buzzwords fall flat onto the stones beneath our feet. Not thc grand reveal that Hal had hoped for.

"You'd better not be using AI," I say. "It's destroying the planet, way worse than eating meat."

"Of course we're using AI. How would we get funding without it?" Hal says. "You don't understand the funding landscape."

Astrid slides in. "We're building an app to help friend groups become more diverse," she says, and we're already hooked in more, both by her accent and by her word choice. "Data shows that most people stay in their little bubbles—politically, geographically, racially, you name it. Our app will match you with people outside your bubble. Expand your world, expand your heart."

"I like it," Tara says straightaway. "Exactly what we need in this divisive age."

She's always the most optimistic judge on our Shark Tank panel. I'm the toughest and love living up to the reputation.

"It's a decent concept," I admit, beginning with praise so the criticism won't smack so hard. "Though definitely don't use the words *diversity* or *inclusion*—everyone knows that movement is dead. And who are your customers? The people who need this app most won't download it. They like their homogeneous echo chambers, cling to them."

"That's true for the extremists," Hal says. "But there's a large segment—the forgotten middle, we call them—that want to meet people from other walks of life; they're just too lazy to put in the work themselves. So they'll outsource it to us, and we'll make it easy for them." She delivers the words with the air of someone who's already raised millions and now can't be bothered explaining herself to commoners like us.

"What's the monetization play?" I ask.

"Monetization isn't important in the early innings," Hal says.

I can tell she's annoyed by my question but respects it too, how I've learned my business lingo. "It's all about customer growth and retention. Once we have people hooked, the options are endless. Subscription model, ad revenue, it goes on."

"Hmm," I say. "I'm not sold." It hinges on the marketing, I tell them. "You could hire me for your launch campaign, if I get an equal split of equity," I say.

"You're insane," Hal says. "No way we're diluting our shares."

But Hal's confidence looks a bit rattled from my grilling, which isn't what I intended.

"Look," I say. "Even if your product was the worst thing in the world—which I'm not saying this is. But even if it was a complete fraud, a total hoax, I'd have faith you could sell it to anyone with a pulse. Maybe a few corpses too."

This cheers Hal right away. It makes me want to drop a few more compliments on her now and then, give her a boost without bloating her ego. "We're applying to a female founders accelerator," she says. "They'd give us some funds as we bootstrap, so say your prayers and cross your fingers."

"You know I don't pray," I say. "But consider my fingers crossed." I twist them together, fingers and toes, until I'm in a pretzel. "You'll get it for sure."

"I know," she says. "Now enough with the distractions. It's time for you to hold up your end of the deal. Show us the script."

"What's the story about?" Astrid asks, as if Hal hasn't told her everything, ratted me out.

"It's nothing really," I say. "It's just inspired by a fight I had with someone the other week. Just a play set in a diner, that's all."

"A breakup script," Astrid says approvingly. "I adore it already."

"No, no, it wasn't a breakup," I correct. "Chris and I have only ever been friends. Not even great friends. We only hang out when I babysit his dog. It's that kind of relationship. *Non-relationship.*" I bumble over my words, cheeks heating.

"Do you think you'll show it to him?" Tara asks. "As a sort of peace offering?"

"Definitely not," I say. "I'm not showing it to anyone. Not yet at least. Besides, it's fiction, I told you."

Astrid is trying to follow the conversation. It makes me hope that perhaps Hal didn't tell her everything, didn't dump my secrets into the pile of jelly beans and clothes they share.

"Wait, what did I miss here?" Astrid says. "Why aren't you dating?"

"Good question," Hal mutters under her breath. Even Tara pinches her mouth, the lines around her lips shaped like two parentheses, encasing the same afterthought.

"An innumerable number of reasons," I say, feeling ambushed. "We'd be here all night if I listed them all."

"I'm not in a rush," Tara says. It's true; she's in a lull between shows and bartending shifts.

"We're not either," Hal adds. "Astrid and I have outperformed our weekly goals already, and it's only Wednesday."

"Good for you," I mutter.

"I didn't mean it like that," Hal says. "I just meant that it would be good to hear why you and Chris aren't together. The real reasons."

I bristle. "What do you mean, the real reasons?"

"Well, as opposed to the fake reasons. You know, like that he has a girlfriend or that he's not your type."

"He does have a girlfriend and he isn't my type," I say. "I'm not making that up."

"I didn't mean fake as in not technically true," Hal says. "I meant fake as in not emotionally true."

"Since when are you one to give lectures on emotions?" I press.

Hal blushes, actually blushes, petal-shaped patches of pink dropping onto her cheeks. It's a sight I've never seen before. She looks at Astrid, then shrugs, like she's done trying not to try. "Since I met this one, I guess."

Astrid purrs, not audibly but with the arc of her body, the elongation of limbs. She leans in for a kiss. It's all very inverse to the mood I'm in. "Get a room," I grumble, looking for backup from Tara. She doesn't say anything, just watches, visibly conflicted.

"We already have a room," Hal says, when she finally reappears from under Astrid's tongue. "You just don't like it when we're there."

"You're right about that," I say. "She hogs all the hot water with that mermaid hair of hers." I say it like Astrid isn't right there, sitting across the table from me.

Astrid tugs on Hal's arms, flicks her eyes away. "Maybe I should go, Hally," she says in a low tone.

"Absolutely not," Hal flares. "EJ is just using this as a diversion tactic so she doesn't have to talk about Chris and how she's fallen in love for the very first time."

I flick off the accusation as if it's just a fly. "I'm not in love with Chris," I say, kneading nonchalance into my voice so as not to stoke Hal's delusion. "And even if I were, it wouldn't be my first love. I've been in love hundreds of times before."

"Name one," Hal says.

"Every time we go to the House of Yes, I fall in love multiple times," I lob back.

Tara pipes up, as if she's been waiting her turn. "EJ, you know that's not really love, right?" she says. "It's just lust, infatuation."

"Of course it's really love," I say, feeling ganged up on. "It's love in its most untainted form, before any resentment or expectations smear the splendor of the initial connection."

"So by your logic," Hal says, "the longer you know someone, the less you love them?"

"For romantic love, absolutely," I say. "And up until now, you two have always agreed with me. Jenni and Lilly used to too . . ." I trail off, feeling lost among the people who first taught me what it was to be found.

Tara puts a hand on my shoulder, gives a few pats. I battle the urge to shrug her away. "Do you think," Tara says, "that if Olivia weren't in the picture, you'd be dating Chris?"

"No," I say, without needing to think about it. "Definitely not."

"Do you think you'd want to be dating him?" she follows up.

Tara, Hal, and Astrid are all looking on, waiting for me to answer. It's like they've already come to their own conclusion and my own opinion doesn't really mean much. Just the garnish to their meal, the lonely parsley sprigs.

"Look," I say, infuriated that I even have to explain myself. But I'm glad of it too, so I can hear myself affirm this. "I'm a liberated woman. The fulcrum of my life is ensuring that I don't have a fulcrum holding me in place. That I can fly however high or low I want, untethered, unlimited. Chris, on the other hand, is a conventional guy who plods along in his corporate job and wants marriage and kids and all that. It just wouldn't work."

"Who said anything about marriage and kids?" Hal says. "We were just talking about dating."

"It's a slippery slope sometimes," I say, shuddering under the crawly candor of it all. "Think about Jenni. So it's better not to even open the door."

The three of them share a look, as if I'm missing something vital.

"EJ," Tara says, her hand still on my shoulder, her thumb stroking circles on my sunburned skin. "I think the door is already open."

"Wide, wide open," Hal chimes in.

"No, it's not," I snap, but I know she's right. I feel it in the way the words sweep in the debris of relief.

The door with Chris opened the first time I walked inside his apartment, when Arnie jumped up to greet me. Before that, even.

Maybe it was when he opened the door of the Red Rocket for Olivia, that time that I was their Uber driver. Or maybe when I strode through the door of the art gallery, the very first time we met. When he pretended to be my fiancé and I chose to play along, just to see where it might go.

Chapter 21

SOMETIME LATE IN SUMMER, IN THE early morning hours I always sleep through, Hal barges into Tara's and my bedroom and flicks on the lights.

I moan and burrow back into my pillowcase, the cotton slicked with sweat or drool, probably both.

"What's going on?" Tara asks groggily from the bottom bunk. "Is there a fire?"

"Something close," Hal says. "Just found *this* in our mailbox." She's waving a sheet of paper, too fast to read even if my eyes were working so soon after waking up. "An *eviction warning* from the landlord," she elaborates.

Tara springs up in bed to examine the notice.

"That's why you shouldn't check the mail," I say, still half asleep. "Nothing good comes from it."

"Then I guess you won't care about this other one addressed to you," Hal replies. There's a small envelope in her other hand. "It's handwritten."

"That's for me?" I ask, blinking my eyes open.

I can't remember the last time I received mail that wasn't a bill, a brochure, or a letter from a scammer. This one will probably be a frilly invite for my niece's first birthday party, planned months in advance. Or maybe a wedding invitation from a college friend, someone who knows I'll decline but expects me to send a present anyway, having heard I'm living in New York City and thus jumping to conclusions about my ability to buy the whole registry when I actually can't afford anything except a toxic rubber spatula, plus two coffee mugs if I'm stretching. "Bushwick" doesn't mean much back in Michigan. Its antithesis to Manhattan is unknown and unwanted. No one wants the curtain lifted on their glitzy dreams, the gritty truth exposed.

Leaning over my top bunk, I reach out for the letter. Hal doesn't hand it over.

"Not until we've come up with a game plan for the apartment," she says. "We've been short on rent the past three months. Larry's turning on us, even with the extra weed I got him last month." She huffs at the injustice of our landlord's immorality. "EJ, don't take this personally, but you're the weak link as far as the finances go. Me and Tara have been covering you for a while now."

"You haven't had an actual income in years," I scowl to Hal.

"True, but I've mastered the art of winning entrepreneurship grants," Hal says. "It's not much but covers costs."

"I give you all my profits from driving Uber and working at Kora," I say. It's nearly correct, after you deduct the portion I spend on healthcare and gas and food and drinks and subway fare and myriad other costs of keeping yourself alive as an adult in this day and age. "And I nearly always cover the tab at the House of Yes. You're penalizing my generosity."

"I don't want to get into the weeds of it all," Hal says. "You just need to find a way to contribute your eight hundred per month. Can you do that?"

It feels like a threat. "Or what?"

"Or Astrid will move in to fill the difference," Hal says swiftly, like this wasn't a spontaneous ambush at all. Like it was a planned coup. If Tara didn't look so disoriented, eyes all puffed and wide, I'd think she was in on it too. "Your pick," Hal says.

"Eviction is expensive for landlords," I say. "And the law is on the tenants' side in New York. His threat is empty. We've got a few more months at least."

"Maybe," Hal says. "Maybe not."

"I don't mind the Astrid idea," Tara says. She's operating from fear, imploding too soon. "We'd have four of us again."

"That's out of the question," I say, and then go on to suggest that we start charging Astrid for when she stays over, thirty dollars a night or something like that. "It's peanuts compared to the billions of dollars that your start-up will be worth."

Hal bites back, says the business isn't out of stealth mode yet. "We won't be revenue-positive for another twelve months at least," she says. "Empires aren't built overnight, EJ."

"I'll pay the eight hundred," I say, after a few more arguments that loop around my waist like Hula-Hoops, falling to the ground with a rattle. "I just need a little more time."

"It's August nineteenth now," Hal says, arms folded. "You have until the thirty-first."

"No problem," I say. "I'll speak with my financial advisor about having some funds transferred from my investment accounts."

"You don't have a financial advisor," Hal snaps. "Or investment accounts."

"Sure I do." Accidentally, I think about Chris and how I used to think he'd be there to help me with my taxes, my least favorite thing in the world. Loss presses into me again, like it's leaning on me for balance. Or maybe it's the other way around. Maybe I need the sorrow to stand, to fill the space that's been singed. "I just don't want to liquidate my assets given the current bull market dynamics in US equities," I say.

Hal appears pleasantly stunned. It's always insulting how she thinks I don't know anything about money and business. Even if I did only learn this much from the financial podcasts she blares in the garden, plus some articles I read back when I was trying to learn more about Chris and what he does all day.

"Look, I'm sorry for being harsh here," Hal says. "I just don't want us to have to move out of the Dunge Inn."

"Me neither," I say. The thought of having to relocate terrifies me. The Inn is where the Redstockings belong. It's our headquarters.

"Good," Hal says, turning to leave. "Oh, and here's that letter." She tosses it up so it lands on my messy sheets.

The handwriting is sticklike and scruffy, no return address label. The envelope is secured with little pieces of tape, as if the sender didn't trust the seal of their own spit. Opening it, I find a page of perforated lined paper. It looks to have been torn carefully from a work notebook, folded exactly in half. Eyes skipping to the bottom, I see the signature. *Chris.*

Only then, once it's confirmed, do I allow myself to backtrack to the hope that this might be him offering the olive branch I was never going to give. It takes forever to decipher the note—not because I'm poring over each word or anything, but because his writing is just chicken scratch.

It's an apology but not a stellar one, just a few quick sentences about how he took his emotions out on me, and how that was wrong and he hopes we can still be friends. I read it over a few times before making my judgment because I'm fair like that. In the end, I decide I don't like it at all, mostly because who writes a letter to someone who lives in your same city? It's a total cop-out. Also, if he actually felt bad, he'd write more. I mean, I churned out sixty-seven and a half pages about him—not that I mailed them to him, but still. It feels like the bare minimum, just a wimpy little confession to ease his Catholic guilt.

I head out for a walk to throw away the letter. No need for it to clutter up the Inn. Each garbage can and dumpster I pass, I think about tossing it in, but I don't like the idea of someone rummaging through the trash and reading it. By the time I get to the Williamsburg Bridge, I still haven't found a suitable disposal location.

I walk onto the bridge and halt when I'm partway across. It's rare for me to be up this early. The tangy morning air with a newness you don't get by noon. Crepe-paper clouds strewn about the baby-blue sky. The Manhattan skyline spliced by chunky rays of sun, or maybe the sun spliced by the skyline.

Cars rumble below, cyclists whiz past. It's almost hard to tell if they're the ones moving or if I am. The theory of relativity can really get you sometimes, but the point is everyone's rushing to get nowhere except me. I'm standing still to get somewhere.

I drink in the summer morning like a cold beer. It washes down easily, stirs in me some forgotten knowledge about the scale and scope of the world and why I was dropped into it.

Not that there's any greater purpose, any divine intention. I was randomly born, just as I'll randomly die. Just as Luke randomly died, leaving Chris with the memories and mutilations that come from loving mortals, from being stupid enough to attach ourselves to other humans, delicate champagne flutes that cut us with jagged debris once they're destroyed and we're forced to keep standing. Clinging to old cuts, tracing new ones just to remind us of what once was, what will never be again.

The impermanence of it all, the futility, makes me want to smooth things over with Chris. I type out a text and nearly send it, but I don't. I delete it letter by letter until no one will be able to prove it was ever there at all. Then, with the quick flick of my wrist, I toss Chris's letter over the side of the bridge, through the grated guardrails. It flutters, then falls.

There's a wrench of remorse for polluting the river—not that it really matters since the earth is being destroyed by humans anyway. A single piece of paper isn't to blame. One little person can't wreck anything, can't fix anything.

On the walk home, I pass one of my favorite street performers who always camps out on Knickerbocker Avenue, just outside the laundromat. Elijah is his name. He's this older guy who wears the same

Christmas tree sweater vest even in summer and plays the trumpet like he's at Carnegie Hall.

The music hits extra hard today, or extra softly I should say, because it gives me the feeling that my bones are gelatin, like I'm just learning how to walk again or something. I have to sit down on the cigarette-and-candy-wrapper-littered curb to regain my balance. But Elijah's gritty trumpet melodies keep knocking me over again, one note at a time.

The jackhammers and wind gusts and car horns try to drag the music away, but it has a hefty quality, staying put. Like it's trying to remind me of something I've intentionally forgotten and have no desire to remember. Because as much as I despise the status quo, I guess I don't like change that much either.

Chapter 22

IN THE DAYS AFTER HAL'S LECTURE about needing to make rent, I take on more shifts at Kora's. It doesn't help much because the more I work, the more I go out and blow my paychecks on drinks and gummies. Nothing breeds recklessness quite like restraint.

One night, the three of us head out to the House of Yes. There's nothing dramatic, no notable difference, but the magic is gone. The whole thing feels cheap and overdone, a high school prom with a poodle updo and too much eyeliner.

The next day's hangover is extra bad. Everything throbs. The strobe lights are still there, blinking like red traffic lights at a four-way stop. I'm late to Kora's, barely making it there at all.

Someone taps my shoulder, awakening me before I realize I've fallen asleep standing up, leaning against the counter.

"EJ," a voice says.

My eyes blink open. It's Chris, standing right in front of me, dressed in a white button-down and a blazer. The edges of him are too crisp to be a hallucination, but I still reach out and touch his arm to be sure. He's solid, the linen of his shirt too stiff, in need of fabric softener.

"What're you doing here?" I ask. There's no time to organize my emotions, delineate which section needs to go where. Everything spills out, spills in.

He tells me that he went to my apartment but Hal said I was over here. "Did you get my letter?" he asks.

"What letter?" I fiddle at the cash register, gripping the paper bills just for something to hold, something to tear.

His forehead creases. "I wrote you an apology. Thought I got the address right . . ."

"Oh, that letter," I say, as if only just remembering. "Yeah, I got it."

Hands in his pockets, feet shuffling in place, he waits for me to continue.

He looks so earnest and awkward that I want to put it all behind us and forgive him, but of course I can't do that. "Some might say that letters are a coward's best friend," I say.

He flinches at that. It doesn't feel as rewarding as I'd hoped. "I thought it was the most respectful way to get in touch," he says. "To give you space."

"You mean so I couldn't yell at you through the phone or send an angry text right back?" I clarify. "*You* were the one who wanted the space, Chris."

"Maybe that's true. Look, I'm sorry for how I reacted." There's a glitch in his voice, a rasp that's not usually there. "I just have a hard time talking about Luke, and I felt like I was being backed into a corner."

The words ripple through me like a fan, cooling my temper a few degrees. "I was really just trying to help you," I say.

"I know you were. In your own Emily Jane sort of way."

I'm pleased he's back to calling me by my full name. My smile breaks out from behind bars. I whip us up a couple of almond milk lattes, though seeing Chris is a shot of caffeine in itself.

"Best coffee in the city," Chris says, sipping from the cardboard cup. "Going to tell everyone at work about it."

"Please don't," I say. "The last thing Bushwick needs is a Wall Street invasion. Rent is going up enough as it is."

My tone might reveal more about my money woes than I intend, because Chris asks if I can watch Arnie this weekend.

"I'll have to check my calendar and get back to you," I say.

"Come on, we both know you don't keep a calendar," he replies with a warm smile.

It's a delicious feeling, how well he knows me and how I might not have to say goodbye to him after all.

"Aren't you working today?" I say, realizing that it's the middle of a weekday.

His pasty cheeks color like my words have given them a good pinch. "I left the office early," he says, talking into his coffee cup. "Got all my meetings done and figured ducking out early wouldn't do too much harm."

"You left work early?" This is a big deal in Chris's world.

"Am I a rebel yet?" he asks, lips twitching.

"You'd have to unbutton your shirt, for starters."

To my surprise, he does. Just the top button, but it's something.

"Better," I say. "I'm not hitting on you, by the way. I'm just protecting you against getting suffocated by your own shirt. The risk looked pretty high."

"Don't worry about that," Chris says. "I know you'd be the last person in the world to hit on me."

"Right," I say hastily, mopping up a puddle of coffee I've spilled on the counter. "Obviously."

"Come by Thursday evening?" Chris says. "Arnold will be excited. You're his favorite babysitter."

The unspoken comparison to Olivia hits me like victory. "Well, you have a very intelligent dog."

I expect to get another smile out of him, but his face catches in a tangled net of emotions. "What is it?" I ask.

"Arnold's not really my dog." Chris glances up, then down again. "He was Luke's."

I let the statement sink in slowly. Suddenly it all makes sense.

Why Chris is so overprotective about Arnie. Why Arnie gets so out of sorts when left alone. The little pup must have abandonment issues.

Knowing this, the fact that Chris entrusts Arnie to my care means even more. It makes me want to scoop Chris into a big embrace, and Arnie too. Usually I'd fight it, but this time I walk out from behind the counter and let myself hug Chris. It feels a lot like being a kid again and giving in to sleep on New Year's Eve after hours of trying so hard to stay awake until midnight.

Chris hugs back, just briefly, before pulling away. "No need to get all sentimental," he says. There's a fissure in his voice, like it wants to crack but can't.

"I'm not getting sentimental," I say. My eyes are dry but my nose is stuffy. "It's just seasonal allergies. Fall is on the way."

"Right," Chris says, smiling at me in that way he does that reaches down into my toes, making them curl, making them dance. "Just allergies."

Chapter 23

A COUPLE WEEKS LATER IN EARLY September, Hal plans a no-special-occasion Redstocking picnic in Prospect Park.

"I know I've been wrapped up in work recently," she says as we pile into the Red Rocket, the yellow paint sufficiently chipped. Hal is driving and I'm riding shotgun. Tara climbs obligingly into the back, carting the food.

"And wrapped up in Astrid," I say.

"It's hard to have it all," Hal laments. "The high-profile career, thriving love life, vibrant friendships."

I frown at her ranking system. "Why did you list friendships last?"

"There was no order to it," Hal says, a little too innocently. She stomps on the pedal and the Rocket lurches into motion down Knickerbocker Avenue. "Don't go getting all sensitive. All I'm saying is I want to get us all together for some sisterhood bonding. And to celebrate how you've stepped up for us with rent, EJ. It's impressive, really."

Praise from Hal always makes me warm and glowy, even if I've made up my mind to be cold and muted. "It's only because Chris overpaid me for watching Arnie," I say, looking out the window at a blur of run-down warehouses and For Lease signs tacked on cracked windows.

I stayed over in Tribeca to watch Arnie while Chris was out of town. It turned into the end-of-summer bright spot I didn't know I needed. Arnie and I were in the middle of watching a movie when Chris got back Sunday night, and rather than shooing me out, he plopped down on the couch with Arnie and me and watched until the end, all the way through the credits, which I never watch.

"Guess I've coached you well on your negotiation skills, then," Hal says, happy to sponge up the credit. "And you too, Tara," she says, calling out to the back seat, her voice rivaled by the roar of the aging engine. "It's great to see how your coaching venture is taking off."

Tara's income is at an all-time high. She's started giving acting lessons now that her résumé has enough credentials on it. "I don't know," Tara says. "I feel like I'm selling out by coaching all these rich white kids. I wish I could get more clients in Bushwick, but no one's willing to pay and I can't afford to do it pro bono."

"You can start a nonprofit down the road," Hal says. "There's nothing wrong with making money from rich people. It's the only way to tax them, really, since they shelter all their investments in overseas accounts."

We start across the Williamsburg Bridge. "I thought we were going to Prospect Park?" I ask, frowning. The park is southwest of us in Brooklyn, so there's no need to cross over into Manhattan.

"We're picking up Jenni first," Hal says. "Thought I mentioned that."

"No," I say, feeling tricked. "You didn't. You said it was a Redstocking picnic. Jenni is an *ex*-Redstocking."

"Come on, EJ," Hal says, as if I'm the one who's being unreasonable here. As if she hadn't been on my side too, until Astrid came into the picture and distracted her. "Just because Jenni broke the Anti-Marriage Pact doesn't mean she's exiled. The Redstockings existed way before the pact. Tara agrees." Hal glances up into the rearview mirror for validation from the back seat.

"I'm just glad we're all getting together again," Tara says, hopscotching around the conflict like usual. "It's been way too long."

Tara goes off and sees Jenni on her own; I've known that and tolerated it for her sake. But Hal absconding too and dragging me along? That's just too much.

"Does that mean you want to bring Lilly back into the Redstockings too?" I ask coolly. My optimism for the day is receding like a tide under a fast-moving moon.

"No," Hal says. "Lilly was hardly ever a Redstocking. We were clearly just a blip to her. She hasn't invested anything in keeping our friendship alive."

Lilly has ghosted the rest of the Redstockings ever since getting married, and it's brought me a dark sort of glee.

"But Jenni's genuinely been trying," Hal goes on. "And she's still in our same city."

"Manhattan and Brooklyn are not the same city," I say. I don't want to have to act like everything's fine, like we're still close. But I'm not going to be the downer who ruins it for Tara and Hal. I'm too old for that game, though I'm good at it.

"Why do we have to pick her up?" I ask. "Can't she at least just drive herself or take the subway? It would be faster for all of us."

"The whole point of today is that it's like old times," Hal says. "The four of us back together, crammed into the Red Rocket, spilling Oreo crumbs in the seat cushions."

"You're making me nostalgic," Tara says. Out of the corner of my eye, I see her clearing the junk off the seat next to her so Jenni will have a comfortable spot. It makes me sad for her, how tightly she's clinging to something that doesn't exist anymore. But it makes me sad for me, too, that I've already let it go so readily, shed it like a snakeskin that you can't crawl back into even if you want to.

"Fine," I grumble, secretly glad to be having the reunion as well, to see Jenni and who she's become since walking the marriage plank. "But I'm Venmo-requesting Jenni for the gas money."

We sit in bumper-to-bumper traffic, snailing our way across the congested Manhattan avenues until we reach the Upper West Side.

The land of new money. Hudson River–view towers, thousand-dollar strollers, and architectural insanities.

"This is her building," Hal says as we sputter to a stop in front of a soulless skyscraper. Tara texts Jenni that we're outside, and Jenni emerges a moment later, a doorperson escorting her out like she's the queen of England.

Jenni is donning a pleated dress with a frilled, flappy collar as big as a bib. Right away I can see she's fully fallen victim to the wealthy way of life, all its duties and dungeons. Peering up and down the street, she tries to locate us.

From the rolled-down window, Hal hollers, "Jenni! Over here!"

Jenni spots us, and her expression tilts. "What happened to the Red Rocket?" she hollers as she gets in the back seat. "It's all *yellow*."

"We thought it was time for an upgrade," I say, hoping she'll feel the pang of the dig. "It's much improved, don't you think?"

"It's hideous," Jenni says. "And what's that *smell*? Did something die in the rafters?"

"It's a new Chanel perfume," I lie. "Like it?"

I wait for Jenni to get offended, but she trills over in laughter instead. "How I've missed you, EJ," she says. "All of you ladies. Today is just what I've needed."

She buckles up and loops her arm through Tara's. "Turn the music up," she orders. Hal happily obliges, and soon enough eighties rock, the Go-Go's and Tom Petty, is blaring as we crawl down the West Side Highway. They're all singing along. I'm only humming, determined not to enjoy myself too thoroughly. From the back seat, Tara reaches up and gives my shoulder a squeeze from behind my headrest, as if she knows the internal battle I'm waging. It's enough for me to release my death grip on my grudge, but I can't drop it altogether.

Finally we get to Prospect Park and circle around a couple times until we find a parking spot. We unload blankets and munchies from the trunk and haul everything into the grassy acres until we find a sequestered spot to set up our picnic. The grass is long, drizzled with dandelions and clovers, just how I like it.

"This is the life," Jenni says. She stretches out on the blanket and double-dips a Dorito in goopy cashew cheese sauce. "I haven't had time to just relax in so long."

"What do you do all day?" I ask, hoping the question comes across as the composite of curiosity and critique that it is.

"My photography business has been picking up," Jenni says. "What with all the baby photo shoots from our friends and all. I do SoulCycle three times a week, weight training two days, and then Thursday lunches at the Colony Club."

"The Colony Club?" Hal says. "As in celebrating colonialization?"

"Of course not," Jenni says, with a serration that implies Hal's ignorance. "*Colony* isn't a dirty word. New York was a colony before it was a state, that's all."

"A colony with slaves," I add, looking at Tara, who's sifting through clovers in the grass, looking for the four-leafers.

"New York never had slaves," Jenni says. "It was more progressive right from the start."

"They might not have had plantations," I say, googling it on my phone right there to verify my intuition. "But household slaves were definitely a thing."

"That's true actually," Tara says.

"Oh," Jenni says, looking like this news is something of an imposition. "Sorry."

"Not your fault," Tara says. "I don't find the word *colony* offensive, just for the record. But anyway, sounds like you're pretty busy these days," she continues, steering the conversation onto safer ground.

"I really am," Jenni says. "Fridays and Saturdays we're out in the Hamptons, at least while the weather's still nice, and on Sundays I volunteer at the children's liturgy at church. Peter's an usher. It's a lot."

"Sounds it," I say, but Jenni doesn't seem to pick up on the sarcasm. "Since when do you go to church?" Her life has changed so much that I shouldn't be surprised but still am.

"I always used to when I was a kid," Jenni says. "Just fell out of it in college and the years after. It's been really good to find it again, rejuvenating for the soul. Especially in a rat race like New York. Peter and I are considering moving to Greenwich soon. Get away from all the— " She makes a general sweeping motion, as if encompassing everything about the city, including us.

"Have some wine," Hal says to Jenni. She, too, appears eager to avoid having the picnic become an evangelist assembly, an ambush to save our souls and stab us with white picket fences. Sloppily, she pours a bottle of red into a red Solo cup, hands it to Jenni.

"I'm actually going to stick to seltzer today," Jenni says. She whips out a can of sparkling water, one of those trendy new brands that took the market by storm overnight and will fizzle out just as fast. She probably paid nine dollars for it.

"So you're too good for Trader Joe's wine now?" I ask Jenni.

"No, it's not that." Her face screws up. She bobs up and down as she sits on the picnic blanket. "I'm pregnant."

We stare and stare. It's almost like the moment when she told us she was married. Like then, Tara is the first to regain her composure. "Jenni!" she says. "Congrats, that's huge."

"Life-changing," Hal says, catching my gaze, snagging on the prickers and adding her own.

"We only just found out, so don't tell anyone yet," Jenni says. "It only made sense to start trying, really," she goes on, like she feels the need to explain herself. Like we asked any questions about it. "Fertility isn't something you can take for granted, especially as we get older." She says it like we're approaching forty, not thirty. "I'm not trying to scare you girls," she adds quickly. "Since I know you probably don't want kids."

"Right," Tara says, but there's a whiff of something wistful. It hits me squarely in the chest, like it's trying to trick me into introspection. But I know better than to go there.

"So that's why we might be moving to Connecticut," Jenni goes on. "Get more space for the little one, be close to Peter's parents."

The image of Jenni sipping a detox smoothie, suntanning by the pool of a Connecticut country club, infiltrates my mind like a parody with none of the solace of comedy.

"But enough about me," Jenni says, though she looks like she'd be delighted to keep gabbing on about her own charmed life, chained life, for hours more. "What about you ladies? I need all the love life updates."

I'm annoyed that this is the first question she asks. It reinforces the societal view that women are only as successful as their romantic relationships. When Jenni lived with us, she used to know better, used to spit in the face of convention, flick it off with her feral fingers. Now, all pious and manicured, she's melted right into it.

"Astrid's still perfect," Hal says with a fluttery sigh. "It's actually frustrating because my life was great without her. But now that she's in it, I don't think I could ever go back." She scoops a whole handful of Oreos from the sleeve, stuffs them in her mouth to distract from the confession.

This is the first time I've heard Hal say something so serious-sounding about Astrid, or maybe just the first time I've listened. Either way, it's not exactly music to my ears.

"Well said." Jenni applauds. She and Hal share a look that feels like it's intentionally leaving me out. Tara too.

"Nothing to report from my end," Tara says, and I can feel her heart pinching at Hal's words. "I just play other people's romances onstage and then have zero leads in real life." She smiles in a self-effacing way that belies the bruises underneath.

"That's objectively false," Jenni says. "Every person in the audience falls in love with you. You're just too humble to notice."

"Exactly," Hal seconds, and Tara blinks twice.

"Maybe a few fall in love with my character," Tara replies after a beat. "But not with the real me. The Redstockings are the only ones who embrace my offstage awkwardness." She gives a goopy, thanks-for-sticking-by-me sort of smile until we're all piled into one big group hug.

I'm the first to duck out of the ring. "Alright, enough with the sap, it's not maple syrup season yet."

"How I've missed that biting wit," Jenni says, giving me a playful nudge as I slurp wine straight from the bottle.

"What?" I say, watching Jenni judge my manners. "No need to create more trash by using a plastic cup too."

"There's this thing called recycling," Jenni says.

"Recycling is a scam," Hal says. "Haven't you seen the documentaries? It's all just wasted, sent to landfills anyway."

"It is pretty wild," Tara says. "That we've sent rovers to Mars and yet can't figure out how to set up functional recycling systems."

"An abomination," I agree, liking how I've won the argument, how Hal and Tara have got my back even for the little things like this.

"Well," Jenni says, moving on. "Guess there's no point in asking for an update on *your* love life, EJ."

"Why not?" I ask.

"If there's anyone I can count on not to change, it's you," Jenni says.

What once might have felt like a compliment now lands as an insult and detonates. I don't like the implication that I'm static, predictable.

"I've changed," I say, chin jutting out defiantly. "I've changed the most out of anyone."

Jenni looks skeptical as she sips on her seltzer, expensive lipstick residue smudging the rim. "Is that so?"

She looks to Hal and Tara to disprove my comment.

"It's true, actually," Hal says, and I feel a surge of affection for her, though it dissipates upon her next words. "EJ is in love," Hal tells the group, with even more drama than Jenni's pregnancy announcement.

"I'm not in love," I sneer. "I just don't really do short-lived flings anymore, that's all."

"Right, because you're in love with Chris," Hal says. "So no one else lives up."

"I'm with Hal on this one," Tara says. The betrayal stings, but their assumptions feel oddly welcome too, like I have a permission slip to admit what they've already accepted as fact.

"Chris even came by the Inn the other day to look for EJ after a fight," Tara tells Jenni, as if this clinches things.

Jenni looks like she's unsure if we're scamming her, orchestrating a prearranged stunt. "Who's Chris?" she asks. "Wait a second . . ." The gears in her head are turning, and I don't like the direction. "This isn't the guy you met at the art gallery way back when? The one you dogsit for?"

"We've developed a *friendship*," I say. "That's all." Usually I'd embellish nothing into something, but now I'm trying to fold something back into nothing.

"That's how Peter and I started too," Jenni says. "Innocuous chats at the coffee maker in the office, and now look at us." She pats her stomach affectionately.

"Chris and I would never work," I say. "I'm an artist and he's an accountant. Have you ever heard of a more ludicrous match?"

"You balance each other out," Jenni says. "Like Peter and me. The men are the steady shores, we're the waves."

"You do realize how misogyny is baked into that entire statement, don't you?" I say.

"I disagree," Jenni says. "Everyone's trying to say there are no differences between women and men, but there are and those should be celebrated. Our femininity is getting stamped out of us in the name of feminism, which is trying to mold us into little men in the name of equality."

This is the proof we all didn't need that Jenni has officially crossed to the dark side. "So you're not a feminist?" Hal asks.

"Of course I am," Jenni says. "I just think some strands of feminism have gotten distorted, that's all."

"Go easy on her," Tara says. "She's pregnant."

"Pregnancy hormones have nothing to do with this," Jenni refutes.

The conversation somehow sloshes back to Chris and me. "Like I said, we're polar opposites," I say. "A different species, really. And besides, he has a serious girlfriend."

Jenni raises a laminated eyebrow. "Since when has that stopped you?"

"Since now," I sling back. "Chris is a good person. He doesn't deserve the EJ tornado ruining his life."

"Damn," Jenni whispers, as Hal and Tara give her an I-told-you-so sort of look. "You do love him."

I try to laugh at the words, but I'm closer to crying instead.

"It's okay," Tara says. "Loving people is a good thing."

"Not when they don't love you back," I mumble.

"But Chris *does* love you back," Hal says, making my stomach lurch with a hopeful sort of fear, or a fearful sort of hope. "You should've seen how nervous he looked ringing the doorbell at the Inn the other day. He was completely torn up."

Jenni asks what happened, so I fill her in on how Chris's brother died in a car crash a few years ago and he never talks about it, and I pushed too far but he realized he was the one in the wrong after all.

"Men," Jenni says, as if that single word explains it all. "Sometimes it's like knocking my head against a brick wall when I'm trying to get Peter to open up. I love him so much, of course, but sometimes I just miss my girls."

"We're still here," Tara says.

"Yeah, you're the one who left," I point out. Even when I want to be nice, I can't help the venom that slips out.

It just makes Jenni laugh, and the others too. "If only you could be this blunt with Chris," Jenni says. "You'd be the next one breaking the Anti-Marriage Pact."

"Never," I say, spine pricking with surprise. "That's the most ridiculous thing I've ever heard."

"Don't take this the wrong way," Jenni says. "But you're a pretty ridiculous person."

I grin at that, and the four of us fall into laughter. It feels like landing on a soft trampoline and springing up together into the air.

"You're not wrong about that," I say.

It's true that I'm not someone who follows patterns, so maybe the most authentic thing I could do is something opposite to what everyone expects. And what I expect. I don't mean marriage or anything that extreme. Lifelong commitment still feels far too confining. But perhaps I could fall in love with someone who might love me back, not just in the darkness of the night but in the brightness of the day.

My gut gives a nudge, like I'm on the right track. I prefer not to be on a track because I'd rather blaze my own trail, but this feels like a pretty good one, still wild and overgrown and riddled with venomous snakes.

Chapter 24

FALL BURSTS ONTO THE NEW YORK scene a bit late this year. It's not until October that the humidity drains from the air and the leaves morph from green to amber to maroon, like a time-lapse science experiment on triple speed.

I suggest to Chris that I become a daily dogsitter. No need for him to hustle home to walk Arnie at lunch, like he usually does. I can take Arnie out and give him some company during the workweek. Now that I know the story of Arnie and Luke, it makes me want to work even harder to give the pup a stable homelife. The thought of him being alone for hours at a time yanks at my heartstrings. Chris agrees, and I hope it's not just because he feels bad about how I'm always scraping by for rent.

One day, Arnie and I are engaged in a highly competitive game of tug-of-war with his rope toy when Chris gets home. I don't always wait for him to get back from work before I leave, but sometimes I do when I think he could use the company. He's looking a little haggard today and has that corporate hunch about him, like someone has laid a thousand invisible bricks on his shoulders.

"Ruff day?" I ask as Arnie leaps on him in joy. "Pun intended."

His lips quiver into a smile, but it's devoid of its usual arch. "It was a grind," he says, setting his briefcase onto the counter with a resigned sort of thud. "We're in the fourth quarter of the fiscal year, and all the division leaders are coming to me wanting me to make exceptions so their year-end financials can look better. But it's against the accounting rules, so I have to tell them no."

"I never pegged you as the bad guy," I say, enjoying picturing Chris as the villain. "If you ever need any reinforcements, I'd be happy to lend a hand. I'm a CPA, you know."

"Are you really?" Chris asks. It means something that he doesn't immediately tell me I'm lying. That he thinks there's actually a chance I've passed the million exams required to be a certified public accountant.

"Of course I am," I say. "It stands for Chief People Aggravator, right?"

That gets a laugh from him, one of those deep ones that comes up from his belly and makes me feel proud of myself for excavating his personality from the depths of the ocean.

His phone rings. "Sorry," he mutters. "Another work call, have to take this."

He heads into his bedroom to take the call. Through the door, I eavesdrop on the tedious-sounding conversation, packed with acronyms and phrases like "accrue for" and "taxation compliance."

"That sounded riveting," I deadpan when Chris emerges back into the living room. "Should have recorded it and played it back before bed for the nights when insomnia strikes."

"Always appreciate how you build me up," Chris says, and I'm glad that he's giving some sass back to me. It's a mark of how we've gotten closer over the year and a half we've known each other.

"Why do you let them bother you when you're out of the office?" I ask. "Do you get extra money for working overtime?"

"If only," he says. "We don't get overtime, but if I'm not available at all hours, I might get fired."

"They're not going to fire you," I say, finding the idea outlandish.

He grimaces, like he thinks there's a good chance of it. "My biggest fear is failing," he says, eyes catching on mine when he says it. "Letting people down."

"Well, what if you're so determined not to let other people down that you let yourself down in the process?" I pose.

I get the sense no one's ever asked him that before, or if they have, he hasn't valued their opinion enough to pause and really think about it. He's thinking about it now.

"I guess when other people are disappointed in me, I'm disappointed in myself," he says. "So the two are intertwined."

"Sounds like codependency to me," I diagnose. "You need to set boundaries."

I rack my brains for ways to help him free himself of his people-pleasing tendencies, reclaim his autonomy. "Maybe you should think of yourself as an actor," I say. "And while you're at work, you play the role of Accountant Chris. But then when you're home, you're Actual Chris. So when someone gets mad at you at work, only Accountant Chris is affected. Actual Chris is unfazed."

Chris considers it. "I don't think that would feel authentic, though," he says. "Pretending like that."

"It's not really pretending," I say. "You'd still be genuine at work; you just wouldn't bring your *entire* self. They don't deserve access to all of you. So you'd keep some boundaries up to protect you from being dragged down by the corporate zombies at all hours of the day and night."

"I don't know," he says, still looking wary. "I pride myself on being a good worker. It's who I am."

"No, it's not," I say, getting snappy. "It's what you do. Your job isn't your identity. Debits and credits aren't life-or-death."

"They're not?" A self-effacing smile ekes out, and then he gets more serious. "Look, I know what I do isn't that important. I'm not an emergency room doctor."

I wonder if Chris is thinking about Luke and the ER doctor who might have treated him after his accident. The one who tried to save his life but couldn't.

"I'm not trying to diminish your work," I say. "It's a good thing that you care about what you do." It's true, actually. I have a lot of respect for how hard he works to try to do a good job. "Just remember, most people in the world don't even know what a balance sheet is and we manage to survive."

"You do know what a balance sheet is, though," Chris says. "You just mentioned it."

"I mean, I know the high-level basics of balancing assets, liabilities, and shareholders' equity," I say, not being able to keep from showing off a bit. "But none of the gory details." I took an accounting class in college and the information has apparently stayed wedged in some cranny of my brain. Forgetting has never been my strong suit.

It makes me preemptively sad as I consider Chris and the day that I'll want to, have to, forget him.

"I should get going," I say, giving Arnie one last belly rub and then springing up to my feet. "Olivia will be here soon."

"How did you know she's coming over?" Chris asks.

"It's Thursday. She always comes over on Thursday nights."

If he's surprised at my newfound attention to days of the week, he doesn't let on. "You don't have to rush out," Chris says. "Olivia knows you watch Arnold."

"And how does she feel about that?" I ask.

"She doesn't mind," he says, faltering. "It's my job to take care of Arnold now that Luke's gone. I can choose who watches him."

"Of course you can." I get the feeling that Olivia has made the grievous mistake of referring to Arnie as "the dog" or perhaps even "our dog" in front of Chris, and that he hasn't taken well to it. The prospect of trouble in paradise excites me more than it should. I really do want to be a decent friend but just don't seem to have the right wiring.

There's a knock at the door. "Doesn't she have a key?" I whisper to Chris, so she won't hear from the hallway.

He shakes his head as he walks to the door. "Not yet."

Chris officially gave me back the original spare key when I started dogsitting again, and the knowledge that I have an (ethically obtained) key to his place and his own girlfriend doesn't produces quite the thrill. That, plus the way we're whispering to each other in secret.

I head out, passing Olivia on her way in. I feel her looking after me, throwing her glare like a freshly sharpened axe. But I'm too deep in my own delight to feel the cut. The blade just ricochets right off me. It makes me wonder if perhaps the strongest armor is no armor at all.

Chapter 25

MY FRIENDSHIP WITH CHRIS IS IN such a good spot that I have no desire to tilt the balance and do something unruly. Or I guess I have every desire to do that; I have just enough self-restraint not to. Maybe you can't fully lose someone if you never really have them, but you can lose them partway, the fractions shattering in a way that whole things don't.

This means I make an effort not to make an effort with him. I spend more time back at Lone Wolf and the House of Yes, stirring up feelings for other people like a witch perched in front of a new cauldron when she knows her last batch was better, more potent.

Leaves drop from the sparse city trees onto the sidewalk, and cold weather surges into the battered Bushwick streets, clapping back at steaming manholes. There's not much bliss on the home front. Hal is all angsty about how Astrid's student visa is expiring at the end of the year.

"Her entrepreneurship visa got denied," Hal moans one afternoon in early December. We're eating s'mores that Tara has baked in the toaster oven to keep us warm. Blustery squalls batter the basement windows, testing the seal, searching for an in. It's the first snowstorm of the season.

"Astrid's role as cofounder of your stealth-mode start-up didn't make the cut?" I say, unable or maybe just unwilling to take the matter seriously.

"Cut it out, EJ," Hal says. "This isn't a joke. It's my entire future crumbling before me."

"Don't blame me, blame the political system," I say.

And so she does, ranting about all the quacks who are threatened by immigrants when all of the country's best innovators have been foreign-born, and even the Founding Fathers were immigrants from Europe and the entirety of America is stolen land. "The hypocrisy is too preposterous to even analyze," she fumes, then proceeds to dissect it nonstop.

"I'm on your side," I assure her when she pauses long enough to stuff two charred marshmallows into her mouth, cheeks puffing like a chipmunk storing up for hibernation. "But I really don't know why you're so distraught. You couldn't ask for a better excuse to break up than deportation. It's all neat and tidy. Sounds like a dream to me."

"I wouldn't expect *you* to understand," Hal retorts, writhing around on the couch as if spiders are crawling inside her flannel pajamas. With a surge of practicality, she plucks herself from her spasm. "We'll just have to house Astrid here at the Inn," Hal goes on. "She'll get a fake ID and evade the authorities until we can find her a permanent solution. What do you think, Tara?"

Of course she'd try to manipulate the situation and go for Tara first. I interject, "No thank you. We won't be housing a criminal." I'm thinking less about the trouble it could get us into, which is admittedly intriguing, and more about the way it would ruin the whole dynamic of the Inn. With Hal and Astrid living here as a couple, I'd feel like a third wheel in my own home.

"I asked *Tara*." Hal glowers.

"There's no way Tara wants Astrid here either," I say. "It's putting all of us in danger."

"Since when have you cared about danger?" Hal shoots back.

"Are you going to listen to what I have to say about it?" Tara asks.

Hal and I quiet down. I'm proud of how Tara is sticking up for herself. But the pride quickly mutates to dismay as Tara speaks.

"I could get behind the idea of Astrid staying here," she says. "Sure, there's some risk involved, but it would be walking the walk when it comes to our view on immigration policy. In the absence of governmental progress, we have to be the change ourselves."

"Exactly," Hal says, nodding vigorously as if Tara has seen the light. "That makes two against one. Sorry, EJ, you're outnumbered."

"I could tip off the police," I say. "That you're housing a fugitive."

"Good luck paying rent if Tara and me are locked up," Hal says.

It smacks hard. "I'd find a way," I say, but I know she can feel that my threat is an empty one. All of us can.

Hal rises from the couch, pulls on her frayed snow boots and a puffer jacket, and heads out into the storm, just like that.

"Good thing I'm not the only dramatic one in the friend group," I say sardonically to Tara.

Tara tries to smile but doesn't quite succeed.

"Do you really want Astrid to move in?" I ask Tara.

"Not really," she says. "But it's better than the alternative of Hal moving out."

"Hal wouldn't move out," I say. "Astrid would go back to Norway, and things would return to their rightful state, just the three of us here."

"I'm not sure," Tara says. "I was watching Netflix with Hal on her computer last night and ads kept popping up for jobs in Oslo. I think she's been looking."

"The algorithm's got it wrong," I say, because it has to be so. "They must've heard Astrid talking about having to go back and find a job in Norway."

"Maybe." Tara looks doubtful, tugging at her hair, long and

braided these days. "But you've got to admit, Hal has never been this way before."

"Certifiably insane, you mean? I agree, it's a new level, even for her."

"I just don't want us to lose her." Tara loops her arm through mine, like she's leaning on my leadership.

"We won't. I'll come up with a solution. Don't worry."

Tara passes me the tray of dilapidated s'mores. "You're the glue, EJ," she says, "that holds us all together."

The praise makes me more committed than ever to figure things out, to keep Hal with us. Maybe it wouldn't be the worst thing to let Astrid stay at the Inn. Sometimes a small loss is worth preventing a bigger one. I'd bet all my savings I'm right about that. I know that means I'm not actually betting anything, but that's the great thing about being broke. You can risk it all without losing anything.

Chapter 26

MOST OF THE TIME, FEAR GETS the worst of people, but once in a while it gets the best of them too. It's like this for Astrid, who decides she doesn't want to hide as a fugitive or chance deportation, so she books a flight back to Norway, set for mid-December.

Hal is distraught, but it'll blow over; all breakups do. Not that they're technically broken up. They're going to attempt long-distance. I give them three weeks, maybe four.

Buoyed by my relief to be rid of her soon, I start being much kinder to Astrid, insisting even that we throw her a little goodbye dinner at the Inn. I ask what food she's going to miss the most. It's not the pizza or bagels; she doesn't eat those. Sweetgreen salads and sweet potato fries, she says, so that's what I order, all leaves and grease. Tara picks up a cookie cake from a bakery too, one of the ones where they scan photos on the frosting. It's a picture of Hal and Astrid sitting in the egg chair together. It makes me giggle, the thought of smearing their happy little faces with our forks, smacking the frosting against my lips and swallowing it until they disappear.

Hal's been over at Astrid's helping her pack, but she bounds into the Inn now with an energy she hasn't had in weeks. Astrid's right behind her, wearing a bedazzled tiara and in an equally fizzy mood. Maybe they thought this was a theme party.

"Greetings!" Hal calls. "EJ and Tara, please assemble on the couch. We have an important announcement."

Tara and I look at each other, assessing if we're equally in the dark. It seems that way. "Maybe an investor for their start-up?" I mumble to Tara as we make our way to the sofa. It would mean Astrid might get her entrepreneurship visa after all.

Hal takes a deep breath, looking uncharacteristically shy. "Don't overreact to what I'm about to tell you," she says. "It's not going to change anything. We're just facing extenuating circumstances and have to act fast to keep Astrid from being deported."

Tara slips her hand into mine and gives it a nervous little squeeze. Neither of us like the sound of this. "Just spit it out," I say.

Hal goes quiet and looks to Astrid, who finally comes out with it as calm as can be, trying to gloss over it with her accent, smooth the serration. "We've decided to get married."

It's like a mousetrap springs, snapping the hammer down on us. Tara's hand goes limp in mine.

Hal jumps in fast, trying to justify the unjustifiable. "It solves the visa issue," she says. "I don't know why it took me so long to think of it."

It doesn't take me long to regain my bearings. The stakes are too high to dawdle in shock. "Hmm, it couldn't be because the Redstockings made a lifelong pact to never get married," I say, attempting sarcasm but not executing it right. My tone contorts into bitterness, not that I try to mold it back. "No, that would be far too reasonable of an answer."

"But ours isn't an old-fashioned marriage like we meant in that pact," Hal says. "We're tying the knot to thwart the government's evil authoritarian regime that's tossing Astrid out of the country, and we're also fighting back against how queer rights are being stripped. What's more progressive than that?"

I call Hal's bluff on that. "Does that mean you'll be getting divorced once Astrid can get another visa?" I ask.

"Of course not," Hal says, as if I'm the crazy one here.

Astrid chimes in, says she never would've thought she'd be

getting married to a woman, but she's come so far in her time in America and it's all thanks to the Redstockings. "I'm so very grateful," she says, eyes aglow with enlightenment-gone-wrong.

It's such warped logic that it's not even worth my rebuttal. Tara's quiet too, like she's trying to convince herself that she's taken too many hallucinogens. I'm hoping I'm seeing things too, but I know I'm not. There's an eerie realism pulling me down into the scene—grippy socks, not ballet slippers.

Of all of us in the pact, I was sure Hal was the safest, the most loyal. The Hal I knew would never do something like this.

"Come on, EJ, don't overblow this," Hal says when I tell her that. "We're evolving into real adults who don't need a juvenile pact to tie us together. It's the next phase of our journey, that's all."

Letting go of Tara's hand, I ask if that's how she feels too, that the Anti-Marriage Pact was nothing but a phase, a childish game. "No hard feelings," I say. "I'll just pack up my stuff and be out the door."

Tara says no, the pact is a lifelong commitment that she's taking to the grave. Turning to Hal, Tara pleads, "Don't give in to marriage. You're too much of a free spirit for that. There's got to be another option here."

I can feel Tara's hurt and it's even deeper than my own.

"You're both blind," Hal says. "I'm not falling into the trope of a conventional marriage. I'm actually dissenting more than you are, resisting the patriarchy from the inside, full Trojan horse–style." Cozied up next to Astrid, she goes on to say that nothing will change, that we'll still be the Redstockings.

"That's false and you know it," I say. "Remember Jenni? She swore marrying Peter wouldn't come between us, but that's all it's done. At the end of the day, marriage is marriage no matter how you spin it. It places a romantic partner above platonic friendships and that's heresy, end of story. Looks like the Redstockings were just another of your start-ups. A novelty to throw yourself into and then leave in the dust to start something new."

Looking at Tara, I know we've already lost. Even if Tara never marries, never leaves me, we'll still be two people against the world. Two is that despicable number that belongs to couples and conformity. In an effort to overcorrect for all the lesbians they wrongly deemed roommates over the centuries, my biographers will probably assume I was sleeping with Tara, that we were lifelong lovers. If I even get a biographer at all. Probably not because there's suddenly nothing original about me or my contributions to society. The Friendship Soulmate Revolution is as good as dead.

Hal decides she's done trying to earn my approval and puts on her business voice. "We're going down to city hall tomorrow morning to make it official," she tells Tara and me. "You're welcome to come if you want; it would mean a lot. But don't bother if you're going to be all judgy about it."

Hal goes on to say that she was hoping that Astrid could move in here so we could all still live together, but based on our reactions, she's reconsidered and decided it's best if she moves to Astrid's apartment in Washington Heights.

Washington Heights is an egregiously long subway ride from here—might as well be Washington State. I carve my stoniest expression and tell Hal and Astrid that unfortunately I have a prior engagement tomorrow. "But I wish you the very best in your little prison cell together, I really do."

Without tying my boots, without zipping my coat, I head out the door. I don't slam it on the way out, don't even close it. I leave it open, letting the frozen air strike until Hal has to get up and close the door herself, like she's already done on us.

It's very late by the time I return to the Inn, already morning. Tara has texted me to say that she's gone down to city hall to be there for Hal and Astrid.

I don't love it obviously but want to support Hal, she says. *Lmk if you want to come too. We've still got each other and always will.*

Tara's too soft for her own good; it's sad to watch. I shut myself in our room, covering my head with my pillow because I'm basically buried already. Everything I stand for is going to the grave that some people call the altar. It's hard to breathe and I wonder for a second what it would be like if I just stopped inhaling altogether. The thought makes me angry that I even entertained it. I'm not someone who gives up; I'm someone who gets up.

So I wind up going to city hall too. It's not like I've had a change of heart about giving my blessing or anything; I just want to catch a glimpse of Hal and Astrid so I can process that it's actually happening. It's proven that seeing the dead body is a necessary stage of grief to help process it, so that's all I'm doing. Seeing the cadaver.

City hall is down in the Financial District, next to Tribeca and not far from Chris's apartment. I'm not thinking about him; it's just a random fact that pops in my head as I'm trying to distract myself from the ghastly scene before me.

There's a line outside city hall. Apparently everyone wants their modern little elopement to make them feel better about how they're about to be legally tethered to another person.

I hide in the crowd without having to hide at all. That's probably the best thing about Manhattan. The ability to not be seen. It's the worst thing about it too. How no one ever sees you.

Finally Hal and Astrid emerge from the hall. Hal is in this penguin tux she got who knows where, and Astrid's in a white calico frock with a faux fur capelet. They unleash the PDA right there on the steps, a flamboyant dip and kiss. The other people in line to get married are hooting and hollering, and Tara's there snapping all these photos.

I try to feel outraged as I watch it all go down, but there's an envy rearing up instead. I try to tell myself I'm just jealous that Astrid is stealing Hal away, but I'm worried I might actually be jealous of both of them together and the life they're skipping off to with real commitment, more than our pact ever meant apparently. Jealous of how they're leaving me behind, a relic of a past era but too recent for antique shops to ascribe any value to.

There's the temptation to walk over to Hal and let her know that I came after all, but my body won't let me. So I just stand there and watch them twirl around for the camera. They eventually head off into the crowd and Tara texts me that they're going back to Lone Wolf if I want to join them for drinks.

I don't move, just stay and watch the other couples come streaming out of city hall with their new spouses, everyone beaming like they've won the fucking lottery. It makes me wonder, just for the briefest of moments, if I'm doing something wrong by not buying my ticket too. The whole scene has an unexpectedly rebellious vibe to it. No fuss over the seating arrangement, no meltdowns because the centerpieces came in the wrong shade of beige. It's the way I'd go about it if I had to get married. But I don't have to—that's the whole point. Plus, I'm seeing people at the very peak of their married life, the fleeting euphoric aftermath. It's all downhill after this.

Just for the absurdity of it, I picture what my wedding would look like. I'd be skateboarding down the courthouse steps in a white suit. I can't tell who I'm getting married to, but Arnie's there so that gives me a bad feeling but also a good feeling. It's the exact opposite of what I want, but given all my contrarian shit, I'm not sure if that means I actually hate the idea or just hate the idea of the idea.

Zigzagging through the streets now, I find myself near Chris's apartment and I nearly go up so I can take Arnie out for a walk. But I'm still holding firm to my efforts to distance myself from Chris, what with how attached he's become and all, so I just pause outside the Windemere and keep walking all the way up to 14th Street, my head winning the battle against my feet by not turning around.

I take the L train back to Bushwick and trek into Lone Wolf. Hal and Astrid are there, all gaga and drunk and swaying to the jukebox as they toast their icons. "Elizabeth Cady Stanton, RBG, Taylor Swift, and Dianna Agron," Hal hoots, raising a shot glass. "Next pickleback, please. My wife is thirsty!"

Right when she catches sight of me, Hal comes over and wraps me up in a wobbly hug. "You came," she says. "I knew you would."

I nearly admit that I was at city hall too but decide against it, in favor of just downing a shot of bourbon without a chaser. The burn is exactly what I need right now. It makes me believe I'm still flammable.

Tara's not working; she's just sitting on a barstool keeping to herself. She seems to have sunk into one of her moods where her fears physically compress her posture. Plunking down on the stool next to her, I jingle her dangly earrings like I'm ringing a bell.

"I give it six months," I tell Tara, hoping it'll cheer her up.

Tara doesn't turn her head. She seems out of energy for that. But she slides her eyes toward me. "What do you mean?" she asks.

"I mean that I give Hal and Astrid's little toy marriage six months before they break it off and Hal comes back to us, single as ever," I say. "It's a green card wedding, just one big theatrical act. Nothing more than that."

"You don't actually believe that," Tara says. "You know we've lost Hal for good. You know it, EJ."

I respect Tara, how she faces the facts head-on and lets them toughen her up, not tear her down. I'm not one to sugarcoat things so I can't really object. "So," I say to Tara. "When are you getting married too?" I say it lightly but feel it heavily.

"Never ever," Tara insists, and I hope this isn't just because she can't picture being with anyone but Hal. I hope it's because she still believes in the foundational principles on which the pact was founded. "Hal getting married just makes the pact that much more important," Tara says now. "I need the security of knowing I'll always have you as my best friend and partner in crime, EJ."

I feel the same way, so I bury my head in her shoulder and go on about how it's not so bad if it's just the two of us. "We'll still have each other to come home to at the end of a long day and can go around having these fantastic love affairs. So it's still the best of both worlds—the stability of friendship plus the adrenaline of romance."

Tara's mood doesn't really improve, but at least it doesn't plummet any lower.

A bit after that, who shows up at Lone Wolf but Jenni. Her baby bump is mostly camouflaged by a flowy dress, and she has a sleek blowout that doesn't fit in with the dive bar aesthetic. She rubs down the barstool with sanitary wipes before she sits and orders a club soda.

Jenni makes a show out of how joyful she is for Hal and Astrid. I know it's mostly because it eases her guilt, if she still has any. Probably not.

"EJ," Jenni says, leaning in close so we can hear each other over the twang of the rock song that's ricocheting out from the jukebox. "I've been meaning to ask you something."

"No, I will not drive you home tonight," I say. "I'm off Uber duty, can't you see?" I take another pickleback shot and cringe as it goes down.

"It's not that," Jenni says. "Peter and I were wondering . . . Will you be the baby's godmother?"

I stare at her, stunned into silence. "You're joking, right?" I ask when my voice comes back.

Jenni says no, she's very serious. "I've been praying about it, and your name keeps coming up. I think it's a sign."

"A sign that this pregnancy is making you insane," I say. "How can I be a godmother if I don't even believe in God?"

Jenni doesn't have a good answer for that, just asks me to think about it. I tell her I will, only because I've dealt with enough today and deserve some rest. She heads out again in no time flat, some rubbery excuse about needing to wake up early for a prenatal wellness retreat in the Catskills.

At some point in the night, Hal and Astrid scoot off to their honeymoon suite at the Sofitel Hotel, this swanky place in Midtown that Astrid booked. It was supposed to be a surprise, but Astrid spilled the beans after two drinks or six, who's counting.

Back at the Inn, I tell Tara that she should sleep in Hal's bed tonight and enjoy all the extra space. She kind of perks up at this, so she takes over the queen in Hal's room and I'm solo in the bunk bed.

It feels all echoey, too quiet and still, a tunnel with no trains. I've slept here a bunch of times when Tara has been out and about, but it's different knowing it's a permanent arrangement. All the extra space smothers me. I'll get used to it, though. I'm very adaptable, just not tonight.

Sometime later, I hear Tara pitter-patter into my room. "What's wrong?" I ask, peering over from the top bunk.

"It was just hard to sleep without you snoring and sleep-talking," she says. "Do you mind if I stay in the bunk bed one more night?"

"I don't mind," I mumble, which is basically the understatement of the year, maybe even the century.

Chapter 27

I DIP INTO A LOW PLACE with Hal gone.

I keep repeating all the reasons I'm living my best life and that's how I know I'm not. The silence sloshing around the Inn feels very loud. I toss new paint on the walls to cover up some of Hal's calligraphy quotes, but everything still feels off, stale and monochrome.

Tara asks if we should think about moving to a one-bedroom place to save on rent. "Absolutely not," I say. "We can't surrender the fort now; we've got to hold the line."

Tara's relieved at that because she doesn't want to leave this bunker either.

I try to negotiate lower rent since it's just the two of us now, but the landlord isn't having it. We're already getting a steal of a deal, he tells us, making some lippy comment about how he'd double the price if it wasn't rent-controlled.

"Not to worry," I tell Tara. "I'll just ramp up my Uber shifts, and I'll sell a script soon too. I've got so much material to write about, what with Hal's betrayal and all."

After getting married, Hal assured us that she'd still come by every Friday for a Redstocking dinner. But she misses the first two weeks, and that's all the proof I didn't need that she's gone for good. Tara copes by throwing herself into casting calls while I hurl myself into more bottles and bodies. The goal is to overstimulate myself with distractions, and it works pretty well.

One morning I'm doing a walk of pride back to Bushwick, after waking up in the bed of someone I met the night before. My low-battery phone rings. It's Chris.

I haven't seen him in a while now, and it's pretty clear he's missing me and wants to set up a time to see each other again. I might as well indulge him.

"Yes?" I say, all cold and expectant when I answer the phone. I don't want him to get the wrong idea that I'm just waiting on his beck and call. He's going to have to grovel for it; that's the fun part.

His words rush out in a panicked slur. "There's been an accident," he says. "Arnold got hit by a car and I'm just leaving my work meeting in Connecticut, but I won't be back for a couple hours. Is there any chance you could get to Reade Street Animal Hospital in Tribeca and see how he's doing? Please, Emily Jane."

It feels like I'm being stabbed by ice picks from all sides. And all I can think of is how Arnie's little paw reaches up onto my back when we're cuddling on the couch. He's teasing when he does it but also kind of serious. It's just the sweetest thing in the world and now I might lose him forever.

I order an Uber straight there. There's not much traffic and no time to play around with subway delays, so it's worth whatever it costs. I keep Chris on the phone on the drive over; he says it makes him feel like he's doing something. I prefer it too because I can't sit alone with my fears or they'll paralyze me.

"What happened?" I ask Chris. He says he'd hired a dog walker and just got a call that Arnold had been clipped by a car on the West Side Highway.

Twenty-six minutes later, I get to the animal hospital. I'm watching the clock; it's excruciating. Hopping out of the Uber as it's still moving, I storm inside and demand to see Arnold the Australian shepherd. "I'm his surrogate guardian. Now tell me where he is."

The woman at the front desk asks too many questions, so I walk away mid-conversation and start pushing open all the doors in the place until I find Arnie. He's sitting up on a medical bed, getting a splint put on his paw. He barks when he sees me. Such a mischievous bark that I could cry with relief, but I don't. I just kiss his ears and then his snout too. It's all there, as perfect as ever.

The vet says he'll be fine: It's just a broken paw, and there's no sign of a concussion or internal bleeding, which is very lucky given the scope of the accident.

On speakerphone, Chris starts asking the vet all kinds of follow-up questions, and I get this rush of affection for Chris and how detail-oriented he is. It makes me feel bad about how I haven't really been there as his friend recently, even if it was for my own good.

I FaceTime Chris so he can see for himself that Arnie's alright. Arnie doesn't quite get the concept of FaceTime. He can hear Chris's voice, which gets him all riled up, sniffing at my phone, trying to locate Chris. It's adorable.

"Where's the criminal?" I ask, noting that the inept dog walker who nearly killed our little Arnie is nowhere to be found. My mind races forward to how Chris and I can prosecute the villain and use the profits to take Arnie on a tropical vacation. Somewhere he can run free on the beach and not have to worry about cars.

Chris tells me to let it drop. The important thing is that Arnie's okay.

"Lesson learned not to hire a dog walker who's not me," I tell him. A faint smile tickles his face, and mine too. I nearly ask why he didn't ask me to dogsit, but I don't want to add any more tension to the day so I let it slide.

"Lesson learned," he agrees and says he'll be back as soon as he can, but would I mind bringing Arnie back to his apartment to get him fed and situated? "Olivia's home," he drops casually. "I'll call her now and fill her in on the accident and how you'll be swinging by and everything."

There's a wonderfully rotten stench about all of this. It just doesn't add up, how his girlfriend is just a few blocks away and yet he had me come over from Brooklyn instead. "Why didn't you call Olivia to come check on Arnie?" I ask. "Why did you call me?"

Chris doesn't have a good answer to that, which is the very best answer there could be. He just babbles on with some lightweight excuses about how Olivia has grad school finals coming up. It's all so frothy that I turn the camera toward Arnie because I don't want Chris to see me and my huge grin.

I hate to be benefiting in any way from Arnie's accident, but it's a pretty spectacular feeling to be the person someone calls when their dog is hit by a car. It reveals a lot about their subconscious priorities. Freud would have a field day with it.

Chris has already been through enough, so I don't give him a hard time about it. I just tell him that it's no problem, that I'll get Arnie home and fed and everything. The vet says he can walk normally, but I carry Arnie anyway, the whole five blocks back to Chris's apartment. I'm not taking any chances with the cars. Arnie's too big for me, but I'm stronger than I look.

Once I can tell that he's the same old Arnie as always, I start giving him a stern lecture about not running out in traffic. "I know you're probably just trying to be like your rebellious mom EJ, but there's a time and a place to be wild, and running across a four-lane highway isn't one of them. You hear me, you beautiful little pup, you?"

I let myself into the apartment. This is why I still keep Chris's spare key on my key chain. Olivia is there doing Pilates in the living room like it's just a regular day. Not meeting my eyes, she thanks me for taking care of "the situation." That makes me growl because Arnie's accident isn't just a situation to be handled. It's a family catastrophe—not that she'd understand.

She says she can take it from here, but I tell her that I'm staying until Chris gets home, that he asked me to. That last part isn't exactly true but it's close enough. I get Arnie the filtered water from the fridge and a full bowl of food, plus some treats to help him recover from the trauma. After he's done eating, I keep him on my lap on the couch, trying to explain the concept of rest to him. How sometimes we just need to lie low for a while before we can play tug-of-war again.

Olivia says she's going out for brunch with a friend and that she'll be back in a bit.

"Sounds good," I say. "If you want to bring back some pancakes for me, that would be most appreciated. I could use some carbs right now. What a day."

She gives me a smile that's as thin and sharp as a razor, then glides out the door.

Olivia has moved in for good. I can tell by how there are even more photos of her and Chris peppered around the place and some stereotypically feminine touches. Lavender throw pillows, lacy white drapes filtering light from the windows. I let Arnie chew on one of the throw pillows. He's been through a lot and has expensive taste. That's not his fault; he's a by-product of how he's been raised. Aren't we all?

Chris gets back soon after that. He bursts through the door, a ball of sweat and stress. Getting down on his knees in front of the couch, he examines Arnie up and down to make sure it really is just the little boot on the paw, that nothing else is wrong with him. Arnie is wagging his tail like crazy and nudging the pillow toward Chris to show off just how much of the expensive fabric he's ripped through. *Look, Dad, aren't you proud?* I can basically hear him saying it.

"See," I tell Chris. "He's all good. The same little troublemaker as always."

Chris's face scrunches up like he's trying not to cry. I remind him that real men express emotions, but he just goes into the bathroom, and when he comes out, his face looks like it was just splashed with cold water. He thanks me for being there today, launches into the apology I thought I wanted about how he's sorry he hasn't been in touch recently.

"I've been a shitty friend too," I say, because I'm in a generous mood. Nearly losing Arnie has put things in perspective, I guess. "Let's call it even?"

Chris nods. "Maybe someone was watching over Arnie today," he says.

"Maybe," I say, wanting to soothe Chris but not delude.

We sit there on the couch for a while, not talking. It's not awkward silence or sexually charged silence, just comfortable silence. I don't usually like being comfortable given how routine it feels, but I like this.

"So Hal's gone off and gotten married," I tell Chris because making it all about me and my problems should help distract from his harrowing day. I'm empathetic like that. "Another one bites the dust."

He asks who she married so I tell him a bit about Astrid.

"I didn't know Hal was lesbian," he says.

"Yeah," I say. "Though we don't really love the LGBTQIAXYZ labels. Celebrating liberated love and yet jamming it into those little boxes. The hypocrisy."

"I thought it helped people feel seen, to have those labels?" Chris says, like he's reciting something from one of those *How to Be an Ally* corporate handbooks.

"It was probably a helpful stage, sure, but we're beyond that now, or should be. The labels just affirm that being straight is the default, that being anything else is the 'other' and in need of a disclaimer. Which is hilarious because everyone's a little bit gay. No one's really fully straight."

"I am," Chris says. His internalized homophobia stands between us like a wall, relying on me to disassemble it brick by brick, scraping off the mortar with my fingernails.

"Right," I say, deciding today is not the day to enlighten him on compulsory heteronormativity and how he was conditioned to be straight, how it was chosen for him just like everything in his life was. "So you're proposing to Olivia at Christmas?"

It's a guess but it's not a wild one. That's the next step for people like Chris who like things to follow a linear path. And I can only imagine the hints Olivia has been dropping on him. She seems like someone who'd have a complete meltdown if she wasn't married by thirty.

Chris fidgets. "Did Olivia tell you that?" he asks, confirming I'm right.

"No, Olivia didn't say anything. I've just gotten good at sensing when a wedding is around the corner after I've lost my best friends to matrimony. It's sort of like a sixth sense I've acquired. I don't wish it on anyone."

Chris admits that yes, he's planning a holiday proposal so long as the ring gets finished in time. I make a scoffing sound that insinuates how ridiculous it is to have a rock symbolize love. Even if I were into monogamy and marriage, I wouldn't be on the diamond ring bandwagon. The industry is the worst culprit of child labor; everyone knows that. Not to mention the environmental calamity of ravaging the earth with mining.

"I'm sure you'll be very content marrying Olivia," I tell Chris. The kindest thing I can say without being fake.

"You say it like it's a bad thing," Chris says.

"Well, contentment is basically a synonym for complacency, isn't it?" I say. "Real happiness has an intensity that's impossible to sustain over a long-term romantic relationship. Sorry to be the bearer of bad news; it's just my personal view. There's a statistically insignificant chance that I'm wrong, so don't read into it too much."

It's clear that Chris is reading into it, though, which is pretty flattering. "But can't you live a content life with moments of more intense happiness?" he asks. "They're not mutually exclusive."

"Theoretically, maybe, but I don't see it playing out in real life,"

I say. "From my research, I've found that married people are either never fighting or always fighting. They have no passion or they have vindictive passion. They're totally bored of each other or wanting to chop off each other's heads. Or both, like my parents. But hey, maybe your marriage will be better. There's always hope."

Chris goes on defense. "Olivia's not boring," he says.

"I never said she was," I point out. "But if you're asking for my opinion, then I'd say yes, she definitely is. There's really nothing controversial about that observation."

"You're wrong," Chris says, and I like how he's really taking a stance on this. "Boring is in the eye of the beholder. If you think someone's boring, it says more about you than it does about them. No one is actually boring; you just need to get to know them deeply enough to understand how interesting they are."

It's a nice little rant but I'm not buying it. Some people are objectively dull. Most people are, actually. It's just a fact, but I don't feel like arguing anymore. I'm too tired for that.

"I've got to get back to Bushwick now," I tell Chris. "I haven't been home since yesterday."

He seems to take in my outfit for the first time, the glittery bodysuit under my coat and my knee-high boots that I haven't taken off despite his no-shoes policy. He asks where I stayed last night.

"That's a good question," I say. "I fell in love at the House of Yes and woke up somewhere in East Williamsburg. I don't remember the details."

He looks like he's waiting for me to say that I'm kidding but I don't. I think he knows I'm not lying; he can always seem to tell. It's probably even easier today because I'm not wearing my contacts since I was planning to go straight back to the Inn this morning. It's a naked feeling not having the extra layer of color to protect me.

Chris tries to pay me for my help, but I say no, don't think about it, I'm just glad Arnie's alright. "He's basically my family by now too. Isn't that right, my little pupper?"

Arnie looks all pleased about it, like he's been trying to plot some *Parent Trap* thing to get Chris and me together. He can be a real rascal sometimes.

"I hope you and Olivia have a long and happy marriage," I say when I'm already halfway out into the hall. I purposely say "happy," not "content," to make a point that I'm not being stubborn, that I really am wishing them the best.

"We will," he calls out. There's a kick to it, like he knows I wasn't telling the truth. Like he knows that I'm actually a lousy enough person to hope they are perfectly miserable together.

Chapter 28

TARA TRIES TO DECORATE THE INN for Christmas.

She even paints a wreath on the front door—'tis the season and all—but it feels very empty. I'm almost glad to go back to Michigan just for the change of scenery. I expect the usual assailment to come, with my mom grilling me about when I'm going to settle down and how all the good men are dropping like flies and I'd better get snapped up soon and start getting my act together. But it ends up being kind of the opposite. I'm thirty now and something about the number seems to have made my family accept that the train has irrevocably left the station. It's a lost cause. I'm a lost cause.

There's a freedom that comes when people no longer have any expectations for what your life should look like, but it's not as happy a feeling as I'd hoped. It's like you can't disappoint them anymore because they've thrown out all their hopes about you in the first place.

My little niece is one year old now and already walking and sort of talking too. The first word she learned to say was "no," which tickles my heart, though my sister tries to spin it and insist she was saying "ma" instead. It's the type of suburban delusion you'd expect.

My body has that hot-itchy-burny feeling the whole time I'm back, and I do my best to detach myself the whole trip. I keep my phone tucked under the table at Christmas dinner at my parents' house, continually refreshing my socials to see if Chris has posted his engagement photo with Olivia yet.

By the time I get back to New York, there's still no sign of it, but I douse the rising embers of optimism, spray a hose in the firepit until the wood is soggy and useless. They'd be that type of couple that gets engaged privately and then does an entire coastal photo shoot before posting about it, just to ensure that they elicit maximum jealousy among exes. That would be Olivia's thought process, not Chris's. He wouldn't want to make a fuss but wouldn't push back either, complicit in the pageant-queen crime.

Tara and I gear up for New Year's Eve at the House of Yes. They're having something called the Surrealist Ball. "Fancy fantasy, psychedelic styles, grandiose illusions" is the tagline—exactly what Tara and I need. She's been in a slump too, first with Hal leaving us and then with rejection after rejection for new roles. She has it in her head that she's already peaked, that her nibble of success will have to sustain her hunger for the coming days, the coming decades.

"Stop that," I tell her, as she talks herself down during our pregame at the Inn. "We're just in a bit of a trough right now. It'll make the highs that much better once they come."

"I don't know," Tara says. "I just feel like the gap between where I am now and where I want to be is too wide. I thought it would feel smaller as I got older, more manageable to wrap my arms around, but it's the opposite."

"Well, who wants a small world?" I challenge. "Isn't the whole point of life that it keeps getting bigger?"

"I guess you're right. It's just kind of demoralizing sometimes, that's all."

"Until you realize it's all a simulation and we've been holding the remote control the whole time," I say. "We *are* the remote controls."

She smiles, like I've lost her someplace beautiful, a coral reef or a field of daisies.

It's just the two of us tonight. Jenni and Peter are having a low-key night, what with the baby coming and all, and Hal and Astrid are doing some kind of hackathon for their start-up. And even if they weren't, they would've bailed for another reason. That's just the rhyme scheme these days.

The general admission party doesn't start until 2 a.m. Tickets for the earlier thing are sold out. I could talk my way in but why bother. Nothing good happens before midnight anyway.

We've got the record player spinning to Tina Turner and we're both hollering along, inventing new notes as we go. The upstairs neighbors, a cranky couple always in their dressing gowns as if reincarnated from a Charles Dickens novel, come down and bang on our door, threatening a noise complaint. It lifts our evening into the stratosphere, catapults us out amongst the stars, amongst ourselves. We take it as proof that we're slaying it on our own, that we don't need the others.

I'm taking the fancy fantasy theme seriously, which is to say frivolously. Candy-colored necklaces, a tasseled headdress, and netted gloves, plus the light-up boots that I paid $3.50 for after bargaining them down from the thrift shop's ten-dollar discount rack. One of my best-ever purchases.

I'm hardly even drunk. It'll be a long night, and morning and afternoon too if I play my cards right, so pacing is important. As I'm pressing lightning bolt flash tattoos into my collarbones and Tara's too, Chris's name pops up on my phone screen. My heart jolts up before I can tell it not to, then does a jagged nosedive once I remember he's calling to tell me about the engagement. I nearly let it go to voicemail but change my mind at the last second. Better to just rip off the Band-Aid.

"Congratulations!" I blurt into the phone, wanting to beat him to the punchline, avoid having to hear him say the actual words.

There's a pause on the other end and I wonder if he butt-dialed me. But then he speaks, his voice more coarse than cottony, not what I'm used to. "I haven't asked her yet," he says.

"What do you mean?" My breath bounces back into place, toes unclenching.

He says he kept meaning to do it over Christmas but it never felt like the right time, and now Olivia's given him an ultimatum to propose before midnight or it's over.

I check the clock on my phone, giddy when I see the time. "That's eleven minutes from now."

"I know," he says. "She's out with our friends and I'm supposed to be there too, but I haven't left the apartment yet. Emily Jane, I don't know what to do."

"Of course you do." I go into my bedroom and close the door, Tara listening from the other side. "Let's look at the facts. You could be in an Uber en route to Olivia, but instead you're still at home calling the most anti-marriage person you know. I mean, it's not like you thought I'd talk you into proposing to Olivia. Did you, Chris?"

Silence squeezes out, the last drops of a dried-up lemon. "I do want to marry Olivia, though," he says.

"Is that what you want or what you think Luke would've wanted?" I press.

He tightens up at that, asks what I mean. I dive into some of the stuff I've alluded to before, back at Bubby's diner. I don't want to drive a wedge between us again, but there's no time to hold back now.

"Look, Chris," I say, padding my voice so he'll know it's safe to fall, safe to break. "I'm no psychologist, but I still think you might be coping by living out Luke's dream life and calling it yours."

My words seem to hit him harder than I mean for them to. Perhaps that's the only way for them to stick. "I'm not trying to talk you out of proposing to Olivia," I say. "I'm trying to talk you into being honest with yourself. Can you really tell yourself that it feels 100 percent right?"

"Nothing's ever 100 percent," Chris says. A rebuttal of the lamest flavor. "That's not realistic."

"How about 90 percent then?" I ask. It's the most I've used numbers in a while, but that's the language Chris speaks. Like raves and rants are for me, or used to be at least. "If you're not even 90 percent sure, that might be a red flag. But this is all just my perspective. You and I see the world very differently, obviously, so you can take it or leave it."

I'm proud of how balanced I'm being. My natural tendency would be to tell Chris that of course he shouldn't propose, that it would be a lifelong prison sentence. But I'm overcoming that inclination and trying to impart some advice that actually helps him, not just me.

"You can't bring Luke back by following in his footsteps," I go on. "But you can carry him forward by letting him inspire you to blaze your own trail."

The line comes out nicely and I file it away to put in a script one day. A long pause follows. I worry that Chris has hung up the phone and gone to chase after Olivia because she never gives him lectures like this. But then he asks what I'm up to tonight, if he can tag along in any of my crazy schemes. "I just need something different," he says. "While I think it all over."

Different is a promise I can deliver on, just about the only one I can. "Yeah, sure, whatever," I tell him, quietly dripping with joy at the prospect. "You can meet us at the House of Yes if you want. We'll get there around two if you can stay up that late."

"Great," he says, no delay. "See you then."

I'm convinced that he won't actually show, that he'll talk himself out of it. But when Tara and I walk over through the flutter of snowflakes just starting to stack up on the pavement, Chris is already there, standing in line by himself, hands in the pockets of his dark-wash jeans. It's like he knows he's out of place, and that's the proof that he's actually in the right place, the right time, the right line.

It's the first time Tara and Chris have ever met, but Tara wraps him in a hug right away. "Finally," she says. "I've heard so much about you, Chris."

"That's not true. I only really mention you in passing when I can't think of anything else to talk about," I say to Chris, popping out my tongue to let him know I'm kidding, not that I need to be that overt about it. Chris is fluent in my sense of humor by now, took long enough.

"And I only talk about you when I'm looking to get into trouble," Chris says with an equally mischievous grin. I'd expected him to be downtrodden and stressed, but here he is all spunk and fun. His usually pale cheeks are ruddy, and there's a luster in his eyes, like he's ready for whatever comes next.

We cut the line and slide inside, touching and teasing the party before we see it. Chris joins the coat check line but I say no, that's not how we do it. I whisk him up the side stairs, shove our coats in the usual spot between the radiator and the wall. "You're doing it the EJ way tonight," I say when Chris looks hesitant. He comes around.

Back downstairs, we pass the mirrors to the main room, giant chunks of glass reflecting what's been washed up and washed down, the sediment still swooshing, no place to go. It's strobe lights and black lights, stage dancers and trapeze artists, balloons and burlesque headdresses.

The dance floor is crowded and cramped, reminding me why I don't like New Year's Eve. All the posers coming in from Manhattan, cluttering up the space. But I can't even scrounge up a bad mood tonight. It's too good seeing it all through Chris's eyes. In sensory overload, he swivels his head every which way like he's stepped through the Narnia wardrobe, which I guess he has.

Tara ditches us pretty quickly. I don't like how it feels like she's trying to give us privacy, but I get a rush from it all the same. Chris and I do some laps around the place, up to the roof and down again. I want to show him everything.

"I can't believe I've never been here," he keeps saying.

"I can," I mutter because guys like Chris don't go to the House of Yes. But tonight I'm starting to see that Chris is Chris, not a guy like Chris.

I hook the bartender's attention, reeling him in until our fireball shots appear. "My treat tonight," I say, when Chris takes out his wallet. "Next time I'm in Manhattan, you can buy me a thirty-dollar margarita, and we'll call it even."

There's a thrill to it, making such reckless plans for a future that will never materialize. I try to get him onto the stage to dance with me, away from the crowd. He doesn't like the idea—no surprise given he can't even rotate his hips half an inch when no one's watching. Taking his hand, I lead him off to the side where he won't get stepped on. "Watch and learn," I tell him, lips twisting into their favorite shape of fluidity.

Floating up onstage, I join the dancers. They welcome me in, receive and celebrate the mass that is me, the mess that is me. We feel more than we know that right where we are is exactly where we're supposed to be and there's no such thing as a mistake here. It's all just love, fractals in a thousand forms cascading from the same burning core. We share all that we are, all that we have—the pride, the pellets, the sequins, the secrets.

I throw kisses at the crowd, then pieces of my costume. My necklaces first, bead by bead, then my gloves. I unstrap my bralette too, fling that away so my nipples are free like they were always meant to be. Chris's reaction doesn't disappoint. Dazed and enthralled, like he's sure something so good has to be a dream that he's been conditioned to interpret as a nightmare. Like he's bracing himself for the alarm clock that is bound to go off soon but hasn't yet.

Others in the crowd are hitting on Chris, trying to get him to dance. He doesn't pair up with any of them, but I'm still jealous and I let myself acknowledge the jealousy, swoop into its caves and its cavities, sniff its musty odor, swallow the metallic tap water. No judgment tonight. It's only the truth, ever the truth. Chris has this hold on me, and it's climbing by the second. The lights drench him in the color he's been lacking, or maybe they just reveal some inner color that's been covered up by too many years of black-and-white suits. Either way it's a dazzling sight. He's a dazzling sight.

I'm a race car, outpacing all the others, accelerating on a dirt road, no turns to curb my speed. I'm a witch, flying by broomstick above the cars, filling flasks with the dusty clouds, consummating her potion with spells that got her ancestors burned at the stake. I'm a winged creature way across the world, flying from a snow-capped summit to join back up with Chris. Landing on my legs, I'm human once again.

Chris's eyes slide down me and I let them slide, beg them to slide.

More drinks, more pellets—they're all kicking in, kicking out. "See how free it is?" I ask Chris. "To be so anonymous in a crowd like this?"

"Free," he echoes back, marveling over all that a single syllable can hold. Only the volume of a thimble yet the vibration of thunder. Now that he's finally stopped to smell the invasive wildflowers, he wants to taste them too, suck on the prickers until he has the wounds to prove it.

I take his hand in mine, step close so I can feel him against me, hard. Something unleashes, some kind of confidence that we'd end up here, pressed against each other.

A whisper says not to go through with this, that I'll ruin and regret it. I don't capitulate to that voice, just move Chris's hands onto my hips so he can feel the textures for himself.

"Happy New Year," I murmur, egging him on, egging him up.

He hesitates, sifting through the cons on his list until he gets to the pros, pausing there. When he leans in to kiss me, I'm already there. The balloon has popped, his pent-up energy bursting, no space left to worry about the consequences. Whatever the fallout may be, it's worth the falling in.

Chris is gone by the time I wake up, which isn't until the next afternoon. I'm not sad that he showed himself out. It's better than having to eject him, and it's not like we were going to go out for bagels and coffee and confess our love for each other. This isn't some gross romantic comedy.

Tara asks me about it, says she saw his shoes when she got back last night.

"Yeah, it wasn't a big deal," I say. "I just had to bring him back here because his ex-girlfriend was at their apartment."

"Ex?" she says. "So they broke up?"

My conscience prickles. "I mean, she gave him an ultimatum that expired at midnight, so by definition that means they're over."

Tara looks like she might say more on that but moves on. "Well, I knew something was finally going to happen between you two. Wait till I tell Hal and Jenni. They've been shipping you both since day one."

"There is no shipping going on," I refute. "It was a onetime thing to help Chris through a weird night. We're not going to become a thing or anything."

"Because you don't want to or because he doesn't want to?" Tara asks, bringing me a steaming mug of coffee with a huge dumping of cocoa powder on top, just how I like it.

"Because we both don't want to. Enough with the twenty questions."

"I just want to make sure you're feeling okay about it all."

"I'm feeling great," I say, gulping down the coffee, coughing on the cocoa powder. "Why wouldn't I be?"

It's not true, though. I'm feeling very off, very irritable. I expected that once I got with Chris, I'd have scratched the itch, moved on like I do best. But if anything, it's made the itch worse. I want to scratch it again, now that I know how satisfying it is.

"We're different that way, I guess," Tara says. "I can't help but get attached to people I sleep with."

"Hmm, I wouldn't know what that's like." I try to laugh at myself but am not quite able to. "No one's ever gotten a hold on me that way. It doesn't sound fun."

"No," she agrees. "But the primary point of love isn't to have fun, is it?"

"Of course it is," I snap. "What else would it be for?"

I don't wait for an answer, just make my escape out the door, leaving my footprints in the thin layer of snow resting delicately on the pavement before the exhaust from the cars wrecks it with soot, turns it to slush.

Chapter 29

IN THE DAYS THAT FOLLOW, A sequence of disagreeable events unfolds.

For starters, the heat breaks at the Inn, our radiators as cold as ice queens. Tara and I have to bundle up in scarves and hats inside, with no update from the super on when it will be fixed. Next, I'm all cramped with writer's block, unable to think of any ideas for a new play. Usually I have so many ideas swirling that I just have a hard time getting them onto the page. Now, though, I can't even dream up the concepts. It's like all my creativity has congealed and I can't figure out how to reverse it from solid to liquid to air.

There's no word from Chris either. I figure he's trying to move on from the whole Olivia mess before he comes for round two with me, but I'm not going to sit around and pine—I'm not an evergreen. So I give him a call one night. It goes straight to voicemail. I don't leave a message, just text him something short so he won't think it's serious. *U still up?*

He never replies. I tell myself he's just so stunned by how amazing it was to be with me that his analytical brain is still trying to process it. Chances are slim that he's gone back to Olivia. Who climbs back into their own coffin after rising from the dead?

I'm confident that he'll pop up again soon, but when two weeks go by, my patience chips away with the nail beds I keep biting. When I text him again, I see the message doesn't get delivered. It stays that icky green color on my screen. A weird feeling stirs that he's blocked my number. It's a trick I know all too well from years of doing it to other people. It makes me all paranoid that maybe he hasn't left Olivia yet, that perhaps she's extended the engagement deadline and they're in couples therapy or something.

"He probably doesn't want the temptation," Tara says when I confide in her one night. We're baking snickerdoodles together in the kitchen, consuming most of the dough before it makes its way into the oven, daring salmonella to get us. "That's why he blocked you."

"It's just insane," I say. "That some people fight so hard to stay away from the things that draw them toward them. Life is too short to do what you think is right; you have to do what you *feel* is right."

"I'm with you," Tara says, pressing horizontal fork marks into the unbaked cookies, making neat little crisscross shapes while I stab the forks in, tines first, poking all sorts of air holes in the dough. "But let's remember the life Chris leads. He's not just going to toss everything aside and follow you into the great unknown. He's too risk-averse for that."

She's right, I know, but it doesn't make it any easier. "Well, I'm not going to be derailed by some dull corporate guy who's passed up the best thing to ever happen to him. That's his problem, not mine."

"He'll realize that eventually," Tara says. "Even if he never admits it to you." She passes me the baking bowl, coated with cookie dough scraps. "You have the rest."

"You really know my love languages," I say, scraping the bowl with my fingers.

Tara opens the oven to put the cookies in, warmth leaking into the apartment but not even filling the tiny cove of the kitchenette. "Well, what are the Redstockings for?" she says, and we both feel it, the resilience of a black cat that's been dropped from a skyscraper window but still springs back up and lives.

As January crawls along, the Inn's radiators finally start rattling with heat again, but things still feel cold inside. Something about Chris lingers, something that no amount of scalding showers can wash off.

I think about going over to Chris's apartment and demanding answers, but bad behavior like his doesn't deserve to be rewarded, so I just keep checking his social media. He hasn't blocked me yet. I'm almost expecting to see a post about how his phone got stolen or how he's just waking up from a coma. I'm not wishing for the coma situation, but at least that would explain things. I'd be able to verify that I'm not being ghosted the way it feels like I am, that Chris isn't just another one of those guys who drops off the face of the earth after sex.

He finally posts a photo, geotagged in Punta Cana. Palm trees and the ocean, no caption. It sends me reeling. His audacity to be out there, jet-setting around the world, enjoying his tropical little paradise without me. I wonder who's watching Arnie while he's gone. It gets me so upset that I have to go out for a manic drive along the Bushwick Expressway. Then I come back and get higher than I've ever gotten, but it just leaves me sinking downward, toward all the rocks at the bottom that are trying to attach to my ankles, pulling me down like anchors.

I end up downloading a dating app or three just to have something else to scroll through besides Chris's photos. It reminds me how many millions of other people are out there, how there's nothing that special about Chris, how he's not even my type at all. If I'd seen him on a dating app, I would've swiped no on him within a nanosecond. I start messaging a few dozen of my matches, then ghost them all in one fell swoop. It doesn't feel good, but it feels a little less bad.

Then it happens. Chris posts a photo with him and Olivia hugging on the beach. Preppy outfits nearly matching, blue stripes and linen. Olivia's hand outstretched toward the camera, showing off a ring, something big and vulgar.

She said yes! is all the caption says.

A laugh jabs its way out. I'm not upset; I'm way beyond that. It's just hilarious how Chris nearly liberated himself from the whole marriage thing but then got cold feet and put the noose back around his own neck. What a joke.

Seven hundred forty-eight people have liked the photo so far, and the comments are rolling in. Things like: *World's most perfect couple!!!* and *You two give me hope that love is alive!*

The irony of it is really too heavy to handle. I think about posting a comment like *So great you were able to move beyond the cheating scandal! xoxo.* But that would be petty even for me and I'm not sure what it would accomplish. Chris would just delete the comment or explain it away as EJ the weird dogsitter causing trouble again.

It's all a total sham. I expected more from Chris and really thought he'd have the guts to end things with Olivia. But maybe Chris isn't just living the life his brother wanted to. Maybe it's actually the life Chris wants and I was wrong about all of it. I'm sure I could coax him into having an affair, but that doesn't appeal. It would be tainted. The only thing I back down from is being the backup.

"I've never seen you this worked up," Tara says one night when I'm going off about Chris's cowardice and how he crawled back into his little jail cell just because he likes the comfort of knowing where the walls are. "Maybe it's a sign to tell him how you feel?"

"How I feel is completely and totally indifferent," I spew. "I'm over it, the whole thing. I was never even under it in the first place."

I can't help imagining it in the abstract, though. Crashing their wedding, standing up at the "or forever hold your peace" part. The look on Olivia's face as Chris leaves her at the altar and climbs on the back of my stolen motorcycle.

I know that if he saw me in person, he wouldn't be able to resist. There's something consoling about that and how I'll never put it to the test.

Tara and I are cleaning the apartment, which just means we're rearranging the mess into a new shape, stooping over to brush crumbs from one corner to another with a hand broom, covering heaps of unfolded laundry with blankets, like it's not still there, like we won't have to deal with it eventually when we run out of underwear or need to layer on another fleece.

"What does your intuition say?" Tara asks. I don't particularly like the question because any kind of gut feeling has been missing the mark lately.

"It says Chris isn't worth my time," I say, flushing the toilet three times in a row and calling it a deep cleanse.

"You can do whatever you want, of course," Tara says. "I just wonder if maybe you should sit with it a little longer before you cross Chris out of your life."

"Too late," I say. "He's already deleted, fully expunged."

My statement sits there like an expired bag of Doritos at the back of the vending machine, neither of us buying it. But there's nothing else to believe except that I was used by someone I cared about, someone who never actually gave a shit about me at all.

Chapter 30

SOME WEEKS LATER, TARA GOES TO Jenni's baby shower. It's a girl, apparently. Yippee.

The shower is at the Colony Club, Jenni's fancy Upper East Side cult, so naturally I sit it out in favor of driving Uber. I tell stories to my riders about how one time someone tipped me four hundred dollars and the next day they won the lottery, seventeen million. Correlation doesn't imply causation, of course, but you can't deny the workings of karma. There's as much truth in the story as there is in mainstream media, and people guzzle that down without an ounce of critical thinking, so there's no moral dilemma as I see it.

A few days after, Jenni calls me up to ask if I've decided whether I want to be the godmother. The baby is due in just a couple weeks so she needs to know.

It's ridiculous but also flattering that she still wants me as godmother, especially after I boycotted the baby shower. I'd assumed she would've changed her mind by now, or that Peter would've talked her out of it.

"Look, Jenni, I really don't think I'm the right person for the job," I tell her over the phone. "With me as godmother, she'll be a teen mom in juvie."

Jenni isn't dissuaded. "I know you're up for it," she says, with a level of conviction I haven't earned. "But if you don't want to, I'm not going to force you. We can ask Peter's sister instead."

"Why not Tara or Hal?" I suggest. "They'd jump at the chance, I'm sure."

Jenni pauses, like she's trying to figure out how to phrase it. "I just think, for a godmother, we want someone who's a bit more spiritually connected. Tara and Hal aren't really."

"And I am?"

"In your own way," Jenni says, leaving me more confused than ever. It's like her time away from Bushwick has made her forget everything I do, everything I am.

"Your pregnancy hormones must really be acting up," I say. "I don't have an ounce of religion in my bones."

"I'm not talking about religion in a dogmatic sense," Jenni clarifies, though it only makes things murkier, like the bottom of a lake shrouded by weeds and algae. "I'm talking about a relationship with the divine."

"I'm the only divine entity that I believe in," I say. "And I don't think that kind of self-centered worship counts on the godmother application form."

"Mm-hmm," Jenni says vaguely, almost like she knows something I don't. It's galling, but I can't yell at a woman who's nine months pregnant, so I just decline again, say she should ask Peter's sister and leave it at that.

A couple weeks later, sometime deep into the snow of February, the old group text lights up with the news that Jenni's going into labor. I'm not inclined to go to the hospital but Tara talks me into it, so we meet up with Hal in the waiting room of Mount Sinai on the Upper East Side.

Tara brings a bouquet of balloons, Hal has a stack of politically themed children's books, and I've got a pack of gender-neutral onesies. I even paid more for the organic cotton; the nylon blend wasn't cutting it. A nurse leads us into the room. Jenni is there on the bed, the little sack in her arms. Peter is at her side, massaging her shoulders as they both stare at the baby, all wrapped up in cloth, except for the head that's covered in dark peach fuzz.

Jenni smiles, starts crying when she sees us and introduces us to their daughter. Juniper is the name, very over-the-top. They call her June, a bit better. "My summer in the winter," Jenni says, reduced to tears again, though even I've got to admit it feels like an addition, not a subtraction.

I know it's off-limits, so maybe that's why I think of Chris and what kind of dad he'll be.

Doting on Olivia, giving her back rubs and foot rubs, going grocery shopping to meet all her cravings.

"Well, I've got to run now," I announce to everyone, suddenly oppressed by the mugginess of the room, the humidity of all the affection. "I'm late for my shift at Kora's."

Everyone can hear my lie, but I don't care. I just need to get out of there. It's all too tender, too pure. The love of it all, the loss of it all, all drilling into my temples like a migraine.

Chapter 31

SOMETHING SHIFTS IN ME AFTER JENNI gives birth.

I, too, want to have something to show from my thirty-one years of looping around the sun. Not a baby, no way, but the compulsion takes over to sell a script once and for all. Time to sell out, write a formulaic little rom-com, and sell it to the highest bidder. Then I'll use the cash to take a trip somewhere where it's summer all the time, or maybe winter would be better. The cold sharpens the senses, emboldens the life force so much more than the heat, which only ends up lulling you into a droopy sleep.

After that first success, I'll have the credibility, the freedom, to pursue more creative, less commercial writing endeavors down the line. And I'll have a pot of money and an inbox full of fan mail by that point, the feeling that the world is waiting to see what I do next. Not that I want the lobotomy wine-mom rom-com crowd to be my fans, but I'll take them for starters, then leave them in the dust when the more intellectual crowd catches on to my genius. How's that?

I shut myself in my room for a couple days for a writing lockdown, leaving only for very important things like bathroom breaks, ice cream breaks, smoking breaks, Netflix breaks. By the time the solitary retreat is over, I still only have scraps of a draft. It's an enemies-to-lovers story between a Greek innkeeper and a demanding American tourist, set on the bluffs of Santorini. I can see where the whole story is going by the time I'm on the third page—never a good sign. Inevitably it means I can't bring myself to finish it because it's too obvious. Anyone could fill in the blanks; why make me do the grunt work?

"It seems I'm allergic to fluff," I tell Tara, unlocking my door and rejoining her in the world of the living. She's on the couch, moping too, fresh from her latest callback rejection. "I physically can't write something bad, even if it's commercial."

Tara builds me up, says she applauds my artistic integrity. "It's a rare thing these days. All the scripts I read for auditions are built on clichés, even the dramas," she says. "Could feed a whole country with all the corn in those lines."

"Exactly." I try not to wonder where I'd be without Tara still at my side. "It's a fucked-up industry, one big house of cards."

There's a lurking fear, though, that I'm the one who's fucked up. That my mind is jumping and sticking in all the wrong spots. I just keep thinking about Chris and the way he felt on New Year's. It was a type of touch that cut through the numbness. So safe, too, in a way I didn't even know I could experience.

"Why do we always glorify things that are dead?" I pose to Tara.

"Still no contact with Chris?" she guesses, no transition needed.

"Nope." I don't bother to sound unbothered. "I thought about stopping by his apartment, but there's really nothing to say."

"Sometimes silence is more powerful than words," Tara says. "I'm sure he can hear it."

I do like this idea, but I can't let my mind go there or it'll get jammed in a broken motor, the blades spinning but going nowhere. "It's not like he was even that great in bed," I say. "I'm just replaying it because I know it's forbidden. That's how my home-wrecker mind works, you know that."

"You're the opposite of a home-wrecker," Tara says. "You *create* things, not break them. Just look at this place." She gestures around us, to the Inn with its vivid walls, its slit windows, its calligraphy quotes from Hal that still show through the thin coat of cover-up paint. "It wouldn't exist without you. Neither would the Redstockings."

She's right, of course. I found the listing to this apartment way back when, just like I was the one who built our friend group into the formidable unit that we were.

"Exist*ed*," I correct, the suffix catching in my throat. "Past tense now."

Leaving Tara on the couch, I head outside, my thrift-store moccasins absorbing the dampness of early spring Bushwick. I wonder who owned the moccasins before I did. Maybe a woman who ran out of an abusive marriage and traveled the world solo in a hot-air balloon. The story doesn't soothe or inspire me. It just makes me feel like more of a failure, like I haven't done anything in these shoes for the next person who wears them to really look up to.

I reach the Williamsburg Bridge without realizing that's where I'm walking. Sitting down partway across it, I stay in the middle of the path so the pedestrians and cyclists have to go out of their way to avoid me. It feels like the only power I have left in this world.

Night has hit and the Manhattan skyline is a jagged wall of lights, the kind of thing that strikes you with awe until the awe has ebbed and all it does is strike you raw. Millions of individual hands have to flip these light switches, night after night after night. What's the point, really?

When I first came to the city, everything felt big, endlessly big. I was sure that I'd expand to its size. But now the scale of this place seems to be mocking my smallness, reminding me how many other people are vying for the same exact things. Everyone wants to be the next great playwright; everyone wants to start a revolution. Except there aren't enough slots and I wasn't born into money or connections and I'm abysmal at social media.

I've always thought that I was bursting with potential, that I'd tap it someday. But now I wonder if the only things I'm bursting with are excuses. Maybe I don't have any potential at all. Maybe I've spent so many years trying not to try that now I can't even try when I actually want to. I'm a flawed product of my own head games.

Maybe I just keep deluding myself that my big break will happen someday, but the only thing breaking is my own body. The body I've tried to wash by bathing in mud, and now the mud is dried and cakey and won't peel off.

Scooching to the edge of the bridge, I let my feet dangle over just a little. No one stops to see if I'm okay. Taking my shoes off, I get ready to hurl them over the edge, like I did with that apology note Chris sent me so very long ago, or so it feels with how time is bending and extending.

I throw one moccasin, then the other, with as much force as I can muster; it's not much. They fall with an elegance that hurts to watch. I can't hear them hit the river, but I imagine I can, and I imagine they'll float down the gray water and someone meditating along the rocky riverbank will pick them up and wonder who wore them. I picture that person looking for clues, swabbing the insoles for fingerprints, anything to try to find me. It comforts me a little until I remember it's not real. None of it is.

I'm barefoot on my walk back to Bushwick, trying to cut my feet wide open, trying to step on every broken bottle I can find. Anything to break my skin open. But I already have so many calluses that my feet are just fine. I hardly even feel anything and that's a good thing, I guess. It proves I'm not hurt.

Chapter 32

TARA IS ALL OUT OF SORTS because she hasn't landed a role in a while, so she throws herself into this theater audition. It's a play about the first female African American pastor. Jarena Lee was her name, back in the eighteenth century.

"Jarena preached during a time called the Second Great Awakening," Tara tells me one night when we're ambling around Bushwick together, wearing the stringy and saucy remnants of our Tony's pizza dinner on our chins like matching tattoos. "It sounds like a predecessor to the Redstockings' liberation movement, doesn't it?" Tara's all spunky in that way she only is when a fresh audition is coming up, when there's still hope that everything might turn out bright gold. "Apparently Jarena was a tortured soul, suicidal before she found God."

Tara wants the Jarena part more than I've seen her want anything in a while, but she's worried the casting director will be able to tell that she's got no religious background whatsoever.

"Will you come to church with me? Just for a method acting exercise," she says, seeing my scrunched-nose veto. "I found one in Harlem that's the same denomination as the one Jarena converted to. I've got to study up and I don't want to go alone. I'd feel so awkward."

Usually I'd shoot it down right away, but I'm glad to feel needed by Tara and agree to tag along, just once.

"What're you bringing a pillow for?" Tara asks that Sunday as we make to leave the Inn. It's the earliest I've woken up in who knows how long.

"To sleep, obviously," I say. "The one good thing about church is how it cures insomnia. I'll be in REM within seconds."

Tara shoots me a disapproving scowl, but there's no time to argue so we get on our way, taking the L train to the 2, getting off at 125th Street. Harlem is my favorite neighborhood in Manhattan by a long shot. There's this levity to it that you don't find anywhere else in the borough, like the residents have seen enough heavy shit not to let the little things sag their shoulders or their spunk. It's hardly even springtime but they're celebrating like it's the solstice. Barbecues and picnic blankets packed into slivers of grass that pop up between the concrete, high schoolers playing basketball on hoops without nets. No one seems to mind; they're too busy winning to notice the holes.

Tara walks fast, hating to be late, steering me up to Mother African Methodist Episcopal Zion Church. "Everyone just calls it Mother Zion," Tara says. "Isn't that a perfect name?"

"It's not bad," I admit, lagging a few paces behind. I thought my church days were safely behind me, and my senses are rejecting the prospect of regressing now.

"Mother Zion is the oldest African American church in the city," Tara prattles on, suddenly a tour guide. "Another name for it is the Freedom Church because it was an Underground Railroad refuge. Harriet Tubman and Frederick Douglass were actually members back in the day. How amazing is that?"

Church insanity aside, it's good to see Tara getting more in touch with her Black roots. She got screwed over being raised by white foster parents who thought themselves very charitable for taking in a Black kid, teaching her their ways.

I can't help Tara much with that stuff since my skin insulates me from a whole world of hate. I wish it weren't the case, but I know on some level I like my protection. It's human instinct, I guess, but it tastes gross, worse than boiled veggie dogs slathered in hairy pickles.

Mother Zion looks all traditional and formal from the outside, gothic stone spires and ornate stained glass. That old shame pricks, telling me I'm too blemished to enter. Maybe Tara can feel me clenching up because she links her arm through mine and leads us inside.

The music has already started, swelling to a volume and vibration higher than anything I've heard in church before. No pianos, thankfully, just a brass band. Everyone's singing along, belting and hollering, those carrying the tune outnumbered by those dropping the tune. Hands are thrown up in the air, lots of them, like they're reaching for something that's suspended just a few feet above.

I've never seen anything like this in church. It's like everyone's on mushrooms or MDMA, but there's this undercurrent of reverence that I try to scoff at but just watch in shock, nearly resentful. Even if it's not real, I want to feel whatever these people are feeling. They look high out of their minds, completely unshackled.

Tara and I try to be discreet as we slide into the back pew, but everyone around us reaches over and wrings our hands like they've been waiting for us, praying for us.

Members of the congregation start standing up at random, calling up to Jesus to heal their mother's cancer, to make whole their hearts, to forgive their porn addiction, their affair, their suicide attempt. I'm embarrassed for them, how they're spilling it all, but they don't seem embarrassed at all. They're over the fucking moon.

None of it adds up. I like the mathematical incongruence of it all even if I know the beliefs are nonsense.

Then the pastor gets up front, roams all around, not rigid behind a pulpit. He gives this bellowing sermon about how church is a hospital for sinners, not a museum for saints, and that every single one of us has ugly parts of our past. Every single one of us is broken, but God and only God can put us back together again. He says that if we let the Holy Spirit guide us, we'll finally stop being at war with other people and at war with ourselves.

I get this eerie feeling that the pastor knows me, but then I remind myself that he's just trained to emotionally manipulate the crowd so we'll drop money in the donation basket.

People are cheering and hooting the whole time. The place is buzzing with this energy like no one cares what anyone else thinks of them because they already know they're immortal or at least they believe they are, and what's the difference really? Either way, they're having a rave and leaving me behind.

I don't rest my head on my pillow at all. I just clutch it with my hands, and the flimsy pillowcase is drenched with sweat by the time Tara and I bolt out of there at the end of the service.

"You said church was boring," Tara says, rounding on me. She's got an incredulous look on her face, probably similar to mine.

"That wasn't church," I say, trying to process it. "That was something else."

It feels impossible, offensive even, that the outside world could possibly be carrying on with all its mundanities, but carry on it does. The subway rattling into the station as clumsily as usual. Passengers being sucked into their phone screens with the same zombie-eyed stares and glares.

"How am I possibly supposed to play a convincing pastor?" Tara says as we subway-surf back downtown, keeping our balance without holding on to the poles. We tip a few times, legs jittery. "I can't do *that*."

"Of course you can," I say. "You'll just have to go back for a few more weeks until the energy seeps into your bones and sticks. Maybe I'll go with you again, if you want."

I act like I'm doing her some grand favor, but really I'm looking forward to it the whole week. It's like a new mystery I'm trying to solve.

The next service is just as electric as the one before. It turns out I hadn't imagined the current in the air. When everyone is standing up and yelling things out during prayer time, asking for healing and forgiveness, I've got this weird desire to speak up and confess some stuff too. But I don't believe in confessing my sins because that would mean admitting my sins, and I don't ascribe to the idea of labeling things as right or wrong, even if some things really do feel foul inside. So I stay quiet, but I list a few things in my head, just to experiment.

Chapter 33

TARA REMAINS FIXATED ON THE ROLE, waiting to hear back. One April afternoon, she bounces down the Inn's outdoor stairs and through the front door, brimming with news.

"I got the understudy!" she announces. "For Jarena!"

She's beaming. I'm frowning. I went to cheer Tara on at one of the callbacks, and she blew the competition out of the water. A dolphin gliding among minnows—it wasn't even close. "Why are they having you as the understudy?" I ask. "You should be the lead."

"Shila got it, remember her?" Tara says. "Her range is insane, way better than mine."

It's not true, but I don't want to piss on her excitement. "Good job," I say, standing up from the couch, where I've been drinking alone and talking to my AI app, telling it to write me a three-act play that I can sell for a million dollars. It spits something out, not any worse than what you see onstage, but my pride won't let me steal it. My conscience doesn't have any problem with the plagiarism, but my ego can't handle being outdone. It's a real bitch sometimes. "And I'm sure I can orchestrate something so Shila gets sick or breaks a few ribs the day before the show so you have to fill in," I say. "Not to worry."

"EJ," Tara warns, but she's grinning as I pour her some whiskey.

"The director, Niles, has just got this *vision* for the show. It's going to be incredible."

"Of course it will be, because you're a part of it," I say. Affirming with words is something I'm working on because maybe I didn't do the best job of it with Jenni and Hal. Chris either, not that I'm thinking about that.

I ask Tara how she wants to celebrate. She says she just wants to stay in and practice her lines and watch that new show about the women spies of World War II and the men who stole the credit.

"So are we going to church tomorrow?" I ask, a couple episodes in.

She gives me a curious look. "I wasn't planning to go anymore," she says. "It was just prep for the audition. Now I'll be busy with rehearsals so that'll be my immersion."

"Right." I'm annoyed with my annoyance. "Makes sense."

But the next day I find myself back at Mother Zion alone. I sit up in the balcony this time so I can hide better and also look down and observe more as a third party, trying to pinpoint the root of what's hypnotizing everyone. I even close my eyes and pretend I believe in God just to see if it makes me feel like I'm floating like they seem to think they're floating.

It doesn't work. I'm still alone in my little pew, feet very much on the ground. There's nothing inside me except an abstract emptiness, exacerbated by the fullness that everyone else seems to be experiencing. I can't even feel any connection to my intuition these days; it's like the signal has been cut. Jenni was definitely wrong about me having any kind of connection to the divine.

I find myself thinking about Chris's wedding again, wondering if it's going to be in a church and if he and Olivia both believe in God and throw their hands up like the people here do. Chris and I never really talked about spiritual things, except when he told me he has a hard time believing in heaven after Luke's death. I wish I'd probed more about his beliefs. It feels important now in a way it didn't back then. Olivia will probably want to get married in a church just so her family doesn't bicker. There's nothing I dislike more than people going along with something simply to avoid conflict.

My favorite thing about the people at Mother Zion is that they're not playing it safe or half-assing this Jesus thing. They're bold and loud with their whole heads dunked into water that I still don't believe in, but they do and so I have to respect their grip on the delusion. It makes mushrooms look like child's play, really.

Another Sunday, some weeks later, I arrive late to church and take my usual seat up in the balcony. There's this little old woman sitting next to me and I like her right away. She's poking her cane up toward the ceiling dome like it's a circus baton. Her tiny hips are swaying side to side. She beams at me with tea-stained teeth, says it's so good to see me again, which is odd because I don't think we've ever met, but I guess she's noticed me. It's kind of a nice feeling, like I'm one of the regulars, like I have a place here.

I don't sing or raise my hands or say anything at all; that part hasn't changed. It's not that I'm self-conscious—well, that's part of it maybe—but mostly I just don't want to pretend or fan their hallucinations, however fun that might be.

At some point, though, my foot develops a twitch and starts tapping lightly on the hardwood floor.

"Do you feel her?" the old woman beside me asks, leaning over during a pause between songs. It's possible she's been talking to me for a little while but I haven't heard her over the trumpets.

"Feel who?" I ask.

"The Holy Spirit, of course," she says, reaching for my hand and giving it a little squeeze. Her crinkled skin feels like velvet.

"You think the Holy Spirit is a woman?" I ask. "Shit."

She doesn't seem shocked by my language, so maybe her hearing isn't so great. She just says the Spirit isn't a man or a woman, but the energy feels feminine to her, so she goes with that. "Especially since Mary Magdalene's gospel was omitted from the Bible," the woman carries on. "So this feels like a nice way to even the tables."

"What do you mean?" I ask. I don't recall ever learning much about Mary Magdalene except that she was unclean, a whore, which makes me feel some kind of bond with her.

"Oh yes, her gospel is very real," the woman says. "It was hidden and destroyed, and no wonder. It's all about how we all have the power of God inside us, how we don't need to rely on anything external. Think of how different things might have been for women, for all society, if her words weren't silenced. But men have a way of curating things to encourage hierarchy, don't they?"

"Yes, they do," I agree. Before I can elaborate on how the entire premise of religion is patriarchal, designed to make us obey man-made rules and leaders, the woman is speaking again.

"The Spirit doesn't speak to everyone in churches, you know," she says to me. Her style is very casual, not didactic, which I like. "You might hear her better if you go into the woods. That's what helped unlock the door for me back when I was lost."

Staring at her, I try to determine if she's gone loony, if she's suffering from Alzheimer's, maybe. But there's no time to evaluate. She salutes me like I salute doorpeople and then totters out of the pew as the service concludes. I don't follow her out. I just sit there on the bench for a while, rolling around in the implications. Would I have been more open to believing in something bigger than myself if I hadn't always associated God and church and religion with masculine structures and male leaders? It probably wouldn't have changed things much, but it might have changed them a little. You never know.

I try to talk about it with Tara when I get home but she's all wrapped up with rehearsals, and the rare moments when I do overlap with her, she's going on about the director, Niles, how he says Tara is a "rare talent."

"I've been telling you that for years," I grumble. "Why do you only believe it when some guy points out the obvious?"

"He's not *some guy*." Tara's aghast. "He's Niles Evans and he's world-famous."

"The Redstockings are world-famous too," I remind her. "Or at least we will be someday. Posthumous legends."

I don't believe it anymore, but it's good for morale to keep up the ruse. Retreating into my room, I try to scrape up some sleep. I still haven't gotten rid of my bunk bed. It's the money holding me back, I tell myself, but it might be the memories too.

My dreams are weird that night and keep getting weirder in the days that follow. There's this recurring forest with bright sunlight splashing through the thrashing trees, but I can't reach the light. No matter how fast I run, I just keep tripping over bulbous roots. I wake up all sweaty and itchy, a tightness in my chest.

I want to talk to Chris about my nightmares. I feel like he'd help me untangle them. It's not like he's in touch with emotions or the subconscious or anything—exactly the opposite—but he's got this practicality that would be reassuring. He'd prove that I'm not going crazy, that the dreams can be explained by all the ice cream I eat right before bed or something like that.

I still scroll through his social media; it's just a habit by now. I could stop if I wanted to, but I like feeling connected to him. That's not sad; it's just the way the modern world works. I'm in the power seat here, getting to know what's going on in his life. He doesn't get to know anything about mine because I never post anything. It's satisfying to preserve the air of mystery, let him wonder about me. He wonders a lot, I'm sure, and no doubt has regrets. He's just not brave enough to do anything about them, and that just proves that I'd never take him back. I'm as anti-coward as I am anti-marriage.

Briefly, I consider what would happen if Arnie got in another accident, if Chris's instincts would take over and he'd call me first again. I know he would, but it doesn't comfort me the way I'd hoped. It just gets me distraught thinking about Arnie getting hurt. The little guy has already been through so much, losing Luke and all and then getting hit by the car. He deserves a nice big yard out in the country with two parents who adore him. He shouldn't be cooped up in a Manhattan apartment with a stepmom like Olivia, who just sees him as a nuisance that sheds on her designer wardrobe.

I'd be such a good mom to Arnie. It's a shame that can't happen—not that it would happen even if Chris and Olivia weren't getting married. The stars would burn out centuries before they'd ever possibly align. I picture Arnie's happy face when Chris and I play tug-of-war with him. It makes me wish things might've been different, that I could've loved Chris in a kind of way that lasts. But I don't have those muscles and I don't want those muscles, so there's no point dwelling on it.

Mango and Squid die the same night, both of them floating on the top of their tank when I go over to feed them. I try to tell myself it's something poetic, that maybe Mango was sick and passed first and Squid chose to go too so they wouldn't have to be apart.

Really, I know it's my fault, that I set the water temperature too cold. I contemplate burying them outside in the park, but I don't want dogs to chew them up, so I decide the toilet is the most humane way to go, as anguishing as that flush is, the swirl of their departure.

I have a hard time sleeping after that, mired in guilt and extrapolating about how this is proof I'm not suited to care for anything or anyone. Why did I think I was ready for goldfish?

One night I pick up my phone and I'm about to text any of the hundred people who could cure my loneliness, or at least aid in my procrastination. But I can't do it for some reason, so I go outside and walk backward laps around the block until Knickerbocker Bagel opens. I talk Fred the owner into giving me a free egg bagel with extra scallion cream cheese because of what an integral member of the community I am and all that.

Sitting on the curb, I lick all the cream cheese off first, then go for the actual bagel. I like the feeling of separating two things from each other. It doesn't inject me with joy but it extracts a bit of the venom, so that's something. I'll take it. I'll take anything I can get these days, so long as it's free.

Chapter 34

I STOP GOING TO CHURCH PRETTY soon after I start.

It wasn't like that phase was ever going to last long—it was about the same duration as my mullet chapter back in college. But I still can't shake the gaze of that little old woman. How she looked at me like she knew me. The past me, the present me, the future me, all curled together in one ribbon of smoke. And the real kicker was how it didn't look like the truth shocked her or scared her like it should. It just seemed to affirm that she was glad to see me.

One day on the blurry border between spring and summer, I decide to take the woman's advice to go out into the wilderness, because why not, really? You can't get lost if you've never been found. Maybe that's me being an overdramatic artist but it feels true, truer than anything has in a while now.

So I write that quote on the ceiling of the Inn in black Sharpie, signing my name larger than the quote itself so the attribution isn't missed. Then I load up a backpack with granola bars, water, pepper spray, and edibles. On my way out, I pass Tara. She sizes me up in my athletic clothes and sneakers, asks where I'm off to.

"I'm going hiking," I tell her. "I'll be back in a day or five, don't worry."

"Hiking?" Tara says, like I've just announced I'm boarding a spacecraft to Mars or something.

"I just need to get out and move my legs," I say. "I've been so restless lately."

She probes some more, tells me to be safe, and asks if I have a portable phone charger.

"Yes, Mom." I roll my eyes but actually like how she'd miss me if I was gone. She'd probably be the only one.

I head off to catch the L train into Manhattan. The geography feels too close to Chris. We still haven't had any contact since New Year's, five months that might as well be five years. I don't think of him often anymore, unless you count the times that I think about how I'm not thinking about him. But I don't count those. Why would I?

Transferring to the 4 train, I head up to the Harlem Metro North station so I can skip over the chaos of boarding at Grand Central. Clambering up to the aboveground tracks, I get on the first train that pulls up. It's headed for Poughkeepsie, apparently. I don't buy a ticket. It's not just that I'm trying to save money. That's part of it, but I also haven't decided which station I'm going to and I like that feeling, the open-ended possibility of it all.

I snag one of the last window seats and sit there watching the dirty-looking Hudson. The sharp buildings start to swap themselves out for rolling foothills in the valley. Clouds bandage the peaks in cotton, like they know the earth needs protecting from humans, that parasitic species that doesn't handle anything with care except their own egos.

When the ticket collector comes by, I slip away to the bathroom. It's the oldest trick in the book but it still works, which makes me kind of disappointed that I didn't have to stretch my creativity to find a loophole. But it's also satisfying in a practical sort of way. When I get back to my seat, it's occupied by this repugnant couple, cuddled up and sharing a pair of earbuds, the cord all tangled. I wonder what song they're listening to before remembering that I don't care at all.

I could demand my seat back but it's not worth my breath, so I just find a new one and have some fun trying to decide what stop to get off at. I pick Cold Spring, but as I'm about to get off there, the conductor announces that Breakneck Ridge is next. I've heard of it before but haven't been, and who could resist that name?

Breakneck Ridge wins me over right away. It's such a ratchet little station that you have to hop off the very back of the train to get down to the platform. I leap down like a ninja, and a group of other hikers follows me, picking up on my leader vibes. They've all got those intense hiking boots and high-tech hiking poles and all that other fancy gear like they're climbing Mount Kilimanjaro.

I don't want to follow anyone and I don't want anyone following me. The whole point of this excursion is to be alone, so I storm on ahead.

The trail is flat at first, but then the incline starts and quickly escalates into a full-on rock scramble. I realize why it's called Breakneck Ridge. One wrong slip and I could easily plummet to my death, off the rocks and into the river. Looking back, I spot the other hikers just starting up. They're going slowly like they're paralyzed by the fear of falling, like they're terrified to contemplate death and therefore terrified to contemplate life.

I increase my speed, leaping up from rock to rock, ledge to ledge. My hands and knees get scraped up, just surface cuts, and finally I reach the top. There's this lookout point over the gray-blue river, the deep green hills undulating for miles. I'm pretty impressed with myself for how far I've already climbed, especially since I never do this kind of thing. It reveals my natural talent or willpower, maybe both.

There's a flagpole at the lookout, and it makes me want to fly a Redstocking flag up there, a banner with the red fist pumping through the air. When I get back to the city, I'll make one for me and Tara, maybe even a couple extra for Hal and Jenni to keep as relics from their rebel days. I probably won't gift them to the defectors, but you never know. It's hard to feel spiteful right now when I'm wheezing so much from the hike.

Drinking some water, I dangle my feet over the side of a particularly jagged rock, like the game I play on the Williamsburg Bridge, only better because there are no guardrails here. This time I don't think about where my shoes would go if they fell. I contemplate the outcome for my whole body. It would scrape its way to the bottom, my head thumping against the rocks. I'd be a goner by the time I reached the river. I wonder what Tara would think when she heard the news, and Hal and Jenni and my family too. I hope they'd know I want to be cremated, my ashes scattered from a hilltop like this. They can't know that, though, because I've never realized that's what I want until right now.

There's a tickle of creative energy in my nose. It feels like a big sneeze is coming, so I open the Notes app on my phone and release a big *achoo*. I type up an outline to a play right there. It's about a woman who tumbles to her death while hiking. The entire play takes place in the seconds between when she falls and when she hits the water, but the audience doesn't know that until the very end. Everyone thinks they're watching the woman live out her life after the hiking accident, until it switches back to the woman falling elegantly through the air and then—smack—into the river she goes, dead as can be.

The sobbing audience is left to wonder if all those scenes they saw were flashbacks that she was remembering or things that never actually happened that appeared as regrets in her final moments. It ends very abruptly and that's what gives the play its impact: the finality of it all.

It feels good to have a plot like this flow out of me so easily, even if it is kind of a downer. It's progress at least and affirms my suspicion that my mysterious friend at Mother Zion knew what she was doing by telling me to go into the woods.

The other hikers reach the lookout too and pose for noisy photos. A couple of them look like they're about to ask me to take a group picture but then think better of it. They all scamper onward. It turns out the trail keeps going, a bit inland. I'm only halfway up.

I keep hiking toward the actual top this time. It's cloaked in evergreen trees, and there's this great big boulder in a small clearing, so I shimmy my way up and sit on it. I can't see the river through the trees, but I don't mind. The forest feels like a cocoon, except without the suffocating feeling because the oxygen is so fresh.

Other hikers pass by on the trail, but no one sees me. In no mood to talk to myself, I strike up a conversation with the character I've just invented and then killed off. Peyton, I name her. I dive into her regrets, roll around in them until they rub against my own, sticking like putty.

Shapes start to form in my head. Hal and Jenni and Chris and even my mom and dad and sister. I don't like how they're invading my retreat, so I stamp them out and rummage through my backpack for the edibles. I can't find them even though I know I put them in the outside pocket. Someone on the train must've stolen them when I was looking out the window. I detest the criminal but I also know I would've done the same, so I'm kind of impressed with their stealth too.

I want to call in a helicopter to airlift me back to Bushwick, but that's not exactly an option. I'd get slammed with a healthcare bill that I'd never be able to pay back. So I decide to just camp out here all night and make my own drugs. I'll get high on delusion like the people at Mother Zion do. How hard can it be?

Standing up on the pine needle floor, I rock from side to side and get into full acting mode. I call up to God, only I don't say

God. That word has too many negative connotations ingrained into me, even if I'm playing make-believe. The Holy Spirit does too, so I go with something new, inspired by what the old lady said about Mary Magdalene and the divine feminine.

"Oh, divine woman," I say in as solemn a voice as I can muster, cracking myself up as I go. "Please speaketh. Guide me toward the light."

I don't hear anything back, not that I expected to, but I'm still kind of disappointed. Maybe arms are like antennas and help cut through the static or something, so I hold my hands up in the air. Still no luck. It's dead quiet. Just the birds and the wind and the squirrels and the hikers laughing obnoxiously from down below. It's all so ordinary, nothing divine in the least.

My eyes start to prick after a while. My berry-colored contacts have been in for a while, so I take them out and start to put them back in their case, but it feels too orderly, so I throw them onto the dirt for an impromptu burial. I feel better right away, like my vision is crisper.

Night falls and I spread out on a pine needle mattress, plunking in and out of sleep. Sometime in the middle of the night I wake up to a whining sound. My first thought is that it's Tara on the bottom bunk having a bad dream. Then, remembering where I am, I shine my phone flashlight until I locate the thing that doesn't belong.

It's this dark bundle a little ways away from me. I've lived in New York long enough to immediately assume it's a bomb. But then the sound comes again, and two bright yellow eyes are staring at me, into me. It's not a bomb at all. It's a deer, a tiny fawn.

Turning off the flashlight so I'm not blinding the little creature, I let my eyes adjust to the darkness. The fawn can't be more than a couple weeks old, all covered in spots and seeming totally clueless about where they are or why they're there. I can relate to that. We're in the same boat.

The mom must've left them here while she went out searching for food. It's weird to pick a spot right next to a human, but it's actually quite a compliment to me. Animals always trust me. It makes me miss Mango and Squid and Arnie too, of course. I'm worried the fawn might be cold because the temperature is pretty frosty by now, even though it was hot in the day. I want to give her my sweatshirt, but that might spook her, and I can't blame her. I even scare myself away sometimes.

The little thing is all tense, sizing me up. But eventually she falls back asleep; she can't seem to help it. It's pretty adorable and kind of reminds me how Arnie tuckers himself out by chasing his own tail and then plops down on my lap for a long nap. I think of my little niece and Jenni's baby too. I haven't been in their lives at all, and this feels like a mistake now.

I chew on some pine needles. They've got a nice crunch. Leaning my head back, I get a look through the shifting treetops up at the navy-black sky. It's strewn with stars like someone went crazy with the saltshaker. There's this one star that really pops out, the lead of the cast.

Things are bubbling up within me. It doesn't feel soothing like hot lava; it's just uncomfortable and makes me burp. I'm curious about what else I've got to burp up, what else is inside me that I don't want in there anymore. Opening my mouth, I point it up toward that big star like I'm at the dentist wagging my tonsils. I've got no clue what I'm doing but I know it's right, so I let the star shine down into me on all the parts I usually shove into the shadows.

The starlight doesn't hit me all at once. It diffuses into a million softer particles so I can examine them one by one if I want to, which I don't at first, but then I start to take a look.

I don't like it at all. Even the smallest drop of light is too bright.

I shut my eyes for a while, but I can't resist so I open them again just to take a quick peek back up at the light. It's blinding but somehow I can see clearly, too clearly. There it is, all my shame splitting itself open or splitting me open. What's the difference?

The shame about not being the sweet, obedient daughter my parents wanted. The shame about still having no clue what I'm doing as an adult, flying around like Peter Pan except I don't actually know how to fly; I just crawl along the grimy sidewalk that I call the sky because admitting it's the ground would break me and I've got too much shame for that, though I've always called it pride.

And below that but above it too, far above, far below, is the shame about how I've piled so many toxins into my body and let it be used as a toy. And how I've used other people's bodies as toys too, total irreverence that I passed off as independence.

I'm writhing on the ground now, or at least it feels like I am. It's hard to tell what's happening out there versus in here. I can't control my body; I can't control anything. Maybe I've never been able to.

Keep going, dig deeper, my intuition says, and it's good to hear that voice again, though it couldn't come at a worse time. I'm out here looking for the divine woman or Mary Magdalene and I'm trying to keep the noise at a minimum.

"No thanks," I tell it. "That's enough for now. This isn't a therapy session." This makes my intuition laugh, like it's in on something I'm not.

"What're you smirking at?" I ask it.

Everything falls quiet in a loud kind of way. I look over at the little fawn, fast asleep, this little ball of untouched fur, so innocent like I used to be. Like I'll never be again.

The sound of a piano thumps in my ears. It's loud, too loud. A man's face flashes, pieces of a puzzle fitting into place just so the final image can destroy me, or maybe just destroy the destruction.

It's Mr. Hubert, my childhood piano teacher. The one who

made me hate that instrument for some reason I don't remember. Except that I remember now. The repressed memories unpeel frame by frame, slowly yet too fast.

His hands are on me like it's the very first time, reaching under my frilly pink dress. Touching, coaxing, telling me what a good girl I am. Me pulling away, looking away, closing my eyes. Him pulling me back in, telling me to look at him, that I can trust him.

I wonder for a moment if I'm hallucinating, if I'm inventing some dramatic trauma just to explain how fucked up I've become. But the starlight swears that what I see is true, and more than that, my body remembers in the way it's shuddering and shivering and itching like I'm breaking out in hives.

I'm not in the scene anymore; I'm looking down on it, looking up on it, seeing myself as the little girl she was. The little girl who started dissociating every Monday from 4:30 to 5:15 p.m., deliberately losing track of time because she thought maybe it would be better or just less bad if she wasn't counting down every minute until her mom rang the doorbell to get her.

The little girl whose parents thought she was being a spoiled brat complaining about piano lessons when they were shelling out money for her. The little girl who wanted to tell her parents what was going on but was too scared and soon felt like too much time had gone on. Because it was the little girl's fault too—that's what she thought. She could've done something; she could've stopped him. But she didn't.

Then the scene spirals, it swirls, and there I am back in the first person again, no separation between the then and the now, the third person and the first. My body collapses in on itself like it's finally realized there's nowhere else to go. The only way out of this is straight through.

Everything is burning, a white-hot searing pain. All those old itches and triggers and hollow relationships. The way I can't really be intimate with anyone or even make eye contact with men sober. It's all here, it's all here, unleashed from the underworld.

I want to rip myself out of the memories, bury them again, even deeper this time, but I know I have to stay here another moment. Stare this down to strip its power and reclaim my own.

The truth is heavy but not as heavy as I would expect. It seems it's been living in my body all this time. I didn't really block anything out; I can see that now. It was always all there somewhere, simmering in the subconscious, coating the ceiling of my life in black mold, the kind that the inspectors never catch until it's too late, making me lash out at my parents and my sister because no one understood. And all those people I slept with over the years, hoping the new touch would erase the old, or at least coat over the filth on my skin. All the relationships I sabotaged because it was better to never let anyone get close. All the hate and blame I spewed at my family and other people to deflect it from the true target: myself.

My cheeks are soaked. I look up expecting to find rain clouds, but the sky is still clear, piercingly clear. The star is still there, piercingly there. I'm crying, crying hard. They're my first real tears in years. Everything's coming up and out of me and I wonder what's going to be left of me, if anything, when this tantrum settles down. The thought terrifies me but carries some hope all the same.

The decibels build; the vibrations strengthen. Pure rage pours out of me, extra loud and guttural to compensate for how long it's been locked up.

But it's free now. I'm free now. Laughter tumbles out too, braiding with the rage, metamorphosing into something new, medicinal and militant all at once.

The laughter gains in proportion, wild and uncouth until I can taste my own hypocrisy and giggle at the absurdity of it. Here I've been praising myself as some grand leader leading people into the light, when really I've been controlled by the darkness. I've espoused liberation while keeping my friends chained to my side, forcing them to conform to one small definition of womanhood. I've stripped their choices and slashed them out of my life when they dared to disobey me, all to overcompensate for my own fears and try to create a relationship structure that would keep me safe. Maybe my intentions weren't all bad, but I'm really no better than the dictators who came before me, trying to oppress everyone around them.

Talk about a plot twist I didn't see coming—though maybe I did and I've just been too stubborn to admit it. That's my defining characteristic after all, but perhaps it's not the only one. Perhaps some other traits can hold me together even if I let that one go.

The sound of the piano has softened. It's not making me writhe in pain anymore. It's just accompanying a trumpet and some lyrics for a jazz melody. And in the gap of the bridge, it all clicks.

It turns out I didn't actually have to seek out the divine woman; I just had to recognize her. She's been inside me all along, that pesky feeling I used to call my intuition. It makes me feel pretty dumb but also very brilliant. Most people go their whole lives without making this connection.

The divine woman breathes a giant sigh of relief that I've finally connected the dots after all her hints. The star is dancing now and I'm its partner. I let it twirl me around and dip me to places I've never been, places I've never let myself go. The pain and shame shrivel up to a raisin that I toss into the woods for the birds to eat.

There's a stirring within me, and it's so obvious now how I'm not the center of the universe after all. I'm just a tiny speck and there's a greater force swirling all around us, creating us and dropping little bits of herself in each of us. Strangely I don't feel threatened about being invaded by an outside force. It's comforting, liberating, like a weight has been lifted and I don't have to be my own god anymore. I just have to stand on the shoulders of the higher power and let her carry me through the trials, the triumphs, the tributaries.

I'm aware of my smallness, but not in a way that makes me feel unimportant. It's the opposite actually. I'm enmeshed in the infinite, vast as can be as I roll around on the earth's soil, no longer soiled, never soiled.

In the morning, I wake up to the sight of the mother deer emerging from the trees, nuzzling up to her baby. It makes me think of our old family dog, Melon, and how he would comfort me after my piano lessons, climbing up onto my bed to sleep with me even though that was against the rules.

The fawn stands up, gingerly like she's still getting the hang of it. I can relate because I, too, feel jittery and shaky, like a newborn. Mother and gangly-legged baby amble off together. As they go, the mom turns back to me just for a moment, gives me an appreciative look. It's the best thank-you I've ever gotten. Then they're both gone and I'm by myself again but not alone. It's weird, in a good way.

Everything feels crisper and brighter and it's clear how much I've missed out on looking at the world through plastic lenses. I'm never putting those colored contacts back in. I'm keeping these boring gray eyes forever. And besides, boring is in the eye of the beholder, as Chris says.

Usually I would tell myself that I feel nothing at the thought of him, but now I can admit I do feel something. I feel a lot and that's okay; that's beautiful actually.

"Hey, divine woman," I say, like I'm talking to an old friend. "Thanks for staying with me all this time. It probably wasn't a walk in the park, what with my delightful attitude and all. If the situation had been reversed, I probably would've left you a long time ago. Just being honest."

She chuckles at that. I make my way down the mountain slowly, going on a back trail without any rocks to minimize the risk of plummeting to my death. Everything feels raw—newly precious, newly fragile. It would be a real shame to pull a Humpty-Dumpty now that I've finally been put back together. Or at least now that I'm putting myself back together. I'm still a work in progress—always will be.

Chapter 35

I'M WORRIED THE FEELING WILL WEAR off once I'm back in the city, but it doesn't. It's not as potent as it was under the stars, but there's this quiet understanding that the divine woman will never leave me, no pact needed.

Tara can sense something different about me right away when I walk into the Inn. "What happened to you?" she asks, tossing leftovers in the skillet to give them a makeover. "Are you still high?"

"I climbed outside of myself," I tell her. "Only I burrowed down deeper too. It's all very meta." I give her the gist of what happened on the hiking trip.

"Who are you and what have you done with EJ?" Tara says once I'm done, appraising me like I've been abducted by aliens, which I pretty much have been.

"I'm the same EJ I've always been," I say. "Just without all the parasites inside." I lay a hug on her and hold on longer than usual. "Thanks for sticking by me all this time, Tara," I say. "Even with all my tyrannical antics."

Still looking uncertain, Tara softens and reciprocates the hug. "You don't have to thank me," she mutters. "You've stuck by me too."

"Guess that's true," I say with a grin. "We're both pretty great. And the best part is that it isn't even bragging because we can't take credit for our greatness. Only the divine woman can. So it's not hubris; it's humility."

"Sounds like you found the perfect religion for you," Tara says.

"Oh no, it's not a religion," I say. "It's the exact opposite really, a living and breathing spirit. No dusty old dogma for me."

Tara frowns. "I don't think I'm really following."

"Of course you're not following," I say. "You're leading. We all are." I pause. If it were anyone but Tara, I would probably just stop there, but I keep going, just a little. "Also, I realized or rather remembered something else in the woods. I'm not ready to talk about it now, but I will be soon."

Tara tucks my half-grown-out bangs behind my ears so she can see my eyes. "I think I might already know."

I tense up at that. "What do you mean?"

She takes a beat, then answers. "When we shared the bunk bed, you would talk in your sleep a lot," Tara says, her voice measured. "A lot of times you would be telling someone to get away, to stop touching you, to just let you play." Tara's jaw stiffens and I can tell there's a lump in her throat. "You're a survivor, EJ. Isn't that right?"

I probably shouldn't be shocked that Tara has seen me more clearly than I've seen myself, but I still am. "Why did you never bring it up?" I ask.

"I thought about it," Tara says. "But I just felt like it was something you needed to process on your own timeline. Pushing things out isn't really my style."

"That's not why you're still living with me, is it?" I ask, half scared to hear the answer. "Because you feel sorry for me?"

"No, I'm here because you're my platonic soulmate," Tara says, which is exactly the answer I didn't know I was craving. "And because you know how to bargain the prices down at Tony's Pizza so we get two pies and garlic knots for $9.99." She grins at me, her whole face alive with the same light I feel splashing onto my own.

"It really is one of my specialties, isn't it?" I say proudly. My eyes are damp. Everything is big and warm. Tara knows, or at least knows enough, and she's not running away. Maybe other people won't run away either. And more than that—maybe I won't. Maybe I'll stay. Here in this body, with all its traumas and its tantrums, all its flaws and its fears, all its beauty and its bandages. Maybe the very definition of power is to not let the past define you. To write your own ending, or non-ending, to this crazy script called life.

—

The next time I'm at Mother Zion, I try to find the old lady who sent me into the woods so I can thank her and let her know what grand success I had.

She's not there so I ask around. Someone informs me that she died last week, had a heart attack while tending to her vegetable patch. My eyes fill up because apparently I'm just a watering can these days now that all my valves are open. But I get the feeling the woman knows that she helped me, that she's got some awareness of it. I can pretty much hear her talking to me, wagging her cane. *I told you so.*

—

My awakening doesn't give me a whole new personality or anything. I'm still just as hilarious and endearingly obnoxious as ever. It's just helped unearth the old me, the real me, and it grounds me in the roots that I tried to rip out for so many years.

I used to think that having roots meant you were tethered to the same spot forever, stuck there with no escape. But now I see that to grow tall and thrash your branches wherever they want to go, you have to grow deep too. Otherwise you'll tip over or snap in the wind. I've done both.

The only real change to my appearance is that my eyes are gray all the time—no more colored contacts. It's still uncomfortable to show myself like that, but there are these occasions that make me glad to be ocularly bare, like I'll be whistling my way down Knickerbocker Avenue and then out of the blue, blue sky, someone at the crosswalk will meet my gaze straight on for a second or two. And suddenly we're both inhabiting each other's spirits and I'm feeling all their hopes and all their holes. There's nothing like it. It's vulnerable and achy but pure veneration and ascension too.

The high isn't always fun and games. It hurts a lot. Every texture scrapes. I get scraped by the homeless man curled up on his cardboard bed. Scraped by a group of friends going out for the night hooting with laughter like the Redstockings used to. Scraped by an Australian shepherd tugging on his leash. Scraped by the new moon and scraped by the full moon and scraped by all the slivers of moon in between. Scraped by the sunrise and scraped by the sunset and scraped by the miracle of how the sun does it all over again the next day. Scraped by the past and scraped by the future. Scraped because I got to be born and scraped because I have to die. And scraped because maybe I won't have made it all count.

I complain to the divine woman about how much the scraping hurts, and she says she didn't promise this way of life was going to be easier; she just said it was going to be more beautiful. I can't exactly argue with that because of this feeling of dancing inside my own body and not wanting to claw my way out. Well, it's beautiful—that's what it is. I wouldn't trade it, not a chance.

"Shila has bronchitis," Tara tells me the night before the opening performance for the Jarena Lee show. "She can't sing, so I have to fill in." She asks if this was my doing, if I cursed her.

"Of course I didn't," I say, though I wonder if I did subconsciously manipulate the energetics a bit. It's not a serious illness—Shila will recover just fine—so I don't feel bad about my witchy talents. I just help Tara step into her confidence, let it wash over her like a monsoon.

Tara commands the stage, not with her volume or her movement so much as her tranquility, her stillness. It makes everyone hold on tightly, desperate not to miss a word. The audience starts off expecting it to be a parody of the church. This is New York City after all, and people seem to be hoping for that kind of comedy show; that's why they bought the tickets. But as the play goes on, there's this shift in the theater as it becomes clear that this isn't a satire at all. It's a redemption story that makes God look pretty good. At first it doesn't seem to sit well with the audience. It's like they feel duped. But by the end they're on their feet hooting and hollering. They've had a taste and now they want more.

I throw Tara a dinner party in the garden the weekend after the show wraps. Hal and Jenni are there, and Peter and Astrid too. Niles the director comes too. He's a last-minute invite from me because I can tell how obsessed Tara is with him. Now with the show over, I get the feeling they'd be dating if Tara wasn't worried about disappointing me. But the idea of Tara getting into a relationship or even getting married one day doesn't threaten me like it used to, and I feel myself wanting to let her know that. I hope that's what inviting Niles does.

I serve vegan calzones. Everyone's drinking except me. I've gone cold turkey on the drugs too. The clarity I got on substances was always rimmed with an artificial haze. I never really noticed it before but can't unsee it now. And now that I'm not blocking out all the memories, blacking out isn't needed. It's not that I'm over the trauma—I might never be—it's just that I no longer have to contort myself into broken shapes to prove that I'm okay. I know I'm whole even with all the holes.

I find myself wishing Chris were here at the dinner. It's not just that I want another person at the table so I won't be the awkward ninth wheel. I want Chris in particular. And I want Arnie too, tugging on the garden vines like rope. I'm not suppressing those feelings—they're worthy of recognition—but I try not to linger on them. No point missing someone who doesn't miss you.

The night wraps up early. It's not even midnight by the time the married couples trot on home. Tara asks if I want to go out to the House of Yes with her and Niles, but just picturing all those strobe lights gives me a headache. I tell her I'm just going to stay in, get to bed.

"But are you sure you don't mind if Niles and I go?" Tara asks, like she's walking on eggshells. It's statements like these that make me realize what an autocrat I was back in my pre-liberated or rather faux-liberated days.

"Do whatever you want," I assure her, with none of the old passive-aggressiveness that I used to wield so well. "It's all good, really."

—

Toward the end of summer, I do the thing I've been putting off since the memories resurfaced. I google Mr. Hubert.

I haven't been ready before, but I'm ready now, on a nondescript August day. Out in the back garden sitting on Hal's egg chair that she left behind, I take three huge volcano breaths and type his name into the search bar, then press Enter.

It doesn't take me long at all to filter through and find the correct person, a Robert Hubert of Plainwell, Michigan. The results make my stomach plummet.

He's dead. He died. Mr. Hubert is a goner.

Four years ago he lost his battle to cancer, as the obituary says. The obituary is long and glowing, so much more adoring than the one for Chris's brother, Luke, which just makes me ruminate on the injustice of it all.

In all the internet search results for Mr. Hubert, there are no mentions of anyone reporting him as a child abuser or sexual offender. No mentions of lawsuits, no evidence at all that he was anything more than "a larger-than-life, salt-of-the-earth man who was beloved by his whole community," as the flowery language of the obituary says.

My stomach feels bloated and empty all at once. I sit there swinging back and forth on the egg chair, my legs kicking out. The lack of closure closes in on me.

I'd thought maybe this could give me a sense of purpose, bringing his atrocities into the light, helping protect others against his evils.

But now there is no lawsuit for me to pursue, no poetic justice to serve.

"You coward," I snarl aloud to Mr. Hubert. "Going and dying before I could press charges and make everyone see you for who you really are."

I suppose I could still go public with my story, but it hits differently when you're accusing a dead man. Not just the optics of it—I don't care about that—but there'd be no sense that my trauma was really helping anyone. I could donate to a nonprofit or even start one myself, but the news that Mr. Hubert is six feet under has taken the wind out of my sails.

Maybe it was my ego wanting the attention of a sensational lawsuit, but the motive has some good in it too. Everything is tangled. Isn't that just how life is?

To counteract the rage or maybe just add more, I look up Chris's wedding site to see if he and Olivia are married yet. It turns out they're not, which makes me more relieved than it should, as if I still think there's time to sabotage the whole thing. My ruinous tendencies are still there, but I'm not going to indulge them like I used to.

The wedding will be October 3 at the Plaza Hotel. It's as typical of a venue as I would've expected, all chandeliers and New York opulence. I don't scheme to crash it, just put a card in the mail congratulating them and apologizing to Olivia.

It's not any grand confession or anything. I just tell her that I feel bad that we got off on the wrong foot and I hope we can all do something together soon. I'm not expecting them to take me up on this but I feel better inside, like I've scrubbed away some of the muck that I thought made me cool but actually just made me cruel.

I put in a little gift for Arnie too, a "best man" chew toy. It's pretty adorable. I know Chris will like it and I hope Olivia will too. It's pretty obvious now how Olivia was never to blame at all. She didn't force Chris to be with her. He chose that with his own free will and I was just too jealous to accept it.

Chris ends up calling me to thank me. I let it go to voicemail and I listen to the voicemail a lot of times in a row, but then I delete it. That part isn't out of spite; it's out of respect. He's about to marry another woman and I don't want to tempt him or tempt myself. I unfollow him on social media too.

Tara seems surprised by these developments, says she's proud of how far I've come. "Now you can start opening yourself up to new people who are actually emotionally available," she tells me one morning while we're sizzling up some blueberry pancakes for breakfast. I've started getting up earlier now so I don't miss so much of the day.

"No thanks," I say. The thought of meeting someone new doesn't excite me; it just makes me feel like I let something precious drop through my fingers onto the concrete and shatter. "And what about you? Why haven't you professed your love to Niles yet?"

Her face contorts. "I don't want to mess things up."

"The only way you can mess it up is if you let fear hold you back," I reply, since I've pretty much become a fortune cookie these days. "Now I'm giving you three days or I'll do it for you. And you know I'm not joking."

Tara is cramped with nerves. She rocks her knees back and forth on the couch. I sit down next to her and give her a side hug. "Look," I say. "Maybe I'm not the best role model on the whole relationship thing, but just go for it. You don't want to have regrets. Trust me."

"What about your view that monogamy is monotonous?" Tara wants to know.

"Well, it depends how deeply you dive into another person's spirit and grow with them," I say. "We all have a choice about how boring or interesting our relationships are. Confinement doesn't always come in the form of commitment. Sometimes it's the opposite. And on that note," I go on, "I think it's time to formally announce that I've dissolved the Anti-Marriage Pact."

Tara's brown eyes bulge. Maybe she's been trying to ignore the signs that we were headed that way, headed to the end, which is actually the beginning. I wish Tara could've been up there on the mountain with me and the fawn and the stars. Then she'd understand.

"Here's the thing," I explain, trying to help her see the starlight. "Rules against convention can be just as confining as conventional rules. That's something the divine woman helped crystalize for me. Being free doesn't have anything to do with whether we get married or not. It has to do with how liberated we are in our choices to marry or not marry, and then how we heal and grow and love with someone else and most of all with ourselves."

Tara runs her hands through her Afro, untamed these days. It's like she's trying to convince herself that I'll get bored of my enlightened self and go back to how I was before. I have to admit I'm kind of scared of that happening too, but at the same time I know that it's a permanent shift—that once a blind woman can see, she doesn't wear eyepatches just for the hell of it, except maybe on Halloween.

"So by that logic, you might get married?" she asks me, like she's trying to catch me in my own trap so I'll backtrack on the whole thing.

"Perhaps." There's a thrill at how many doors have been flung wide open. Not just with relationships but with everything else that I'd previously prohibited. "It's still unlikely," I admit. "But I'm open to evolving and you should be open too. If you want to be with Niles, then just go for it. I'll buy you three pints of pea milk ice cream if it doesn't work out. How's that?"

"Pea milk ice cream is disgusting," Tara says. "I'll need the coconut milk kind. And make it five pints, not three."

"You're worth the splurge," I assure her. "Now woman up and tell him how you feel."

Chapter 36

MY PEP TALK MUST BE AN inspirational one because Tara and Niles become an official item soon after. Apparently Niles was wanting to make a move and they were both waiting it out. Life can be like that, one big game of chicken.

Without the clubs and all the love affairs—or lust affairs I guess I should call them, now that I can see their flimsy frames in daylight—I need other things to focus on. I set myself a goal of reaching one hundred rejections of any kind. It feels overly analytical to have a number in mind like that, but I like the clarity it brings. How it'll mean I'm really trying and going for things that I wouldn't have in the past.

I work hard on a script, three full acts. It's an expansion of the concept I dreamed up on the mountain about the woman who falls to her death and confronts all her regrets. It feels good to sit down and see something through to the end. I always kind of knew what I was doing, what I was avoiding, by jumping from script to script, the same way I knew what I was doing by jumping from body to body. But it's amazing how much you can justify and deny your own actions until suddenly it all comes crashing down so you can rise again.

I submit the play to a bunch of contests and theater companies and agents and managers, and by the time September arrives, I've gotten thirty-eight rejections and am waiting to hear from a couple dozen more. Sometimes success doesn't start as success, I keep reminding myself. More often success starts as failure that you refuse to interpret as failure. You look at it as a stepping stone instead of a sunken stone.

It feels good to take a hammer to the walls of fear I've been living within for so long, so I do an audit of the rest of my life to see where else I can shatter old habits. One thing that bubbles up is how scornful I've been of anyone who works a corporate job, even though I've never done it myself. I decide I'll make up my mind about it from the inside, so I apply to a bunch of Wall Street firms in Manhattan because those really are the worst of the worst, all those men sitting around making billion-dollar trades to their fraternity brothers, off gallivanting on their yachts while the rest of us hustle around driving Ubers or pouring coffee or playing drums at subway stations to put a roof over our heads. At least that's the view I've always had.

The job applications ask for a résumé, which I don't have, so I upload a photo of a sunflower whose petals are just starting to unfurl in the sunlight. That's really the most honest résumé there is. Anything else is just ego. I'm tempted to reach out to Chris to ask him for connections in the finance industry, but I don't. This is something I've got to do alone.

I don't get any interviews, what a shocker, but the rejections don't get me down. I just add them to the tally. Then I download one of those apps where you can trade stocks with your own money because who needs the Wall Street gatekeepers anyway?

I buy shares of different companies, diversifying picks so I don't have all my eggs in the same basket. One of my portfolio companies is an airline that's been in the news for having some plane crashes. I load up on that one because I figure they'll get their act together and come back stronger than ever—I know all about that. Then I buy this woman's digital health company and some shares of Uber because I'm hoping they'll pay their drivers more if their stock price goes up. I'm strategic like that.

It's pretty addicting to watch my few hundred dollars go up and down and back up again. Some days I lose half my money but other days it triples; it's quite the rush. I'm still an adrenaline junkie even though I'm off the drugs. I just get my thrills in different ways.

I text Hal for investing advice. She doesn't make any snide comments about how I've been a terrible friend since she married Astrid. She just comes over and we sit out in the garden like old times.

She gets on her high horse telling me all about how I shouldn't be investing in individual stocks because that's way too risky. "You should get an index fund that's benchmarked to the S&P 500," she advises. "And then just let your money sit there for decades without touching it and come back and check on it when you need it for retirement."

"Where's the fun in sitting and waiting?" I ask. "I like to be in the heart of the action, you know that."

Hal gets a kick out of me, says it does seem like a healthier outlet than the booze and the bodies and all that, so she's supportive. "You should join one of those social media forums where day traders talk about what stocks to buy and sell and all that," she says. "You'd be a natural ringleader."

It's a decent idea, so I make an account right there. My username is @RedstockingRebel and I immediately like the forum's energy. Everyone's trying to screw Wall Street and help Main Street. The issue is that nearly everyone on there is a man, so I start a chat called "Women's Revolt." Within a few weeks, there are over five hundred women on there and they're all talking about how they're tired of men making all the money, talking their big games about investing. They want in too. It's about time.

Who knew that stock trading would actually be part of my contribution to women's liberation, but I guess it makes perfect sense because money is power. You can sit back and point your middle fingers at the system like I used to do, or you can wiggle in through the window and make it better from within.

Building a stock trading community for women injects me with a similar type of empowerment to what I was hoping to feel by making Mr. Hubert pay for his evils. It makes me realize that I don't always need to route my rage into direct revenge. I can channel it into different avenues too, different outputs of the same origin.

Hal is impressed with my work. "When our start-up goes public," she tells me, "we can get everyone in your chat to buy the stock and push the price high. Rig the system, but legally."

Tara and Jenni join the Women's Revolt community too, and the whole thing brings the Redstockings closer again. Though it's not really the trading that does that. It's how I've finally gotten out of my own way enough to see that Jenni and Hal didn't betray me by getting married. It wasn't the sword in the back that it felt like at the time, just a blade cutting them free from the ropes I'd tied around their wrists.

Chapter 37

SOME DAYS I FEEL LIKE I have it all figured out, and some days I slip right back down again.

I guess it'll always be like that. Baggage never goes away and I wouldn't want that. That would mean erasing everything that's brought me to where I am today, and I don't want to delete the past; I just want it to be lighter so it doesn't press down on me so hard. Get some baggage with wheels, I guess.

There are a lot of nights when I wake up with these awful flashbacks about the things I did in my past and the things that were done to me. I cringe and sweat and scream at myself.

Maybe that's the final stage of freedom: self-forgiveness. Extending grace to yourself and not just other people.

I'm sort of like a thirty-two-year-old newborn, having to unlearn everything before I can learn it again. It's basically triple the work. I'm not asking for credit, but it would be nice to be recognized for it, that's all I'm saying. The divine woman gives me a nudge to remind me that she recognizes me, and that's the most important approval I can get. It's just like her to yank me out of my sulky mood when I'd prefer to stay and wallow for a while.

I get all jumpy and my body tightens as September scoots along, too fast. October 3 is right around the corner: Chris and Olivia's wedding. It gives me cold feet, which is a ridiculous reaction considering I'm not the one getting married.

I wonder if Chris is having cold feet too. I wonder if he's thinking about me at all. I hope he's not. I hope his feet are nice and toasty warm and he's just thinking about Olivia and how excited he is to build a life with her. When I'm actually prioritizing his happiness above my own and not just pretending to prioritize it, that's when I finally know, or at least admit, that I guess I am in love with him after all.

"Took you long enough to admit it," Tara says when I tell her.

"It's not like I didn't know I loved him," I say. "I was just waiting for my feelings to wear off. But I guess some never do."

It's been over three years now that I've known Chris, and he's still swirling around in my thoughts day and night, dawn and dusk. It doesn't really make sense, but none of the best things do.

Even if I never get to be with him, it's still a big deal to know that I can feel safe around a man. Maybe that was the whole point of getting to know him. It wouldn't be my favorite moral to the story, but it's not the worst one either.

One afternoon, eight days before the wedding, I'm walking around Bushwick, listening to Elijah the trumpet player, still on his same street corner. I hum along loudly, not even to try to annoy other people. I'm just doing it to express some melodies that have been bunched up for years and years and now just want a chance to be out in the air, floating or sinking, whichever is most authentic. The music massages the parts of me I can only see were sick now that I'm starting to get healthy.

My phone buzzes. Chris's name flashes on the screen. I immediately assume something horrible has happened to him or Arnie.

"Chris, what's wrong?" I say, picking up.

"Hey, I'm okay," he says, voice calm. "All good."

I'm relieved, but something still seems off. "What's going on? Why are you calling me?"

"Olivia's gone."

By the way he says it, I can tell that Olivia didn't just leave to go to a hot yoga class or get a five-hundred-dollar facial. She's actually gone. Not dead but the relationship is over, the wedding is off.

I'm not nearly as pleased about this news as I ought to be, which is how I again verify that my love for Chris is the pure kind, the real kind. It's unfortunate, but beautiful too.

"Want me to come over?" I ask. He doesn't say anything, but I can hear him nodding, clenching his jaw.

"Be right there," I tell him and gallop off to the subway station as fast as my feet can carry me.

I find Chris sitting on the floor of his apartment. His back is hunched, resting up against the couch. He's staring at the wall, which is now completely bare, devoid of all the old photographs. Arnie is snuggled up loyally on his lap like he knows perfectly well what's going on.

I sit down next to them. "Was it the pool boy at her parents' Hamptons estate?" I ask, trying to get a smile out of Chris. It doesn't work. Chris just keeps staring blankly at the wall.

"Olivia didn't cheat," he says. "It was my fault."

"You're the one who ended things?" I say it gently, but he winces like I've slapped him, which gives me the sensation that I've slapped myself.

He says that's right. "I don't really know why I did it. I can't pinpoint it exactly."

The fact that he can't find a logical explanation seems to frustrate him to no end. I imagine his analytical brain is going insane trying to understand why one plus one didn't equal two.

He tells me that his anxiety was acting up as the wedding approached, his thoughts kept racing, and he couldn't sleep. "It felt like nothing was wrong, but something wasn't right."

"That's really good you listened to your intuition," I say, because it's true. I'm impressed, and I'm also trying my best to start building him back up. It'll be a long process, but we've got to start somewhere.

I ask if it just happened today and he says yeah, they'd been having conversations for the last few weeks, but it all came to a head this morning when he floated the idea of postponing the wedding to give them more time to figure things out. Olivia freaked out and said that either Chris was ready to commit to her today or he'd never be ready and she wasn't just going to sit around waiting and wasting the prime of her life. "She said she's thirty and wants to start a family soon. And she thought I did too because we've talked about it a million times. So she wanted to know what changed, and I didn't have an answer. I didn't have an answer," he repeats.

My heart kind of goes out to Olivia on that one. She's a victim of the patriarchy and societal programming and the biological inequity of women's fertility. But I also have to come to Chris's defense. He was speaking up even at the risk of conflict. "It's better that you realized you're not the right fit now rather than after you made it official."

We sit there for another stretch of time, five minutes or maybe an hour.

"I kept thinking about what you said about how I was trying to live out Luke's dream life, not my own," Chris finally says. "And maybe there was a little truth in it, at least when it came to Olivia."

This should give me a nice boost—Chris is admitting I was right after all. But it just scrapes me because I don't want this breakup to be my fault. I don't want to have messed with his head. I should've had more tact.

"I'm sorry for overstepping my boundaries," I say. "That wasn't right."

He says no, he isn't trying to put the blame on me or anything; he would've been having doubts anyway. Talking about Luke with me just kind of helped Chris see himself in third person, he says. A boy sprinting his whole life to keep up with his brother. And now when his brother isn't there anymore, the boy—now a man, or at least trying to be—just keeps sprinting faster through the same trees so he doesn't have to pick his head up and see the big forest and wonder where he is and where he's going and why.

"Look who's gotten all introspective," I say.

Chris gives me a scrap of a smile, not much, but I'll take it. I'll take whatever I can get from this man. I don't mean that in a pick-me way or anything. I'm just being honest that I've missed him and little bits of him are better than no bits at all.

"Well, I started going to therapy," he says. "So I guess I have to credit you for that."

"No credit needed. It turns out my own genius isn't even mine. It comes from someplace higher, someplace prettier. So," I say, just about holding my breath. "Are you missing Olivia?"

Chris nods, the kind of nod that says he can't speak because it's too hard to swallow.

"You could still go after her," I hear myself say. I resent the words but I revere them too, if there's a chance they could help Chris feel better. "If you regret it, you could talk through the Luke stuff with her and work it out. You could still get married if you want to."

"Let me get this straight," Chris says, talking slowly. "You, the founder of the Anti-Marriage Pact, are telling me to get married?"

"I'm not telling you to get married. I'm just saying it's still an option," I clarify. "And as for the pact, it's been dissolved. Turns out I was kind of misguided in my views. Sure, marriage can be a cage, but so can being single. It's really a case-by-case thing. Commitment isn't necessarily suffocating if your partner lets you evolve and supports you as you do. At least that's my current perspective. I'm still learning."

Chris looks at me, really looks at me, for the first time all afternoon. His gaze doesn't make me want to close my eyes or hide behind a sarcastic joke like it usually does. I want him to see how my steel shell has cracked open, how my spirit is oozing out of my body like crepuscular rays from storm clouds.

"It's really good to see you again, Emily Jane," Chris says.

"Yeah," I say, still not breaking eye contact. "It's good to see me again too."

This gets him grinning, which makes me grin too.

"And you too," I add. "Obviously."

Chapter 38

AS WE'RE CATCHING UP IN HIS apartment that afternoon, Chris asks what happened to me.

I tell him that I accidentally found the divine woman. "Hiding inside me this whole time, what a prankster," I say with a snort. "Story for another time, but look, I'm just saying if you're having second thoughts about Olivia, I'll support you if you want to get back with her."

He soaks that up and then he says that he doesn't want to get back with her, that there's this whisper of relief at the bottom of the hurt that tells him it was the right thing. "But it doesn't make it easier," he says. "One second I was picturing growing old with her, pushing her around in her wheelchair and putting wool socks on for her when her arthritis gets too bad to bend over. And the next second she's out the door, gone forever. It's just not natural to flip a switch on love like that." He pauses for a breath that seems to get clogged in his throat.

Taking a big gulp, I pay Chris a compliment. It's clunky as it trips off my tongue. "Look, Chris, I'm proud of you," I say. "It's not easy to jump off a speeding train. It takes a lot of guts, and you're doing great. It's a real honor to be your friend."

Chris, too, seems to find my praise jarring but doesn't comment on it. He just asks what I mean about jumping off the speeding train.

"Getting off the life path you were on," I elaborate. "It's a hard thing to change direction against all that inertia."

"Was it hard for you to get off the life path you were on as a kid?" he probes. "The more conventional track?"

It catches me off guard because not many people ask about my past life. Usually I prefer it that way, but not now. I want to tell Chris the truth. Lies don't have the allure that they used to.

"Not really," I say. "I always felt a bit out of place just by existing. I didn't really have friends or that sort of thing. I was ready to be out of the house from the time I was about twelve."

I think about telling him about Mr. Hubert and the piano lessons gone wrong. I don't, not now, but I will at some point. That acknowledgment feels good in itself, knowing that I'm no longer repressing the truth or silencing it, that I'm just choosing to share it another time, on my terms. Tonight is about Chris.

"So when I got to college, I was lit on fire with rebellion," I carry on. "The flames were my savior. It was pretty easy to burn the old order down to the ground. The harder thing has been realizing that okay, maybe I overshot the target. Maybe all men aren't misogynists, maybe all commitment isn't confinement."

I fill him in on my trip upstate and the fuzzy little fawn and how I met the divine woman, or more accurately, how I realized I'd met her long ago. "I'm trying to reconnect with my intuition, which is also the cosmic knowing, which is also the sacred feminine energy in Mary Magdalene's teachings. They're all part of the same divine force," I explain, like I've just received my PhD on the topic and tossed my tasseled cap up into the air for effect. "And I'm actually semi-supportive of Jenni's and Hal's marriages now. I even told Tara to go for the guy she's in love with. They're getting serious, and look, I've barely got any spite." I smile-grimace to prove the point and poke fun at myself.

Chris rests his arm on my shoulder. It makes me jolt. All those years of feeling nothing while throwing myself at strangers, and here I am out of breath just from Chris's arm around my shoulder. I'm getting soft but I like it that way.

"I sure missed a lot while I was trying to stay away from you," he says.

"You were trying to stay away?" I ask.

"Of course I was. Thought you knew that."

"I suspected." This right here is happiness, I decide, the whole basin of it. Knowing you were missed and knowing you don't have to be anymore. "Now let's order some pizza. I'm starving," I say.

Arnie wags his tail at that. I place an order from Dona Bella's. Chris tries to pay but I won't hear of it. "You should never have to buy your own pizza after a breakup. That's one rule I'm holding on to," I say. "Plus, I'm a stock trader now. I've got some earnings to blow through."

I show him the Women's Revolt chat on my trading app. It's up to nearly ten thousand members—not that scale indicates success, but it's still kind of cool. We talk about investing for a bit and Chris says I could teach the guys on Wall Street a thing or two.

"Yeah, I could, but I'd rather teach the women on Main Street," I say. "We're the ones who've been sidelined for centuries."

"Fair point," Chris says and tells me about a woman accountant he hired on his team. He's worried she feels out of place with all the guys and asks for my advice. This says a lot about Chris, that he's thinking about how to help someone else when his engagement and all his life plans have just fallen through.

Chris says it's nice to be able to bounce ideas off me again.

"Yeah, I'm pretty great," I say. "But I have more humility now. Haven't you noticed?"

We share a smile at that, and then the pizza arrives and we eat it right there on the floor. I keep staring at the bare wall. The white paint looks like it's stinging from having the pictures ripped off it so fast. The nail holes are still there, big and gaping. It gives me an idea.

"Hey, Chris, do you care about getting your security deposit back?" I ask.

He tells me he doesn't have a security deposit since he owns the apartment. The way he says it is very unassuming, but I make a face. How could I not? "Must be nice," I say, though I'm happy about it because it means we can have a marvelous time shaking up this place.

Hopping up, I say I'll be back in a few, that I need to run some errands. I zoom over to the craft store down the street and load up on paint, balloons, and glitter. Then I pop into the Patriot Saloon and swipe some darts. It's quite a rush and doesn't even make me feel bad, which makes me feel good that the new me can still enjoy illegal activities on occasion.

"Time to create some masterpieces on the blank canvas of our lives," I tell Chris as I unload the art supplies back at his place. Filling the balloons with paint, I tape them to the wall. Then I roll up the edge of his expensive-looking rug and lay down some plastic bags so we don't fully trash the place. Not that I'd mind, but Chris wouldn't like it.

I put Arnie in his crate so he doesn't eat the paint and get sick. He gets all pouty and I tell him that I know, cages are the worst, but we just have to help his dad feel better and then I'll give him extra treats later.

"Give it a try," I tell Chris, handing him a dart. "Nothing is permanent," I remind him because I can tell he's making an internal list of all the things that could go wrong. "We can always start over without actually starting from scratch."

Chris doesn't join in my philosophical musings. He just takes off his button-down shirt so he's only wearing the T-shirt underneath. He looks better than good. The first dart he throws hardly makes it to the wall, just grazes the very bottom.

"Weak," Chris says, which is exactly what I'm thinking but I don't like it when he's mean to himself.

"Decent first attempt," I say. "You just need more velocity. Try again."

He does and it's a little better but not much. He's still holding back like there's a blockage in his body.

"Watch this," I say, because I can't resist showing off. I throw a line drive right into the middle of a balloon. Bull's-eye. Neon green paint splatters out and runs confidently down the wall. The whole apartment instantly brightens. It's almost like water has been poured over a patch of parched earth, soaking into the cracks.

Picking up the winning dart, I put it in Chris's hand. "Okay, try this," I say. "Pretend like this little dart has never been outside this apartment. And this throw is its one and only chance to break out and fly through the sky, feel the wind, taste the air."

I'm speaking in my theatrical voice, getting all carried away with the drama because I guess I've still got an itch to perform. "And you, Chris," I say, "are in charge of this dart's destiny. Are you going to make it count or what?"

Chris evaluates the dart like he's trying to imagine my story coming true. Then he nods, bites his lip, and throws it like he means it, like he's trying to drill a hole through the wall. It punctures a balloon, and red paint drips down on top of my green. The best part of it all is the look in Chris's eyes as he throws it. *Tenacious*: There's no other word for it.

"How'd that feel?" I ask. He doesn't answer, just picks up another dart and does it again and again and again until the wall is a glorious splatter paint creation. A colorful slice of the cosmos blending the inner world and the outer world until there's no delineation between the two.

"Now that's what modern art should be." I applaud. "We could open our own gallery in Williamsburg and charge tens of thousands for our work."

"I'm not an artist," Chris says. "I'm just an accountant."

"False," I say. "Everyone's got both parts inside of us. The problem is that society makes us believe that we're actually only a half circle on our own, that we need another human to complete us. So people go around clipping their own wings so they don't ruffle someone else's feathers. Or worse yet, they never even realize they have wings. They just waddle around like flamingos, birds that can't fly their whole lives."

"I'm a flamingo then," Chris says, all dejected.

"Of course you're not," I snap, a bit harsher than I mean to be. "That wasn't my point at all. You're on a brave and colorful flight, and moving on from Olivia is part of that journey."

I wish I hadn't brought her name up. Chris's energy slumps and I know he's thinking about her, feeling her absence and all the lonely days that are on their way. "I should get some sleep," he says.

"Okay, sure," I say quickly. "I've got to get home anyway." I'm wishing he'd offer up the spare room, but it's best for both of us that he doesn't. "I have morning yoga with Tara tomorrow," I add. "I can touch my toes now if I bend my knees. It's pretty impressive."

After giving Arnie his treats, I pocket one of the darts to keep as a souvenir and show myself out.

Chapter 39

IN THE DAYS AND WEEKS THAT follow, I check in on Chris here and there, and we go on a couple walks with Arnie, but I make sure I'm not his emotional crutch. That wouldn't be helping anyone. I understand more now about the value of grappling with the silence inside yourself before you can figure out who you are, what you want, and all those other juicy existential questions.

It means I devote more time to the Redstockings. I tell Hal and Jenni what I remembered up at Breakneck Ridge. Hal brainstorms different businesses I could start—a nonprofit or a sexual offender tracker app or a song production platform to help people heal through music. I have no desire to pursue any of those, but it's still nice knowing she's on my side, seeing my own fury and hurt bubble up in her blue eyes. Jenni hugs me for about two hours straight and then showers me with gift cards to expensive vegan restaurants, which is pretty great too.

All of it helps the Redstockings spring back from the dead with weekly potlucks in the garden all fall. Attendance is pretty good and there's a lot to celebrate. Hal and Astrid raise fifty thousand dollars in pre-seed funding for their app. That sounds like a shit ton of money to me, but Hal says it's just baby dollars, that they've got a long way to go.

"Okay, Hal, but don't be so laser focused on the destination that you forget to do some cartwheels on the journey," I advise, because I'm quite the sage these days.

Jenni's got updates too. She's thriving as a new mom, says she's found her passion after all this time. The way her whole body lights up when she says it, I can tell it's the path that's truest for her, at least in this season, and I feel some guilt for all the judgmental things I used to say about stay-at-home moms. I probably stunted Jenni's path a bit, but she got there in spite of me and it makes it all the better.

Tara and Niles are going strong, and I ask Tara if he might want to move into the Inn. It would help me save on rent but it's more than that. I want to show that I approve of their relationship so I don't wind up pushing Tara away like I did with Jenni and Hal.

"Niles and I are actually thinking about getting our own place," Tara tells me, looking sheepish as can be. "It's obviously nothing against you or the Inn. We just feel like we're ready for that step."

The news hits me harder than I thought it would. "Good for you," I mutter, sardonic spice sprinkled back on. I can't help my injured instincts. It's not like I hadn't suspected this was coming, and it really is good to see Tara taking such big leaps. Her choices are reflecting her hopes, not her fears. But I still put up a good pout because this means I'll have to move out of the Inn. I have no interest in finding a new roommate; it would be too much of a letdown after the Redstocking era, and I can't swing the rent on my own even being the savant of a stock trader that I am. Equities have been tumbling down recently, a ruthless bear market.

"You don't need to move out," Hal says as we're talking about it over dinner one night, chowing down on falafel and breadsticks. "You just need to find a way to monetize the Inn. It's basically a historic landmark as the Redstockings' headquarters. You could charge people for tours."

"Yeah, I anticipate massive crowds lining up to pay big money to see a grimy basement apartment where four unknown women lived," I say wryly.

"Hal's onto something, though," Tara pipes up. "This garden is incredible. You could open up a restaurant."

"Except for the fact that I hate cooking and our kitchen would never pass the health and safety exam." I feel myself withdrawing behind my armor. I hate the habit, but it's one I don't think I'll ever fully get over. Even now that I'm enlightened, I don't feel light all the time. The darkness is still there; I just have greater peace that it'll pass soon if I let it, which I don't always want to.

"You could turn it into a bar," Tara goes on. "Recruit the Lone Wolf crowd over and have your own speakeasy. I'd bartend for you."

"I appreciate the help, but I'm going to start looking for a studio apartment. Or maybe I'll just rent out someone's closet and put a sleeping bag in there," I say to elicit maximum sympathy. "It won't be that bad."

It feels bad, though—very bad. The Inn is the first place where I've ever really felt at home. The only place that's made me feel truly safe and like I was enough. It's how the walls wink joyfully at me, how the floorboards never make me feel like I'm taking up too much space, how the sun gushes through the tiny windows to illuminate the shadows, how the double lock on the front door never falters.

"I've got it," Jenni says. She's looking around the garden like she's seeing it for the very first time. "You can turn this place into an outdoor theater."

The rest of us stare at her for a second, trying to digest the suggestion.

"I can't believe I never thought of it before," Jenni prattles on. "The stage can be there." She points to a spot in front of the ivy-lined wall. "And then some folding chairs here. And then we can serve drinks back there."

Jenni's swiveling her head this way and that, and Tara's nodding along. "It's perfect, EJ," Tara says. "You can write the scripts and then see them come to life right here. Charge people for tickets. You'll have your own theater company."

"A one-stop shop," Hal says, joining in. "You'll stick it to the bureaucratic theater industry for shutting you out for so long. Just like you skipped over gatekeepers to bring stock trading to the masses. You can call it the Populists' Playhouse."

"The Populists' Playhouse," I repeat, peeling out of my bad mood like a ripe banana.

So I start planning it out hypothetically. I run the numbers and determine that to cover rent plus utilities, I'd need to sell eighty-three tickets a month at thirty dollars a pop, and that's not even counting the cost of the chairs and stage and all that. The garden could probably fit twenty people, maybe twenty-five, and I could write a new script every month and perform the same show one or two nights a week.

But I don't find the answer in the math; I find it in the aftermath. How I'm bouncing off the walls like a kid on a sugar high. I've got to go for it and if I fail trying, it'll still be less of a failure than not trying. Or at least that's what I keep repeating to myself.

My first play will be a short, I decide. It'll just have two actors and be about fifteen minutes. Start small and scale up from there, as Hal says. This also means I won't have to pay for a cast because Tara and I can do it all ourselves.

With this grand plan underway, Tara feels less guilty about leaving me. She and Niles move into their own place in East Williamsburg. It's not far away, but I shed some tears because it still marks the end of a chapter I wasn't done reading.

On my first day as the Dunge Inn's lone resident, I go into the garden and do some yoga on my own to adjust to the new energy. It's not as lonely as I thought it would be because the divine woman is still there. I can never shake her and that's one of my favorite things: how I can't sabotage our relationship no matter how hard I try. She's EJ-proof and that's no small feat.

During a wobbly tree pose, my mind wanders to how many years I spent accidentally imprisoning the Redstockings. I start getting all self-critical, but then the perspective shifts and I can observe it from the outside without the icky attachment. And it hits me that this is the greatest plotline for a play.

After savasana, I open up my computer and type up a ten-page satire from the perspective of a zookeeper who gets some cheetahs to believe they're living in the wild African savannah when really she's keeping them trapped in a tiny backyard in central Florida. The dialogue is between me (the zookeeper) and Tara (one of the cheetahs who's caged). It's this amazingly self-aware critique, totally brilliant.

Tara isn't sure what to make of the script at first, but once she sees me laughing about it, she starts laughing too and can't stop. "I wasn't sure if you meant it as a comedy or not."

"Of course I did," I say. "I'm very self-aware these days. It makes for delicious satire."

"Proud of you," Tara says, and I know she's not just talking about the script.

Opening night is the beginning of November, that lovely time of year when the leaves are still tacked on the trees but the air is crisp and cool. I've sold twenty-three tickets and budgeted a 10 percent no-show rate, per Hal's recommendation, but everyone who RSVPs shows up, and even two more buy tickets at the door. I guess it should be a vote of confidence, but it makes me nervous instead.

Jenni has arranged the garden perfectly. She's brought back the

Christmas lights that she stole and strung them again. Instead of chairs, we decided on cushions on the ground for people to sit on. It's more relaxed and helps everyone in the back see better since we don't actually have a real stage. Tara and I are just going to imagine we have a full-blown set and trust the audience to catch up.

It's a motley crew that shows up, a bunch of locals I recruited. It wasn't hard with a name like the Populists' Playhouse; there's never been anything more Bushwicky. Elijah the trumpet player is there and my landlord comes too. I gave him a free ticket so he can see how I'm turning our building into a cultural mecca and in hopes that he won't put a stop to all the fun or evict me if it's a total bust and I come up short again for rent.

Then there's the Manhattan crowd. It's easy to spot them, all collars and ties. Chris bought tickets for the eight people he manages at his accounting firm. It'll be a good team-building outing, he's told me—more inclusive than golf, right?

It's pretty great to see how he's supporting me, though I'm not sure I want him here. It makes the stakes feel higher. He wishes me luck and sits down on his cushion and doesn't even look too worried about his pristine suit getting dirty. He's come pretty far, Chris has.

Hal's cousins are there too, visiting from South Dakota and soaking up the satisfaction that comes from experiencing a locals' night out rather than falling into the Times Square tourist trap.

It's BYOB, and everyone's got their wine bottles and flasks. Just because I'm all on my high horse about being sober doesn't mean I don't want other people to guzzle down the alcohol. They'll be a much easier crowd that way and I'm really not sure how good the play is. That's one of the not-so-great things about staying away from the drinks and drugs. I overthink things more.

"Welcome, everyone, to the grand opening of the Populists' Playhouse," I say from the stage, too jittery to breathe through my mouth, so I'm just taking these nasally inhales. "This play is called

The Zookeeper's Downfall. It's loosely inspired by a true story. Hope you enjoy it, and stick around after to mingle. We've got to mix the Brooklyn and Manhattan people. Right now we're like oil and water." I ramble on because it's no secret that's what I do when I'm nervous. "Let's not forget we're all humans here, all woven from the same divine fabric."

Chris's coworkers exchange skeptical looks. But then the show starts and I tune out everything external. I just drop into myself as Tara and I channel our boldest Broadway dreams, the ones we haven't let die a natural death. The ones we've kept on ventilators and have now nursed back to full health despite the odds.

I can't tell how it's going while I'm performing and I don't try to because I know the show will lose something, lose everything, if I pop out of myself and start analyzing. We take our bows at the end and then it's over. Everyone is on their feet and maybe it just means Hal and Jenni are good at working the crowd, but I think it's something more. I think we nailed it.

There's real hope for the Populists' Playhouse to be featured in the Redstocking museum one day, though the idea of a museum feels less important now that I have a concept of how I might live on even after I'm dead. My physical death hopefully won't mean my actual death so long as I keep myself open enough that my spirit can spill out of my corpse and keep soaring.

People stay to mingle afterward. Some of the ties and suit jackets come off, which is a good sign. Slowly, everyone trickles out so it's just the Redstockings and Chris left. He's stuck around even though I haven't gotten to talk with him yet. I've been too inundated with admirers; it's a tough problem to have.

Chris chats with Jenni for a while but then Jenni's hugging me, telling me how little June is so lucky to have an aunt like me. It makes me almost wish I'd said yes to being her godmother, but aunt is better, really. Less pressure, more play.

Tara and Niles peel off with Hal and Astrid. It's clear what they're doing, trying to leave me alone with Chris. It's not going to work, though I wish it might.

"Don't you have to wake up early for work tomorrow?" I ask Chris as I'm unplugging the light strands. The garden is dark, lit only by the splash of interior lights from apartments bordering the courtyard.

"Are you trying to kick me out?" he says.

"No, I just know sleep is important to you," I reply.

"This is important to me too," he says. "You were amazing up there."

It's been a few months since the breakup with Olivia and he looks good, better than I've ever seen him actually. But maybe I'm just riding the rosy glow of how I just launched my own theater company and collected the money in cash so I don't have to pay taxes. It's hard to distinguish between the factors at play.

"Hope your coworkers didn't hate it," I say. "I know it was kind of out of their element."

"They loved it," he says. "So did the endings match up?"

I frown, confused. "What endings?"

"The first time we met," Chris says. "You told me how the ending the characters want and the ending the audience wants can't be the same. But it felt like they were the same in the play tonight. Both groups ultimately wanted the cheetahs to be set free, right?"

I can't believe he remembers that conversation we had way back when at the art gallery. It tickles me in a giggly kind of way. I try to think up a rebuttal, a way to point out a flaw in his argument, but I don't feel like being a contrarian tonight. "Yeah, I guess they can be aligned sometimes," I say. "If the playwright is a real genius and the audience aren't all idiots."

A smile drips out of Chris's closed-faucet face. He's getting closer, right in front of me. I want to kiss him but I can't. It'll ruin it, I'll ruin it, and Chris doesn't deserve that.

It happens fast. My knee goes into his groin. He loses his balance and yelps in pain, falling backward onto the wall of ivy. I stand there and watch, babbling some lame apology.

Chris cuts me off once he regains his breath. “You don’t need to explain yourself,” he says. “I got the message.”

His eyes are cold and glazed. It’s a horrible sight. I’m locked inside myself again, unable to find the key in time, or maybe I’m just not looking. Maybe I’ve lost it again on purpose. “Things are great as they are,” I say. “Let’s just stay friends, okay?”

“Sure,” he says. “If that’s what you want.”

I show him out the front gate. Then he’s gone and I’m sitting there trying to soak in the success of the night, but all I can think about is how I just pushed away one of the only people I’ve ever wanted to pull closer. I might be healed in some ways, but I’m still broken in others. I guess I always will be.

As I take a shower that night, the water lurches from cold to hot to cold again and I burn with both extremes. When my skin is red and shriveled, I finally turn off the shower and want to bash my head against the tile wall as retribution for how I fucked up everything with Chris. But I don’t give in to that desire.

I just reach for the softest towel off the rack and wrap myself up as gently as I can.

Chapter 40

IN THE DAYS AND WEEKS THAT follow, Chris and I both seem determined not to let anything change between us. I know he might meet someone else anytime now, but I'm just not there yet. I haven't had enough time rolling around in the sacredness of my own self to think about adding another person to the equation.

There's a lot to focus on other than that because I start putting on two performances a week at the Populists' Playhouse. Demand is greater than supply; we're sold out just about every night. Word of mouth spreads from the first shows, and then I post about it in my Women's Revolt stock trading forum and some of those people start coming too and telling their friends and it's this amazing intersection of New York's corporate and creative sphere. Everyone's bursting out of their little bubbles and nothing's better than the sound of a good pop.

By the time December rolls around, I'm able to afford space heaters for the garden and start paying Tara and myself a small salary. We even get written up on this website that reviews indie shows and concerts in New York. I'd have a lot of cash stockpiled by now if it weren't for all these itty-bitty clothes and playthings I keep buying for June. That stuff adds up but it's worth it; I love that little goon. I've declared myself co-godmother and Jenni agrees, says she knew I'd come around.

One night after a show, I'm walking around in the garden alone.

Everyone has cleared out and I have a whim to call my parents to share the news of how their delinquent daughter is making it in the big city after all. My mom picks up the phone right away. She's all freaked out, asking if I'm okay. It kind of cuts me to realize that I call so rarely, they assume it must be from the emergency room. She puts me on speakerphone and my dad comes over and joins. I tell them about the theater company I've founded, though I leave out the name of it. No need to get them riled. I expect them to ask when I'm getting a real job or a husband who can support me, but they're actually pretty interested, or at least pretend to be.

We could end the conversation right there, pocket the win, and avoid conflict. I nearly say goodbye, but my tongue catches and I know what I'm being asked to do.

"I need to tell you something else," I tell my parents over the phone. "It's about the piano lessons I took when I was little."

"Yes, we know you blame us for forcing you into hobbies that you hated," my mom says in a tired voice, anticipating the same old attacks. "But it didn't ruin you too badly. Look at what you're doing now."

"No," I say. "It's not about that."

I lay it all out there as minimally as I can, just the cold, hard facts, no gory details or anything, but my mom starts bawling and my dad drops more expletives than I've ever heard, even when the Lions lost the Super Bowl. They're aware that Mr. Hubert died—he was their neighbor after all—but they begin talking about how we should press charges against his widow because leave it to them to blame a woman somehow. I'm just kidding, sort of. I really do appreciate their outrage but I say no, I don't want to do that, I just want to move on. I'm not going to use the abuse as an excuse.

"Yeah, it was awful and it hurt me," I say. "It messed me up in ways I probably still don't fully understand, maybe never will. And I think I've been punishing both of you for this thing that you never even knew about."

"Well, of course you've been punishing us, honey, as you should," my mom says between hiccups. "Does your sister know?"

I say no, she doesn't, but this is why I fought so hard for her not to take piano lessons too, even though she resented me for it. I tell them that I don't want to keep circling over the past, I just want to live in the now, and it would be good if maybe our family could sort of start fresh?

"How about a family vacation soon?" my dad suggests. It sounds very quiet in the background, like he's turned off the TV, or at least muted it. "I start collecting Social Security next month. I can treat us all to a Caribbean cruise."

The suggestion feels like a big hug from him, the kind I used to wriggle out of but vow not to anymore. "I don't do cruises," I say. "But a beachside villa and swimming with dolphins wouldn't be the worst thing."

They say they would like that very much, or at least I think that's what my mom says. It's hard to understand her since she's still choked up, and my dad is all congested with emotion too. The old me would be thrilled about how worried they are about me, how they're beating themselves up over this thing that happened so long ago, but the new me doesn't want suffering to beget suffering. Though I have to admit it's a nice feeling to be heard and cared for in a way that I never thought I would from my parents ever again. They stopped showing up for me long ago, but maybe it was partially because I stopped giving them a chance to show up for me. It was easier to suffocate the shame in a coffin than let it air out in the cold. Easier to twist my parents into caricatures, complicit in the crime, than to see them as the complex characters they are.

After we say goodbye, there's this peace rippling around me, rippling in me. I have the urge to swat it away or do something dramatic to disrupt it because peace is boring, right? Peace means you're content with the way things are, and where's the inspiration or innovation in that? But the longer I breathe in the peace, the more I want to keep it, nurture it.

Maybe Chris has a point about contentment. Maybe contentment can carpet your life and free you up to do cartwheels and handstands and backflips without worrying about cracking your head on the cement because you know you'll have a soft landing no matter what. It's an interesting theory. I'll have to test it out a while longer, but for now at least I'm not feeling like contentment and happiness are rivals the way I used to think they were. It feels truer to me that contentment is a prerequisite for real happiness. I mean, how much can you really enjoy the flight up in the sky if you know you're going to shatter the second you hit the ground again?

Chapter 41

TARA PROPOSES TO NILES ONE NIGHT when they're drunk. It spurts out and sticks.

"I was going to take it back the next day," Tara tells me when we're together at home, recounting it all. "Because I thought I'd pressured him into it by popping the question out of nowhere. But he'd already posted about our engagement on his socials, so there was really no going back."

"You could still go back," I say. "If you're having doubts."

"I'm not," she says. "I mean, I'm nervous about the scale of the change, sure. But I have no doubt he's the person I want to build a life with. It's way scarier thinking of life without him than life with him."

"Damn," I say, feeling only slightly slighted at how I'm not that person for Tara anymore. "You're the queen of confidence these days."

"Learned it from you."

"Not when it comes to romantic relationships."

"I really am sorry to be doing this to you," Tara says, and it's clear she's been nervous about my reaction, no matter how supportive I've been of her and Niles. "Walking the marriage plank and leaving you by yourself."

"I'm not by myself, I'm with myself," I say, laughing at the cheese of it, the truth of it. "Besides, I don't really see marriage as a death plank anymore. It's more of a bridge that can be wobbly or well-built, depending on the people. And I have faith in you and Niles. I'd bet all my investments on your marriage, and that actually means a little something these days."

"Thanks, EJ," Tara says, both of us sloshy in the eyes. "I'll try not to let you down."

"It's no big deal if you do," I say. "Just don't let yourself down or my whole Redstocking reign would be a total waste."

Soon after, I go back to Michigan for my annual holiday trip. It hits differently this time, sort of like I've escaped the need to escape. Christmas Eve Mass no longer sends me spiraling. I just take it for what it is and think back to my first Communion at this church, what a trusting little kid I was. My heart rips for her, but I get the sense she'd actually be pretty proud of where we are now. Every life has dents; every life has detours. I'm not special really, though I like to think I am because my ego is still there; I can be objective about that.

Afterward we have dinner and my parents hardly even argue over how spicy the chili should be, though they do argue a little, just for the tradition of it. Then we take a family walk around the neighborhood to see the lights. My sister's husband stays back with the baby, a snarky toddler now whose favorite word is still "no," which makes me very glad to see. So it's just the four of us—my mom, my dad, my sister, and me. The originals.

When we pass Mr. Hubert's old house, my mom takes my gloved hand in hers and gives me a squeeze through the knitted wool.

I look at the green shutters, the nondescript gray siding, the snow-covered shingles in need of replacing. My head feels the spin, the stress, the sadness. But my body stays calm, not clamping up or burning or itching. It's like I've finally metamorphosed the abuse into fuel, expunged the evil to make space for openings, or something like that. Healing isn't linear—it's like I told Chris when we were talking about his brother—but for the most part my trajectory is upward, with a few jagged spikes because those shapes are more interesting than straight lines.

There's a For Sale sign in the snowy front yard.

"Mrs. Hubert must be moving," my sister observes. "Downsizing now that Mr. Hubert has taken up residence in heaven."

My dad snorts loudly. My sister says, "Bless you," but I know it wasn't a sneeze.

"Oh, I don't think he's in the good place," my dad says, very loudly, too loudly. His whole body seems to be quaking, tectonic plates ready to erupt.

My sister frowns. "Why not? He seemed like a nice enough guy. Not that I'd really know, since I never got the chance to take piano lessons." She huffs lightly.

My parents meet my eyes, taking the lead from me, which I appreciate. I shake my head imperceptibly. Now is not the time. I'll fill my sister in soon, over fresh mangos and melons in Hawaii. We have our family trip planned for the spring. No need to spoil the holiday cheer, and besides, my sister has enough on her plate with motherhood. Though to her credit she complains less than she used to, or maybe I'm just more perceptive to the positive things she says too.

"It turns out Mr. Hubert had a dark side to him," my mom tells my sister. "But we don't need to dwell on it."

"What do you mean?" my sister asks, looking hopeful that she's stumbled across a scintillating story she can share with her mom friends at *Bachelorette* watch parties. "Was he smuggling drugs or something?"

"Far worse," my mom says, her voice colder than the icy air, her jaw clenched into a pointy profile. "He was a murderer."

My sister gasps dramatically. "A murderer! In this neighborhood?"

My mom's words trickle over me as truth. She's right. He murdered innocence. He murdered girlhood. He murdered trust. He murdered dreams and princesses and pirates and possibilities.

And he nearly murdered my younger self—wonderful, spunky little Emily Jane. But he didn't, and what sweet victory is that. Reclaiming power after someone has stripped you, degraded you. Not doing it to prove anything to them but to prove everything to yourself. The flavor is tangy and sweet and salty all at once. I could bottle it up into the world's best barbecue sauce and make millions, but that's not really the point.

"Merry Christmas to you, old Hubert," my dad says, nearly spitting. "Hope you're feasting on flames in hell."

It gets me all shades of giddy to see my parents on my side like this. I felt the energy over the phone, but witnessing it in person is something else.

My sister is bug-eyed. "Dad!" she says, shocked. Then she turns to me. "But I mean if that's true, then it's a good thing you made it out of his house alive, Emily Jane."

A snowflake lands on my face, melting in the tears that I feel forming. I hope my parents and sister can hear my expression, translate the dampness into the *I love you* that it is. Judging by their faces, I think they can. I've never really thought I look like my family at all, but I think I look like them now. More than a little. A whole lot, really. It doesn't make me panic. It gives me peace.

"Yeah," I say, as we keep walking past Mr. Hubert's house, looping back toward my childhood home where we'll make a fire and put cider on the stove. "It really is."

Chapter 42

AFTER THE HOLIDAYS, I HEAD BACK to Brooklyn and curl up in the coziness of winter, cradling the creative flow that hasn't plugged up yet.

The garden shows are still selling out, even with the snow and sleet and subway delays. It seems my genius is weatherproof. I always had an inkling of that, but it's nice to see the proof, feel the evidence as cold, hard cash.

"You have groupies," Tara tells me one night as we clean up after a performance, stacking the foldable chairs against the garden wall. "That's when you know you've made it."

My insides swoop up like they're on the trapeze swing at the House of Yes, only better because I know I won't wake up with a headache tomorrow.

"*We* have groupies," I correct, since Tara is still doing all the shows with me. I'm gearing up for a bigger cast for a spring play, a parody about a dysfunctional Midwest family with an unreliable narrator. What would I know about that?

Tara squeals at that. "We have groupies," she repeats, and we start spitballing ideas for how we can amp up the effects of the courtyard theater.

"You know, Tara," I say, dead serious. "It's pretty great to see you putting more effort into our play than your wedding planning."

Tara frowns, like she's doing something wrong.

"I don't mean that in a spiteful or competitive way," I say. "It's just nice to see that you haven't been absorbed by the wedding industry's capitalistic, patriarchal pressures, that's all."

"I mean, I don't see the point of spending two years planning a six-figure party," Tara says, shrugging. "Niles and I have decided on something casual at the theater where we first met. The second weekend of February."

"Isn't that a little soon?" I say, feeling a tug to backtrack and tell her maybe she should spend a bit more time planning the wedding after all.

"I mean, we already made the big decision of committing to each other, so we both want to make it official sooner rather than later," Tara says. "I don't like how the engagement period kind of feels like limbo."

"You're not in limbo," I say. It seems to me like maybe Tara's rushing because the wedding is triggering old abandonment wounds. I nearly point this out to her, but I just swallow the seeds of critique and say, "Look, if that's what you want, then go for it." It feels pretty amazing to realize I'm not in charge of other people's choices or outcomes. My only job is to love her and be there for her no matter what. "And I guess there are some tax benefits to an accelerated timeline, too, since you and Niles can file jointly."

"You're like Hal with all that business jargon," Tara teases me.

"And you're like me with all those eye rolls," I reply.

We crack up at that, how we've all sprinkled bits of each other into our splintered parts. And even when we're not physically together, the changes stick, the new traits stay. Like alchemy, except it's actually real. No fraudsters here.

Tara's not doing bridesmaids, thank goodness, but she gives me a plus-one. I just RSVP for myself, though, no plus-one. I'm happy being the only single Redstocking left standing. Being the odd one out actually affirms my strength more than if the rest of my friends were single too. I'm not just going along with the pack.

But as Tara's wedding gets closer, something doesn't feel totally right. I go for a swim in my spirit to find the epicenter of the weirdness. Turns out that even though I'd have a grand ole time solo, I want to take Chris to the wedding as my date. I want to toss him a dramatic eye roll when Tara and Niles start crying during their vows, and I want to steal his sweet potato fries from the plant-based burger place that's catering. I want to spin him around the dance floor and loosen up those accountant hips of his and rest my head on his shoulder at the end of the night after I've wowed the crowd.

I'm not exactly pleased that this is what I want. It feels like it's following a script that someone much less talented than me wrote. But then the divine woman chimes in, warns me not to trap myself back in that little box of what I expected liberation to look like. *Didn't you watch your own play?*

I know, I know, I spray back, a mixture of snark and salt.

I call Chris right then. It feels accidental yet also more intentional than anything I've ever done. He picks up in the sliver of space between the second and the third ring. "Emily Jane," he says, and the way he says it feels more like an answer than a question.

"Hey," I blurt. "So you know how Tara and Niles are getting married this weekend? I was wondering if maybe you'd want to come to it. I know this is super last-minute, so no worries if not. Just thought I'd check."

I try to keep my voice casual, but then I remind myself it's okay not to be casual. It's okay not to be chill because being chill is basically the same thing as muting your feelings, pretending your emotions don't exist. And who wants that? Not me, not anymore.

Chris takes a while to answer. It's probably only one and a half seconds but it feels like forever, and in that forever I'm confronted with the terrifying truth of how badly I want him to say yes. I don't need him to, but I want him to and there's this raw vulnerability and raw power in that. Those two things aren't opposites like I used to think. They're actually quite connected. The more vulnerable you are, the more powerful you are, really.

"Would I be going as your date or as your friend?" Chris asks.

"Take your pick," I say, but then I make myself jump from the airplane and pray that the parachute comes out. "I was hoping for the first option."

"You want me to come as your date?" Chris clarifies.

He's really taking a while to catch on, but I guess I can't blame him considering how I rebuffed his kiss and karate-chopped him in the nuts. "That's correct," I say and then keep going because I'm past the point of no return. I've been past it for a while now. "I'd like you to be my date to the wedding, Chris. Or if you can't come to the wedding, I was hoping we could still go on a date sometime. I like you as a friend but also in other ways; that's what I'm trying to say here. There it is. Do what you want with that information."

I'm cringing with each word, wishing I could take it back but glad I can't. Chris's voice swings up after that. He says in that case, he'd love to come to the wedding; he'll just have to find someone to watch Arnold, but that's no problem. He'll ask his new neighbor; they have an Australian shepherd too who gets along great with Arnold.

I know how Chris likes to plan things out, how curveballs can make him anxious. But he's prioritizing this, he's prioritizing me, and I'm bouncing on my toes now. Everything is bubbling up, molten again.

"But just so we're on the same page," he says. "I shouldn't try to kiss you?" He's trying to keep the tone light, make a little joke of the whole debacle last time, but I know it's a real question and that he feels as exposed as I do right now.

"Kissing at your own risk." I hope he can hear the invitation in my voice.

"Understood." His smile is audible.

Arnie is barking in the background like he's giving his approval, and that just widens the grin on my own face. It's one of those oversized smiles that I used to find obnoxious on other people because I was bitter about their bliss, but now that I've got some for myself, I swear I'm never going back to my curmudgeonly ways. I'll be annoying people with my goofy grin long after I'm dead.

"I went to visit Luke's grave last week," Chris says, and the tone shifts but doesn't fall; we're both still airborne. "First time since the funeral," he adds. "I've been scared to face it before, I guess."

This is a big deal, but I act like it's not so he won't shut down. "Oh, how was that?" I say, like he told me he spent the morning at Whole Foods, diligently squeezing avocados to find the optimal ripeness.

"Tough," he says. "But good." He tells me that he sat at the tombstone for a while and talked to Luke as if he was still here. He couldn't hear anything back, but by the end he still felt a little closer to him.

"I mentioned you in the conversation," Chris says. "Told him the story of how you kicked me in the balls when I tried to kiss you, figured he'd get a good laugh out of that. But also I think he'd be proud of me for taking that chance. For stepping out of his shadow and figuring out my own path, or at least starting to."

"You're carrying him forward without staying stuck in the past," I tell him. "That's not easy."

"'Give me a free life, not an easy life,'" Chris says.

It's one of the lines from my play, and it's quite a thrill, hearing my own quote repeated back. "What cultural icon said that?" I deadpan.

I tell him, too, that I think there's a pretty decent possibility that Luke is still out there somewhere, or in here somewhere. "It's hard to explain, but that night on the hiking trip I just saw how time was an illusion," I say. "How we're already dead and also haven't been born yet and also are here, living right now."

"I'm not sure I'm really following," Chris says.

"That's fine," I say and tell him that it's really just Newton's laws in action: Energy can't be created or destroyed, only transferred. "I'm not trying to give you false hope, though maybe there is no such thing as false hope. Maybe all hope is real, by definition."

"Maybe," he says, and I do feel like he's a bit brighter after that, though maybe that's just my own confirmation bias.

We talk a bit more about the wedding, the dress code and location and timing, and I let Chris hang up first. Turns out I don't need to be the one in control of saying goodbye anymore.

The Redstockings have a field day when I text them that I'm bringing Chris as my plus-one. I expect them just to light up the group chat with a few emojis, but they all descend on the Inn within the hour. They don't bring their partners; it's just the four of us again, like it was in the beginning.

"I think you're blowing this out of proportion," I say as we demolish three pizzas, dribbling sauce onto the canvas of the couch, our favorite artwork. "You're acting like this is Armistice Day or something."

"It pretty much is," Tara says. "You've been fighting yourself for years trying not to fall for Chris."

"Don't you have a wedding to be getting ready for?" I ask Tara.

"Not for three more days," she says, unstressed. "Still time to make it a double wedding." She winks.

"Perfect," I say dryly. "All I'll need is a mirror. Because I'm marrying myself, obviously."

They giggle at that, and I do too, but it's kind of spectacular how there's some truth in it. How I can look at my reflection now and not shrink or shudder or shut my eyes anymore. I hardly ever even pee in the dark anymore, except sometimes I still do just because it's kind of relaxing, like a meditation room.

"We're just happy to see you taking a risk, that's all," Tara tells me.

"My whole life has been about risk-taking," I say, though I know that's not really true. I've actually been trying to avoid hazards, avoid hurt by hurling myself into things I never had any real hope for.

I have real hope for Chris. The thought that it might all end in heartbreak makes me reach out for Tara and Hal and Jenni, pull on their earlobes to make sure they're still there, still solid.

"I think I deserve some applause for all of this," Jenni says. "If it weren't for my bravery being the first to break the pact, you'd all still be trapped in that little zoo."

It makes me strangely proud of Jenni, how she's grown enough to take credit for her crimes.

"But it was really my exit that gave the resistance any momentum," Hal says. "One is a glitch, two is a trend."

"And three is a movement," Tara says, grinning. "A rebellion against our original rebellion."

"Well, maybe I'll stage a rebellion against the rebellion of the rebellion," I say. As far as I'm concerned, marriage still isn't in the cards for me for a very long time, if ever. I'm just going to see how it feels to have a plus-one and start there. "And I'll have six dogs and write satirical plays about your marriages and divorces."

"EJ," Jenni scolds, covering her ears at the *d* word.

"What?" I say. "I'm not wishing for that. I'm just saying the stats aren't great, and I'll be here if it happens. EJ, the Great Witch of the Dunge Inn, haunting Bushwick with her brilliance."

"There are worse fates," Hal says.

The four of us bring in our fists for our old Restocking handshake.

"To liberated love," I say. "In whatever form or non-form it takes."

They all gobble it up, affirming that I'm still the leader even if our group doesn't exist in the same way it used to. The bond is still there, the particles reorganized, never obliterated.

The others head out soon, back to their other lives, but their presence lingers in the vents and the vaults of this basement that bloomed into a home under the shoddy care of girls trying to become women, women trying to remain girls.

I turn on the record player and dance around the living room, slow-dancing with myself. There's clarity, like a knife has been removed from me, and instead of bleeding out, I'm bleeding free. I'm surrounded on the outside by the immortal art painted by my immortal friends, and I'm surrounded on the inside by all the immortal songs that I can finally hear. It makes me wonder where my life is going, what's the next scene and the one after that. I'm glad I don't know because it would ruin the surprise.

I walk out onto Knickerbocker Avenue. The sky is crying like it's just had its own awakening, and the pavement is glowing like it knows something good is coming, like something good has already arrived.

An antique shop has just opened down the street, and I feel a nudge to walk there now. There's a piano in the window, a beautiful ivory thing. I've never seen it before.

My feet carry me inside. A bell jingles in the doorway like it's Christmas. Without asking for permission, I sit down at the piano bench and set my hands on the black and white keys. Taking two deep breaths, I prepare myself that I won't remember anything, that this is pointless.

But then my mind gets out of the way and my fingers start moving, start flying. It takes me a moment to realize what I'm playing. It's my old favorite ballad, Frank Sinatra's "The Way You Look Tonight." My prized masterpiece that I learned as a kid, the one I practiced so much and performed at a recital.

I'm ecstatic that I still have access to it, but I'm anguished too. Because if the muscle memory is there for the beautiful things, it must be there for the brutal ones too.

Up and down the keys my fingers dance. My feet know what to do with the pedals, though I haven't practiced in decades. I bob to the beat, my spine bending like a puppet, but there's no one pulling the strings. It's just me.

When I finish, my whole body is tingling like I've just been electrocuted, four lightning strikes in one.

The store owner comes up and asks if I'm interested in purchasing the piano, says it seems made for me.

"Not today," I say, though the vision of a piano in the Inn flashes through my mind like a prophecy. "But this was just what I needed. Thanks for letting me play." I tip him five dollars because I carry real bills now, thanks to the Populists' Playhouse cash-only policy. Then I bounce out of the shop, feeling lighter than I have in ages.

I take the Red Rocket for a spin, driving down toward the Williamsburg Bridge.

It's a gray sort of day. Gray clouds are blotting the gray cables of the bridge that are framing the gray water of the East River that's sloshing up against the gray steel of the skyline. In the rearview mirror, my gray irises are looking back at me. I don't flinch or blink or look away. I hold my own eye contact.

The Rocket's crusty old windshield wipers are working like new again, keeping the view clear as I drive across the bridge, slower than I've ever driven before. The tires hardly have any tread left and I don't want to skid. There's too much to lose these days. There always has been; I can just finally see it.

The car behind me honks. It's one of those long-drawn-out screeches that's trying to make a statement for the whole city to hear. The sound doesn't faze me; it just makes me tap the brakes. I'm going to move through this life as slowly or as quickly as I want. I'm a free woman, after all. Three cheers for that, or however many cheers you want. It's really not my decision to make. It's yours.

Acknowledgments

Bringing this book to life didn't feel like writing. It felt like channeling. The flow state was beyond anything I've experienced before.

I wrote the first draft in 2020, while my agent was pitching my debut novel to publishers. I poured my anxiety into creativity and found a level of liberation I hadn't accessed before. When my first publisher told me this book was too edgy—that it didn't fit neatly into the rom-com box they wanted to keep me in—I was disappointed but patient. I trusted that the right moment would come.

Over the years, I kept returning to this story, revising it, listening to it, and letting it evolve alongside me.

Thank you to my agent, Emma Parry at Janklow and Nesbit, for understanding the vision the moment you read the manuscript.

Thank you to the team at HarperMuse, especially my editor Kimberly Carlton, for believing in this project, honoring its gritty texture, and helping bring it into the world with such care.

To my friends—for the conversations, the late-night existential crises, and the unfiltered honesty that inspired so much of this book. You mean the world to me.

To the parts of myself I excavated while writing these pages—I'm so glad we've met, and I promise I will never silence you again.

To God—for co-creating this book with me, and for trusting me as a vessel for these ideas. I am deeply grateful.

To New York City—one of my forever muses. To the strangers I met in Brooklyn coffee shops, on subway platforms, and on street corners: Your eye contact, your smiles, your stories have inspired me more than you'll ever know.

To my family—thank you for supporting my creative dreams and for seeing what I'm trying to do. Not just write books, but expand my own consciousness and help guide others toward self-actualization as well.

And to you, dear reader—thank you for being here and for devoting your precious time and attention to this story. I hope you'll carry the spirit of the Redstockings with you and out into the world.

Discussion Questions

1. Have you ever been part of a "pact"—spoken or unspoken—like the Redstockings' Anti-Marriage Pact? What did it offer you at the time, and what did it cost you?
2. Going into the book, who did you expect would be the first to break the pact? Why do you think you made that assumption?
3. Which of the four Redstockings did you relate to most, and why? How did your feelings toward the characters shift over the course of the story?
4. Many readers find EJ unlikable at first. Did you? What do you think shaped that reaction? When did you begin to sense the softness beneath her scaly exterior?
5. In what ways was EJ attempting to be a liberated leader—and in what ways was she inadvertently acting like a tyrant, forcing her friends into a new kind of box?
6. The piano appears throughout the book as a recurring symbol. What does it represent in EJ's life, and how is its meaning foreshadowed early on?
7. In a culture that often frames women's choices as "tradwife" versus "never marriage, never kids," how does this novel honor choice as the truest form of liberation?

8. How does the book celebrate breaking out of boxes—relational, professional, spiritual, or otherwise? Where do you feel pressure in your own life to be a certain kind of woman?

9. Animals often bring out the most tender parts of people. What role does Chris's dog, Arnold, play in the story—and in EJ's growth?

10. How would you describe EJ's spiritual orientation by the end of the book? Have you experienced a spiritual awakening of your own or a shift in worldview that mirrors hers?

11. What do you imagine happens next—for EJ and Chris, and for the Redstockings—after the final page?

12. What do you think this book ultimately says about modern feminism and what it means to be a liberated woman today?

From the Publisher

ARE EVEN BETTER WHEN THEY'RE SHARED!

Help other readers find this one:

- Post a review at your favorite online bookseller
- Post a picture on a social media account and share why you enjoyed it
- Send a note to a friend who would also love it—or better yet, give them a copy

Thanks for reading!

About the Author

Photograph by Alyssa Sonnevil

LINDSAY MACMILLAN is an author, speaker, and creative entrepreneur. Before carving her path in the creative world, she was a Vice President at Goldman Sachs. Lindsay graduated magna cum laude from Dartmouth College. This is her fourth published novel.

Visit her online at lindsaymacmillancreative.com